D0615616

PARTY Crashers

By Stephanie Bond

PARTY CRASHERS
KILL THE COMPETITION
I THINK I LOVE YOU
GOT YOUR NUMBER
OUR HUSBAND

STEPHANIE BOND

PARTY Crashers

AVON BOOKS

An Imprint of HarperCollinsPublishers

This is a work of fiction. Any references to real people, events, estab-lishments, organizations, or locales are intended only to give the fiction a sense of reality and authenticity, and are used fictitiously. All other names, characters, and places, and all dialogue and incidents portrayed in this book are the product of the author's imagination.

AVON BOOKS
An Imprint of HarperCollins*Publishers*
10 East 53rd Street
New York, New York 10022-5299

Copyright © 2004 by Stephanie Bond Hauck

ISBN: 0-7394-4226-0

All rights reserved. No part of this book may be used or reproduced in any manner whatsoever without written permission, except in the case of brief quotations embodied in critical articles and reviews. For infor-mation address Avon Books, an Imprint of HarperCollins Publishers.

Avon Trademark Reg. U.S. Pat. Off. and in Other Countries, Marca Registrada, Hecho en U.S.A.
HarperCollins® is a registered trademark of HarperCollins Publishers Inc.

Printed in the U.S.A.

Acknowledgments

The opening, closing, and merging of various department stores in Atlanta caused me grief in writing my previous book, *Kill the Competition,* and again in *Party Crashers,* because some of the scenes reference or take place in department stores that were defunct by the time I turned in the manuscripts. But simply changing the names of the department stores can create other problems. In the store originally featured in *Party Crashers,* the men's and women's shoe departments were together. When that store announced it was closing, I changed the setting to Neiman Marcus. If you're a customer of Neiman Marcus, you know that the men's and women's shoe departments are in separate areas of the store, but I left the shoe departments in proximity to each other. I hope you don't mind the liberty I took for the sake of the story.

With every book there are people to whom I turn for answers to obscure questions. For *Party Crashers,* I'd like to thank Tim Logsdon, Steve Grantham, and Chris Hauck for their unblinking resourcefulness. Many thanks also to my wonderful agent, Kimberly Whalen of Trident Media Group. And there aren't words to thank my editor, Lyssa

Keusch, for allowing me to run with my ideas and providing insightful feedback to make my stories better. Lyssa, your trust is humbling.

Also, many thanks to my readers who send notes of encouragement just when I'm ready to throw my hands in the air—you help me to muddle through. I hope I'm keeping you entertained.

Stephanie Bond

One

"It's like, I can't decide between the Kate Spade slides and the Via Spiga T-straps, you know?"

Kneeling on the floor of the Neiman Marcus footwear department, Lenox Square, Atlanta, Georgia, Jolie Goodman peered at the tortured coed over a mountain of overflowing shoe boxes. Jolie's knees were raw and carpet burned. Her arms twitched from relaying stacks of shoe boxes to and from the stockroom. Her fingers ached from tying laces and finagling straps to ease shoes onto malodorous feet. Yet her considerable discomfort was apparently minuscule in comparison to the momentous decision weighing on the young woman's mind.

Jolie reached into her sales arsenal and pulled out a persuasive smile. "Why don't you take both and decide when you get home? You can always return a pair later."

The woman's shoulders fell in relief. "You're *right*. I'll take them both. Oh, and the Prada flats, too."

Jolie nodded with approval, scooped up the boxes, and trotted to the checkout counter before the girl could change her mind. Michael Lane, a senior sales consultant, waited for a receipt to print. He eyed the three boxes in her hands with an arched brow. "You're catching on," he murmured. "You just might last after all."

Only through the holiday sales season, Jolie promised herself. Eighty-one more days, if one were counting. The salary and commissions would tide her over until the housing market picked up after the first of the year and she could resume building her real-estate business. She had hoped the experience would sharpen her sales skills . . . She hadn't counted on the bonus of raising her threshold for pain.

Michael ripped off the long sales receipt and handed it to his customer with an ingratiating smile. "Thank you for shopping at Neiman Marcus." As he turned toward Jolie, he said, "Don't forget about the sales meeting tomorrow morning at nine. I know you're not on until noon, but everyone is expected to be there."

Jolie groaned inwardly. She'd been planning to assemble a mailing to her former customers the next morning—one day into her temporary job, and she was already neglecting her primary goal. She rang up the slightly enormous sale, swiped the young woman's credit card, then sent her on her way with a brimming Neiman Marcus shopping bag. The satisfaction over the big fat sale was short-lived, however, because she had to straighten and clear thirty-some boxes of discards before she could move on to the next customer.

Discards—that was a laugh. The boxes held some of the most exquisite designer shoes available, each stuffed and wrapped with form-holding stays, some swathed in cloth bags, some with registration cards. In her previous unenlightened world, she hadn't known that people actually registered their footwear, but she had since learned that when consumers forked over hundreds of dollars for a pair of shoes, they expected prestigious, if hollow, bonuses.

Jolie stooped, ignored the twinge in her lower back, and began repackaging the shoes. She reminded herself she should be thanking her lucky stars for landing this position. According to Michael, the shoe department ranked high in dollar sales per customer, and was always busy. She could do worse for a temporary job. While she repacked a pair of Anne Klein mules, she scanned the customers for the person who seemed most eager to be waited on. They were in the midst of a Columbus Day sale, and the temperatures had begun to dip in earnest, so Atlantans were rushing to the mall in droves to replace their sandals with more substantial fare. And six-hundred-dollar faux crocodile stiletto-heeled boots would definitely keep the chill at bay.

Her gaze skitted over the after-five crowd, then caught on a familiar dark orange ball cap. Her heart stalled. *Gary?* The man stood several yards away, his profile obscured by other shoppers. In a split second, her mind rationalized it could be him—he certainly had preferred shopping at the upscale stores in this mall. Her heart jumpstarted, thudding in her ears. What would she do first—confront him or call the police? Kiss him or kill him?

Jolie craned for a better look just as the man turned. Her pulse spiked, then a fusion of disappointment and relief shot through her. It wasn't Gary. Again. She dropped her gaze and stared at the box in her hand until her vital signs recovered. She felt like a fool all over again, just like a month ago when she explained to a dubious officer that her boyfriend—and her car—had simply disappeared. But

Gary drove a Mercedes—why would he want her Mercury? In her mind, her car being stolen and Gary dropping out of sight were mutually exclusive. The uniformed man hadn't been nearly so magnanimous when he'd told her flat out that she'd been royally scammed.

Squashing the train of thought, she gave herself a mental shake—she couldn't afford to be distracted, not now, when she needed to be on her sales game. She resumed scanning for ripe customers.

Her gaze landed on a tanned and rumpled sandy-haired man, strangely dressed in holey jeans and an expensive sport coat, hovering near a sleek blonde to whom Michael was showing a strappy shoe that Jolie hadn't yet memorized—Stuart Weitzman? Stubbs and Wootton? Her head swam with trendy monikers. From the restless look on the man's rugged face, he was a salesman's worst enemy—a "straggler," the person who accompanies the primary shopper and shifts from foot to foot until the shopper moves along. Interesting face or no, he wasn't useful to her.

Scan, scan—*stop*. Jolie cringed.

Ten feet away, Sammy "Sold" Sanders, real-estate agent extraordinaire and Jolie's ex-boss, scrutinized a Manolo Blahnik bootie with laser blue eyes. Jolie's pulse hammered as she imagined the belly laugh that Sammy would enjoy when she discovered that her employee who had quit in a puffed-up huff over the questionable ethics of a deal had been reduced to selling shoes. Jolie had hoped to see Sammy again, but not until the Jolie Goodman Real Estate Agency was well into the black . . . or at least had letterhead. She stacked boxes high in her arms and lifted them to obscure her face as she hurried toward the stockroom. Maybe she could hide out until Sammy left.

During the two hundred or so trips she'd made to and from the stockroom that day, Jolie thought she had the path and its obstacles memorized. *Apparently not,* she realized, as she collided with something solid and bounced back. She teetered on the heels of her sensible pumps, trying to stabilize the boxes that swayed one way and then the other. She failed spectacularly and acrobatically, falling hard on her tailbone while propelling the boxes into the air so high, she had time to envision the sound and sight of the merchandise crashing to the ground before it actually happened.

Except it was so much worse than she'd imagined.

The shoe boxes landed on and around Jolie in a thudding avalanche. Everyone within earshot turned to stare, including Sammy Sanders, which was bad enough on its own, but since Jolie sat on the floor with her legs spread and her skirt rucked up to her thighs, it was the stuff of which nightmares were made. In those first few seconds of stunned silence, she was afraid everyone was going to start clapping, like the time she dropped her tray in the school lunchroom in the seventh grade. But no one clapped: The customers of Neiman Marcus simply seemed annoyed that she'd interrupted their pristine environment.

"I beg your pardon," a deep voice said.

Jolie bent her head back to find the sandy-haired man with the holey jeans standing over her, his hand extended.

A smile played on his mouth. "I wasn't looking where you were going."

Afraid that she might pull him down with her when she tried to stand, Jolie rolled over on her side and pushed herself to her knees before accepting his hand and being helped to her feet. His gentlemanly behavior, she noticed, didn't keep him from stealing a peek at the expanse of leg she had on display.

"Thank you," she chirped, yanking down her hem. She'd managed to lose one of her own shoes in the aftermath, and proceeded to toe it upright and stick her foot inside before anyone noticed it wasn't a brand that came with a registration card.

"Are you okay?" the man asked.

She nodded, cheeks flaming. "I should be asking *you*. I just clobbered you with five thousand dollars' worth of shoes."

One side of his mouth lifted. "I'll live."

But it was the smile in his brown eyes that made her tongue do a figure eight.

Michael Lane rushed up. "Are you all right, sir?"

"I'm fine."

"Please accept our deepest apologies. This is Jolie's first day on the job." Michael shot her a frown that indicated it might also be her *last* day on the job.

"No harm done," the man said smoothly.

"Jolie? Jolie Goodman, I *thought* that was you."

Jolie closed her eyes briefly, then turned to face the music. Sammy Sanders glided toward them in all her pink and white blonde glory.

"Hello, Sammy."

Sammy's gaze landed on Jolie's lapel badge, and her eyes rounded. "Are you *working* here?"

"Yes."

Sammy made a distressed noise, as if she were stepping over a homeless person, and touched the arm of Jolie's jacket with a manicured hand. "Jolie, it doesn't have to be like this. Come back to the Sanders Agency and we'll let bygones be bygones."

Jolie glanced down at Sammy's hand, then pulled away. "Excuse me while I clean up the mess I made."

Sammy's face reddened, then she tossed her pale hair. "While you're in the back, Jolie, fetch me this little number in a size seven, will you?"

Fetch . . . like a dog. Sammy had been having her fetch things for years—would she never be able to get one up on the woman?

The man she'd plowed into stepped in. "I believe the lady was helping me."

Sammy flicked her gaze over him, then conjured up an ingratiating smile. "I'll wait."

He looked around and picked up the nearest men's shoe, a lustrous Cole Haan loafer, quite a contrast to the battered tennis shoes he wore. "Do you have this in size eleven?"

Jolie gave him a grateful look. "I'll check." She stooped to grab an armful of shoes, lids, and boxes, and scrambled toward the stockroom.

Michael was on her heels with a second armload. "Do you know who that is?"

"My former boss, Sammy Sanders."

"I mean the *man*."

"No. Should I?"

"That's Beck *Under*wood."

She dropped her load on a table. "Of Underwood Broadcasting?"

"The same. His family owns more media outlets and production companies than anyone on the East Coast."

Egad—she subscribed to their movie channel. "I've seen his father and sister on the news," she said, suddenly realizing why the woman with him seemed familiar, "but I don't remember him."

"He's been away from Atlanta for a few years, living in Costa Rica, I believe."

Which explained the longish hair and the deep tan.

"Carlotta told me he was back in town."

"Carlotta?"

"Carlotta Wren—she works upstairs, usually in the Prada department. Hard-core celebrity groupie, knows everyone who's anyone in Atlanta. She'd wet her capris if she knew Beck Underwood was in the store."

Jolie held out the requested size-eleven loafer. "Maybe you should handle this sale."

"I'm handling the sister," Michael reminded her, pulling Jimmy Choo boxes from the shelf by twos. "I'm counting on you to keep *him* busy while I sell *her* the entire fall line."

"Will you cut me in on your commission?"

"No, but I won't fire you."

She swallowed. "Deal."

"Besides," Michael said with a wry grin, "the man probably owns nothing but jungle footwear—maybe you can sell him some civilized shoes." He gave her the once-over, then squinted. "You might want to . . . *fluff* or something." Then he walked out, laden with enough shoes to shod the Rockettes.

Jolie glanced into the mirror on the door of the employee bathroom and groaned. Her short dishwater-blonde hair, curly and fine textured, was unruly under the best of circumstances. But after a confrontation with the carpet, the stuff was a staticky, high-flying nest. Her dark jacket and skirt were lint covered, and the makeup she'd applied so carefully this morning had vanished. She resembled one of the mannequins in sportswear—prominent eyes and knees, with a chalk white pallor—and she felt as insubstantial as she looked. For someone who prided herself on her fortitude, she conceded that six hours on her feet, plus the false sighting of Gary, plus the scene she'd created, plus the run-in with Sammy Sanders . . . well, it was enough to wear a girl down.

Weighing her options, she glanced at the doorway leading back to the showroom, then to the fire-exit door leading to a loading dock. She had the most outrageous urge to walk out . . . and keep walking.

Is that what Gary had done? Reached some kind of personal crisis that he couldn't share with her, and simply walked away from everything—from his job, from his friends, from her? As bad as it sounded, she almost preferred to believe that he had suffered some kind of breakdown rather than consider other possible explanations—that he'd met with foul play, or that she had indeed been scammed by the man who'd professed to care about her.

The exit sign beckoned, but she glanced at the shoe box in her hands and decided that since the man had been kind enough to intercept Sammy, he deserved to be waited on, even if he didn't spend a cent.

Even if people with vulgar amounts of money did make her nervous.

She finger-combed her hair and tucked it behind her ears, then straightened her clothing as best she could. There was no helping the lack of makeup, so she pasted on her best smile—the one that she thought showed too much gum, but that Gary had assured her made her face light up—and returned to the showroom.

Her smile almost faltered, though, when Mr. Beck Underwood's bemused expression landed on her.

She walked toward him, trying to forget that the man could buy and sell her a thousand times over. "I'm sorry again about running into you. Did you really want to try on this shoe or were you just being nice?"

"Both," he said mildly. "My sister is going to be a while, and I need shoes, so this works for me."

At the twinkle in his eyes, her tongue lodged at the roof of her mouth. Like a mime, she gestured to a nearby chair, and made her feet follow him. As he sat, she scanned the area for signs of Sammy.

"She's behind the insoles rack," he whispered.

Jolie flushed and made herself not look. The man probably thought she was clumsy *and* paranoid. She busied herself unpacking the expensive shoes. "Will you be needing a dress sock, sir?"

He slipped off his tennis shoe and wiggled bare, brown toes. "I suppose so. I'm afraid I've gotten into the habit of not wearing socks." He smiled. "And my dad is 'sir'—I'm just Beck."

She suddenly felt small. And poor. "I . . . know who you are."

"Ah. Well, promise you won't hold it against me."

She smiled and retrieved a pair of tan-colored socks to match the loafers. When she started to slip one of the socks over his foot, he took it from her. "I can do it."

"I don't mind," she said quickly. Customers expected it—to be dressed and undressed and re-dressed if necessary. It was an unwritten rule: *No one leaves the store without being touched.*

"I don't have to be catered to," he said, his tone brittle.

Jolie blinked. "I'm sorry."

He looked contrite and exhaled, shaking his head. "Don't be. It's me." Then he grinned unexpectedly. "Besides, under more private circumstances, I might take you up on your offer."

Heat climbed her neck and cheeks. He was teasing her—his good deed for the day. Upon closer scrutiny, his face was even more interesting—his eyes a deep brown, bracketed by untanned lines created from squinting in the sun. Late thirties, she guessed. His skin was ruddy, his strong nose peeling from a recent burn. Despite the pale streaks in his hair, he was about as far from a beach boy as a man could be. When he leaned over to slip on the shoes, she caught a glimpse of his powerful torso beneath the sport coat.

She averted her gaze and concentrated on the stitched design on the vamp of the shoe he was trying on, handing him a shoe horn to protect the heel counter. (This morning Michael had given her an "anatomy of a shoe" lesson, complete with metal pointer and pop quiz.)

The man stood and hefted his weight from foot to foot, then took a couple of steps in one direction and came back. "I'll take them."

A salesperson's favorite words. She smiled. "That was fast."

He laughed. "Men don't have a complicated relationship with shoes."

She liked his easy laugh, it was a happy noise that drew attention—including Sammy's, Jolie noticed. Her former boss came over, her pale brows knit in frustration. "Jolie, were you able to find the shoe I wanted?"

Jolie glanced in Beck's direction. "Go ahead," he said. "I'll wait."

"Give me just a minute," Jolie murmured, then manufactured a smile for Sammy. "A size seven, wasn't it?"

"Yes. And please hurry—I have a big closing in thirty minutes."

Embarrassment flooded Jolie, setting her skin on fire. For the thousandth time, Jolie thought how attractive Sammy would be without her permanent smugness. "Yes, ma'am." She returned to the stockroom, her ego smarting.

Despite the fact that she'd worked for the Sanders Agency for over a decade, it had been inevitable that she and Sammy would part on bad terms. Edgar Sanders had hired her as a receptionist right out of high school, and from the beginning she had clashed with the man's daughter. Sammy was a few years older than Jolie and on the fast track to realty royalty. She'd hated Jolie at first sight. Mr. Sanders, on the other hand, had rewarded Jolie's hard work by moving her up through the company. The two women had developed an uneasy relationship based on avoidance. Jolie had managed to put herself through night school, to become an experienced agent, and three months ago, to obtain her broker's license with an eye toward commercial real estate. Unfortunately, it had coincided with Mr. Sanders' retirement, and suddenly, Jolie had found herself working for Sammy.

Remarkably, the woman's personality seemed to change overnight. She'd been downright helpful to Jolie . . . and two weeks ago, Jolie had discovered why. In order to close a big deal, Sammy wanted Jolie to pass information to the buyer that would breach the company's confidentiality agreement with the seller. Gary had been missing for a few days, and Jolie was already stressed. In fact, she had a feeling that Sammy had purposefully targeted her during a vulnerable time, thinking she would cave. Jolie didn't, and Sammy threatened to fire her. Instead, Jolie had quit.

Sammy said Jolie'd lost her mind—no one left the Sanders Agency voluntarily.

And now Jolie was selling shoes. Boy, she had really shown *her*.

She sighed and scanned for the pair that cost more than her week's salary selling shoes, then removed two boxes from the shelf. She carried them out to Sammy, who apparently had taken advantage of the opportunity to introduce herself to Beck Underwood. The oversize Barbie doll had extended her business card in his direction and he was accepting it, although somewhat reluctantly, Jolie noted.

"We only have a size six and a half and a size seven and a half," Jolie said to Sammy, holding up the boxes. "Would you like to try them?"

Sammy made a face and waved her hand. "No, that's okay. I really was only killing time until my big closing."

Jolie nodded. "It must be a really big closing, since you've already mentioned it twice."

Sammy's eyes narrowed. "Happy *shoeing,* Jolie."

Jolie watched Sammy sashay away, her stomach churning over the way she'd handled the situation. This was a bad time to be starting her own brokerage company, and she had very few resources to fall back on. Considering how many agencies were struggling, if she couldn't get enough business going in the next few months, she might have to go crawling back to Sammy or start at square one somewhere else.

She glanced down at the boxes in her hands. She didn't seem to have much of a future in shoes.

"I sense history between the two of you."

Jolie glanced at Beck Underwood, who sat patiently

with his new shoes on his lap. He had put his old tennis shoes back on, and Jolie wondered about the ground those battered shoes had covered, places she hoped to see someday.

"Former boss," Jolie murmured, then reached for his new shoes. "I'm sorry you had to wait. Do you need anything else?"

"Yeah." Then he smiled. "But it'll give me an excuse to come back—this is the most excitement I've had since I returned to Atlanta."

She managed a shaky smile, thinking she didn't know how much more excitement she could take today. She just wanted to go home and soak her feet, and maybe call her friend Leann to report on what had to be the world's worst first day on the job.

She set aside the shoes Sammy had passed on and carried Beck's loafers to the counter to ring up his sale.

A willowy black woman wearing chinos and a dark jacket walked up to the counter.

"I'll be right with you," Jolie said.

"Jolie Goodman?"

Jolie tensed. "Yes."

The woman opened her coat to reveal a silver badge. "I'm Detective Salyers with the Atlanta PD. I need to speak with you."

Two

Jolie stared at the detective and her stomach caved. "Is something wrong?"

"I just need to talk with you, ma'am."

"Is this about Gary?"

"Yes." The woman's expression gave away nothing.

Jolie's mind reeled. She looked up and saw that Beck Underwood had overheard everything and was watching her carefully. Across the sales floor, Michael Lane stared curiously in her direction. She glanced at her watch, then looked back to the detective. "My shift ends in fifteen minutes. Can you wait?"

The woman nodded. "How about meeting me at the Coffee Shack in the food court?"

Jolie swallowed hard. "Okay." She watched the policewoman walk away and wanted desperately to run after her. Her heart slammed against her breastbone, and her hands were shaking so badly, she could barely finish ringing up the sale.

She looked up and tried to fix her face in a natural expression. "Will you be using your Neiman Marcus card?"

Beck was staring at her. Slowly, he reached for his wallet and flipped through before removing a platinum bank credit card. "There isn't a Neiman Marcus where I've been living."

She ran the card and handed him a receipt to sign. While she bagged his purchase, her gaze drifted toward the mall entrance. The detective had to have some kind of news, didn't she? And if it were good news, the police would have called, wouldn't they? Or Gary himself?

"Jolie?"

She started, then took the signed receipt he extended. "Thank you."

He cleared his throat. "This is none of my business, but is everything okay?"

She nodded and held up his shopping bag. "Thank you for shopping at Neiman Marcus." Then she gave him the best smile she could manage. "Please come back and I'll try not to bulldoze you."

He hesitated, then took his bag. "Take care."

She maintained a cheery smile until he turned away. Then she grabbed the Sammy rejects and checked the floor for debris she might have overlooked from the crash. In the stockroom, she spent the last few minutes of her shift methodically returning the jumble of boxes, lids, and shoes to order.

Snippets of Gary Hagan kept popping into her head—his crooked smile, his curly black hair that he kept gelled in place or covered with an orange cap, the cell phone that was at his ear more often than it was in his pocket. He was wiry and athletic, with an electric personality, always moving. Gary had been the most thoughtful man she'd known—he'd never missed an opportunity to celebrate an occasion, and often had brought her flowers for no reason. But the police didn't understand any of those things.

She climbed onto a stool to reshelve the boxes, and unbidden tears clouded her vision. She swayed, then grabbed the edge of the shelf to keep from falling.

"Jolie?" Michael Lane was behind her, his hand against her back. "Are you okay?"

"Just a little light-headed," she said, allowing him to help her down.

"Who was that woman? She asked me to point you out to her."

Jolie hesitated, but if Michael was left to concoct his own answer, he might come up with something worse than the truth. "She's a detective from the police department. A guy I was dating disappeared a few weeks ago."

"Disappeared?"

She nodded. "The detective must have news, because she wants to talk to me. I asked her to meet me when my shift ended."

"Go," he said, pointing toward the door. "I'll put everything back. I hope she has good news."

She nodded gratefully, then retrieved her purse from a locker in the break room and walked out across the showroom toward the entrance to the mall. She resisted the urge to look for Beck Underwood. In the space of a few minutes, he had learned that she was a hopeless klutz, estranged from her former boss, and that the police wanted to talk to her. The man probably thought she was a total drama queen. He'd never know how much she'd appreciated his concern.

She nodded to the security guard at the doorway and hurried out into the mall, instantly assaulted with voices, music, and crowd noise reverberating between tile floors and glass ceilings. Because of Columbus Day, kids were off school and had been at the mall all day in full force, cruising for attention and trouble. The girls were squeezed into provocative clothes and looked old enough to do things they shouldn't. The boys looked overwhelmed.

A far cry from her own sheltered upbringing. She had been an only child, a change-of-life baby, and her frugal parents had harbored rather old-fashioned notions about child-rearing. But even if she hadn't worn the most fashionable clothes or obtained her driver's license until she was eighteen, she could thank her parents for loving her and for giving her a good value system. She'd lost them both to illness when she was in her early twenties. Work had been her solace, and night school had kept her plenty busy. Oh, there had been occasional dates and sporadic boyfriends, but Gary Hagan had been the first man who had made her think about sharing her future. He was an orphan too, having lost his parents to a car accident. She thought it had made them closer, their aloneness.

Would her parents have approved of Gary? She'd asked herself this question many times over the months they had dated. In the beginning they would have been uncomfortable with his exuberance, just as she'd been. But eventually, they would've been won over by his relentless cheerfulness.

At least she liked to think so.

Through gaps in the crowd, Jolie saw the lady detective up ahead, pacing in front of the coffee vendor.

Pacing . . . that couldn't be good.

Jolie drew in a shaky breath and strode forward, eager to get the meeting over with. Detective Salyers spotted her and stood still, waiting until she came close enough to speak.

"Would you like a cup of coffee?"

Jolie shook her head.

"I'm going to get a cup, why don't you grab us a table?"

Another delay. Jolie found a table for two away from the din and studied what looked to be cookie crumbs left from the previous occupant. It was a trick she'd learned: Focusing on mundane details allowed her to get through difficult times because they were reminders that life went on. No matter what the detective had to say, life would go on. Tomorrow someone else would be sitting here, maybe falling in love for the first time, or contemplating what to cook for dinner. And Gary would either be dead or alive.

"Here you go," Dectective Salyers said, sliding a cup of caramel-colored coffee in front of her. The woman smiled. "I thought you might change your mind."

Jolie thanked her.

The detective claimed the opposite seat. "Ms. Goodman, you're a difficult woman to track down. You weren't home, and we have your employer listed as the Sanders Agency."

"I left there a couple of weeks ago."

"We contacted the woman you had listed as your closest relative on the missing person's report you filed on Gary Hagan—a Leann Renaldi in Jacksonville?"

"Yes, she's a good friend." And she was probably frantic by now.

"She told us where we could find you."

Jolie sipped the coffee, flinching when the scalding liquid

hit her tongue. "Did you find Gary?" she blurted. "Is he alive?"

Detective Salyers sat forward, her long, dark fingers wrapped around the paper cup. "No. And we don't know."

Jolie heaved a sigh of relief and frustration. "What's this all about then?"

"We found your boyfriend's car."

"His Mercedes? Where?"

"In the Chattahoochee River."

Jolie's heart jerked. "In the river? Where?"

"Near Roswell." The detective wet her lips. "And we found a body inside."

Jolie inhaled against the sharp pain in her chest and covered her mouth with her hand. "I thought you said—"

"It's not Mr. Hagan. It's . . . a woman. Belted into the passenger seat."

Jolie's mind spun in confusion. "A woman? Who?"

"The body hasn't yet been identified. I was hoping you could give us some idea who it might be. She's Caucasian, dark hair."

Jolie shook her head, trying to make sense of what the woman was saying. "I don't . . . I can't . . . think . . ."

"His sister?"

"No. Gary was—*is* an only child."

"Mother?"

"She's deceased. As well as Gary's father."

"Business associate? Secretary, maybe."

Jolie shook her head. "Gary worked for himself and he worked alone."

Detective Salyers sipped from her coffee cup. "Perhaps an old girlfriend?"

Jolie bit her lip and closed her eyes briefly. Nothing

about this situation sounded sane. A woman was dead . . . in Gary's car . . . He was missing . . . *and so was her own car.* She hadn't wanted to believe that Gary had stolen her car, couldn't imagine why he would have needed it. But now . . .

"I don't know any of Gary's old girlfriends." She touched her temple. "Although he did mention once that he'd had problems with a girl he'd dated."

"Problems?"

She frowned, trying to remember. "It was an offhand comment about a fatal attraction."

Salyers looked interested. "Did he mention a name?"

"No. You'd have to talk to his friends."

"You're my first stop. Since you filed the missing persons report, I assumed you two were . . . close."

Jolie paused, wondering how she could best describe her relationship with Gary. Friendly lovers? Loverly friends? "We dated, but Gary kept company in . . . high circles. I never met any of his friends."

"You didn't find that to be suspicious?"

She could feel the older woman's censure. "I got the feeling that he wanted to keep that part of his life separate."

"You mean, that he was ashamed of you?"

Anger sparked in Jolie's stomach. "Actually, I thought he might be ashamed of *them*."

Salyers put pen to paper. "I need names."

Jolie shook her head. "I'd tell you if I knew any, but I don't."

The detective pursed her mouth and withdrew a notebook. "Would you mind if we started from the beginning? I inherited this case, and I'd like to get some fresh notes now that we have a new lead."

Jolie shrugged, suddenly very glad for the coffee.

"Your boyfriend's name is Gary Hagan—H-A-G-A-N, right?"

"Yes."

"When was the last time you saw Mr. Hagan?"

"A month ago, September tenth."

"Do you remember what day of the week that was?"

"Friday."

"What was he doing the last time you saw him?"

"He dropped me off at my apartment around eight thirty."

"And was headed where? Do you know?"

"To Buckhead. We'd had an early dinner near my apartment. He said he had a few things to take care of and that he'd call me the next day. He wasn't specific."

"Was that typical, for him to go out after the two of you had had a date?"

Jolie frowned. "I wouldn't say it was typical, but it had happened a few times."

"Did he seem different to you that night?"

"What do you mean?"

Salyers shrugged. "Had he received a phone call that upset him? Was he overly tired? Had he been drinking?"

She had replayed her last conversation with Gary so many times, looking for clues as to his frame of mind. "He seemed a little . . . irritable."

"Had you argued?"

Jolie shrugged. "It was nothing, really. Gary was a bit of a slob, and I was picking up after him. He snapped at me."

"So he had a temper."

"I'd heard him raise his voice during phone calls, but he'd never lost his temper with me."

"Until that night?"

Jolie nodded.

"Did you break up?"

She bit her lip. "No."

"Did you get the feeling that he wanted to stop seeing you?"

Yes. "Maybe. He'd grown distant in the previous few days, and when he snapped at me for picking up after him . . . Well, I remember thinking it was the kind of nit-picking that couples go through when they're on the verge of breaking up."

"Was he wearing a hat when you last saw him?"

Jolie's heart jumped. "Why?"

"We found a man's hat in the car."

"H—he liked to wear an orange ball cap, one of those rounded ones that fit close to the head, with a gray bill. Is that the cap you found?"

"After that much time in the mud, it's hard to say what the original color was, but the shape is similar."

Jolie covered her mouth, the image of Gary's body submerged in the thick muddy water of the Chattahoochee too awful to imagine.

"Ms. Goodman, what exactly was Mr. Hagan's occupation?"

Jolie squirmed—it was the one point of contention between her and Gary. "He was vague about what he did, but he called himself a services broker."

"A services broker?"

"Gary had this incredible network of acquaintances. If a person wanted something special, they called Gary. He said he could arrange a ride in a traffic helicopter, or courtside seats for the Hawks, things like that."

Salyers nodded, making notes. "Did his services extend to supplying drugs or prostitutes?"

Jolie winced. "What? No, of course not."

"Are you certain? If he were deliberately vague about what he did, maybe he was covering up."

Jolie didn't know what to say, so she simply lifted a hand. "I suppose anything is possible."

"Did the two of you ever do drugs?"

"*No*."

"Were you aware that Mr. Hagan has a record for dealing coke?"

She felt nauseous. "No. When?"

"Eight years ago in Orlando."

"I didn't even know he'd lived in Orlando."

The look that Salyers gave her made her feel stupid and susceptible. "Did Mr. Hagan own a gun?"

Anxiety eddied in her chest. "If he did, he never mentioned it."

"You didn't see a gun at his apartment, in his car?"

"I only visited his apartment a couple of times, but no."

Salyers made more notes. "Okay, you said that Mr. Hagan left that night to go out—what happened next?"

"I watched TV, then I went to bed. I got up the next morning and when I went out to run errands around nine o'clock, my car was gone."

"Were there signs that the car had been broken into—glass on the ground, for instance?"

"No."

"Did Mr. Hagan have a key?"

"Yes. I had locked my keys in the car once, so we made a copy for the sake of convenience."

"Was that your idea or Mr. Hagan's?"

Jolie squinted. "Gary's, I believe—why?"

"Just asking." She consulted her notes. "You drove a 2001 gray Mercury Sable Sedan, is that right?"

"Yes."

"But you didn't make an immediate connection between your car missing and Mr. Hagan?"

"No. After I called the police to report my car stolen, I called Gary, but he didn't answer his phone. Several hours later, I began to suspect that something was wrong, except I was worried about Gary, not my car."

"You called his cell phone?"

Jolie nodded. "He was never without it. He didn't even have a land line at his apartment."

"And he lived in Buckhead?" The woman turned back a few pages in her notebook and read off the address.

Jolie nodded. "That's right. But there was a fire at his complex a few days after he . . . disappeared."

Salyers heaved a sigh. "It seems like we had an apartment fire every week this summer. We have two serial arsonists in custody. His unit was damaged?"

"And almost everything in it."

"Almost?"

"I called the manager to tell him that Gary was missing when I saw the news about the fire. The manager called me a couple of weeks ago, said he had salvaged a box of Gary's things and if I wanted them, I should stop by." She frowned. "When I got there, he tried to extort the overdue rent but wound up giving me a box of things that probably came from Gary's fireproof desk—photographs, piled-up mail."

"Did you keep them?"

"Yes, the box is at my place."

"The same address listed for you on the missing persons report?"

"Yes, near Roswell," she said, and she realized she had repeated the name of the area where Gary's car had been found.

"Would it be possible for you to bring the box by the midtown precinct tomorrow?"

Jolie nodded.

Salyers made a note of it. "Ms. Goodman, when did you report Mr. Hagan missing?"

"The following Wednesday, I believe."

"That seems like a long time to wait."

Jolie bristled at the woman's accusing tone. "Gary is an adult. I didn't keep tabs on him."

"But you still didn't believe he had anything to do with your missing car?"

"No. I thought it was a coincidence. Gary had a nice car—I couldn't imagine why he would have wanted mine." Then again, it hadn't occurred to her that he'd just rolled his own vehicle into the river and needed a getaway car.

"It didn't cross your mind that he might simply have sold your car for cash?"

Jolie shook her head. "He wouldn't have done something like that."

Salyers pursed her mouth. "How long had you been seeing Mr. Hagan when he disappeared?"

"About four months."

"How did you meet him?"

"I was working for the Sanders Agency. He came in one day to ask for directions."

Salyers smiled. "And he got your number instead?"

Jolie nodded, smiling for the first time. "Gary was very . . . persuasive."

"Were the two of you serious?"

"What do you mean?"

"Did you date other people?"

Jolie rolled one shoulder. "We never discussed it—I didn't date anyone else, and I guess I just assumed that he didn't either."

"In the box of personal effects that the manager gave you, do you remember seeing an address or schedule book?"

"No, but I didn't go through the box closely."

Salyers frowned. "Really? If my boyfriend was missing, I'd have gone through it with a fine-tooth comb."

Again, the censure. Jolie tried to ignore the prickly nervousness that gathered around her pulse points. "Gary had a Palm Pilot, but he kept it with him—it wouldn't be in that box."

The detective studied her as if she were trying to size her up. Her entire life, Jolie had felt as if people were sizing her up, trying to figure her out. It unnerved her because she wasn't nearly as complicated as people thought she was. She wanted the same things in life that other people wanted . . . except she hadn't yet figured out how to get them.

"Has your insurance company paid the claim for your stolen car?"

"Not yet." Jolie angled her head. "What are you getting at?"

Salyers sighed and pressed her hand against the table. "Ms. Goodman, this is no longer a missing persons case. This is now a homicide investigation."

"Homicide?"

"And your boyfriend is a fugitive."

"Fugitive?"

"And if you know more than you're telling, you could be charged as an accessory."

Alarm squeezed Jolie's chest. "Accessory? I don't know what you're talking about." Her voice escalated until people around them turned to stare.

Salyers adopted a calming expression. "All I'm saying is that if Mr. Hagan came and knocked on your door that night and asked for your car, now is the time to say so, before this gets any worse for you."

She knew her mouth was open—she could feel the air on her tongue. She snapped her jaw closed and pushed to her feet. "When I filed the report on my car and the missing persons report on Gary, you people made me feel like an idiot. I was patronized and told that I'd been conned." She was shaking. "I didn't see Gary later that night, or any time after he left my apartment Friday. Now, if you don't have anything else to tell me, I'd really like to go."

Salyers stood. "Ms. Goodman, I'm giving you this information for your own protection. If Gary Hagan is a dangerous man and he's still alive, you could be in danger yourself." She handed Jolie a card. "If he tries to contact you, call me."

Jolie stared at the card, seeing nothing. She just wanted to escape to a quiet place where she could think. She shouldered her purse and stalked away, blinking rapidly. Nausea ebbed and flowed in her stomach. After threading her way through the food court, she stepped into the main corridor of the mall, into a stream of shoppers heading toward the exit. Dozens of people passed her, going in the opposite direction, brushing her shoulder, bumping her purse.

She searched their faces, desperately hoping to see Gary in his orange ball cap, laughing, saying everything had been a huge misunderstanding. But they were all strangers to her, giving her a fleeting glance, if that. People staring past her and through her, shuffling toward their respective destinations. Life went on.

Then her gaze settled on one familiar face a few yards away, walking toward her: Beck Underwood. He was walking next to his sister, who was talking, her blonde head turned toward him. He was laden with Neiman Marcus shopping bags—apparently Michael had scored a fat sale. At that second, Beck's gaze landed on her, and recognition registered on his face. Recognition and concern.

Jolie quickly turned her head and walked faster, carrying herself past and away from the man with the perceptive brown eyes. Unreasonable resentment flickered through her body—people with as much money as the Underwoods didn't have to worry about things the way that normal people did. If they were wrongly implicated in a crime, they'd simply make a couple of phone calls and the problem would disappear. Gary had called it the "Buckhead Bubble"—a magic bubble, he said, that surrounded the country-club set that lived in the ritziest part of Atlanta.

For a few seconds, she fantasized what it would be like to walk in the designer shoes of the rich and famous . . . to have all doors and possibilities and pleasures at your fingertips. It was an attractive daydream when her own humdrum life seemed so precarious.

Swallowing past a lump in her throat, her mind jumped to who the dead woman could be, and why she had been in Gary's car. Where was Gary, and why had he implicated *her* by stealing her car? And could Detective Salyers be right? Could she herself be in danger?

She pushed open the door leading to the parking garage

and stepped out into the uncharacteristic chill of the evening. It wasn't quite 7 P.M. yet, but the days were getting shorter, and the sunlight was already fading. In the parking garage, the light was even more diffuse, and two flickering bulbs didn't help to dispel the darkness in the corners. She jumped when the heavy metal door slammed closed behind her.

The garage was full of cars, but empty of people, except a few who were unlocking trunks for their shopping bags. She walked down the ramp a half level to where she'd parked her car, her pumps clicking against the concrete, sending rhythmic echoes around her. Jolie pivoted her head right and left, telling herself it was good policy to be alert, that the detective's words hadn't spooked her. But when she spotted her rental car, she found herself walking faster and faster.

Footsteps sounded behind her, and a shadow fell upon hers. She walked faster and the footsteps kept coming. Her heart thrashed in her chest and she whipped around. A man walking a few yards behind her held up his arm, aiming something in his hand. A scream gathered at the back of her throat just as his thumb moved and the car next to hers bleated, the lights flashing in response to a keyless remote. Oblivious to the fact that she was on the verge of cardiac arrest, the man nodded briefly, then walked past her and opened his door and swung inside.

Jolie slumped against the door of her own car in abject relief, chiding herself for letting the detective's words get to her. No doubt that Gary, wherever he was, was in a lot of trouble, but she had no reason to be afraid.

Then she wet her lips and listened to the blood rushing in her ears. So why was she?

Three

Jolie scooted into the tan Chevy Cavalier rental and closed the door behind her. When she pulled the seat belt across her shoulder, she had a grisly vision of a faceless woman belted into the passenger seat of Gary's Mercedes, the clawing fear she must have felt when she realized the car was going into the muddy river, the car filling up with water—

Her cell phone rang, sending her pulse and imagination into overdrive. Gary? She pulled the phone out of her purse with a shaking hand and checked the screen: Leann. With a sigh of relief, she flipped up the receiver. "Hi."

"The police called me looking for you!"

"They found me."

"What's going on?"

"They found Gary's car."

"You're kidding. Where?"

"In the Chattahoochee River." She bit her lip, loath to say the words. "There was a body inside the car . . . a woman."

"What? Oh, my God, who?"

Jolie released a shaky sigh. "No one knows yet."

"Did . . . did they find Gary?"

"No, just his hat."

"So they think he's still alive?"

"I believe so. They seem to think that he stole my car after sending his into the river."

"Omigod."

"It gets worse. They think I know something about . . . what happened. That I gave him my car so he could get away." She swallowed a wad of tears, but her voice still wobbled. "A detective told me I could be charged with accessory."

"To *murder*?"

"To whatever they charge him with."

"I can't believe this. Are you going to get a lawyer?"

She felt faint. "With what?" Her laugh sounded hysterical to her own ears. "My savings is gone from trying to get my business off the ground. I'm already eating into my credit cards. Besides, wouldn't that make me look guilty?"

"Possibly." Leann sighed. "I should be there for you."

"Your sister needs you right now."

"I know, I'm just sorry about the timing of this visit."

"I'm fine. A little shell-shocked, but fine." Salyers' warning about her safety reverberated in her head, and she looked over her shoulder at the dim, deserted parking garage. "I just keep hoping that Gary will turn up and this will end."

"What are the police going to do next?"

"I didn't ask," Jolie admitted. "They're trying to identify the woman."

"Did they give you a description of her?"

"Only that she was Caucasian with dark hair."

"Hm. What kinds of questions did they ask about Gary?"

"It was just one detective, a woman, and she asked me a lot about Gary's job."

"What did you tell her?"

"Not much—like I told you before, Gary was vague about that part of his life." Jolie hesitated, then said, "Leann?"

"Yeah?"

"I know you only met Gary a few times, and I know you didn't exactly click with him, but did you ever get the feeling that he was capable of . . . murder?"

"He was a little manic maybe, but capable of murder? I just don't know." Leann made a rueful noise. "On the other hand, Jolie, you have to admit that you might be a little gullible where men are concerned."

She blinked and allowed that painful tidbit to sink in.

"I'm sorry, Jolie, I shouldn't have said that."

"No," Jolie said in a hoarse voice, "it's okay. But I should go. I'll call you soon."

She disconnected the call and turned off her phone, then focused on the designs on her windshield made from various bugs whose lives had ended suddenly simply because she'd been going in the opposite direction. The randomness of it all was mind-blowing. She was assailed with an overwhelming sense of "float," that her life seemed to be shifting out from under her.

Maybe Leann was right. Maybe she was gullible where men were concerned . . . where Gary was concerned. She'd taken his smiles and stories at face value, and when red flags had raised in her mind, she hadn't probed or pushed because . . . Why? Because she felt special that someone like him wanted to be with someone like her and she didn't want to risk breaking the spell?

Waves of shame rolled over her. Forget what Gary had gotten himself into. What had *she* gotten *herself* into?

She had obviously overestimated Gary's feelings for her—but had she also overestimated her feelings for him? Maybe she intentionally turned a blind eye to the problem areas of their relationship because he had been such a source of moral support for her, he had constantly encouraged her to break out of her shell, to take on the world. Her shyness and aversion to new people and new situations had confounded Gary. Over and over he had said she had the makings of a successful individual—she simply needed to crash through her self-imposed barriers. She had believed him, had started making changes in her life even after his disappearance . . . only now to discover that he'd left her saddled with this unbelievable debacle.

She inhaled a cleansing breath, then started her car and eased her way out of the parking garage and into traffic. The worst of the rush hour was over, but there were still plenty of cars to weave through from where the Lenox mall was located in Buckhead north to her apartment complex in Roswell. Her route took her over a section of the muddy Chattahoochee River, running high from recent rains. Her throat convulsed as she gazed over the broken, angry surface of the rushing water.

Shortly after she'd met Gary, Mr. Sanders had put together an outing for the employees of the agency and their families that included an afternoon of "tubing" down the 'Hooch. Single employees were allowed to invite two guests, so she'd asked Leann and after much hesitation, Gary, to sit in an inner tube and float, butt in water, down the river. Leann had taken an instant dislike to Gary, but Jolie had felt the first stirrings of something deeper as he made jokes and entertained them all afternoon.

A memory chord strummed . . . Gary teasing her about

her fear of the brown, frothy water, about not knowing what was beneath the surface.

"*The 'Hooch would be the perfect place to dump something you wanted to get rid of,*" he'd said. "*There's no telling how many cars and guns and bodies are just beneath us.*" Then he'd reached over and grabbed her bare leg like a snake striking, howling with laughter when she'd let out a little scream.

Had he remembered his observation when he was looking for a place to dump his car and a body? Had the woman already been dead? The likelihood of him being near the river bank and accidentally driving into the water seemed remote, and if it had been an accident, why hadn't he contacted the police?

Fear took root in her stomach, slowly encompassing all of her internal organs. Denial warred with reality. Had she allowed a cold-blooded killer into her home and into her bed? Was it only happpenstance that had kept *her* from being the woman strapped into his car and sent to a watery grave?

When the enormity of her gullibility hit home, tears threatened to engulf her. She gripped the steering wheel and gulped for air until she gave herself the hiccups. By the time she pulled into her assigned parking space in the apartment complex, the day sat on the precipice of darkness, and she was thoroughly spooked. She gathered her things and swung out of the car in one motion, slamming the door behind her. She trotted to her first-floor apartment door, warily looking for movement, shadows, anything.

Looking over her shoulder, she stuck her key in the lock and turned the deadbolt, then practically fell into the dark interior. A ringing phone pierced the silence. She fumbled for a light and scanned the kitchen and living room for intruders. Seeing none standing out in the open, she pulled the door closed behind her and clambered for the phone. She yanked up the cordless unit, her heart hammering. "Hello?"

"I'm sorry," Leann said.

Jolie's shoulders yielded to the pleading tone in her friend's voice and she dropped into her favorite chair, an overstuffed wingback, with a heavy sigh. "It's okay."

"No, it isn't. You've probably had a nightmarish day, and I go and say something stupid like that."

"It wasn't stupid," Jolie said miserably, kicking off her shoes. "It's true—I'm gullible when it comes to men, else how could this have happened?"

"We've all been fooled by men," Leann said, her voice wistful. "Let's just pray the police leave you out of this."

Jolie murmured her agreement.

"So . . . how was your first day as a shoe salesperson?"

"Exhausting. I never knew how much there was to know about shoes. Oh, and get this: Sammy Sanders stopped by."

"Ew. Was she terrible?"

"Oh, yeah."

"Well, between her and the police officer, were there any bright spots?"

Beck Underwood's interesting face flashed into her mind. "Well, I crashed into a guy while I was carrying an armload of shoes."

"That doesn't sound like a bright spot."

"The bright spot is I didn't get fired."

Leann laughed. "I admire you, Jolie—no matter what life hands you, you simply take it in stride."

"Give me an alternative," Jolie said lightly. "How's your sister?"

"Bloated, nauseous, and depressed."

Jolie hummed her sympathy. "Do you know how much longer you'll be there?"

"At least five more months, unless the baby comes early. This sounds selfish, but I keep thinking about all the clients I'm losing to other interior designers." Leann sighed. "And now this business with Gary. Listen, you probably just got home, so I'll let you go. But call me if you need to talk about it."

"I will," Jolie promised, said goodbye, then returned the phone to its cradle. She sighed, missing her neighbor friend. They had met only months ago at the apartment laundry room, but they had become fast friends, bonded by Leann's occupation in interior design and her own job in real estate. Even though she was seeing Gary, Jolie had made time to foster the new friendship because she appreciated the other woman's plain-talking wisdom. She sent good thoughts toward the ceiling for Leann's sister's problem pregnancy. As she pushed herself up from the chair, the phone rang again—classic Leann.

Jolie picked up the phone and smiled into the receiver. "What did you forget?"

Silence greeted her.

"Leann?"

Someone was there, she could hear the openness of the connected call, a faint rustle in the background. "Leann, is that you?" When there was no answer, her heart skipped a beat. "Gary?"

The rustling sound grew louder, then a click disconnected the call. Jolie swallowed and listened to the dial tone for a few seconds, then set down the phone and looked toward the darkened bedroom. Unbidden, a horror movie came to mind, the one about the cute coed receiving threatening calls all evening, only to have the police to call her later and tell her they'd traced the calls as coming from inside the house.

She wasn't a cute coed, and for the life of her she couldn't remember how the movie had ended. *For the life of her?* Bad choice of words, she conceded, moving toward the bedroom as quietly as possible. She had her cell phone in her right hand, ready to punch the speed dial button for 911. Remembering something on an airline safety report about shoes being a ready weapon, she scooped up one of her chunky-heel pumps and wielded it in the other hand, thinking that if Gary Hagan was crouching in the bedroom, he would be more likely to die from laughter than from any wound she might inflict.

Moisture gathered around her hairline as she pounced on the light switch. When she stepped into the doorway, though, the most dangerous-looking thing in her bedroom was the multi-outlet strip in the floor overloaded with a spaghetti knot of appliance cords. She scoffed at her foolishness and sat on the mossy-colored duvet to remove her pantyhose, thinking she had to get a grip on herself. Gary Hagan wasn't a murderer. It was more likely that he'd been drinking and somehow had driven into the river, then panicked when he couldn't get his companion out.

Except why would he have been near the river, so far from his apartment, so far from his neighborhood of Buckhead? And who was the dead woman?

Her gaze landed on the book that Gary had given her to read—the sales bible, he had called it. *The Magic of Thinking Big* by David J. Schwartz. She had gotten a couple of chapters into it, but had quit reading it when he disappeared, because she'd begun to feel patronized . . . not by the author, but by Gary. He was always pushing her to think about the future, to become her own boss. *"Don't spend the rest of your life working for someone else, Jolie. Why spend your energy making someone else rich?"*

It was one of the reasons she had quit the Sanders Agency; when Sammy had made a snide remark about Gary absconding with her car, quitting had seemed like both a way to defend Gary and a way to follow his advice.

Now who felt like a big, broke fool?

She rubbed her temples and decided there was no warding off the headache that had been coming on all day. Backtracking to the kitchen, she tossed down a couple of aspirin and peered into the freezer for dinner options. One chicken breast and a package of frozen whole-wheat waffles.

The waffles won. She dropped two in the toaster, then walked to her desk and flipped on her computer. She'd missed the early local news, but suspected she'd be able to find something online about the discovery reeled out of the Chattahoochee River. She glanced at the to-do list next to her computer and frowned.

Have business cards printed
Photocopy flyers for customer list
Pay E & O insurance premium
Pay fees for MLS

The errors and omissions insurance was a must to prevent an honest contractual mistake from wrecking her real-estate career, but thankfully, it was affordable. A lifetime membership to the Multiple Listing System to access home listings online would be less expensive in the long run, but five grand stood between her and that option. For now, she'd have to go the monthly subscription route. And advertising on a shoestring budget meant lots of postcards, flyers, and good old-fashioned cold-calling. She was tempted not to do anything until this bizarre situation with Gary was resolved, but when the holidays were over, the brokerage company had to be up and running. Life would go on, and she needed to be able to support herself.

Assuming she wasn't in jail, of course.

Jolie was halfway through the waffles when she found the story she was looking for on a local news web site:

CAR AND BODY PULLED FROM CHATTAHOOCHEE RIVER—A local fisherman alerted Roswell authorities that he'd found what appeared to be a late-model car just below the water's surface near the Morgan Falls Dam. A 2003 silver Mercedes sedan registered to Buckhead resident Gary Edward Hagan was pulled from the Chattahoochee River. Authorities found the decomposing body of an unidentified woman inside. A warrant has been issued for Hagan's arrest. The local and state police are asking that anyone who knows of his whereabouts contact them.

She clicked on the link to photos and inhaled sharply at the color picture of Gary's car being pulled from the water by a winch, yellow water gushing from the fender wells. The next photo showed a black body bag being loaded into a van. A lump clogged her throat at the graphic nature of the photo—from the way the body handlers held the bag, the body seemed especially unwieldy. But when Jolie hit the button for the next photo, the air fled her lungs. Gary's license photo. He was a handsome man, dark-headed with smooth brown skin, pale eyes, and a charming smile. But the DMV photo made him looked heavy-lidded and surly. Any person who saw that photo would think him capable of murder.

The waffles forgotten, Jolie stared at the photo for the longest time, her eyes watering and her doubts rearing.

Was he?

She returned to her bedroom and opened the closet door to stare down at the box of Gary's belongings that the apartment manager had given to her. She debated whether she should sort through everything or not before delivering the box to Detective Salyers—after all, if she didn't look, she could always plead ignorance.

On the other hand, Detective Salyers already believed she *had* looked.

She heaved the box to the bed and gingerly lifted the lid, releasing a smoky odor into the room. Her heart squeezed with the thought that, fugitive or no, Gary's life had been reduced to this cardboard box. She sorted through bills and junk mail and set them aside, unopened. A wire tray held more mail, but the envelopes appeared to have been opened, she assumed by Gary. A check of the postmarks confirmed that they were received the week he disappeared. She uncovered his cell-phone bill, and a half dozen credit-card invoices, all with overdue amounts that were breathtaking. Gary was either slothful about bill paying or was deeply in debt.

There was a cube of yellow note paper, on the top of which he'd scribbled, "extra door key for Gordon." She didn't remember him mentioning anyone named Gordon, but if Gary was giving him a key to his apartment, they must be close. A neighbor? A cleaning service?

There were various flyers and postcards advertising all

kinds of happenings in Buckhead, midtown, and down-town Atlanta. Concerts, art shows, restaurant openings, club events, open houses. It was how he kept up with everything, she presumed. He was on the mailing lists of the Museum of Contemporary Art, the Woodruff Arts Center, the High Museum of Art, the Fernbank Museum, the Falcons, the Braves, the Thrashers, the Hawks, and every college in the vicinity. She turned over each flyer, looking for highlighting or more hand-scribbled notes. On the back of the postcard for the High Museum, he had written—illegibly—what looked like "hardy manuals." The nonsensical words meant nothing to her.

There were sales papers, random coupons, and other ir-relevant pieces of mail. She almost missed a small enve-lope the size of a gift card. The envelope was blank, but contained a tiny pink card. Outside it read, "Missing you," and inside it read "Missing me?" The card was signed, not with a signature, but with a lip imprint in pink lipstick. The imprint was smeared, badly . . . purposefully, but by the sender or by the receiver? Was it a message from his "troubled" ex? Since the envelope had no address or stamp, the sender had obviously delivered it in person, or left it where Gary would find it.

She returned the card to its envelope, then delved through the rest of the box's contents—a couple of base-ball caps, although not the burnt-orange-colored one he wore most often. A couple of sports-themed paper-weights, a Swiss Army knife, a handful of matchbooks from local restaurants, some bottles of over-the-counter painkillers, a few music CDs he'd burned and labeled himself—80s ROCK, 90s ROCK, DELTA BLUES. She winced when she thought of his extensive music and movie col-lection being melted down by the fire.

At the bottom of the box was a dusty framed photograph of his parents, a Midwestern-looking couple dressed in sensible clothes, smiling as if they were having an appropriate amount of fun. She thought of her own parents and how frantic they would be if they had lived to witness this. A wry smile curved her mouth as she wondered which would consume her mother the most—her proximity to a hideous crime, or utilizing her hard-won college degree to sell shoes.

There was a small photo album, which surprised her because Gary didn't seem like the sentimental type. The photos in the beginning were dated and yellowed—various shots of him growing up, labeled on the back in a neat, feminine script, and she guessed that Gary's mother had started the album and perhaps he had added to it after her death. The more recent pictures were mostly snapshots of him with various well-dressed people she didn't recognize. The women were numerous, but none of them seemed to have been singled out by the camera. As she turned pages, however, the faces of four *men* seemed to occur more often than others—and the men appeared to know each other. Could one of them be the Gordon who was to receive an extra key? She slipped out each photo, but none of the recent pictures was labeled on the back.

There were also a couple of photos of Gary by himself outdoors. In one he was sitting on a rock, dressed in hiking gear and mugging for the camera. The next was of the same location, but a closer shot. Fingers obscured the lower edge of the picture—a woman's fingers, with nice nails. The picture was dated a year ago by the film developer, but again not labeled. Was the photographer the mysterious pink-lipped ex?

She turned pages and scanned photos of holiday parties, then she smiled, surprised to see photos taken during their inner tube float down the river. She had felt awkward giving them to him, had been afraid he would think she was trying to force the issue of them being a couple, but had reasoned that the shots were group shots, not just of her and Gary. They were all smiling, everyone wet—even Sammy—having a good time. Jolie turned the page and stared at the last photo, then her smile evaporated.

This was another group photo from that summer day, except Gary's tube was bumped up next to hers. She remembered the moment, had reached out to playfully push him away. But the way her hand rested on his arm looked proprietary.

And it obviously had disturbed someone who had viewed the picture, because her face had been obliterated by a slashing red X.

Four

"Is Detective Salyers available?" Jolie asked, setting the box on the counter lip in front of a thick window that she assumed was bulletproof.

The cop behind the counter pulled on his chin. "She's out on a case. Can I help you?"

"My name is Jolie Goodman. She asked me to drop this off. It's related to a case she's working on."

"Hold on." The man rummaged for a pen and paper, then slid both underneath the half-inch gap at the bottom of the window. "Write her a note, will you?"

Jolie took the pen and scrawled, "From Jolie Goodman re: G. Hagan," and added her cell phone number. She stuffed the note down in the top of the box, and the man came through a side door to take it from her. "I'll make sure she gets it."

Jolie thanked him, then exited the bustling station and jogged toward her car. If traffic wasn't too bad, she *might* make the sales meeting on time. She slid into her seat and closed the car door, fighting the urge to skip the meeting, to skip her shift—hell, to skip the entire day.

But that would only make things worse. In fact, she really should be around people today, around crowds, to take her mind off the events of yesterday that were threatening to consume her. She started the car and turned it in the direction of Lenox Square, stifling a yawn, a result of the sleep she didn't get last night.

She'd placed a giant cactus beneath her bedroom window and slept with a fire extinguisher—the only thing she had that could remotely be considered a weapon. She might have to use her employee discount to buy something more threatening today, although at the moment the most dangerous thing she could think of that Neiman Marcus had to offer was the employee discount itself.

She maneuvered back roads to get to the mall and found a good parking place at this early hour. Ten minutes later she slipped into the room where, to her great relief, the sales meeting had just gotten under way. From the front, Michael Lane gave her an approving nod, then pointed to his name badge and back to her. All employees, she recalled, were supposed to wear their name badges while on duty and during company functions.

She retrieved her badge from her bag, and fastened it while the store manager, Lindy, a neurotic redhead with a high-frequency voice, recited numbers from the previous weekend's sale. She recognized individual departments that were performing well, including shoes (Michael beamed), housewares, and women's fine apparel, specifically Prada.

"Speaking of which," Lindy said, her gaze landing somewhere behind Jolie, "here's our star sales consultant for the week, Carlotta Wren. Carlotta just topped the former weekly sales record, which she also set, by the way. Congratulations, Carlotta."

Jolie joined in the smattering of applause and turned to see what a star sales consultant looked like. Carlotta Wren stood behind Jolie's chair, tall, with long, straight dark hair clasped in a low ponytail. Her slender, hour-glass figure was wrapped in a sport-stretch red dress complemented with red platform shoes and a dark denim leather-trimmed Prada tote. She had large, exotic features, including a wide smile with a gap between her front teeth, reminiscent of Lauren Bacall. She took a little bow, then said, "Thank you, thank you," and dropped into the seat next to Jolie, smelling of something musky and mysterious.

"What did I miss?" she whispered.

"Not much," Jolie whispered back, instantly edgy from the nervous energy rolling off the woman.

"You're new. I'm Carlotta." She stuck out her manicured hand.

"I'm Jolie," she murmured, giving the outstretched hand a shake, conscious of her own gnawed-down nails.

"Jolie? Do you work with Michael in shoes?"

Jolie nodded.

"Oh, *you're* the one."

"The one what?"

Carlotta waved her hand. "Oh, honey, we definitely have to talk after this waste-of-time meeting."

Jolie had hoped to spend the time between the meeting and the beginning of her shift at the copy store printing flyers, so she didn't encourage the woman's attention. But when the meeting ended thirty minutes later, Carlotta turned and said, "I'm starving—have breakfast with me."

"Well, I—"

"What time do you clock in?"

"Noon, but—"

"Good," Carlotta said with a gap-toothed grin. "We have plenty of time to get to know each other. I'm meeting my friend Hannah and you'll love, love, *love* her."

Joining them seemed like a foregone conclusion, and the decision was cinched by Jolie's howling stomach—the waffles had been forever ago. "Okay." Besides, she missed having Leann around to talk to. She could use a friend or two.

Carlotta walked liked royalty, her shoulders hyper-extended and her chest thrust forward. She was a head taller than Jolie, and she had the longest neck Jolie had ever seen.

"How do you like it in shoes?" Carlotta's voice was nasal and clipped.

"My first day was a little rough," Jolie said.

"You'll be great—you have the perfect look for selling shoes."

Jolie glanced down at her non-designer uniform of khaki-colored skirt, pale blue blouse, black blazer, and low-heeled sandals. "Okay."

"Relax, I meant that in a good way. You look . . . ap-proachable. That's important for shoes. Now where *I* am, in designer wear, it's best to look *un*approachable. That scares off the riffraff who want to waste your time trying on things they can't afford. Only the people with serious money have the balls to come up to me."

Jolie was beginning to see why this woman was a star sales consultant. "How long have you worked retail?"

"For most of my adult life, and trust me, it doesn't get better than Neiman's. Are you working part-time?"

"Yes, through the holidays."

"Did your company downsize? We've gotten a lot of part-timers from the telecom layoffs."

"Um, no, actually, I'm in real estate."

"Ah. Say no more. Plenty of my good customers are re-altors, and they're hurting, skipping trunk shows and buy-ing clearance instead." She sighed and shook her head. "It's so sad."

Jolie could only nod.

"On the other hand, there are just as many women who can no longer afford their shrinks or their Zoloft, so they're practicing shopping therapy." Carlotta grinned. "It all evens out."

The mall wasn't as busy today and the food court was nearly empty. Jolie eyed the spot where she had met De-tective Salyers and felt a stirring of anxiety.

"We're meeting Hannah at the Crepe Cafe," Carlotta said, nodding toward the end of the corridor.

Jolie groaned inwardly, wondering how big a dent breakfast would put in her wallet. She'd lain awake most of the night wondering what she could sell if she needed an attorney, but all she could come up with was a kidney. She was a frugal person—she could get by on one.

"Hannah knows the chef here," Carlotta said, "so we'll eat for free as long as we leave a nice tip."

The woman was either a mind reader or she thought Jolie looked poor. Regardless, Jolie was grateful.

Carlotta's friend hadn't yet arrived, but they were shown to a cloth-covered table in a sunny alcove. Carlotta flirted outrageously with the waiter and asked for Pellegrino bot-tled water. Jolie asked for hot water and lemon, and scanned the menu, which sported some rather alarming prices.

"So, Jolie," Carlotta said over the top of her menu, "I must hear all about your encounter with Beck Underwood."

Jolie lifted her eyebrows, and the man's face came into her mind. "My encounter? I sold him a pair of shoes."

"No, back up," Carlotta said, waving her hand. "I haven't seen a picture of him in ages. What does he look like these days?"

She recalled that Michael had said Carlotta was a bona fide celebrity groupie. "Um, he was sunburned, mostly."

"Come on, is he still gorgeous?"

Jolie shrugged and her cheeks warmed. "I wouldn't say 'gorgeous,' maybe . . . striking."

Carlotta grinned and her shoulders shook with a dramatic shudder. "You know he's one of the most eligible bachelors in Atlanta."

"Um, no, I didn't."

"Do you have a boyfriend?"

Jolie swallowed hard and shook her head.

"Really? You're so pretty. With the right makeup, you could pass for Charlize Theron. I met her once at a club—her skin is, like, perfect."

A little overwhelmed, Jolie simply nodded. "Where are you from?"

"Here. I grew up in Virginia-Highland."

"That's nice," Jolie said, referring to the area of Atlanta and to Carlotta's circumstances. The woman was obviously from money. Old money.

"You?" Carlotta asked.

"I grew up in Dalton," Jolie said.

North of Atlanta on Interstate 75, Dalton, Georgia was the carpet capital of the Southeast. Both of her parents had retired from flooring factories, and she wasn't the least bit ashamed, although she was prepared for the woman to wash her hands of her.

Instead, Carlotta's eyes lit up. "Do you know Deborah Norville?"

Jolie smiled. Newswoman Deborah Norville was Dalton's other claim to fame. "I met her once at a charity walk, she seemed really nice."

"Darn, I'd love to have her in my book."

"Your book?"

Carlotta reached into her bag and pulled out a small, pink, leather-bound book. "I started when I was a teenager—I met Jane Fonda at a Braves game, and it changed my life." She flipped through the book, showing Jolie the tabbed pages. "I record who I meet and where, and every category has its own alphabetized section: actors, athletes, singers and musicians, politicians, newspeople, businesspeople, and personalities."

"Personalities?"

"You know—people you recognize, but you're not really sure what they do . . . like Fergie, Duchess of York. Who, by the way, I would *kill* to meet."

This woman would have loved Gary, Jolie thought. He could have introduced her to all kinds of celebrities. Jolie nodded toward the well-worn book. "So who's the biggest celebrity you've met?"

"Hmm, it's a toss-up between Antonio Banderas and Elton John, but since Elton has a home here, I guess I'd have to say Antonio. And maybe Bill Gates."

"Wow. How did you meet Bill Gates?"

"At a party. Elton I saw at a restaurant. And I've met lots of celebrities at the Sunglass Hut right here in the mall."

"No kidding?"

"Yeah, everybody famous needs sunglasses. Atlanta is a fabulous place to spot celebrities because there aren't that many places for them to go, and they usually don't have a paparazzi guard with them because it's the South and most people don't really care who they are as long as they wipe their feet."

Jolie laughed, grateful for the woman's entertaining banter. The waiter brought Carlotta's Pellegrino and Jolie's hot water, and while Jolie squeezed the lemon wedge into the steaming cup, Carlotta looked up and waved at someone behind Jolie. "Oh, here's Hannah."

Jolie turned in her seat to see a woman with short black-and-white-striped hair coming their way. She wore a white culinary smock, jeans, and black combat boots. A plain canvas bag slung over her shoulder hung almost to her knees. She smiled and swung into the seat adjacent to Jolie. "Hiya."

Carlotta made introductions. Hannah Kizer was more reserved than Carlotta, but adventuresome, judging by her hair and the silver barbell through her tongue. Jolie was so fascinated, she could barely focus on what the woman was saying. When the waiter took her drink order, they placed their food orders, and Hannah excused herself to say hello to the chef.

"Is she a chef too?" Jolie asked, watching her walk through the swinging doors of the kitchen.

"She's still a culinary student," Carlotta said. "But she works for one of the best caterers in town, and she flat-out knows food."

A minute later, Hannah came back and settled into her chair. "Sorry I was late—MARTA is running slow this morning." She tapped short, neat nails on the table and Jolie caught a slight whiff of cigarette smoke.

"We were just getting to know each other," Carlotta said. "Jolie works in shoes, so when you're ready for a new pair of ugly boots, she can help you out."

Hannah smirked, and Jolie, a loner all of her life, admired their teasing relationship.

"Have you heard about the bash at the High Museum tomorrow night?" Hannah asked, her tone slightly mocking.

Carlotta leaned forward, her eyes shining. "No—what is it?"

"A wine tasting for the big contributors, eight o'clock. The guest list is hush-hush, so I'm guessing there are some important people attending."

"We have to go!" Carlotta said.

"I have to work it," Hannah said, sounding disappointed.

"Jolie will go with me," Carlotta said, then turned to Jolie. "Doesn't it sound like fun?"

Jolie felt sheepish. "I'm kind of on a tight budget."

Carlotta pshawed. "I got you covered. Do you know where the entrance ramp to the museum is?"

Jolie nodded.

"Meet me there, eight thirty sharp."

Her mind raced and it occurred to her that the kind of people that Gary had worked for could be found at such get-togethers. Who knew? She might be able to find out something about his "work," and maybe a clue to the identity of his scary ex.

When her practiced excuses not to socialize rose in her mind, Jolie reminded herself it meant she wouldn't be sitting at home alone, imagining herself with a big red *X* on her head. "Okay . . . but what should I wear?"

"A black dress and great jewelry. Oh, and bring a biggish purse."

Five

The next evening Jolie was lucky enough to find parking along Peachtree Street, a mere block from the High Museum of Art. When she climbed out of the car, her stomach fluttered with nerves. Had she worn the right dress? Would she say the right things? Would she stumble across someone who knew Gary? And more immediate, how much, if any, of the story of Gary should she share with Carlotta?

She had sidestepped Michael Lane's questions at work, thinking that even if he'd seen the news, he couldn't possibly connect a car and a woman being pulled out of the river with her comment that her boyfriend was missing. She'd simply told him they were checking in with her. In fact, in the light of day, it was easy to convince herself that everything would work out all right. In was only after the sun set, like now, that her imagination went into overdrive, projecting all kinds of atrocities onto the slightest sound or movement.

She had taken only a few steps down the sidewalk when

from the depths of her "biggish" purse, her cell phone rang. She stopped under a streetlight to remove the phone. She didn't recognize the local number, but she punched the CALL button anyway.

"Hello?"

"Ms. Goodman, this is Detective Salyers. Is this a bad time?"

"Um, no," she said, stepping back to allow a well-dressed couple to walk by.

"I'm sorry I didn't get back to you sooner, I got slammed yesterday and today. I did have a chance to go through the box of items you dropped off. I assume you looked through them, too."

"Yes, I did."

"Did anything jump out at you as being odd?"

"You mean other than the photo with my head crossed out?" she asked wryly.

"So you *did* see the pictures?"

"Yes."

"Do you think that Mr. Hagan was the person who drew that *X* over your picture?"

Jolie sighed. "I just don't know. I can't imagine why he would do something like that. Unless . . ."

"Unless?"

"Unless he was getting ready to break off our relationship, and that mark was some kind of joke."

"Did you recognize anyone in the other pictures?"

"No."

"Did you send Mr. Hagan the note with the lipstick print?"

"No."

"And you don't have any idea who might have?"

"That's right."

"Did you realize that Mr. Hagan was heavily in debt?"

"We didn't discuss our finances with each other."

"When you were out together, did he use cash or credit cards?"

She squinted, trying to remember. "Cash, mostly."

"His bank account is overdrawn. I ran a check on Mr. Hagan's credit cards, and they haven't been used since that Friday before his disappearance. Does he have access to any of your cards?"

Jolie frowned. "No, and I didn't give Gary one of my credit cards, if that's what you're asking."

"He might have stolen a card. Have you noticed unusual activity on any of your accounts?"

Jolie opened her mouth to say no, then realized she hadn't received this month's statement on her VISA and American Express. She'd been in such a hurry to get inside her apartment the last two nights, she hadn't even stopped to check the mail. "I . . . haven't noticed, no."

"Have you heard from Mr. Hagan?"

"No," Jolie said. "But . . . I had a hang-up on my home phone Monday night."

"What time?"

"Between seven thirty and eight."

"You don't have Caller ID?"

"Not on my home phone."

"Do you think it was Mr. Hagan?"

"I don't know," Jolie said. "I'm just trying to keep you informed."

Salyers sighed into the phone. "Ms. Goodman, I want to believe that you had nothing to do with this, but I talked to the woman who lives above you. She said she had her window open one night a few weeks ago and heard you and a man arguing on your doorstep."

Jolie frowned. "Mrs. Janklo? The woman has a hearing aid."

"Well, she must have had the volume turned up. She said the two of you were arguing about your car."

Jolie's mind spun, trying to recall what the woman might have overheard. A memory surfaced, and she gave a little laugh. "Oh, one night when Gary left, he was teasing me about how boring my car was, and I got a little indignant. That must have been what Mrs. Janklo heard."

Salyers made a little snort of disbelief. "Do you remember when that conversation took place?"

"Not really . . . maybe a week before he disappeared."

A voice sounded in the background and the detective covered the phone to say something to someone, then came back on the line. "I have to take another call. But we'll be talking again, Ms. Goodman." Then she hung up.

Jolie frowned at the phone, irritated that she was being cooperative and the woman still seemed intent on implicating her in this mess. In fact, the more information she shared, the more the detective seemed to misinterpret. Detective Salyers' response made her feel determined to find out more about Gary on her own. Maybe she could find him herself, encourage him to give himself up . . . and maybe return her car.

She stashed her phone and resumed walking toward the museum, which was lit up like a big luminaria adorning midtown. The building sat back from the street on a rise, and the long, sloping, ramped entrance was part of its architectural grandeur. A spectacularly dressed woman as tall as Carlotta Wren waited near the bottom of the ramp, but as Jolie drew closer and slowed her pace, she realized the woman was blonde.

"Thank God. I thought you had left me hanging," the woman said.

Jolie squinted and walked closer. "Carlotta?"

The woman laughed and touched her Marilyn Monroe-like hair. "Sorry—I should have told you that I might alter my appearance."

"Is that a wig?"

"Of course—don't you have wigs?"

"No," Jolie said, feeling rather stodgy.

Carlotta waved her hand. "Well then, let's get a look at you."

Jolie stood stock still while Carlotta walked around her, perusing her modest black swing dress, clucking like a hen. "Not bad—are those real pearls?"

Jolie nodded and touched her throat. "My mother's . . . mine now."

"Nice touch." Then Carlotta looked down and frowned. "But your first purchase with your employee discount really must be shoes—what *are* those?"

Jolie squirmed and looked down at her chunky-heeled slingbacks. "I don't know—I've had them for a while."

"Hmm. Remember, vintage is good. *Old* is not good. But your makeup is great, and your hair is fabulous—what did you do to it?"

"Washed and combed it."

"Hmm. If you tell me it's naturally curly, I'm going to kill you."

"Trust me, curly hair is much more trouble than it's worth."

Carlotta sighed in obvious disagreement. "Let's go in before all the booze is gone."

Jolie took a deep breath and followed the woman up the

ramp. Carlotta had not adhered to her own advice to wear a black dress—her zebra-striped coatdress fairly glowed, and would have been almost loud, except it was overshadowed by her strappy pink and rhinestone shoes.

Jolie gaped. "Those are the shoes kept under glass by the register."

Carlotta looked down. "Oh, right—the Manolos. Limited edition. Aren't they amazing?"

"Yes," Jolie murmured, stunned that star sales consultant or no, the woman could afford a two-thousand-dollar pair of shoes. Then she remembered that Carlotta had inferred that she'd grown up with money. Maybe she had a trust fund. Jolie trailed her to the entrance, where a woman in a staid suit eyed Carlotta suspiciously. "Tickets?"

"Of course," Carlotta said, producing two long tickets and extending them with a glib smile.

The woman frowned and lowered her reading glasses from her forehead to her nose. "Those aren't the right tickets."

Carlotta laughed, then took the tickets back and opened her purse—which was quite "biggish," Jolie noticed. "I'm so sorry," Carlotta said, reaching into her bag. "I simply have too much on my calendar this week. Are the tickets blue?"

"Yes," the woman said.

"Ah. Here they are." Carlotta withdrew another pair of tickets, this time pale blue.

The woman glanced at them, then nodded and dropped the tickets through a slit into a wooden box. "Have a nice time, Ms. Holcomb," she said with a magnanimous smile.

"Oh, we will," Carlotta said, then clasped Jolie by the arm and pulled her forward.

"Are the Holcombs friends of yours?" Jolie asked.

"Hmm? Oh . . . I guess you could say that."

They walked down the narrow foyer, which made an abrupt left turn and opened into an extensive atrium, open to the top story of the museum. Suited men and decked-out women mixed and mingled on a shiny white marble floor. The room whispered *money*. The hum of voices and low, sporadic laughter were background to a quartet playing cymbal-brushing jazz. Wine and perfume wafted on the air, tickling Jolie's nose. In the presence of so much privilege, her pulse picked up. Tanned, glowing skin abounded—as well as severe, highlighted hair, waxed and gelled into individual little works of art. Everyone was trying hard—trying to jockey for a good position to be seen while casting furtive glances over their wineglasses in search of better people. Jolie noticed that *she* didn't garner more than a glance, but almost everyone stopped to consider Carlotta in her outrageous designer outfit and platinum blonde wig, although more than one mouth twitched downward.

"All I see are stiffs," Carlotta murmured. "Let's get some wine and find out where the interesting people are hanging out."

Jolie started to take a step toward the bar when Carlotta ducked into an alcove next to a bronze sculpture. At a loss, Jolie followed.

"Isn't this a stunning piece?" Carlotta asked, stepping in front of the sculpture with her back to the corridor.

Jolie looked at the stack of cubes seemingly melting into one another. "I'm not an art connoisseur, but yes, it's interesting."

"Step closer," Carlotta urged, and Jolie obliged.

"Keep talking as if we're having a conversation," Carlotta said out of the corner of her mouth.

"I thought we *were* having a conversation," Jolie said, then noticed that Carlotta had opened her purse.

"Don't stare at my purse," Carlotta hissed. "Keep talking."

Bewildered, Jolie jerked her gaze back to the sculpture. "Y—you don't have a gun in there, do you?"

"What are you, crazy? Of course I don't. Talk, for heaven's sake."

Jolie swallowed. "As I was saying, my knowledge of art is pretty limited. I know some of the names, but I have a difficult time—"

"Here you go," Carlotta said, nodding and smiling while pressing something hard and cold against Jolie's hand. "You don't have to look down, it's a wineglass and a napkin."

Jolie curled her fingers around both items, now thoroughly confused. "What for?"

"It's a wine tasting," Carlotta said through clenched teeth.

"And we have to bring our own glasses?"

"Unless we want to pay a hundred dollars for one of theirs," Carlotta said, still smiling. "How do you think they make money at these events? Just come with me and do what I do."

Jolie watched as Carlotta casually peeled off, carrying her empty wineglass in her right hand, a cocktail napkin held beneath the stem with her pinky. Jolie made her feet move and she lifted her glass similarly, although it took her a few seconds to get the pinky thing down. She followed Carlotta past the table where a gloved waiter was handing wineglasses to patrons in return for one-hundred-dollar bills, then joined one of the lines behind a semicircle of tables where stewards poured an inch of wine from any of a dozen bottles before them.

Despite the encouraging glances from Carlotta, a sweat broke out along Jolie's hairline. What if someone had seen them? She looked around, fully expecting a security guard to bound over and oust them.

"It's just a little wine," Carlotta whispered. "They'll never miss it."

Jolie nodded and tried to smile, but her palms were slick against her glass as she watched Carlotta hand the steward the smuggled stemware. The young man seemed a little too dazzled by Carlotta's curves to pay much attention to the glass. Carlotta gestured to a bottle of chardonnay, and he nodded happily, pouring the requisite inch, then adding an extra splash. Carlotta twisted and smiled prettily, then winked at Jolie when she turned to walk away.

"What can I get for you, ma'am?" the young man asked.

Jolie jumped. "Oh . . . the merlot would be fine."

He smiled and gestured. "I need your glass."

She flushed. "Of course." She handed it over, her chest tight.

He held up the glass and frowned, sending her heart pounding. "You have a smudge," he said finally, then polished the glass with a cloth.

She exhaled in relief and silently willed him to hurry as he poured the berry-colored wine into her glass. "There you are," he said, nodding.

She thanked him, then joined Carlotta, who was walking back toward the crowd.

"See, that didn't hurt, did it?"

Jolie sipped the ill-gotten wine. "It wasn't exactly honest, but I suppose the tickets to get in were expensive."

"I suppose," Carlotta said with a secret little smile.

"Did your friends the Holcombs simply give them to you?"

Carlotta shook her head, her lips wet with wine. "Jolie, I don't know anyone named Holcomb. My brother printed those tickets for me on a laser printer."

Jolie blinked and almost choked on her wine. "You mean, we're . . . party crashers?"

Carlotta laughed. "You should see the look on your face. It's not a crime, you know."

"But it's . . . it's . . . dishonest."

"It doesn't hurt anyone," Carlotta said, then swept her arm toward the crowd. "Do you think anyone in this herd cares?"

Indeed, no one seemed to be paying them any mind.

"Then why do it?" Jolie asked.

Carlotta shrugged her lovely shoulders and pursed her mouth. "Because it's exciting to see what you can get away with."

"You do this a lot?"

"Yeah, usually Hannah and I hit a couple of gigs a week. She knows every catered event in town."

"But how do you know about the tickets?"

"Every place in town uses the same printer. This museum uses the same ticket format on either white or blue paper."

"That's why you had two sets of tickets."

Carlotta answered with an exaggerated nod.

"Do the Holcombs even exist?"

"Somewhere," Carlotta said. "I always use an old Atlanta last name. That way even if someone suspects me, they're usually too intimidated to ask questions." She grinned, revealing her gapped teeth. "Come on, let's mingle."

Jolie fell into stride beside her. "What if someone asks who I am?"

"Well, I never give out my real name, but that's up to you. Tonight, I'm Carly Holcomb."

"Do you always wear a wig?"

"No . . . sometimes I wear glasses or do other things to change my appearance if I feel like it. It's fun to pretend to be someone else for a few hours." She nodded to a food-laden table. "And tonight I feel like being someone who eats Beluga."

"Have you ever gotten caught?"

Carlotta shook her head. "It's all about the attitude. The trick to party crashing is to act as if you belong. Oh, there have been times when people suspected I'd crashed, but who's going to bounce someone who's entertaining the guests? I talk to people, work the room. When I go to someone's home, I fawn over pets, and I always take a hostess gift." She grinned again and lifted her glass to herself. "I'm so gracious, who wouldn't want me to crash their party?"

Jolie was in awe of the woman's chutzpah. Carlotta made her feel as if she'd been living her life in a very small way. While she was squirreled away in her apartment eating frozen waffles, Carlotta was cruising upscale soirees eating caviar.

They filled tiny saucers with bite-sized delicacies, and Jolie's stomach rejoiced. Carlotta had impeccable manners, she noticed, eating precisely and blotting with her napkin between bites. The woman knew how to behave in polite society.

"Do your parents still live around here?" Jolie asked.

Carlotta's expression changed. "No, just me and my brother. Will you be okay if I split to find Hannah and say hello?"

Jolie nodded and watched Carlotta disappear into the crowd, wondering if she'd hit a nerve. She downed one more stuffed mushroom, then handed her plate to a passing waiter, feeling like a heel that she was there under false pretenses and being waited on. She glanced around the room, suddenly antsy as she surveyed the expensive clothes and winking jewelry, watching everyone moving with regal restraint as they sipped and nipped and glad-handed people around them. Everyone seemed to know everyone else, and she had the feeling that she was observing carefully trained animals. It was morbidly fascinating to watch them interact—this was the interplay that Gary had hinted at, the ongoing drama of the rich and famous.

Remembering her initial reason for coming, she opened her purse and slipped out the one group photo from Gary's album that she'd kept. It showed the four men that seemed to dominate the photos, and three women, plus Gary. She scanned each face, memorizing features that wouldn't have changed, then returned the photo to her purse. After fixing her expression into one of faint concern, she worked her way around the room, methodically glancing at faces while craning her neck as if she were looking for a lost friend. Face by face, she eliminated most of the crowd, then something about one man standing a few yards away made her look again. Early thirties, receding hairline, dark slashes for eyebrows . . . one of the men in the photos, she was almost certain. Then he lifted his drink-holding arm to rest it on the shoulder of a man next to him and her mouth went dry—it was the same pose, except in the photo he'd been leaning on Gary's shoulder.

"Did you find the person you've been looking for?" a man said near her ear.

Jolie jumped and turned to see Beck Underwood standing there, holding a one-hundred-dollar wineglass full of what looked suspiciously like beer.

Six

"Jolie, right?" the man asked, then pointed to his shiny new loafers.

She looked down, and on the way back up noticed that he'd traded his holey jeans and sport coat for a dark gray suit and collarless cream shirt. His brown eyes danced, and a smile played on his mouth. Jolie had heard people described as breathtaking before, but she'd never actually had the mere sight of someone squeeze the air out of her lungs. She opened her mouth and dragged in a deep breath. "Yes. And you're Beck . . . Underwood."

He nodded, then tsked. "Except you're one up on me— I don't know your last name."

Carlotta's advice not to use her last name flitted through her mind, but Jolie decided there had been enough deceit for one night. "Goodman."

"Well, Jolie Goodman, what brings you to this roaring bore of a party?"

She glanced inadvertently at the man she recognized

from Gary's photographs, then back. "Actually, I came with a friend."

"Ah. A male friend?"

"No."

He gestured vaguely to the crowd with his wineglass. "Am I keeping you from finding her?"

"No, she'll find me. In fact, she's rather eager to meet you."

His eyebrows lifted. "Me?"

"She says you're a celebrity."

"And why would you be spending time with an outrageous liar?"

She laughed. "We work together."

"In retail or in real estate?"

Suspicion suffused her chest. "Retail . . . but how did you know that I'm in real estate?"

"Your former boss gave me her card."

She felt foolish. "Oh. Right." Remembering the events of that ghastly day, she sipped her wine and glanced back to the man from Gary's photograph.

"Is Roger a friend of yours?" Beck nodded toward the man who had caught her attention.

"Um, no . . . but he looks familiar. Do you know him?"

"Roger LeMon. He and my sister Della dated years ago."

Jolie wet her lips, feeling like a gumshoe. "Do you know anything about him?"

"Old family, made their money in banking—I think Roger is a venture capitalist, but I've been away for a while." He grinned. "I've also lost my touch, if I'm standing here answering questions about another guy."

Her cheeks blazed. "I'm . . . just trying to place how I might know him."

He looked philosophical. "He's not available anyway—

the poor guy is married." Then he frowned. "At least he used to be. I've been gone too long to know for sure."

"Someone said Costa Rica, is that right?"

"Yeah. Wonderful place."

"What did you do there?"

"I went there to facilitate an agreement to broadcast in San Juan, but that didn't pan out, and I . . . stayed."

She took in his tanned skin, his sun-bleached hair, and felt a tickle of resentment—or was it envy?—that he had the means and the guts to simply pick up and live in a foreign country for a few years. She wondered idly if Costa Rica was by chance experiencing a shortage of real-estate brokers. Or shoe salespersons. "Why did you come back?"

He lifted his shoulders in a shrug. "I missed my family. My sister was going through some things I wanted to be here for." He lifted his glass, topped with a two-inch head of foam. "And I missed the cold beer."

Jolie laughed. "I thought this was a wine tasting."

"I found a sympathetic bartender." His smile dimmed a little, then he leaned forward. "Listen . . . I've been worried about you."

He was close enough for the earthy undertones of his cologne to reach her nostrils. Her skin tingled with awareness and she resisted the urge to take a step backward . . . or forward.

"Are you in some kind of trouble?" he asked.

She was struck by his protective stance and the sincerity of his gaze. The man emanated power and money and . . . security. She pressed her toes against the soles of her shoes to counter the inclination to lean into him. The urge to trust him was overwhelming. She wet her lips. "What if I am?"

"Well," he said slowly, "depending on what kind of trouble it is, I might be able to help."

Her breathing sped up, her chest moving up and down as she mulled the ramifications of taking Beck Underwood into her confidence. His accessibility to the people Gary knew would be helpful, but would he close ranks when he found out why she was asking questions?

"There you are," Carlotta said, gliding up to stand next to Jolie. Her wineglass was newly filled and she only had eyes for Beck. "Aren't you going to introduce me to your friend, Jolie?"

Jolie couldn't decide if she was happy or irritated to see her friend, but she splayed her hand. "Beck Underwood, this is Carlot—"

"Carly," Carlotta cut in, extending her hand. "I'm Carly."

If Beck was taken aback by Carlotta's flamboyant appearance, he didn't let on. "Nice to meet you, Carly."

"It's nice to meet you too," she said, batting her eyelashes. "Are you glad to be back in Atlanta?"

His eyebrows went up, but he nodded. "Yes."

"The city has changed so much in the last few years. Have you decided what part of town you'll be living in?"

He glanced at Jolie and said, "Actually, I'm in the market for a place. Do you think you could help me out?"

Jolie froze. Yes, she needed the business, but she wasn't sure she wanted to spend that much time alone with Beck Underwood. "I, um . . ."

"Of course she can help you," Carlotta oozed, then gave Jolie the evil eye before turning back. "Jolie is a real-estate whiz. She's only selling shoes at Neiman's for the holiday discount. Isn't that right, Jolie?"

Jolie stared. It was scary how the woman ad-libbed. "I,

um . . ." She looked up at Beck, drawn in by his eyes . . . and the dollar signs in her own eyes. "Sure, I can help you . . . find a place."

"Great." He smiled, then pointed over his shoulder. "I have to leave, but do you have a card?"

"No, but—"

"But I do," Carlotta cut in, flashing a toothy smile. "Jolie can write her contact information on the back." She dug in her purse and came up with a card and a pen. The card was pale yellow and read simply "Carly" with an e-mail address and cell phone number. Jolie turned the card over and wrote her own name and cell phone number, then handed it to Beck, feeling flushed and a little unwell. "Mornings and evenings are better for me. And I'm available on Sundays."

"I'll call you," he said, then lifted his hand in a wave.

Jolie nodded and watched him walk away until she realized that Carlotta was watching her watch him. She glanced over and Carlotta grinned triumphantly. "Well done. You managed to snag the attention of the most eligible pair of pants here."

Jolie shook her head. "I'm only interested in selling him a house. People like that make me nervous."

"You mean people with money?"

Had she just put her foot in her mouth? "Well, I—"

"Don't ever let people with money make you nervous," Carlotta said, her voice suddenly level. "But always be suspicious." She scanned the crowd. "Did you know the governor is here? And Arthur Blank? All the carats and the cash in this room would be easy pickings for a thief."

Her eyes were serious and her voice was tinged with a mixture of resentment and excitement that made Jolie wonder how much of a thrill seeker Carlotta was. She had a feeling the woman was more complicated than she pretended to be.

Jolie spotted Roger LeMon. "Carlotta, do you know that man in the yellow shirt?"

Carlotta squinted. "Yeah—Roger something or another. I see him out all the time. He's a big Buckhead muckety-muck. He's hit on me a couple of times. Why?"

"I think he and I have a mutual friend."

"Well, let's go see."

Carlotta barreled toward the knot of people where the man stood talking, and Jolie followed, her heart thudding in her ears. The man was in a mixed group, but was seemingly alone and disengaged, standing a half step back and constantly surveying the room.

"Excuse me," Carlotta said, touching his arm.

He pivoted his head and when he saw Carlotta, turned away from the group all together. "Hel-*lo*."

"Hi," Carlotta said with a flirty smile. "My name is Carly, and this is my friend, Jolie."

He glanced at Jolie and nodded. "Hi there." But his attention snapped back to Carlotta. "I'm Roger LeMon." He put the twirl of a French pronunciation on the last name, and he might as well have said, *"I'm* zee big cheeze." He wasn't wearing a wedding ring, she noticed.

"So, Roger *LeMon*," Carlotta said, mimicking the pronunciation and improving upon it, "my friend Jolie thinks you two have a mutual acquaintance."

He looked back at Jolie, his thick eyebrows raised high on his forehead. "Who would that be?"

Jolie tried to affect a casual tone. "Gary Hagan?"

He drew back slightly, his eyes narrowing, then he recovered and shook his head. "Hagan, did you say?"

"Yes, Gary Hagan."

He made a noise in his throat. "No, the name doesn't ring a bell. Why would you think I would know this Hagan fellow?"

Unprepared for his flat denial, Jolie chose her words carefully. "It was a photo I saw—you look like one of the men in it with Gary."

He gave a little laugh. "Well, they say everyone has a twin somewhere. Who *is* this Hagan guy?"

"Just a friend," she said, her breathing shallow.

He squinted. "What did you say your name was again?"

Fine hairs rose on the nape of her neck. "Jolie Goodman."

He nodded, then drained his wineglass. "Ladies, it was nice meeting you," he said, edging away. "But this is, after all, a wine tasting, and I need another taste." He lifted his glass, turned and strode away.

Carlotta gave her a wry smile. "I guess you were mistaken." Then she frowned. "It's weird, but the name Gary Hagan sounds familiar to *me*."

Jolie's heart rate picked up, but she tried to maintain a steady voice. "You know Gary?"

A furrow formed on Carlotta's forehead, then she shook her head. "No, I'm thinking of another guy I used to know, Gary Haggardy." She shrugged and looked around, already bored.

Jolie watched Roger LeMon moving through the crowd. His pace seemed more hurried than someone who was chasing a drink refill. Indeed, instead of stopping at the bar, he strode past and veered off down a hallway. Curious.

"I'm going to the ladies' room," she murmured to Carlotta.

"I'll meet you at the food table," Carlotta said. "Hannah said they were getting ready to put out lobster cakes."

Jolie barely heard her as she walked away. Keeping an eye out for Roger LeMon, she traced his steps through the crowd and down the side hallway. A twin bank of pay phones sat at the end of the hall, just before the entrance to the restrooms. Roger LeMon stood with his back to her, a black phone receiver pressed to his ear. From the angry, chopping gestures he made with his other hand, she gathered he wasn't talking to his mother.

Thankful for the carpet, she walked quietly toward him. As she drew closer, she could hear his agitated, lowered voice.

"—recognized me from a photograph . . . Hell, I don't know . . . She said she was a friend . . . Goodman, Jolie Goodman . . ."

At the sound of her own name, Jolie's feet faltered and her knees threatened to give way. She spun around to make a silent retreat, but as she rounded the corner, the wineglass slipped out of her hand. She clawed the air, but the glass tumbled and bounced on the carpet, spilling wine in a red arc. Jolie stared at the glass, knowing if she retrieved it, she'd be in LeMon's line of vision—and if he'd heard the noise, he would most likely be looking. Instead she turned and racewalked back through the crowd until she reached the food table.

Carlotta, in her look-at-me ensemble, was hard to miss. She grinned. "Jolie, try the quiche—"

"I have to go."

Carlotta frowned. "Is something wrong?"

"I'm . . . not feeling well," Jolie said. Which was true. "I'll s–see you tomorrow—thanks for the ticket."

She turned and practically trotted toward the exit, sending panicked glances over her shoulder for Roger LeMon. She flew by the ticket taker and stumbled down the entrance ramp, walking as fast as her shoes would allow along the dimly lit sidewalk to her car. She gulped air as she fumbled to get her key in the lock, then realized she'd forgotten to lock the door. She grabbed at the handle and opened the door, then practically flung herself inside and slammed it shut.

She gripped the wheel, inhaling and exhaling slowly to calm her vital signs, trying to figure out what to do next. Call Detective Salyers? The woman's suspicion resounded in her head. Would she accuse Jolie of grasping at straws, or maybe lying altogether? Jolie hesitated, then reached for her purse.

"Jolie," a man said. *From the back seat.*

She froze, and terror bolted through her body at the realization that someone had been lying in wait for her. The muscles in her legs bunched and her arm flew to the door handle.

"Jolie, it's me—*Gary.*"

Seven

"Gary?" she whispered on a breath that seemed to be pulled out of her.

"*Don't* turn around, Jolie."

She stopped, mid-turn, her heart thudding in her ears. "Wh–why not?"

"So that when the police ask if you've seen me, you can say no." His voice sounded reedy and unfamiliar. Terrifying.

Her fingers curled around the metal door handle. "W–what happened to you?"

"I don't have time to explain now, but I want you to know that I didn't do what the police are accusing me of. I was set up." His voice ended on a choke.

Think, think, keep him talking. "Who . . . who was the woman in your car, Gary?"

"I can't tell you. The less you know, the better."

"But . . . where have you been?"

"Staying out of sight. They think I'm dead, and I want them to keep thinking it."

She frowned. "Who is 'they'?"

"Like I said, the less you know, the better." He sounded more agitated. "If anyone asks you about me, I simply disappeared."

"With my car," she reminded him.

"I'm sorry about that. I'll pay you back, I swear. Money, at least, isn't a problem."

She pulled the door release as far as it would go, without making noise. "How did you know I was here?"

"I followed you from your apartment. It was too dangerous to talk to you there. They would expect it."

Her skin crawled and her mind raced with questions. "Gary . . . if you were set up, why don't *you* go to the police? The detective I've been talking to—"

"Jolie, if anyone knows I'm alive, you could be in danger. That's why I had to do this—to warn you."

She swallowed. "Why would I be in danger?"

"Because of the envelope."

"What envelope?"

Silence, then . . . "Oh, God, maybe they intercepted it." He sounded desperate, making mewling noises.

"Gary," she said carefully, "what was in the envelope?"

A scrambling noise sounded from the back. "I have to go, Jolie. I'm sorry that I got you involved. I'm sorry for a lot of things." He sounded almost philosophical, as if he were talking about something in the very distant past.

"Wait, Gary—don't go. Let me drive you to a police station."

"*No.*"

"If you're in danger, they'll put you in protective custody."

He scoffed. "That only means I'll be alone when they come to kill me."

"*Who* is 'they'?"

"Bye, Jolie. Promise me you won't say anything to the police. Both of our lives depend on it."

She pressed her lips together and shook her head, fighting tears.

Suddenly he came up over the seat and put his arms around her, pressing his cheek against hers so she couldn't move her head. She screamed, but the sound was lost against the hand he cupped over her mouth. She sucked air through her nose, jerking in her attempt to fill her lungs. His hands smelled grimy, his rough beard pricking her skin. He had her arms pinned to her sides. He had never behaved aggressively toward her, and the possibility of him being high on cocaine blipped into her panicked mind. She struggled and tried to bite his fingers.

His grip tightened like a vise. "Jolie, for God's sake, I'm not going to hurt you, but you have to promise me you won't go to the police. *Please*," he begged, his voice tearful. "I need time to get my ducks in a row, then I'll go to the police."

His despair reverberated in the small car. Real or imagined, he was indeed afraid for his life. She nodded against his hand.

"Thank you," he breathed, then slowly released her mouth. "I'll be around, keeping an eye on you, but be careful, Jolie."

She gasped for fresh air and glanced in the rearview mirror, but she saw only the outline of his head and shoulders. The door slammed, sending a vibration through the small car. She clawed at the controls on the door panel until she heard the comforting *thwack* of all four doors locking, then she laid her head on the steering wheel, giving in to shuddering breaths and waves of relief . . . frustration . . . confusion. Nothing remotely like this had ever happened to her before. How had she, a normal, hard-working, *good* girl, suddenly become enmeshed in a murder investigation?

She massaged her temples, trying to chase away the fear, to clear her head enough to think. Gary was obviously terrified, but was it possible that he'd become mentally unstable—sometime before or after he'd driven his car into the river and killed that woman? And was he doing coke? With all the talk about what "they" would do to him, he'd sounded clinically paranoid. She'd promised him she wouldn't go to the police, but that went against her every gut instinct.

And what if he was telling the truth? What if he *had* been set up by some kind of drug ring and the police couldn't protect him? Roger LeMon had seemed intent on hiding his relationship to Gary, although the man didn't strike her as a criminal mastermind. If he were a successful investment broker, he might simply be worried about his reputation if the media tied him personally to a murderer.

Common sense itself kept pulling her away from Gary's fantastic tale of being set up. Wouldn't denial be a likely first line of defense? On the other hand, if he were guilty of murdering the woman in his car, why would he stay in Atlanta? Why not flee to another state, or to Mexico? He'd made it sound as if he were going to try to resolve the situation himself and go to the police afterward. What if he was right—what if she went to the police and their interference only made things worse . . . or cost him his life?

A knock sounded on the window. Jolie gripped the steering wheel and screamed until her tonsils quivered, then turned her head.

Beck Underwood stood there with his hands up, his eyes wide. "Didn't mean to scare you," he shouted, his voice muffled by the window.

Her shoulders fell in relief, but she'd had enough of men sneaking up on her for one night. She rolled down the window and demanded, "Are you following me?"

He looked perplexed. "What? No." He gestured in the direction Gary had gone. "I was coming back from walking my sister to her car and I saw you sitting here. Are you having car trouble?"

She looked up at him and burst into tears—a first for her, ever. And she wasn't sure who was more horrified, her or the man standing outside her car. While she tried to pull herself together, he squatted down to her level and placed his hand on the car door. He had big, strong hands that matched his physique . . . capable hands . . . capable of harm? She retreated a few inches, suddenly suspicious of everyone.

He sighed. "Look, Jolie, I don't know what kind of trouble you're in, but it's clear to me that you're scared of something. Does this have anything to do with that police officer coming to see you the other day?"

His voice pulled at her with a promise of comfort. Once again she had the overwhelming urge to confide in this stranger. But as the seconds ticked by, the desire to spill her guts was overridden by the fear that Gary might still be watching her, might even be within hearing distance. "I'm fine," she said, dragging a tissue from her purse. "I'm not feeling well, that's all." Now accustomed to the man seeing her at her worst, she blew her nose noisily.

"Let me drive you home," he said.

"No." She stuck the key into the ignition and turned

over the car engine. "I'll be fine. I just need a good night's sleep."

"I'll follow you home," he said.

"*No*," she said, more vehemently than she'd intended. What kind of mess was she that in the space of a minute she could find him suspicious, then trustworthy, then suspicious again?

"Good night," she said quietly, then buzzed up the window, displacing his hand.

As she pulled away from the curb, she glanced in the side mirror and watched him standing with his hands on his hips, staring after her. He had to be thinking she was the most bizarre woman he'd ever met.

Considering her current predicament, she would have to concur. In the past couple of days, she felt as if she'd entered the Twilight Zone. As she proceeded north on Peachtree Street, she scanned the sidewalks for any sign of Gary on foot, while keeping an eye on her rearview mirror for headlights. She wiped the corners of her eyes and exhaled heartily, then turned on the air conditioner full blast to dispel the faint smell of cigarettes and body odor Gary had left behind. How long had he been following her, waiting for her? She shivered, remembering the desperate edge to his voice.

What had been in the envelope he'd sent her—money? Drugs? And was this "they" he was talking about intercepting her mail? If so, "they" had already made a connection between her and Gary. Who were "they" . . . friends of his? People who knew about the missing person's report she'd filed? Police officers? Was that why Gary was afraid for her to go to the police, because they were involved somehow? Of course, the missing persons report was a matter of public record, for anyone to access.

She shook her aching head, realizing she was buying

into Gary's thin explanation of a conspiracy. Because, despite evidence to the contrary, she wanted to believe him, needed to believe him. Because she needed to justify her decision to become involved with him? Otherwise, what kind of a woman would she be if she could be conned by a con man?

Gullible? Or, in this case, *criminal*?

She reached for her purse and rummaged with one hand until she came up with her cell phone, her heart hammering against her ribs. Her thumb hovered over the number pad as she tried to decide whether to call Detective Salyers.

But what information could she provide really—other than the fact that Gary was alive, which the police already suspected? He'd given her no names, no specifics at all, to support his contention that he was set up. Salyers would probably dismiss his ramblings as those of a strung-out fugitive, then have him hunted down. And maybe haul Jolie in for good measure.

If he *was* guilty and she didn't call Salyers, he would eventually be found and brought to justice. If he was innocent and she didn't call Salyers, he might be able to gather more information in his defense before the police closed in.

So in reality, there was nothing tangible to be gained from telling Salyers about Gary's sudden reappearance. And if she implicated herself further, the police would pester her to no end. Gary's warning to be careful rang in her ears . . . The police couldn't help her there, either, other than to reiterate his warning . . . and maybe make things worse if "they" thought she was cooperating with the police.

She glanced down at the phone, wavering. When she

stopped at the next intersection, she punched in a number and waited while the phone rang one, two, three, four times.

"Hello," Leann said, sounding out of breath.

At the sound of a familiar voice, Jolie's blood pressure instantly eased. "Hey, it's me. Did I catch you at a bad time?"

"Just dealing with some throw-up," Leann said with a tired sigh.

Jolie cringed. "Your sister sounds miserable."

"Almost as miserable as I am," Leann murmured. "I thought you were going to a party tonight."

"I just left." She flipped on her signal, then merged onto Roswell Road.

"Wow, it must have been a bomb."

"No, it was fine," Jolie said. "A little ritzy for me, but . . . okay."

"Your new friend must be ritzy, too."

Was that a touch of jealousy in her voice? Jolie gave a little laugh. "Carlotta? Get this. She had fake tickets to get us in, and smuggled in wineglasses so we wouldn't have to buy them for the wine tasting."

"You *crashed* the party?"

"Yes."

Leann howled laughing. "I don't believe it! *You* crashed a shindig at the High Museum?"

Jolie frowned. "Yes." At this point, she didn't want to admit she'd been bamboozled into being bad. "Apparently, Carlotta and her friend are both serial party crashers."

"Sounds fun. So why did you leave early?"

She didn't feel like recounting the story of Roger LeMon, especially when there were more important things to report. "I was tired. But when I walked back to my car . . . Gary was waiting for me."

Leann gasped. "Gary? Are you shitting me?"

"No. He was in the backseat, hiding."

"Omigod, omigod, omigod. Are you all right? Did he hurt you?"

"No, he didn't hurt me, but he nearly frightened me to death."

Leann sputtered. "Tell me everything! Where has he been?"

"He didn't say, only that he's been hiding out. He said he's innocent, that he was set up for the woman's murder."

"Who set him up? And who was the woman?"

"He wouldn't tell me anything. He said the less I knew, the better. And he begged me not to tell the police that I'd talked to him."

"So why did he come to you at all?"

"He said he wanted to warn me that both our lives will be in danger if I go to the police."

"Gee, Jolie, he's either crazy or crazy in love if he'd risk his life just to talk to you. Do you believe him?"

"I don't know . . . maybe. He was definitely scared."

"*Tell* me you're going to the police."

Jolie bit into her lip. "I've been going back and forth trying to decide . . . but I don't think so, not yet anyway. Gary didn't tell me anything useful, and he said he needed some time to get his ducks in a row."

"You mean, like to get away?" Leann asked dryly.

"If he wanted to get away, he's had plenty of time to do that. I think he's trying to gather evidence against the people who set him up. He said then he'd go to the police himself."

"Jolie . . ." Leann's voice petered out.

"I know—you think I'm being gullible."

"Jolie, for God's sake, he's a fugitive. You could get into big trouble."

"Leann, I'm not harboring him."

"Do you know where he's staying?"

"No—if I did, I would definitely call the police. But they're already accusing me of knowing more than I do. If I told them I talked to Gary and that he didn't tell me anything, do you think they would believe me?"

"That actually makes sense. Either that or I'm sleep deprived. Do you think you'll see him again?"

"I don't know. He said he'd be keeping an eye on me, to make sure I'm safe."

Leann made a choking sound. "Doesn't that creep you out?"

"A little," she admitted. "But he actually sounded . . . protective."

"I didn't realize you cared so much for this guy."

Jolie sighed. "It's not a matter of how much I care for Gary. When that detective accused me of being an accessory, I felt helpless. If Gary is innocent, I don't want to be the person to make things worse. You had to be there, Leann, to hear his voice."

Leann made a rueful noise. "I'll support you if you're sure."

"I'm not sure of anything these days."

"I just don't want to see you wreck your life over someone like Gary Hagan."

Jolie gave a wry laugh as she wheeled into her parking place. "That would imply I had a life to wreck. I just pulled into the complex. Thanks for keeping me company on the way home."

"No problem. Look, Jolie, I know you're not big on guns, but think about getting a dog or something." She sighed. "I hate not being there—is there someone you can call if you're in real trouble? Your party-crasher friend, maybe?"

The thought of Carlotta coming to her rescue was so absurd, she almost laughed. Then, unbidden, the face of Beck Underwood popped into her mind. That protective air, the note of concern in his voice.

She swallowed. "There's . . . someone. But only if I'm in real trouble."

"Good," Leann said. "Look, I hate to run, but I think I hear my sister calling. Stay in touch, okay?"

"Okay." Jolie disconnected the call and exhaled a shaky breath. She looked all around the parking lot until she was satisfied that no one was lurking in the shadows. After gathering her purse, she opened the car door and pushed herself to her feet. She slammed the door with all her strength to warn any would-be attackers that if assaulted, she could at least make a lot of noise, then trotted to the bay of metal mailboxes next to the sidewalk. Her neglected six-by-six-inch box was stuffed full. She yanked the envelopes and catalogs out by handfuls, shoving them into her purse until she could scrutinize them in the light.

A noise behind her sent her heart to her throat, but it was only a neighbor's air-conditioning unit kicking on. Even so, she galloped to her door and unlocked it as if the devil were on her heels. Then she walked from room to room, slapping on lights and checking windows and lifting the dust ruffle on her bed. Satisfied that no one was lying in wait, she walked back into the living area and flipped on the television for comforting noise. Then she dropped into her favorite chair to sort through the mail.

Junk mail, catalogs, flyers, bills. A reminder from her doctor for her annual checkup, a schedule of adult education classes from a local university, a copy of the *Atlanta Business Chronicle*. She flipped through and sorted everything twice, but there was nothing from Gary. And while her credit card statements showed disquieting balances, there was no unusual activity.

But then hadn't Gary said that money was no problem?

She squeezed her eyes closed, trying to remember everything he'd said, and wondering if she should have handled things differently. So many questions orbited in her head, she could barely separate one from another. Was Gary involved with drugs? Who was the woman in his car? Had he been set up? And was she truly in danger?

She sat back in the chair and pulled her knees up to her chin. She'd been alone most of her life—an only child, a solitary student, an introverted teenager, a reserved adult. And she'd never minded, not really. Loneliness had a comfortable, insular quality that could lull a person into feeling secure in a distorted kind of way . . . secure in the knowledge that she'd never have to expose herself to another person's failings. If she didn't trust, she'd never be betrayed, and if she didn't love, she'd never be rejected. In fact, she had counted herself lucky, because while women around her seemed to be drowning in melodrama with their parents and their roommates and their boyfriends, she was immersing herself in school and work, positive she'd come out ahead on the other end.

Except here she was at thirty-one, losing ground.

Leann had once called her fatalistic, which was laughable now, considering the circumstances. But she'd preferred to think of herself as vigilant. She favored list-making, slow transitions, and backup plans. Then Gary had come along, with his winning smile and irresistible spontaneity and just enough detachment to make her believe that they had something in common. Except the side she concealed was emotional; and the side he concealed might be criminal.

Jolie hugged her knees to her chest and fought the swell of tears that pushed at her throat. Crying wouldn't help anything. Her lapse in front of Beck Underwood had been so humiliating, she wasn't sure she could face him again. It wasn't like her to lose control, and certainly not in front of a virtual stranger. And of all the virtual strangers in the world, why did he keep popping up when she needed someone the most—and the *least*?

Eight

Jolie tried to hide a yawn behind a shoe box lid as she repacked a pair of Christian Dior "padlock" sandals. The right shoe sported a tiny silver-tone padlock, and the left shoe, the miniature keys. After a gander at the price tag, she understood the gimmick—if someone paid that much for shoes, they needed to keep them under lock and key.

Fifteen minutes until her break, then she'd find a display to crawl under for a nap if she had to. She bugged her eyes, trying to shake herself awake, thinking that if she made it until the end of her shift, she was likely to fall asleep at the wheel on the way home. The lack of sleep was wearing on her—that and the strain of looking over her shoulder all day, after Gary's impromptu appearance last night. Her nerves were shot. Her neck ached and her eyes burned from constantly scanning the crowd for Gary, or anyone matching his build. If he had grown a beard, he might have done other things to change his appearance. Suddenly she felt a finger peck on her shoulder. Jolie stiffened and whirled around, her pulse skyrocketing.

"Remember me?" a young woman asked, holding up a Neiman Marcus shopping bag. "Kate Spade slides, Via Spiga T-straps? My dad made me bring back the Prada flats."

Jolie's memory stirred, then surfaced as her muscles relaxed. The coed from Monday who couldn't make up her mind. Jolie tried to maintain her cheerful smile. A return. The last time she'd handled a return, she'd accidentally processed a refund for over a million dollars. "Just a moment, I need to get a supervisor."

She signaled Michael, who was helping an elderly woman find shoes that would work with her orthopedic inserts. He excused himself, then walked over and spotted the bag. "Will you be exchanging these today?" he asked the young woman. Always the salesman, trying to salvage the sale.

"No, I'd like a refund," she said, then pointed to Jolie. "When she sold me the shoes, she said I could bring them back if I changed my mind."

Jolie squirmed, but Michael gave the woman a tight smile. "Yes, if the shoes haven't been worn outside, you may have a full refund."

"Oh, they haven't been worn outside," the girl said cheerfully. "Just in my house, trying to convince my dad how cute they looked with my outfit." Then her face fell. "But he didn't go for it."

Michael removed the shoes from the box and inspected the soles carefully, then, apparently satisfied, nodded and talked Jolie through the refund as she punched the appropriate buttons on the computer terminal/cash register. When the woman's refund had been processed, she flitted on her way.

"You have to be careful," Michael said. "Some customers buy a pair of shoes they can't afford, wear them once, then try to return them."

"Really?"

"Happens all the time—people buy an outfit for a big occasion, wear it, then bring it back the next day for a refund."

"What do you do?"

He sighed. "We handle it case by case. If they truly bought the wrong size and simply want an exchange, of course we'll do that because it's partly our job to make sure the shoes fit properly before the customer leaves. But if the shoe clearly has been worn and the person wants a refund, we have to apologize and explain the refund policy. If they're a good customer, we'll usually give them a store credit. It's only the ones that are out to cheat us that get upset." He looked past Jolie's shoulder and angled his head. "Well, look who's slumming."

Jolie turned to see Carlotta striding toward them wearing her normal smug smile, stunningly swathed head to toe in pea green—a color, Jolie noted, that would make *her* look like a zombie. Carlotta was carrying a shoe box and an inventory slip. She gestured toward the nearly vacant sales floor. "I see it's dead down here, too."

Michael nodded. "Everyone's holding out for the Blahnik appearance on Saturday."

"That's right," Carlotta said. "It'll be a zoo." She held up the box, marked SIZE 7. "You'll want to put these back right away."

Michael frowned. "Your customer didn't want them after all?"

"No," Carlotta said ruefully. "Pity, too—they looked great with the dress she picked out."

Michael opened the box and peeled back the tissue paper. Jolie swallowed her gasp—the limited edition pink and rhinestone shoes that Carlotta had worn the night before. She lifted her gaze to Carlotta, who was staring back with one eyebrow raised ever so slightly.

Michael removed the shoes lovingly and set them on the counter. Indeed, they looked pristine. "They'll sell Saturday after Manolo signs them." He removed a key from the cash drawer and unlocked the glass case next to the counter, then situated the sandals next to a pair of alligator slingbacks, and relocked the case. "Carlotta, we're going to need some extra help down here Saturday. Would you like to pitch in?"

"Sure. I could bring a dozen pairs of my own shoes for him to sign."

Michael wagged his finger. "No carry-ins for the autographing. Only shoes purchased during the event, and *maybe* a pair you're wearing, at Manolo's discretion."

Jolie looked back and forth between them. "The man is going to sign shoes?"

Michael grinned. "Hundreds of pairs, hopefully. And I need for you to come in as early as you can to help me set up ropes to control the lines."

Jolie balked. "There's going to be crowd control?"

"Oh, there will be lots of extra security, and Manolo will have his own crew, too. But it's always better if we try to maintain as much order as possible, set up a separate area for the media, that kind of thing." He glanced across the showroom. "I'd better get back to my customer. Jolie, you look exhausted. Aren't you due a break?"

She nodded gratefully, and stifled another yawn.

He winked. "I hope you were out doing something fun last night."

"She was with me," Carlotta said.

He scowled. "Don't corrupt Jolie—she's a good girl."

Carlotta stuck her tongue out at him, and he returned to his customer. She glanced at Jolie and frowned. "You look ghastly."

"Thanks."

"Are you still sick from last night?"

"I . . . haven't been sleeping well," she said evasively.

"Well, you left too soon. Guess who I saw!"

"Who?"

"Michael Stipe!"

Jolie squinted.

"Michael *Stipe*—the lead singer for R.E.M.?"

"Oh. Right."

Carlotta sighed and leaned on the counter. "You're slightly hopeless, you know."

Jolie blinked back sudden moisture in her eyes, then looked away, mortified.

"Hey, I didn't mean that," Carlotta said, her voice low and soft.

Jolie waved her hand. "Trust me, it isn't you. It's . . ." She looked back to see real concern on the woman's face. "I'm exhausted, that's all."

Carlotta made a cooing sound. "Come upstairs with me to the lounge—you can take a catnap. And something just arrived that I think will look sensational on you."

Jolie managed a laugh and followed her across the showroom. "Right."

"You should perk up your wardrobe a little, wear bright colors."

"I'm more comfortable in dark colors."

"Comfortable isn't fun," Carlotta fussed, stepping onto the up escalator. "You're too young to be comfortable."

Jolie pursed her mouth. "Those shoes you gave to Michael—were they the same shoes you were wearing last night?"

Carlotta's mouth twitched, then she nodded. "You're not going to tell on me, are you?"

"No. But why risk it?"

"It's *fun*," Carlotta said. "You're going to have to add that word to your vocabulary. F-U-N, fun."

"Fun, like the party crashing?"

"Exactly. I get to wear fabulous shoes, the shoes get exposure—a dozen women asked me where I got them. I bring the shoes back, someone comes in to buy them, everybody wins." She lifted her arms to underscore the brilliance of her logic.

"How do you keep them looking so new?"

A sly smile curved her wide mouth. "I have my little tricks—I tape the bottoms so they don't get scarred up, and I leave in the cardboard stays so the leather doesn't crease."

"That can't be comfortable."

"Like I said, comfortable isn't fun."

Jolie marveled at the woman's aplomb. As she followed her to the cool, hushed area of the fitting rooms, she observed that Carlotta's entire bearing was stamped with self-assurance. People turned to look at her, stepped aside so she wouldn't have to. Her hair was loose and flowing today, a dark curtain down her back. Far from classically beautiful, she had more presence than a roomful of models . . . yet she was enigmatically single, irresistibly aloof.

Carlotta led her to a spacious dressing room with lush carpet, and pointed to an upholstered chaise. "There. Lie down and take a nap. I'll come back in thirty minutes."

"Are you sure I won't get you into trouble?" Jolie asked, looking at the chaise with longing.

"I'm sure," Carlotta said with a laugh. "Besides, you're no good to Michael if you're dead on your feet. There's the light switch—get some rest."

She closed the door and Jolie hesitated only a few seconds before extinguishing the light and feeling her way toward the chaise. She removed her jacket and stepped out of her shoes, then eased onto the plump surface, reveling in the coolness of the smooth fabric against her skin. She turned on her back and exhaled slowly, flexing her feet to stretch her twitching leg muscles, then relaxed into the softness. Heaven. She closed her eyes to allow the haze of exhaustion to lull her into semiconsciousness, but her mind fought her body's need for rest.

The events of the past few days rose to haunt her, racing through her brain, merging and morphing until Gary had turned into a monster. He was taunting her, laughing at her fear of what lay beneath the surface of the brown, foamy Chattahoochee River, strapping her into the passenger seat of his car, then sending her rolling downhill into the water. First she was floating, then the water rose higher and higher, pulling at her clothes. She tried to free herself, but her arms were pinned to her sides. She was going to drown. A tremendous hatred for Gary seized her . . . until she turned her head to see him strapped in the driver's seat, also trapped. His eyes were big, apologetic, innocent . . .

Jolie jerked awake, the sheen of perspiration cool on her brow and neck. She inhaled deeply to relieve her squeezed lungs and to slow her elevated heartbeat. Closing her eyes, she wondered how long she'd been asleep—

five minutes? An hour? She didn't care, she just wanted to lie there for a few more minutes in the blessed dark.

Voices came to her, agitated and low . . . threatening. Slowly she recognized one of the voices as Carlotta's. She was arguing . . . with a man.

"—ever come here again, I'll call the police."

"Do that, *Lottie*. I'm sure the people you work with would be interested . . ."

Jolie sat up and scooted closer to the wall, where their voices were being funneled through an air vent.

"—*dare* threaten me," Carlotta said in a hoarse whisper.

A man's harsh laugh sounded. "You know that I don't make idle threats. Two grand by next Friday."

The stone-cold tone of the man's voice sent a chill down Jolie's neck. The silence stretched on, then Carlotta murmured, "H–how will I find you?"

"Don't worry, Lottie," he said. "I'll find *you*."

Footsteps sounded against the tile floor, then receded. Jolie held her breath, wondering what kind of trouble Carlotta was in, and what was going through the woman's mind right now. A couple of sniffles sounded, then a thump, as if Carlotta had brought her hand down on the counter in frustration. Jolie felt an instant kinship, then shook her head at the absurdity of suddenly feeling aligned with the woman because they both were in dire straits.

A light knock at the dressing-room door sent Jolie scooting away from the wall.

"Jolie, it's me," Carlotta said, then opened the door and stuck her head inside. "Are you awake?"

"Yes," Jolie said, then stood and flipped on the light. She blinked against the glare and glanced at her watch. She'd been asleep for twenty-five minutes.

"Were you able to get some rest?" Carlotta asked, showing no signs of being threatened only a moment ago.

"Yes, thank you so much," Jolie said, then slid her feet into her shoes and reached for the jacket she'd shed.

"Wait, I want you to try on something."

Jolie gave her a wry smile. "I don't have the time or the money."

"Oh, shush, Michael can spare you for five more minutes. Get a load of this." She held up a sleeveless butternut-colored Ultrasuede jumpsuit with wide legs and a silver-tone belt that hung low on the hips.

Jolie's lips parted and she felt an irrational gush of appreciation for the designer. "Oh, my."

"It's perfect for you; try it on."

"No, I couldn't."

"Sure you can," Carlotta said, stepping in and closing the door behind her. "Just *try* it."

Jolie wavered, then reached forward to touch the fabric and was lost in the exquisite liquidity of the cloth. "Okay, but I'm *only* trying it on."

Carlotta eased the jumpsuit off the hanger while Jolie undressed a bit self-consciously. Carlotta hummed and eyed her figure critically. "Wow, if you were a few inches taller, you could be a model."

"I've lost weight recently," Jolie said, glad that at least her Wal-Mart white underwear matched, but knowing it made her look bluishly pale. "I guess I haven't adjusted to my new schedule."

"How's your real-estate business coming along? Have you called that hunky Beck Underwood yet?"

Jolie stepped into the jumpsuit, nervous at the mere sound of his name. "He's supposed to call me." She didn't add that she'd left her cell phone turned off all day. She wasn't sure who she wanted to hear from less: him or Detective Salyers.

"Are you kidding me?" Carlotta gaped. "Do you know how many realtors in this city would sell their soul to be Beck Underwood's agent? We're talking a multimillion-dollar home. The commission would set you up for a year!"

She'd told herself the same thing a thousand times. "I know."

"You act as if you're afraid of him," Carlotta said. "Or is it men in general?" She wet her lips. "Um . . . Michael told me that your boyfriend is . . . missing."

Jolie glanced up from shrugging into the top of the jumpsuit.

Carlotta winced. "Don't be angry with Michael—he thought you could use a little moral support."

So that was why Carlotta was being nice to her. Jolie wondered if everyone would be as supportive if they knew all the details of her "missing" boyfriend.

"You don't have to talk about it if you don't want to," Carlotta murmured.

In answer, Jolie dropped her gaze and allowed Carlotta to fasten the silver-tone buttons running up the front from waist to breastbone. In light of the conversation she'd overheard, the woman had her own problems.

"There," Carlotta said, then stood back. Her face lit up, then she turned Jolie around to look in the wall mirror. "You," she said over Jolie's shoulder, "look like a goddess."

Okay, "goddess" was stretching it a bit, Jolie thought, studying her reflection with wide-eyed wonder. But "good" was not inappropriate. She slid her hands into the hidden side pockets and drank in the sight of herself in the luxe designer outfit. The style, the color and drape of the fabric—everything about the jumpsuit was perfect for her figure type and skin tone. She didn't look like herself. The woman staring back looked . . . accomplished. Situated. As if she knew who she was, and other people be damned.

With the impact of a thunderbolt, Jolie suddenly realized the attraction of haute couture: it wasn't how high fashion made a woman look, it was how high fashion made a woman *feel*.

"Well, was I right?"

She glanced at Carlotta in the mirror and nodded miserably. "It's incredible, but I couldn't possibly afford something like this. How much is it?"

Carlotta fidgeted. "Well . . ."

Jolie picked up the dangling tag and her heart dropped. "Oh. My. God. This is more than the Blue Book value on my car." A car that she didn't even have. She began fumbling with the buttons. "Carlotta, I shouldn't even be trying this on."

"Relax, Jolie . . . relax. I'll help you work out the financials. You simply must have this outfit."

"Even with my employee discount, it's an impossibility."

Carlotta put her hands on Jolie's shoulders. "I have a system."

Jolie was instantly wary. "What do you mean?"

"Buy the outfit at your discount, wear it to a big bash tomorrow night that you simply *must* attend with me, then return it." She lifted her arms in a happy "see?" shrug.

"I can't do that," Jolie said, shaking her head. "It wouldn't be honest." Then she squinted. "What bash?"

"It's a big reception for journalists—some kind of award nominations are being announced. I'm going, and you have to go with me."

Jolie gave her a wry smile. "You mean *crash* with you?"

Carlotta grinned. "All the best people will be there."

She thought of Roger LeMon. "Some of the same people that we saw the other night?"

"Sure, that pack runs together."

She'd like the chance to get close to Roger LeMon to find out more about his relationship to Gary, and why he cared that she had connected them. But how could she do that when he already knew who she was?

Jolie looked back at her reflection . . . *She didn't look like herself.* "Carlotta, do you think I could borrow one of your wigs for tomorrow night?"

Nine

Jolie sat slumped in her car, questioning her judgment for agreeing to meet Carlotta in the parking garage of the hotel. Sitting in the dimly lit structure, she was an easy target for anyone who might have followed her. Not that she'd noticed anyone following her, but between Gary's stealth, Roger LeMon's secrecy, and Detective Salyers' perseverance, she couldn't be certain.

Except surely Gary wouldn't have the kahonas to tail her in her own car.

She glanced at her cell phone display: 2 MISSED CALLS. Salyers had called twice yesterday, twice today. Jolie wondered if she were breaking some kind of law by not answering and not returning the detective's calls, but she'd promised herself that she'd call Salyers tomorrow about Roger LeMon, regardless if she learned something solid tonight. She picked up the folded sheets of paper she'd printed last night after researching her subject on the Internet.

Roger LeMon was thirty-four years old, graduated from

Vanderbilt University with a degree in finance, worked in the Buckhead office of LeMon and Pride, Ltd., the investment company his late father had founded. By all appearances, the man was a success in his professional and in his personal life. Recipient of various humanitarian awards for philanthropic contributions, winning member of an Atlanta tennis club, on the board of a local business college, on the vestry of his church. Married Janet Chisholm in 1995, lived in a gated neighborhood in Buckhead, no children that Jolie could find a record of. And no direct link to Gary that she could pinpoint, other than the photograph.

On the opposite end of the parking garage, headlights appeared, then a dark sedan . . . slowly climbing the ramp . . . turning into the aisle where she had parked. Carlotta had told her to look for a white Miata convertible, so she slumped lower and watched in her side mirror for the sedan to pass by.

Instead, it stopped . . . directly behind her car, trapping her. Tinted windows hid the face of the occupant. Realization of her stupidity hit Jolie full force, and she scrambled for her cell phone. The hypocrisy of calling the police now was not lost on her, but she didn't care. And how petty was it that she was thinking if she were shot wearing the jumpsuit, she wouldn't be able to return it?

The tinted window started to buzz down just as she punched in 9-1-1. Oh, God . . . "they" were going to get her. Her heart pounded in her ears so loudly, she could barely hear the phone ringing.

"Nine-one-one. Where is the emergency?"

Jolie opened her mouth to unload on the answerer, her eyes riveted on the car window as the top of Carlotta's head appeared, then her gapped grin. Jolie sighed in relief. "Operator, I'm so sorry, I made a mistake."

She disconnected the call, then climbed out of the car, irritated with herself. "I thought you were driving a white convertible!"

Carlotta frowned. "My battery was dead. I had to borrow my brother's car."

"Oh." Jolie gave herself a mental shake. She was either going to have to go to the police or calm the heck down.

Carlotta handed a Mui Mui shoe box out of the window. "I have your shoes, but put the box in your car so you'll have it to make your return tomorrow."

Jolie put the empty box in the trunk, already dreading the return tomorrow. Would Michael know she'd worn them tonight?

"Get in," Carlotta said, "and I'll find a place to park."

She locked her car doors, then shouldered her "biggish" purse and checked to make sure the shocking price tag of the jumpsuit was still secure, tucked down inside the bodice beneath her armpit, held in place with a tiny safety pin.

She climbed into the sedan and closed the door. The interior was luxurious and clean, but reeked of cigarette smoke. "What does your brother do?"

"He's a hacker," Carlottta declared. "Mostly he plays computer games, but sometimes he'll get in the mood to work, help companies with their security, things like that."

"He must be smart."

"Yeah, especially for a nineteen-year-old."

Jolie's eyebrows went up.

Carlotta sighed as she turned into a parking place. "Yes, there's a big age difference. Mother thought another baby would help their marriage."

Jolie could tell by the tone of her voice that it hadn't. "Sounds like you're close to your brother."

She shrugged. "He lives with me." Then she turned off the ignition and smiled with approval. "You look great."

"Thanks. So do you."

Carlotta preened in her "borrowed" red bugle bead jacket over a silvery three-quarter-length dress. Her lustrous dark hair was skimmed back and twisted into a chignon. Against her black, black hair and her olive skin tone, her blue eyes were captivating.

Jolie leaned in. "I thought your eyes were brown."

"Tonight they're blue."

"Contact lenses?"

"Yeah, I have green ones, too, and a pair that looks like cat eyes—those freak everyone out a little. Are you ready for your shoes and new hair?" Carlotta had already turned to retrieve a bag from the backseat. "Here are the shoes."

When Jolie opened the bag to find the soles of the silver-colored cut-out leather pumps covered with several layers of tape, she worked her mouth from side to side. "I feel like a thief."

"Let's don't go through that again. Come on, we're going to be late. Remember to leave in the cardboard stays."

Jolie removed the low heeled sandals she'd worn and pushed her feet into the yummy shoes.

"Put your other shoes in your bag, just in case you have to . . . leave in a hurry."

"You mean in case we get caught crashing and are chased out?"

"It's rare, but it happens," Carlotta said with a sniff. "It's just best to be prepared. Here's your wig." She hoisted a medium-brown pageboy wig, then angled her head. "But your hair looks great—are you sure you want to do this?"

Jolie nodded, then, using the visor mirror, tucked her

curls into a hairnet that Carlotta handed her and stretched the wig over her scalp. She tugged at the ends until all was even. The transformation was startling. She touched her face to prove to her brain that she truly was looking at herself.

"Let me see," Carlotta said, then gasped when Jolie turned her head. "You look . . . completely different. Your boyfriend wouldn't even recognize—" She stopped. "I'm sorry, Jolie, I didn't mean to upset you . . . Wait a minute." She gestured vaguely toward Jolie's getup. "Does *this* have something to do with *that*?"

Jolie's throat constricted. "Maybe."

Carlotta squinted. "At the museum the other night when you were talking to Roger what's-his-name, was the mutual friend you mentioned your boyfriend?"

"Yes."

"But Roger denied knowing him."

"He lied." Jolie hesitated, then pulled from her purse the photo she'd saved from Gary's album. "Gary is the one standing next to Roger. They look chummy to me."

Carlotta hummed her agreement. "But why would the man lie?"

Jolie was silent, knowing she could use an ally, but not sure if she could trust a woman who "borrowed" merchandise from the store and was having money problems. Then she glanced at herself—bewigged and wearing her own "borrowed" outfit—and realized that she was in no position to cast stones.

Carlotta looked up. "What's your boyfriend's name again?"

"Gary . . . Hagan."

"He's cute. I don't recognize him, but wow, that name still sounds so familiar."

Jolie took a deep breath. "You've probably heard it on the news. His car was pulled out of the Chattahoochee River earlier this week."

Carlotta's big blue eyes got even bigger. "He's dead?"

"His body wasn't found," Jolie said carefully. "But there was . . . a woman's body . . . in the car."

Carlotta gasped. "Who?"

"The police don't know yet."

"*Christ.* Oh, you poor thing." Carlotta reached out to touch her arm. "You must be going crazy."

Jolie sighed. "I'm muddling through."

"Do you think he's alive?"

"The police do. My car was stolen the same night Gary disappeared."

"*Christ.* He killed somebody, then he stole your car?"

Jolie wet her lips. "Actually . . . I don't believe he killed anyone."

"You think it was an accident?"

"I don't know," she said, weighing her words. "Gary had friends in high places. I'm thinking maybe he got in the middle of something, maybe he was . . . set up."

Carlotta's jaw dropped. "Christ, this is like something on TV. Are you on a mission to clear the name of the man you love?"

Jolie squirmed. "Well—"

"Christ, the police don't think *you're* involved, do they?"

"Well—"

"They do?"

"Not directly. But . . . the detective who questioned me practically accused me of giving Gary my car to get away."

"Christ, Christ, Christ." Carlotta bounced in her seat. "Your life is so much more exciting than mine!"

The woman's exuberance alarmed her. Jolie looked all around and lifted a quieting hand. "Carlotta, please . . . I need the job at Neiman's. If Michael or anyone else there thought I was somehow linked to a murder—"

"Say no more," Carlotta said, suddenly sober. "I hear what you're saying about the people you work with knowing your personal business."

Jolie remembered the quiver of fear in Carlotta's voice yesterday in the conversation she'd overheard from the dressing room, and wondered if she should tell Carlotta that she'd inadvertently overheard. But since she wasn't in a position to help the woman monetarily, she felt sure that Carlotta would rather not know that she knew.

"Thank you for understanding," was all Jolie said.

"So are you hoping to run into Roger LeMon again tonight, ergo the disguise?"

"Right. I shouldn't have given him my name. If I do see him, I'm hoping he won't realize I'm the same person he talked to the other night."

Carlotta tilted her head, and the tip of her tongue appeared. "Hmm . . . I know!" She pulled out a small case. "Wear my green contact lenses. They don't have a prescription, and they've just been cleaned."

Jolie hesitated. "I don't know . . . having something in my eye."

"It's like a tampon, you won't even know it's there."

Although the imagery did not soothe her qualms, Jolie agreed to try them. Carlotta coached and after much poking and blinking and tearing, they were in. She stared in the mirror, marveling how much the color did change her appearance. "My mascara is a wreck, though," she said, pulling her makeup kit from her purse.

"Do you have an eyebrow pencil?"

Jolie checked. "I have mascara, powder and lip gloss."

"Lip gloss? What are you, in the sixth grade? Here." Carlotta removed a makeup case the size of a loaf of bread from her purse and unzipped it. She rummaged, then withdrew a gold-tone case and twisted up a lipstick the color of cinnamon. "Try this."

Jolie eyed her bag. "That's some arsenal."

"Don't underestimate the power of the right shade of lipstick."

After smoothing on the color, Jolie had to admit Carlotta was right.

"Now, about your eyebrows . . ."

Jolie frowned. "What about my eyebrows?" They were pale, practically nonexistent.

"Eyebrows are the most distinctive feature you have—did you know that your eyebrows keep their basic shape from the time you're born unless you pluck them?"

"No."

She held up a brown pencil. "Give me a couple of minutes, and I promise, no one will recognize you."

Jolie acquiesced and a few pencil strokes later, sported darker, fuller eyebrows with an artful arch. That did it—she did indeed look like a different person.

Carlotta clapped her hands. "What else can I do to help?"

"Do you recognize anyone else in the picture?"

Carlotta turned on the overhead light and studied the photograph again. "No . . . wait, this woman looks familiar," she said, tapping the face of a smiling brunette standing on the end. Pretty, with a mod haircut.

"You don't know her name?"

"No, but she might be a customer. That's a seven-hundred-dollar Ralph Lauren Black Label sweater."

Jolie peered at the woman's yellow sweater—beautiful, but brand-unrecognizable to her untrained eye.

Carlotta drew the picture closer to her blue, blue eyes. "Hmm."

"What?"

"That picture on the wall behind them—I've seen it before."

Jolie studied the picture, which appeared to be an illustration of a pig wearing a suit—a page from a children's book? "Do you remember where? Was it a bar, or someone's house?"

Carlotta frowned, then shook her head and handed back the photo. "I can't remember."

"Okay," Jolie said on an exhale. "Well, I've held us up long enough. I have no idea what I'll say to Roger LeMon if I see him, but I guess I'll just play it by ear."

"Wait—a name, you need a name!"

"Right. How about . . . Linda?"

"Okay, and I'll be Betty." Carlotta grinned. "I've always loved that name." She opened her purse and removed a small white container. "I have a little disguise of my own."

Jolie watched her withdraw what looked like a retainer, then insert it into her mouth. When Carlotta turned and grinned, the gap between her front teeth was gone, replaced by perfect, sparkling white incisors. A slight adjustment, a remarkable change.

"Wow," Jolie murmured.

Carlotta shrugged. "My dentist is always after me to get caps, but I kind of like my smile. My father always said it gave me character." Her voice dropped an octave when she mentioned her father.

"Are your parents still living?" Jolie asked quietly.

"Yeah," Carlotta said with a stark laugh, opening her door. "If you can call it that. Ready?"

Jolie sensed more to Carlotta's story, but nodded and opened her own door, reminding herself that she had a reason for attending tonight's party besides bonding with Carlotta—although that idea suddenly held more appeal than dogging Roger LeMon. She stood, adjusted her clothes, and took a few tentative steps in the stiff shoes. "I hope I don't fall."

"You'll get used to them," Carlotta said.

But by the time they made it to the elevator and rode down to the ground floor, her feet were already chafed from the cardboard stays. The guilt of wearing the pricey outfit and the unfamiliar snugness of the wig seemed to weigh her down, making each footstep more difficult.

"You look like you're in pain," Carlotta chastised.

"I *am* in pain."

"Just think of how good you look and that'll make you feel better."

"At least we don't have far to go," Jolie said, turning toward the glass door that led from the garage into the hotel.

"We're going this way," Carlotta said, pointing in the opposite direction.

Jolie frowned. "What are you up to?"

Carlotta gave her a secret smile. "You'll see."

Jolie followed her to a side exit of the garage and out onto the sidewalk, then looked around to get her bearings. They were past the hotel and around the corner. In fact, most of the cars turning down the side street were taxis and limousines presumably circling back around to Peachtree Street after dropping guests at the hotel. Carlotta turned to the right and headed toward the street corner, farther still from their destination.

Clutching her bag closer to her body, Jolie was besieged by a sudden case of nerves, wondering how she'd made the leap from nice and predictable to . . . here.

Maybe Sammy Sanders had been right. Maybe she *was* out of her mind to leave her comfy job. What did it say about her that she could let Gary's disappearance throw her life into chaos? She wasn't even sure how she still felt about him, but his disappearance had been a catalyst in her life. Carlotta's earlier words resonated in her memory, in her heart. *"Your life is so much more exciting than mine."*

A few steps ahead of her, Carlotta stepped to the curb and flagged down a shiny black limo, then leaned in a lowered window and spoke to the driver. The woman's body language was pure flirtation. Suddenly she turned and beckoned Jolie forward. "Come on, we're going to arrive in style."

Jolie blinked the swimmy contact lenses into place, scooted forward in her stiff shoes and murmured, "Suddenly, *my* life is so much more exciting than mine."

Ten

Jolie slid in next to Carlotta on the long, black bench seat of the limousine. "We're taking a limo around the block?"

"It's all about perception," Carlotta said. "People will assume we're somebody important if we arrive in a service."

Jolie wasn't about to argue, because her feet were screaming for relief. And although the ride was over before her tootsies could get a break, Jolie conceded a little thrill of excitement when a gloved hotel doorman opened the door and helped her out onto the carpet under the canopied entrance, and people turned to look. "Are you ladies here for the broadcasters reception?"

"Yes," Carlotta said in a clipped voice, ringing with unmistaken authority. "Could you point us in the right direction, please?"

"Straight ahead to the lobby, then left," the doorman said, beaming at the women.

Carlotta folded a tip into his hand. "Thank you indeed."

Jolie was conscious of other people's heads pivoting

with interest as they walked toward the open double doors. The women seemed intrigued; the men were more blatant with their admiring looks. For a few minutes she forgot how much her feet hurt.

Out of the corner of her eye, a car on Peachtree Street caught her attention—a gray Mercury Sable sedan . . . Hers? Her breath caught in her chest at the thought of Gary following her. She craned for a better look, but the contact lenses moved on her eyes, obscuring her vision for a few seconds. She blinked furiously, but by the time she had focused, the car had already slid into traffic and out of sight. She exhaled a long breath, telling herself there were hundreds of cars like hers in the metro area. Surely Gary wouldn't risk being caught driving a stolen car along the Peachtree-Street corridor at night when the police patrols were in full force.

She wondered if he would be waiting for her when she returned to her car tonight, or if, as Leann had suggested, he had used the bought time to get the hell out of Dodge.

Was she being a colossal, gullible fool by believing him?

"Are you okay?" Carlotta asked.

"Fine," she murmured, and resumed walking.

They were directed down a lavishly tiled hallway that opened up into a spacious foyer with a small, tasteful sign that welcomed guests to the reception for the Broadcasters and Journalists Association of Georgia. Jolie's palms were moist when they chained onto a line of beautifully dressed guests waiting to give their tickets to a rather stern-looking middle-aged gentleman. She grew even more nervous when Carlotta, casting inconspicuous glances at the tickets people around them were holding, turned a little gray around the gills.

"What's wrong?" Jolie whispered.

"I was misinformed," Carlotta whispered back. "I had my brother print up the wrong tickets."

Jolie felt a full-fledged sweat coming on, and out of fear of staining the rented jumpsuit, concentrated on trying to contract her pores. "What are we going to do?"

"Follow my lead," Carlotta said just as the couple in front of them moved on and the ticket taker held out his hand.

"Tickets please."

"Forgive my ignorance, sir," Carlotta said in a distinct British accent. "This is the first time I have attended such an event, and I wasn't aware that I was supposed to bring the vouchers."

Jolie stared. The woman was a chameleon.

A wrinkle formed in the man's brow. "I'm not supposed to let you in without a ticket, ma'am."

"Oh," Carlotta murmured, fluttering her hands. "I'm quite embarrassed, still adjusting to American protocol and all of that." She turned to bestow a beatific smile on the people behind them. Then she turned back to the ticket holder. "Isn't there something you can do, sir? Check my name on a list, perhaps? Betty Halverson, CNN. And guest."

Jolie did her part, nodding as if she were indeed the guest of British-born Betty Halverson, CNN, although her neck itched and the contact in her left eye was beginning to feel like a tampon all right—a tampon in her eye.

The ticket taker leaned in to speak to Carlotta conspiratorially. "I asked for a list, ma'am, but they didn't give me one."

Carlotta made a rueful noise in her throat. "This isn't your fault, good sir, it's mine, all mine." *Flap, flap* went her false eyelashes.

Jolie could practically hear the man's resolve crumbling. "I think it would be all right this once," he murmured.

"You are a true gentleman," Carlotta crooned, and floated through the opening.

Jolie followed with a grateful American nod. When they had moved out of earshot, she looked at Carlotta. "What was that?"

"Accents will open doors," Carlotta said with a lovely shrug. "People with a British accent sound smart and trustworthy."

"You're scary," Jolie said.

"We're in, aren't we?" Carlotta said, then scanned the room full of milling guests. She stopped and inhaled sharply. "Oh, my God."

Jolie froze and tried to blink her contact lens into place. "Do you see Roger LeMon?"

"No, it's Thomas Roberts—CNN anchor." She sighed. "That man puts the 'ooh' in news."

"Maybe you should go introduce yourself to your coworker," Jolie said wryly.

Carlotta made a face and continued to survey the room. "I'm going to be able to add to my book tonight. Without moving, I see Paul Ossman, Monica Kauffman, and Clark Howard."

"The consumer reports guy?"

"Yeah." Carlotta frowned. "Someone should tell him that his advice to shop discount stores is not only bad for the economy, but bad for the Atlanta fashion scene."

"Oh, no," Jolie said with a laugh. "It's better to buy something and wear it, then return it."

Carlotta frowned harder. "I told you, this is good advertising. Do you know how many people are looking at you right now?"

"They're looking through me to get to you," Jolie said, then nodded toward the bar. "Since you hired the limousine for our long journey, I'll get us drink tickets."

"Wait," Carlotta said, clasping Jolie's arm. She stared at the table where tickets were being sold and murmured, "Yellow." Then she angled her body toward Jolie, opened her purse, and pulled out six yellow generic tear-off tickets. "Three for you, three for me."

Jolie's eyes widened, and her errant lens popped back into place. "You brought your own drink tickets?"

"You can buy them in rolls at any office supply store."

"How did you know the tickets would be yellow?"

"I didn't—I brought red, blue, *and* yellow, just in case."

"You really have this down to a science, don't you?"

"I prefer to think of it as an art," she said with a smile, as they walked toward the bar. "By the way, don't get red wine or anything to eat with red sauce—you know the old saying, 'If you break it, you buy it'?"

"Yes."

"Well," Carlotta said, gesturing at the jumpsuit. "If you stain it, you've just obtained it."

Jolie swallowed. "Got it." They joined the line at the bar and Jolie glanced around the ballroom. Even to her unsophisticated eye, this crowd seemed more affluent compared to the crowd of two nights ago. "What's the biggest event you've ever crashed?" she whispered to Carlotta.

"The governor's inaugural ball."

Jolie's eyes bugged. "How did you manage that?"

"Hannah loaned me a chef's coat to wear over my outfit. I walked in through the kitchen, picked up a tray and carried it to a table, detoured through the bathroom to remove the coat, stuffed the coat into my bag, and joined the party."

Jolie shook her head in amazement.

"By the way, Hannah will be here in an hour," Carlotta said, looking around, "so I need to find a side door to let her in."

"Oh . . . kay," Jolie said, moving up in the bar line.

"But the most *fun* I had," Carlotta said, on a roll now, "was watching the Hawks. I printed up a press pass, borrowed my brother's camera with a big honking lens, and parked myself courtside."

"When was that?"

"The entire 2000–2001 season."

Jolie gaped. "No one ever questioned you?"

"Nope. Of course, now, security at the big venues is too strict for someone like me to get in."

"Don't you think that's probably a good thing?"

"I suppose so," Carlotta agreed, then stepped up and handed the bartender one of the generic drink tickets in exchange for a gin and tonic.

Jolie got white wine, tipped well to assuage her conscience and then began to scout the room for Roger LeMon or one of the others in the photograph.

"I'll check out the other side of the room," Carlotta murmured. Jolie nodded and watched the men watch her friend as she glided across the room. When she realized she was getting a few looks of her own, she reached up to touch her hair and encountered the unfamiliar texture of the straight wig. The knowledge that tonight she didn't have to be mousy little Jolie Goodman shot through her. Tonight she could be anybody she wanted to be.

"Beautiful outfit," a woman next to her said.

Jolie smiled, then wet her lips. "Why thank yaw," she said, but her British accent came out sounding like Scarlett O'Hara with her mouth full of peanut butter. She cleared her throat. "I mean, thank you," she said in her normal voice, then felt compelled to add, "Neiman's."

The woman pursed her mouth and nodded, then turned back to her group. Jolie sipped her wine and moved around the room, forcing herself to join knots of people and make small talk about the weather and traffic, and to congratulate the people who wore colored badges, designating a nomination for broadcasting and journalism awards.

She introduced herself as Linda, an attorney—why not? She'd wondered what it was like to walk in the shoes of the rich and famous, and now she was getting a taste of it. Her feet had progressed beyond painful; they were anesthetized, allowing her to accept compliments graciously, plugging Neiman's at every opportunity. A couple of men tried to latch on, buy her a drink, and while she enjoyed the attention, she made excuses to keep moving.

For some reason, Beck Underwood's face kept popping into her mind, and she wondered if she'd see him tonight. Mixed feelings danced in her chest over the fact that if he did put in an appearance, she wouldn't be able to talk to him and not blow her cover. Which was probably for the best, she told herself. The last thing she needed was to develop a crush on Beck Underwood simply because he had a hero complex and was bored with being back home.

Blaming that disturbing mind tangent on the fact that her brain was trying to pump blood to her numb feet, she wiggled her toes (at least she thought she did) and forced herself to move on.

Everywhere she turned, she was drawn into light conversation. She attributed the warm reception she received to the clothes and the shoes, although she couldn't blame people for treating her differently. She *felt* different.

Taller, sexier, wittier. She was well-read and had observed local politics for years, but had never put herself in situations to engage in clever party dialogue. The wine and the new persona she'd adopted made her brave. In one crowd she ventured a joke that garnered bursts of laughter, to her great surprise. The attention was absolutely heady, more powerful than the wine. She caught a glimpse of herself in a mirrored column and was stunned at the woman who was reflected—self-assured, poised, polished. Was this the person she might have become, under different circumstances?

Jolie turned away and sipped from her glass, unnerved at her train of thought since arriving. She'd never wanted to be anyone other than herself until this mess had landed in her lap. In fact, people with money and power had always made her uneasy, and she'd do well to remember that the same people who had laughed at her jokes wouldn't give her a second glance if she were wearing her normal discount-store clothing and selling them shoes.

And that some people in this social echelon—perhaps in this very room—might be responsible for what had happened to Gary . . . and the woman in his car. Bolstered by a second glass of wine, she canvassed the room with new resolve. And then she spotted Roger LeMon, wearing a tuxedo, one hand wrapped around a drink, the other in his pocket. He was talking to a man who was wearing an award nomination badge, and they seemed to be deep in conversation. But what sent a stone to her stomach was the fact that the second man, a stout, round-faced fellow who looked prematurely gray, was also familiar. He too was in the photo in her purse.

"Do you see what I see?"

Jolie jumped and turned her head to see Carlotta, her intense blue eyes wide with excitement. "You mean Roger LeMon? I just saw him. Do you know the man he's talking to? He's in the photo too."

"I've seen him around, but I don't know who he is."

"He's wearing a nominee badge."

"Then by all means, let's go congratulate him."

Jolie touched Carlotta's arm. "Wait. What if LeMon recognizes us?"

"He's not going to recognize us," Carlotta said, then wet her lips. "Especially not *this* English rose," she said in her perfect British accent.

"How did you learn to do that?" Jolie asked as they made their way through the crowd.

"I had an English nanny."

More clues to her blueblood upbringing. Jolie followed her friend through the crowd, sensing the master party crasher had had a troubled life. Why else would she delight in mocking the class of people that would probably welcome her with open arms? Only a powerful resentment could drive a person to go to so much trouble to pull one over on a group of people who would never realize they'd been had.

The closer they got to Roger LeMon, the harder Jolie's heart pounded. His voice and his words from the other night reverberated in her head. *"She said she was a friend . . . Goodman, Jolie Goodman."*

She had to force herself to walk closer, terrified that he would recognize her, that he might even have found her dropped wineglass the other night and know that his conversation had been overheard. By the time they were near enough to the men to strike up a conversation, her tongue was immobile. Part by part, her body was becoming paralyzed. Not that she had to worry, with Carlotta in the vicinity.

"Hallo," the woman purred, stepping between the men. They stopped mid-conversation. LeMon seemed perturbed by the interruption, and took the opportunity to drink deeply from his cocktail. Carlotta directed her attention— and accent—to the unknown man. "I'm Betty, and this is my friend Linda, and we wanted to say congratulations on your nomination."

The plump man raked his gaze over Betty and interest flared in his eyes. He switched his drink to his left hand— the one with the wedding ring—and shook Carlotta's hand with his right. "Thank you. I'm Kyle Coffee. This here is Roger LeMon." His speech was slightly slurred, and he seemed to be well on his way to being toasted.

"How do you do, Roger?" Carlotta said. "Do both of you gentlemen work in the industry?"

"I'm in television production," Kyle offered. "My buddy Roger is a money man."

Carlotta smiled. "Ah. Sounds like a most fortuitous friendship. You work together?"

"No," Kyle Coffee said with an exaggerated wink. "I guess you could say we *play* together, wouldn't you, Roger?"

LeMon hesitated, then gave a little laugh and turned to look at Jolie.

She fought the clawing urge to run. The relief that he didn't seem to recognize her gave way to the heebie-jeebies from his lascivious stare. He wet his thin lips, then said to Carlotta, "So, does your friend have that same cute accent?"

Carlotta gave Jolie a questioning look. "Who, Linda? Well—"

"No," Jolie said softly, but emphasized the Georgia drawl she'd been raised with and had worked hard to dispel. "That is, I have a cute accent, but it's closer to home."

They all laughed and Roger moved a few inches closer. The hand in his pocket began to jingle change and his neck loosened with what she assumed was his "hey, chickie baby" stance. "Nice outfit," he said, looking at her boobs.

"Thanks." Her mind raced, searching for a line of questioning that might lead somewhere helpful. "Where do you live . . . Roger?"

He took another drink, as if he were debating on what—or perhaps whether—to tell her. "In Buckhead," he said finally. "You?"

"Vinings," she said, glad that her real-estate training had made her so familiar with the metro area. "I just moved to town. What did your friend mean when he said you were a money man?" She managed a flirtatious smile. "You don't *launder* money, do you?"

Kyle Coffee belly-laughed, blowing his flammable breath all over them. Roger joined in, slightly less amused, a half beat later. "No. I'm an investment broker. What do you do . . . um—"

"Linda," she supplied. "I'm an attorney."

Kyle elbowed Roger. "Maybe she's a divorce attorney." He laughed again, scorching the air.

Roger's thick, dark eyebrows came together. "Maybe you've had a little too much to drink, Kyle."

When the silence began to grow tense, Jolie asked, "So, Roger, do you come to these events to network for clients?"

He shook his head. "No, I come for the same reason that most everyone else is here: to kill time." He lifted his glass for another drink and winced as he swallowed. "Besides, almost everyone here is already a client of mine."

She glanced around to humor him. "I guess that means you deal only with high rollers."

He shrugged. "Well, not to brag, but my minimum investment for new clients is seven figures."

The man was so bragging. But with those requirements and Gary's wrecked finances, Gary certainly wasn't a *client* of LeMon's. "Do you have a business card?" she asked.

He extended his drink for her to hold, and she took it, feeling a little smarmy just by association. She had the feeling that Roger LeMon was used to people doing what he wanted, especially women. And while some women might find his arrogance attractive, she was repulsed. She watched as unobtrusively as she could as he removed his wallet. On his left ring finger was a gold band—a band he hadn't been wearing two nights ago. He made a show of opening his wallet, which boasted a thick stack of bills, then withdrew a business card and tucked the wallet back into his pocket.

Jolie glanced at Carlotta, who had noticed the wad of money and seemed to be deep in thought as she sipped her gin and tonic. Unease tickled Jolie's spine, but she cut back to Roger and offered him a beguiling smile as he handed her his business card.

Feeling bold, she asked, "Is there a private number on your card?"

He pursed his mouth and stared at her cleavage again, then pulled a pen out of his jacket and clicked the end with purpose . . . and a gleam in his eye. He turned over the card and wrote something on it, then reached forward to tuck the card in a small breast pocket on her jumpsuit (proportioned, she presumed, especially for small breasts). "Call me soon."

He stroked her breast as he pulled out his finger and she swallowed against the revulsion that rose in her throat. His hands were long and slender, his nails manicured. The edge of a small black tattoo on his wrist peeked out from beneath his shirt cuff. His smile was cocky as he returned his pen to an inside pocket. Her hands itched to throw the two drinks she held in his face.

"Don't look now, Roger," Kyle Coffee said with an elbow nudge. "Here comes history."

Both men looked over Jolie's shoulder and fixed smiles on their faces at whoever was approaching.

Jolie turned around to greet the arrivals, and nearly choked. Beck Underwood and his sister stood there, both of them giving Roger wary glances. It suddenly hit her that Beck had mentioned his sister had once dated Roger. Jolie ducked her head and frantically glanced around for an escape route, but found herself hemmed in between Roger and a gigantic sago palm tree. Desperate, she held up her wineglass to obscure her face.

"Hi, Della," LeMon said, dipping his chin.

"Hello, Roger," Della replied, her voice surprisingly tentative for an heiress, although based on the dark circles beneath her eyes, the woman looked a little under the weather.

"Hey, Beck," LeMon said a little too loudly. "Long time, no see. I hear you've been living with natives, or something like that."

"Or something like that," Beck said coolly.

Out of the corner of her eye, Jolie saw Roger's hand twitch as he suddenly realized he didn't have a drink—Jolie was still holding his glass. When he reached for it, Jolie felt all eyes land on her, and she dreaded looking up. When she did, newly shorn Beck Underwood, exquisite in a black suit, white shirt, and silvery tie, was studying her, then "Betty." Jolie averted her gaze and hoped like heck he didn't put two and two together and get two—namely, her and Carlotta.

"We came over to congratulate Kyle," his sister said, extending her hand and a smile to the inebriated man. "Dad couldn't be here tonight, but he can't say enough about your work on the *Yesterdays* series."

Kyle Coffee must have realized the significance of the Underwoods' presence because he visibly tried to gather himself. "Thank you," he said, shaking hands with Della, then Beck. "Good to see you b–back, B–Beck," he ventured, but the alliteration was too much for his sloshy tongue to handle and he giggled nervously. "Uh . . . meet our new friends," he said to cover his gaffe.

Jolie was caught.

"Della and Beck Underwood, this is Betty and . . . and . . . *Linda!*" Kyle said, proud of himself for remembering.

Carlotta nodded graciously. "Hallo."

"Oh, you're from England," Della Underwood said. "What part?"

"London," Carlotta said without missing a beat.

"What part of London?" Beck Underwood asked mildly.

Jolie's heart began to trip overtime. He was on to them.

"Liverpool Street," Carlotta said triumphantly.

"Ah. Near the station, or in the city?"

Carlotta's smile faltered for a split second. "Er, near the station . . . of course."

He nodded, then he looked at Jolie and his eyes danced with mischief. "Linda—it *is* Linda, right?"

She nodded, feeling like an idiot.

"Are you from London also?"

"N–no," she stammered in her resurrected Southern accent.

"Linda is an attorney from Vinings," Carlotta offered, trying to be helpful.

"*Is* she?" Beck asked, his eyebrows lifted.

"Beck Underwood," a woman's voice said behind them. "I *knew* our paths would cross again."

They all turned, and Jolie's intestines twisted at the sight of the blonde gliding their way dressed in shocking pink. Sammy "Sold" Sanders.

This night just kept getting better.

Eleven

Watching Sammy Sanders introduce herself around the circle was painful because the woman personified every stereotype that had plagued the real-estate business for decades: cheesy smile, fake boobs, and an elbow-wagging handshake straight out of Realty 101. Jolie decided to take her chances climbing over the palm tree, but came up short when Roger LeMon hooked his arm in hers.

"You're not *leaving* . . . ?" It was more of a statement than a question. He glanced toward Della Underwood for a split second, and it hit Jolie like a thunderbolt that he wanted to make the woman jealous. Her flash of anger dissipated when she considered the ramifications—and complications—of unresolved feelings between Roger and Della. A memory stirred . . . something Beck had said when she'd asked about his return to Atlanta. *My sister was going through some things I wanted to be here for.*

A love affair gone bad?

By the time Jolie had processed the new possibilities,

Sammy was standing in front of her. "I'm Sammy," she said, grabbing Jolie's hand for a pump that would have brought up water from the Sahara.

"Linda," Jolie murmured.

"Hey, Linda just moved here," Kyle Coffee boomed. "Maybe *she* needs a house."

Sammy went from seven hundred and fifty watts to one thousand. "Really?"

"No . . . no," Jolie said as quickly as her acquired drawl would allow. "I don't need a house."

Sammy's face fell, then she squinted. "Have we met before?"

Jolie's heart skipped a beat, then resumed. "No. Like he said, I'm new in town."

"Linda is an attorney," Carlotta and Beck said in unison.

Everyone stared. Carlotta cleared her throat and added, "She lives in Vinings."

Sammy turned back to Jolie. "It's just that . . . you remind me of somebody . . . I can't put my finger on it."

Carlotta couldn't know that Sammy was her former boss, but Jolie suspected that her friend could see the panic on her face.

"Oh, you know what they say," Carlotta said with a laugh. "Everyone has a twin somewhere."

Next to her, Roger LeMon's head jerked toward Carlotta. Jolie winced inwardly when she realized that Carlotta had inadvertently echoed LeMon's response from two nights ago when she'd said she recognized him from a photo with Gary. Had he just made the connection?

His head pivoted back to her and Jolie saw suspicion flash through his eyes. She maintained a wide-eyed expression for his sake and for Sammy's. Then Sammy glanced down at Jolie's shoes and she snapped her fingers. "Did you get those shoes at Neiman's?"

Jolie felt her smile waver, but she managed a nod.

"Were you shopping there this week? Monday maybe?" Jolie managed another nod.

"I'll bet that's it," Sammy said with a big smile. "I probably saw you in the shoe department."

Beck's burst of dry laughter got everyone's attention. He lifted his big shoulders in a casual shrug. "Eventually, you see everyone in Atlanta in the shoe department at Neiman's."

"So true," Carlotta said, jumping on the "save Jolie" bandwagon. Everyone laughed politely, but Roger LeMon kept staring at her. Jolie squirmed and her mind raced for a reason to excuse herself as the sudden lull in the conversation dragged on.

"Linda," Carlotta sang, "I hate to be a damp rag, but we did promise Hannah that we would meet her."

"Right," Jolie agreed in relief.

"It was nice to meet everyone," Carlotta said, backing away and bowing, leaving Jolie to wonder if bowing was still in vogue in England.

Afraid that Sammy would recognize her voice, Jolie nodded her agreement, sending a smile all around. Kyle Coffee waved good-naturedly and Sammy had refocused her fawning self on Beck Underwood, pressing a cream-colored postcard into his hand. Roger LeMon continued to watch Jolie through narrowed eyes with such dark intensity that if he were somehow involved in this mess, she could understand why Gary had sounded so terrified. She tried to smile, but LeMon's face remained immobile.

Her numb feet weren't responding well—she stumbled

past Beck Underwood and he reached out to steady her with his arm. The warmth and strength of his fingers against her bare skin sent a jolt of awareness through her. When she looked into his brown eyes, she saw questions there. She was grateful that despite his obvious bewilderment, he hadn't given them away.

"Thank you," she murmured.

"You're welcome," he said, holding her arm a few seconds longer than necessary before releasing her.

She blamed her heightened senses on the constant stream of adrenaline her body had been pumping throughout the evening, and turned to walk away as fast as her deadened feet would take her. Next to her, she could sense that Carlotta was ready to burst out of her skin. They had barely gotten out of earshot when Carlotta squealed. "Oh, my God, that was so exciting!"

Jolie exhaled. "That isn't a word I would've used."

"Did you find out anything from Roger LeMon?"

"Maybe . . . I don't know." She touched her thumping head. "This entire thing could be a dead end. Maybe I'm looking for a bigger connection than what's there."

"Are you going to call him?"

"I don't know. I'm not sure, but I think he recognized us toward the end."

Carlotta touched her temple. "Because of what I said about having a twin? I'm *so* sorry. That just popped out." She winced. "If I've blown our cover, I'll never forgive myself."

Jolie decided not to make her feel worse by telling her about the phone conversation she'd overheard the other night, and that if LeMon thought they were trying to pull one over on him, he might be incensed . . . to the point of being dangerous.

"It's okay," Jolie said. "I could be wrong about him recognizing us."

"Beck Underwood saw right through us." Carlotta elbowed Jolie. "But then again, the man seems to have radar where you're concerned."

Jolie's cheeks warmed. "I don't know what you're talking about."

"He has a *thing* for you."

"No, he doesn't, and if he did, I'm not interested." Not interested in being a novelty for a man who moved easily in circles she had to crash.

Carlotta pressed her lips together. "Are you still hung up on your boyfriend?" She made a rueful noise. "Of course you are, I didn't mean to be crass. You don't even know for sure if the man is dead or alive."

"R–right." Jolie drained the remaining inch of white wine in her glass. "Did you find out anything about Kyle Coffee?"

"Other than he can't hold his liquor? The only thing I noticed that was odd was that he and LeMon have the same tattoo."

Jolie frowned. "The one on LeMon's wrist? I noticed it, but I couldn't make out what it was."

"Kyle had one in the same place, but I could see his because the slob had lost a cuff link. It was some kind of crest . . . Maybe a college fraternity thing?"

Jolie splayed her hand. "It could mean nothing."

"Did your boyfriend have one?"

"No."

"Hmm. Well, you're right—it could be nothing. I gathered that you knew Realtor Barbie from somewhere?"

Jolie rolled her eyes. "Sammy is my ex-boss."

Carlotta made a face. "Did she fire you?"

"No. I quit."

Carlotta raised her eyebrows, then grinned, revealing her retouched smile. "I like you, Jolie Goodman. You've got chutzpah."

Warm surprise suffused Jolie's chest, and she conceded a little thrill to be accepted by someone like Carlotta, who was such an interesting character herself.

They climbed a short set of carpeted stairs to another bar area where they swapped two more tickets for fresh drinks. "This is my limit," Jolie murmured, already feeling a little light-headed. On the other hand, the guilt of consuming free drinks seemed to dissipate with each one, Jolie noted, sipping the crisp chardonnay.

Carlotta stopped a waiter and whipped out her British accent. "Pardon me, could you direct me to the smoking area?"

"There's smoking outside only," he said apologetically, and pointed. "Down this hall and to the right, out the doors onto a covered patio."

She thanked the man, then pulled out her neon-yellow cell phone. "I'll tell Hannah where to meet us."

While Carlotta talked on the tiny phone, Jolie realized the raised floor gave her a good vantage for spying. She slid a glance in the direction where they'd been standing earlier. Only Kyle Coffee remained, talking to a new group of people, none of whom she recognized. She picked out Beck and Della Underwood a few yards away, shaking hands with more nominees. Beck was hard to miss because he was at least a half head taller than most of the men in the room. His hand hovered at his sister's waist protectively and Jolie experienced a stab of envy over their closeness. If she ever became a mother, she would want more than one child to make sure they had siblings to grow up with and comfort and companionship after she and their father had passed on.

Why those domestic thoughts were whirling through her head now, she couldn't fathom. She had to get through this chaos surrounding Gary before she could move on with her life. But as she watched Beck move, undeniable attraction curled in her stomach. She liked the way he carried his body—with the grace of a natural athlete. It was, she realized, easier to observe him from a distance. When the man was in her proximity, in her personal space, his presence played havoc with her senses.

She wondered if he'd stepped in tonight for his powerful father, and if he'd minded. Was he the prodigal son returning home to pull his weight in the family conglomerate after whiling away a few years in paradise? Had he been summoned home?

His noise about finding a house notwithstanding, would he stay in Atlanta, or be off on another adventure when things became too staid? That kind of freedom frightened Jolie, it was too . . . uncertain. She needed boundaries to be able to organize and guide her life, a measuring stick against which to gauge her progress—a by-product of her blue-collar parents, she was sure. She supposed it would be different if one were raised without financial limitations, which probably explained why money married money . . . being rich was as much a state of mind as it was a state of bank account.

As she watched, a beautiful redhead engaged Beck in conversation. The woman was perfect in every way: perfect hair, perfect smile, perfect figure, perfect clothes, perfect carriage. She angled her body toward Beck in an unmistakable invitation, and he didn't turn away. He was, after all, a man. A rich man who was accustomed to having beautiful women throw themselves at him. Jolie's cheeks flamed that she had even briefly entertained the idea that he might be interested in her.

He laughed at something the woman said, revealing even white teeth, then he glanced around the room and before she could look away, looked up and caught her staring at him. Great. He lifted his chin slightly and a smile played on his mouth before he turned his head to respond to something else the redhead said.

Jolie looked away before she could make an even bigger fool out of herself. Undoubtedly, the man already thought she was certifiable—why not behave like a stalker too?

Keeping an eye peeled for Roger LeMon, she scanned the crowd methodically, thinking she should have watched where he'd gone. A few seconds later, she chastised herself. Just because LeMon gave her the creeps and lied—possibly—about knowing Gary didn't mean he was a criminal monster. He simply could be a run-of-the-mill chauvinistic jerk.

The wisecrack that Kyle Coffee had made about a divorce attorney—had he been hinting that he himself could use one, or Roger? Neither man, in her opinion, presented himself as being prime husband material. Is that what Della Underwood had decided, or had Roger LeMon ended their relationship?

Carlotta snapped her phone closed and stashed it in her bag. "Hannah will meet us outside in a few minutes. Want to come?"

"Sure. Carlotta . . . what do you know about Della Underwood?"

Carlotta pursed her mouth. "Actually, Della and I went to the same private high school for a while."

"Were you friends?"

"No. She was a year ahead of me, and she hung with a very exclusive crowd. Her mother has always been sickly, so she began making appearances with her old man when she was still in high school." Carlotta laughed. "I was wildly jealous of her, we all were."

It was hard to imagine that Carlotta would be jealous of anyone.

"After high school, Della was a social diva—a real party girl, but she had a lot of style, you know? Classy. Dated senators' sons, professional athletes, was always in the social column." She paused and lifted her shoulders in a slow shrug. "Then . . . I don't know, she just sort of dropped off the scene. There were rumors that she was in drug rehab, that she'd had a nervous breakdown, that she'd had a baby—but none of those things were ever verified. She started making appearances again, but she was like this scared little animal, like . . . like she'd been wounded."

"What year was that?"

Carlotta squinted. "Ninety-four, ninety-five."

"What do you think happened?"

Carlotta spoke behind her hand. "Personally, I always wondered if maybe Mrs. Underwood was a mental case, and if maybe Della inherited something." She shrugged. "But that's only speculation on my part."

"She's never been married?"

"No."

"Beck mentioned at the museum the other night that she used to date Roger LeMon."

Carlotta frowned. "Really? I don't remember that. Not that I'm an expert on the Underwoods."

Jolie wet her lips. "Has Beck?"

"Has Beck what?"

Her cheeks tingled. "Ever been married?"

A sly smile curved Carlotta's mouth. "Not unless he got married while he was in exile."

"What do you mean, 'in exile'?"

"Beck worked for his dad, but it was well known that they didn't always get along. Beck was a rebel, a real champion of the working man," she said, her voice heavy with sarcasm. "If you ask me, leading pickets against his dad's companies had more to do with making his old man crazy than with sympathy for the lowly masses, but regardless, Daddy Underwood sent him packing."

Admiration bloomed in Jolie's chest. Despite her best intentions, she stole another glance in Beck's direction and saw that he had been cornered by a reporter and camera crew. Of course anyone covering award nominations for broadcasters and journalists would want to talk to the successor to the largest broadcasting company in the Southeast. A spotlight haloed his wide torso as he spoke into the extended microphone. His body language didn't read like a rebel . . . He looked thoughtful and distinguished, like someone on the verge of taking over the reins of a company he would most likely inherit. A crowd had gathered around him, and from the expressions on their faces, it was apparent that men wanted to be him, and women wanted to be with him.

"He's something, isn't he?" Carlotta whispered with a sigh.

Jolie jerked her head around, then flushed. "He's . . . perplexing."

Carlotta linked her arm in Jolie's and pulled her in the opposite direction. "He's a man, Jolie—trust me, he's not that complicated."

Jolie closed her eyes briefly, trying to sort her jumbled

thoughts. With so many other matters pressing on her mind and her heart, she had no business wasting a brain cell on Beck Underwood.

They followed the waiter's directions through a set of glass doors to a covered patio. A chilly October wind had blown in, raising goose bumps over Jolie's bare arms. She shivered, thinking she should have worn a coat, although she didn't own anything nearly nice enough to wear over the jumpsuit.

Pedestals holding bowls of white sand had been situated around the perimeter of the patio for the smokers. They were a forlorn bunch: social outcasts relegated to a covered concrete pad to practice their vice. The lighting was dim and depressing, and the strident whine of nearby electrical boxes filled the night air. Everyone huddled in their jackets, their backs to the wind, huffing and puffing.

"And to think," Carlotta muttered, "smoking used to be popular." She handed her gin and tonic to Jolie to hold, then opened her purse and pulled out a box of menthol cigarettes. "Want one?"

Jolie started to shake her head, then decided she could use something to calm her nerves and warm her up. "Okay."

Carlotta opened the box and slid out two cigarettes, stuck them both in her mouth and pulled out a slender mother-of-pearl lighter. She lit both cigarettes, then traded one to Jolie for the drink she'd been holding.

Jolie drew on the cigarette until her adenoids stung, then coughed smoke into her hand. "I've never been much of a smoker."

Carlotta exhaled figure eights into the air. "I've quit twenty-seven times. I hate the way it makes my clothes smell." She gestured to Jolie's jumpsuit. "You'll have to turn it inside out and run it on air-only in the clothes dryer for at least an hour. Make sure you tape cardboard around the tags so they don't curl."

Jolie nodded obediently and attempted a more shallow inhale on the cigarette. She glanced over her shoulder, uneasy about the pitch-blackness surrounding the patio. A person could be standing a mere foot off the edge and no one would know it. Gary could be out there, watching her as he'd said. She shivered and took a step toward the center of the patio.

Carlotta looked toward the door, then emitted a little laugh. "Well, if his liver doesn't give out, his lungs will."

Jolie turned to see Kyle Coffee stumbling through the door, holding an unlit cigar that was at least nine inches long. He stopped next to a bowl of sand and set down his drink, then used both hands to search various pockets. Finally he pulled out what looked like one of the postcards that Sammy was handing out, rolled it lengthwise and used it to borrow a flame from the cigarette of the guy next to him. Jolie watched, poised to run in case Coffee set something—or himself—on fire, but he lit the tip of the cigar from the paper, then jammed the card into the sand without incident. He retrieved his drink, drew on the cigar until his face turned scarlet, and exhaled with a happy sigh. He didn't notice them, didn't notice much of anything, Jolie suspected. He seemed to be in a fog, shuffling around the edge of the concrete pad, tapping ashes into the grass.

Jolie looked at Carlotta. "Do you suppose that Coffee is even more chatty when LeMon isn't around?"

"Let's go see, shall we?"

When they approached him, his glassy eyes made it clear that he didn't remember them. They reintroduced themselves as Betty and Linda, and Carlotta congratulated him again on his nomination. He was loud and barely coherent. The cigar smelled like singed hair.

"That's an interesting tattoo," Carlotta said in her perfectly clipped accent, pointing to his wrist.

He frowned and leaned in. "Huh?"

"Your tattoo, what does it mean?"

Her words registered and he clamped the odorous cigar between his small teeth, then yanked back his sleeve to reveal a black tattoo the size and shape of a postage stamp. Jolie leaned in for a good look, and saw a border of what looked like four arms, one melding into another counterclockwise, the tiny hands on the corners. The center of the image was a filigree pattern that she couldn't make out.

"This," he slurred around his cigar, "was the biggest mistake I ever made."

"You don't like having a tattoo?" Jolie asked, enunciating clearly for his benefit.

"Hell, I got a half dozen tattoos," he said. "But this one has ruined my life."

Jolie's skin prickled. "What makes you say that?"

"His wife doesn't like it," Roger LeMon said behind them.

Twelve

Jolie jerked her head around and her heart slammed in her chest at the sight of LeMon's thin mouth pressed into a flat line as he considered their threesome. He walked up and put his arm around Kyle Coffee's shoulder, then pulled the man's head close to his. "Isn't that right, Kyle?" he asked in a tone that might have been good-natured except for his precise enunciation. "Your wife doesn't like that tattoo because it's in a more visible place than the others."

Kyle blinked at Roger dumbly, then nodded. "That'z right, Roger," he lisped around the cigar in his mouth.

Roger slapped him on the back. "I called you a cab, man. It's time for you to say good night."

"Okay," the man mumbled.

"I'll walk you out," LeMon said, and guided his big friend toward the doors. LeMon turned his head to give Jolie a suspicious glare, then herded Coffee inside.

Jolie exhaled.

"Coffee was getting ready to tell us something," Carlotta said. "I just know it!"

"Maybe. I wanted to ask him if he knew Gary."

"So call him. Make up a story."

"Right," Jolie murmured, except she doubted that Kyle Coffee would be as forthcoming when he was sober. And she was starting to feel as if this whole situation was getting out of hand. She didn't know which details might be relevant and which details might take her on a tangent. Plus she was feeling antsy that she hadn't heard from Gary again. She needed to talk to Detective Salyers, try to convince the woman to consider the possibility that Gary had been set up without revealing that she'd seen him. She gazed out into the inky darkness, and nearly swallowed her cigarette when she saw a figure move . . . and approach the patio.

"Hiya," Hannah said, stepping up onto the concrete.

Jolie's shoulders fell and a shiver overtook her. She needed food . . . and her life back.

Even Carlotta looked a little spooked, but recovered quickly. "Oh, hey. You startled me."

Hannah wore skinny black pants and a long flowing jacket that looked a bit vampire-ish. Her hair was slicked back from her slender face and gelled into place. Her makeup was dark and dramatic, and her chandelier-style earrings looked like little swords strung together. Retro Gothica. A fetish, or a lifestyle? Jolie had the sudden sensation that she wouldn't want to encounter Hannah Kizer on a dark street during the witching hour.

Hannah looked at Jolie's ensemble, wig to shoes. "Wow, I wouldn't have recognized you."

"Carlotta helped."

"Yeah, I've told Carlotta if she ever wanted to go underground, she could pull it off."

Carlotta drew on her cigarette. Jolie wondered if she were thinking about the money she'd have to come up with by next Friday.

Hannah looked back and forth between them. "Why are you two so jumpy?"

Jolie sent a warning glance to Carlotta. She didn't want to tell anyone about Gary who didn't need to know.

"This party was a tough nut to crack," Carlotta said, passing her half-smoked cigarette to Hannah, indicating she could finish it. "I'm Betty and she's Linda. If I break into a British accent, just go along."

Hannah shrugged. "Okay."

On the way back inside, Jolie stopped to grind her cigarette into the bowl of white sand and noticed the postcard that Kyle Coffee had used to light his cigar. On impulse, she pulled the stiff, cream-colored card out of the sand and unrolled it, flicking off the charred ends.

A party invitation . . . to Sammy Sanders' house the following evening—the same invitation Jolie had seen her press into Beck Underwood's hand.

You're invited to a champagne pajama party.

Jolie lifted an eyebrow. She'd heard rumors at the agency about the parties that Sammy hosted at her posh Buckhead residence, but of course she'd never been invited. According to the postcard, the attire was sleepwear, the guest list was exclusive, and invitations had to be presented at the door. Apparently Sammy had moved through the crowd tonight, picking and choosing her guests.

Jolie smiled wryly. Even disguised, she wasn't good enough for Sammy.

Tucking the creased invitation inside her purse, she followed Carlotta and Hannah back inside, where no one questioned Hannah's entry. They headed for the food tables as Hannah told them which items to avoid and which items to sample. Jolie filled a small plate with non–red-sauce foods and ate enough to dispel the slight buzz she'd gotten from the wine—she needed to be clear-headed for the drive home.

Beneath the wig, her scalp itched like crazy. The contact lenses felt gritty in her dry eyes. Her feet . . . Well, her feet might never be the same. She longed for a hot soak and a soft pillow and a positive balance in her savings account. She glanced around, expecting to see Roger LeMon lurking in the shadows, watching her. And God help her, she had hoped to catch another glimpse of Beck Underwood. She was sure the man would never work with her now, but she did want to thank him for being discreet, and try to offer some rationalization for her bizarre behavior . . . except she couldn't think of an explanation other than the truth. And she wasn't going to drag Beck into her drama, especially since he had an indirect connection to Roger LeMon through his sister Della.

Jolie pulled herself out of her dismal thought loop and turned toward Hannah and Carlotta.

"The bastard isn't here, is he?" Hannah turned her head for a quick sweep of the room.

"I didn't see him," Carlotta assured her.

"Who?" Jolie asked.

"Her boyfriend Russell," Carlotta said.

"Today I'd had it," Hannah said. "I found out where he

was having lunch and confronted him while he was eating with his boss."

Carlotta gasped. "You didn't."

Hannah nodded emphatically, her knife-earrings jingling. "Sure did. If he thinks he can simply ignore me after all I've put up with, he's insane."

Hearing the bitterness in the woman's voice, Jolie wondered briefly who, exactly, was the sane one. Hannah the Huntress was a tad intense.

"What happened?" Carlotta asked.

Hannah sighed. "He promised he was going to ask his wife for a divorce this weekend."

Jolie choked on a scallop.

Carlotta turned her head and muttered, "He's been promising to leave his wife for a year."

"I heard that," Hannah declared. "Carlotta thinks I'm throwing my life away." She scoffed. "As if her life is going somewhere."

Carlotta cocked her hip. "I'm not the one who spent my lunch hour accosting my married boyfriend."

Hannah leaned in. "When was the last time you *had* a boyfriend?"

"Stalker."

"Prune."

Jolie set down her drink. "*Look* at the time. I guess I'd better be going. I have to go in early tomorrow to help Michael with the Manolo Blahnik appearance."

Carlotta looked disappointed. "Okay. Well, I guess I'll see you tomorrow."

Jolie hesitated, then said, "I was wondering . . . would the two of you like to go to a pajama party tomorrow night? My ex-boss is giving it, so it should be nice, but . . .

we'd have to crash." She had no legitimate reason to go other than it was something fun she could offer up to the girls. Plus she could get one over on Sammy, and the woman wouldn't even know it.

Was that how Carlotta felt when she crashed upscale soirees? That it was enough for *her* to know?

Jolie withdrew the mangled invitation from her purse and handed it to Carlotta, who read it and looked up. "Realtor Barbie is giving a bash?"

Jolie nodded.

"And we're not invited?"

Jolie shook her head.

Carlotta grinned. "Sounds like fun."

"Can you reproduce the invitation?"

"Are you kidding?" Carlotta tapped her finger on the card. "Without raised lettering this won't even be a challenge."

Jolie felt a tiny stab of guilt over planning to crash a private party, but she remembered just a handful of the times that Sammy had dismissed her and the feeling passed rather quickly. "Do you have plans, Hannah?"

Hannah pursed her vampy mouth, then sighed. "No, I'll come."

"Unless her boyfriend calls," Carlotta muttered.

"I heard that."

"I'll see you tomorrow," Jolie said before she could get caught in another round of crossfire.

"Jolie," Carlotta said, "will you be okay walking to your car?"

Hannah gave her a strange look. "Why wouldn't she be?"

"She's worried about my feet in these shoes," Jolie said with a laugh. "Thanks, but I'll be fine. Good night. Oh, and . . . thanks."

Carlotta gave her a secretive nod, then Jolie threaded her way back through the crowd. She kept an eye out for LeMon and other persons of interest, but saw neither. When she walked back through the reception entrance, the ticket taker was still manning his gate and gave her a friendly nod. She waved, once again having misgivings about manipulating their way into the party.

But she did have more information to give Salyers when they talked—Jolie looked at her watch—tomorrow. She'd call the detective tomorrow. After the hoopla at the store, she'd have a few hours before the party. Enough time to put together that mailing to her former customers she'd been putting off. And to discuss a murder investigation concerning her boyfriend.

As she retraced her steps back through the lobby, her thoughts turned to the dead woman in Gary's car. Had she been identified? Did her family know she was missing? Did she even have family? Jolie chewed the tip of a polished nail, wondering if she were to disappear how long it would be before someone missed her. When her rent came due? When the IRS missed her tax return?

She asked for directions to the parking garage and was sent down a hallway and a short flight of stairs to the glass door that she remembered before Carlotta had taken them the roundabout way. She pushed open the door, then walked through another, more industrial door into the parking garage. The cool night air sent shivers through her body. She rubbed her hands over her arms as she waited for the elevator. Halfway up the ramp, a family of four approached their car, their boisterous noisiness a comforting sound in the gloomy concrete structure.

Car doors slammed, then the car with the family backed up and exited the garage. Jolie tapped her foot in the echoing silence, partly to pass time, and partly to send feeling to her toes. The elevator was on its way down, but moving slowly. Fifth floor, fourth. The glass door opened behind her, and a suited man stepped up next to her to wait for the elevator. He looked all around, including at the security camera above them, then stared straight ahead. Tiny red flags raised in her mind. Something wasn't right. His suit was ill fitting, his fingernails were grubby, and—she glanced down—his shoes were scuffed and soiled. Her heart lurched in her chest, stealing her breath. The elevator dinged and the door slid open. He boarded first, then held the door for her.

She stood rooted to the ground.

"Are you comin'?" he asked.

"No," she murmured, then took a step toward the door leading back into the hotel. "I . . . forgot something."

He pursed his mouth, then shrugged. "Suit yourself."

She shot a glance toward the security camera and stayed within its range until the elevator doors closed. According to the lights above the elevator, he rode to the third floor . . . where she had parked. She stood and waited for the man to drive down and exit the garage, but minutes ticked by and no man, no car. Jolie swallowed hard. Was he waiting for her by her car? *In* her car? If he and Gary were both there, the backseat could be crowded.

A foursome came through the glass door and waited for the elevator. She waved them on, and a few minutes later when they drove their car down the ramp and out the exit, the hair stood up on the back of her neck. When she realized the elevator was headed back down, she turned on her heel and jogged back toward the lobby of the hotel, trying to decide between calling the police or hotel security. She stumbled through the door and up the stairs into the lobby, frantically searching for someone who looked official. A guest walked off, freeing one of the women behind the long concierge desk. Jolie headed in that direction, and the panic must have been written on her face, because when the woman looked up, she said, "May I help you?" with a look of concern.

"There's a m–man," she stammered, "in the garage."

"Do you mean the man who's having car trouble?"

"Excuse me?"

"We called an auto service, it should be here shortly."

Jolie touched her temple. "No . . . I mean . . ." She turned and the man from the elevator was striding up behind her.

"I called from the garage," he said. "About the auto service?"

"It's on the way, sir," the woman said. "Third floor, right?"

He nodded. "Thanks."

Jolie watched him walk away and felt like a fool.

"Ma'am, did you need anything else?"

She turned back to the desk. "Um, no. Thanks."

"That's a lovely outfit," the woman said.

"Thanks," she murmured. "Neiman's."

The woman smiled at someone behind Jolie. "Hello, Mr. Underwood."

Jolie winced.

"Hello," he said good-naturedly, then added, "Hi, again . . . *Linda.*"

Jolie turned slowly, and looked up into Beck's amused expression. Her cheeks flamed. "Hi. I, um, suppose you're wondering why I'm, um, dressed like this."

"And going by a fake name?"

"And going by a f–fake name," she parroted.

He crossed his arms, still smiling. "I admit I'm slightly curious."

She swallowed and touched her throat. "Well, my girlfriend and I were just having a little fun."

"You crashed," he said with a grin.

She nodded, thinking how childish it sounded, but willing to let him think she was childish rather than . . . childish and paranoid.

He covered his mouth with his hand. "The other night at the High Museum too?"

She nodded and flushed to her knees. "You must think that's terrible."

He uncovered his mouth and was laughing. "No, just . . . interesting I hate these events—I can't imagine crashing one for the fun of it."

Said the prince to the peasant girl. Cheeks burning, she straightened and walked past him. "I was just leaving."

"Wait—did you drive?"

She nodded.

"Valet?"

She shook her head, thinking he probably valeted his car at the mall. "I'm in the parking garage." The cheap seats.

"May I walk you to your car?"

She remembered her earlier experience and swallowed her pride. "Yes."

He seemed surprised, but fell into step next to her. His stride was one and a half times hers, but he paced himself, then held open the door. He had loosened his tie and unbuttoned the top button of his snowy shirt. He was so handsome that she couldn't look at him, and she couldn't *not* look at him, which only made her feel more like a groupie.

"Am I taking you away from your sister?" she asked.

"No, I was just seeing Della off. I'm living at the hotel for now."

"Oh." Her mind spun at the thought of that bill.

"You can see why I need to find a place to live," he said.

She looked up. "You still want to work with me?"

He grinned and pushed open the industrial door leading into the garage. "Are you a good realtor?"

"Yes," she said as she passed under his arm. "Actually, I'm a broker."

"So you work for yourself."

"Yes. I'm hoping to open an office after the first of the year. For now, I'm working out of my apartment. I can give you a client reference list." She stopped at the elevator and pushed the up button.

"No need," he said. "Anyone who is willing to work two jobs must be trustworthy."

In response, she fidgeted with the blunt ends of her wig. The man made her forget things, like how chaotic her life had become. And how numb her feet were.

The elevator doors opened and she walked inside, thinking when he followed how strange that since Monday, their paths had crossed so many times. She could say it was kismet, and Leann would chastise her for being gullible.

"I assumed your family already had a broker that you worked with." She punched the button for the third floor.

"We do," he said simply.

"Oh." So he was going out of his way to give her his business. Hmm.

"Did you have a good time tonight?" he asked.

Strangely, she had—before the run-in with Roger LeMon, of course. She nodded. "Actually, I did, earlier in the evening. It's obviously rote to you, but I thought it was fascinating to see all those important people in one room and to mingle as if I were one of them." She stopped, suddenly embarrassed at what she had revealed about herself—as if Beck Underwood would be interested in her private inadequacies.

A frown flickered across his face. "As far as I'm concerned, you're just as important as anyone in that room."

She tried to joke her way past her lapse. "You probably say that to all the girls."

But he didn't laugh. "No . . . I don't. But then again, I find myself saying things to you that I'd never say to other . . . women. And I'm not quite sure why that is."

He seemed to be studying her, his eyes filled with a curiosity she'd seen before. He was trying to figure her out. Silently she willed him to see what no one else could see—that she was a common woman looking for an uncommon connection, for a sign that life was more than random physical interactions. She waited, her breath coming in little spurts.

His lips parted, and just when he seemed on the verge of saying something, the elevator chimed its arrival at the third floor.

The elevator door opened and she walked toward her car, embarrassed that the Chevy was so . . . unremarkable, and irritated with herself that she cared what he thought. Their footsteps echoed against the concrete, and for some reason she liked the sound of it—their own pattern.

She closed her eyes briefly, reminding herself that there was no "their" anything. A "their" necessitated a "they," and there was no "they."

She walked up to the car and glanced in the backseat before unlocking the door. Empty. She turned back and smiled. "Thank you . . . for everything."

"I only walked you to your car," he said mildly. In the glare of the fluorescent lights, he looked tired. Which meant she must look like something from a crypt. In a wig.

"I mean thanks for . . . earlier," she said. "Covering for me when Sammy was on the verge of recognizing me."

"No problem," he said, hands in the pockets of his dark slacks. "I got the feeling that it was important to you to hide your identity." He wet his lips. "That there was more at stake than simply being able to crash a stodgy old party."

He looked at her as if she were transparent. She couldn't break away from his gaze.

"Are you interested in Roger LeMon?" he asked quietly.

Her throat convulsed. "Not in the way you think." Again, the urge to confide . . . but again, the overriding urge to protect him, and herself. To protect him from association with a terrible crime. To protect herself from making Beck Underwood a confidante.

"In what way, then?"

Her mind raced. "It's . . . business. Did things end badly between Roger LeMon and your sister?"

"I have no idea what she saw in the man, but I believe he broke her heart."

Was LeMon the source of Della Underwood's withdrawal from society years ago?

"What about you?" he asked.

She looked up. "What about me?"

"Did someone break your heart?"

Her lips parted. Gary's disappearance had left her wary, but heartbroken? On the other hand, it was best to let Beck know that her heart wasn't available, largely because of Gary. "There is a man," she said softly.

He gave a little laugh. "There always is. Is he in trouble?"

She nodded.

"Ah. And does this party-crashing have something to do with it?"

She nodded again.

He averted his gaze, then looked back. "So . . . when can you and I get together? To talk about what I'm looking for. In a house, that is."

Despite her best efforts to be immune to him, her tongue felt gluey. "H–how about here, Sunday afternoon?"

"One o'clock?"

"One o'clock is fine," she said, her heart thumping erratically.

He grinned. "How will I know you?"

She grinned. "Look for Jolie Goodman."

His grin faltered for a second. "I will."

Something happened then . . . an exchange of ions between them. She felt the charge of her body drawing energy from his, and the accompanying carnal tug. From his eyes, she knew he felt it too. She was old enough to know that to Beck, a tug was a tug; but in her confused state, a tug was open to wide misinterpretation, and she couldn't risk giving in to the temptation of his attention.

Jolie hastily opened the car door and lowered herself into the seat, closing the door with more force than necessary. Then she started the engine, backed up, and drove away with a wave. Capturing a glimpse of Beck Underwood in her side mirror, she mulled over the written warning. *Objects in mirror are closer than they appear.*

Hmm.

Thirteen

"Jolie, thank God. I thought you'd never get here."
Michael Lane's anxiety was evident in his voice
and in his hand-ruffled hair. "Customers are already starting to arrive."

Jolie stepped back to keep from being mowed down by
a salesclerk who had jogged into the stockroom to grab
more Manolo Blahnik shoe boxes. She looked at her
watch. "Three hours early?"

"These people are rabid."

Jolie held up the box of Mui Mui shoes. "I had to bring
these back."

He frowned and lifted the box lid. "Wrong size?"

She swallowed and tried not to fidget. "Just wrong for
my feet."

He glanced at the pristine soles, then shrugged and
tucked her receipt in his pocket. "I'll process your refund
as soon as I get a minute. Meanwhile, I'll put them back in
inventory."

Jolie nodded, relieved and a little remorseful for taking advantage of Michael's trust.

He handed her two silver poles with a fat black velvet rope strung between them. "Chain these on where I left off, then start waiting on customers."

Eager to assuage her guilt, she took the hardware, then emerged from the stockroom. Sure enough, a small crowd of people had already gathered on the edge of the shoe department, where signs had been posted to advertise the appearance. The women were tall and leggy, dressed in black so the eye was drawn to their Manolo Blahnik shoes. Both sides of the checkout counter were three-deep with shoppers holding MB boxes, and the floor was a flurry of activity. Jolie groaned inwardly, thinking this did not bode well for her blistered feet. She looked down to make sure none of the dozen or so adhesive bandages she'd applied this morning to toes and heels had crept over the sides of her sensible pumps, then shuffled forward, dragging the poles with her.

The women in line gave her superior looks—ironic, considering she was putting up gates to confine *them*. She pasted on her best sales smile and thanked them for coming, then limped back to the sales floor and waited on women who at the eleventh hour had succumbed to the temptation to own a pair of the infamous shoes so that they could have them signed by the creator. For two hours she sold shoes as fast as she could tote them from the showroom. She kept her mind off her aching feet by concentrating on the commission she was earning. She had just slid off one of her pumps to massage her heel when Sammy Sanders walked up wearing a tight black dress and a pained smile.

"Jolie, do you work on Saturdays *too*?"

Jolie bit the end of her tongue, then nodded.

"Wow, that doesn't leave you much time to sell real estate, does it?"

Jolie tasted blood.

"And, oh, you poor dear . . . I heard about Gary's car being pulled out of the river—with a woman inside!"

Jolie nodded.

Sammy's eyes were large and shocked. "Do you know who it is?"

Jolie shook her head.

"Do they think Gary is dead, too?"

Jolie pursed her mouth. "Did you need some help, Sammy?"

Sammy sniffed. "I understand—you can't talk about it while you're on the clock." She released a musically sympathetic sigh. "Well, I closed a big, big deal this week, and decided to splurge and buy myself another pair of Manolos, something really special. I figured the least I could do was to let you have the commission."

Jolie's cheeks burned, but Sammy seemed ready to spend a lot of money. Being in no position to turn away business, she suddenly had a bright idea. She smiled and removed the glass case key from the cash register. "I know just the thing—we have only a couple of pairs left, and the size seven is on display."

As Jolie expected, Sammy fell in love with the pink-and-rhinestone shoes that Carlotta had worn to the High Museum party a few nights ago.

"I'll take them," Sammy announced, then looked up. "I saw another pair of shoes while I was here the other day . . . silver-colored pumps with cutouts?"

Jolie's mouth twitched—the shoes she herself had worn

last night. "I believe I know which ones you're talking about. Just a minute." She went to the stockroom and returned with the box she'd given to Michael earlier. "These?"

"Yes, those are lovely."

Jolie removed the cardboard stays that had so distressed her feet, then knelt and eased them onto Sammy's perfectly pedicured puppies. Sammy stood and beamed her satisfaction. "I'll take these, too." She lifted her hands. "Gee, Jolie, you seem to have a real gift for retail sales."

Jolie wanted to kick her, but sucked up the backhanded compliment and repacked the pricey shoes. She was, after all, using Sammy to dispose of the shoes that she and Carlotta had "borrowed." "Thanks . . . Sammy."

When they reached the counter, the woman tossed her hair, then said, "The Singer deal fell through."

Jolie looked up. The deal she'd quit over. "Oh?"

"You didn't know?"

Jolie frowned. "How would I have known?"

Sammy shrugged. "I just wondered if anyone had . . . contacted you, asking questions."

Her mind raced—questions meaning someone had suspected Sammy was playing both sides against the middle? "No," she said evenly, and began ringing up the sale, sending inconspicuous glances in the direction of the woman for whom she used to work. Sammy seemed agitated, touching her face a lot, stroking her hair. Jolie had never before seen Sammy rattled. It was kind of . . . leveling.

Jolie announced the total of the sale—over twenty-four hundred dollars, thankyouverymuch. When Sammy opened her small, green Kate Spade bag, Jolie caught a glimpse of metal and remembered with a jolt that Sammy had a permit to carry a concealed handgun. Jolie conceded that being a female real-estate agent could land a woman in remote locations with strangers, but she'd always wondered if Sammy had ulterior motives for being armed, such as protecting herself from anyone she might have double-crossed.

Sammy withdrew a pink lizard-skin wallet and removed a wad of hundreds. Jolie wasn't completely surprised—it would be just like Sammy to keep some of the agency's business off the books and pocket the cash.

Jolie counted the hundreds carefully, then said, "You gave me five hundred too much," and slid the extra bills back toward Sammy.

"That's for you," Sammy said, her expression completely still.

Jolie blinked. "Excuse me?"

Sammy pushed the money back toward Jolie. "Call it severance."

Astonishment bled through her limbs even as her mind was screaming, *Take it! Take it!* She could buy a copier, stationery, a ticket to Cancun. "I . . . can't take that money, Sammy."

"Sure you can."

A bribe in case someone came around asking questions about Sammy's business practices. Jolie hardened her jaw and pushed the money back with finality. "But I *won't*."

Sammy gave a little laugh and folded the extra cash back into her wallet. "That's always been your problem, Jolie—you can't see that sometimes the right thing to do is the easy thing to do."

Swallowing the words that jumped to her throat, Jolie finished ringing up the sale and passed Sammy her change. She reached for the boxes to bag them, and Carlotta materialized by her side.

"I'll do that," she said, then smiled at Sammy. "Nice shoes."

Sammy tilted her head. "Aren't they?"

"Yes," Carlotta said, handing her the shopping bag. "Thank you for shopping at Neiman Marcus. Enjoy the event."

"I will, thank you." Sammy glared at Jolie. "I hope they catch your boyfriend." Then she whipped around and stalked off.

"Brrr," Carlotta said. She was dressed in a black jacket that was longer than her black miniskirt, dark tights, and a pair of black-satin-and-embroidered stiletto demi-boots with tassels around the top. Vintage Manolo. She offered a gapped grin. "I can't *wait* to crash her party tonight. Did I see her trying to give you *money*?"

Jolie nodded. "Hush money."

"You didn't take it?"

"Nope."

Carlotta emitted a dry laugh. "Well, tell me whatever it is and she can pay *me* hush money."

Jolie bit into her lip, knowing her friend was thinking about the money she owed in a few days' time to the man who'd come to see her at work.

"I see you sold our shoes," Carlotta said, changing the subject. "I take it Michael didn't give you any problems?"

"No," Jolie said. "But I feel terrible."

"It'll pass. Christ, this place is a zoo."

Jolie looked up to see Michael directing the placement of enormous bouquets of white helium balloons. Thumping music played over the speakers at a volume that Jolie had never heard in the store. Nervous energy crackled in the air as the conversation level rose from a hum to a dull roar. Black suits abounded as senior management arrived and store security multiplied. The press had been funneled into an area near the front of the line so cameras could capture the frenzy. Reporters interviewed the women standing in line. She saw Sammy put on her Sanders Realty badge and mug for a camera.

"Where's the jumpsuit?" Carlotta murmured.

"In my locker in the break room."

"Let me have it, and I'll process your return while no one is around."

Carlotta followed her into the stock room, quizzing her.

"No stains, right?"

"Right."

"Did you run it through the dryer on air to get out the cigarette smoke?"

"Yes."

"How are the tags?"

"Perfect."

She unlocked the locker and withdrew the black dress bag. "Thanks, Carlotta. I felt like Cinderella last night."

Carlotta pshawed, but Jolie could tell she was pleased. "You didn't leave anything in the pockets, did you?"

Jolie covered her mouth. "Oh my God—his business card. I can't believe I forgot about the card."

"LeMon's?"

Jolie nodded and unzipped the bag. "It might have fallen out in the dryer—no, here it is." She pulled out the card and turned it over to see if the "private" number he'd written was still legible. It was . . . and so was the note he'd scribbled.

I know what you want.

She inhaled sharply, then showed Carlotta the card. "He must have recognized me."

Carlotta squinted. "Wait . . . He gave you the card just as the Underwoods walked up. If he knew who you were, he hadn't figured it out at that point . . . had he?"

"I don't know." Jolie touched her temple, trying to remember the series of conversations and events.

"Maybe the jerk meant it as a come-on, as in 'I know what you want: me.' "

Jolie's shoulders dropped. "You're probably right," she said, trying to convince herself. "Else, why would he have written his number?"

"Right."

"Right." Jolie tucked the card inside her jacket pocket and zipped the garment bag with a shaking hand.

"Jolie," Carlotta said, her voice tinged with concern. "Have you told the police about LeMon?"

"I'm going to call the detective on the case this afternoon." She checked her cell phone—Salyers had called again.

"Jolie!" Michael yelled into the stockroom. "A totem-beaded mule in size six, and a Carmine ankle-tie pump in size nine! Hurry!"

Carlotta hooked her fingers into the hanger and slung the garment bag over her shoulder. "I'll catch up with you later."

Jolie nodded, then scrambled to get the shoes that Michael needed, trying to put Roger LeMon out of her head. When she emerged with the shoes, she was confronted with a crowd that had grown exponentially—the sales floor was a solid mass of bodies, and the line to meet Manolo Blahnik snaked out of the department and through the belly of the store. Jolie handed the requested shoes to Michael, then glanced around to see what she could do to help in the confusion. A bearded face in the crowd caught her attention. Gary?

Her pulse spiked as she stepped to the side to get a better look. But the crowd shifted too, and the face was lost in a sea of shuffling bodies. A droning noise sounded, like a swarm of killer bees, as a murmur moved through the crowd. The mob of shoppers turned collectively to see Manolo Blahnik stride in, flanked by security and his "people." A cheer went up and the older gentleman raised his hand and smiled in greeting. He was a striking figure dressed in a dark suit, his thinning white hair combed back, his jet-black eyebrows setting off inquisitive eyes.

Jolie's first thought was that he looked like a banker. But when the crowd pressed forward and his security inched closer, her next thought was that anything could happen in a crowd like this—shoplifting, pick-pocketing . . . or worse. She scanned the crowd frantically, looking for the face she thought was Gary's. Manolo Blahnik began to speak to the press, and someone jostled her from behind as everyone surged forward for a better spot. She jerked around, jittery now and a little claustrophobic. The air conditioner hadn't caught up with the crush of bodies, and her underarms and neck were moist. She fanned the neckline of her blouse and decided to move toward the front to get more air.

With whispered apologies, she elbowed and sidled through bodies until she was standing a few feet behind the shoe designer. Lights glared on him and cameras rolled, reminding her of last night when Beck Underwood had been interviewed at the reception. She'd sat up like a groupie to catch the fifteen-second spot on the local news.

"Beckham Underwood, son of Lawrence Underwood and heir to the Underwood Broadcasting empire, was on hand to honor the award nominees of the Broadcasters and Journalists of Georgia. Mr. Underwood, who has been living in Costa Rica for the last few years, says he's glad to be home, but is cagey about whether or not he'll stay to take over his father's company."

"I love Atlanta," Beck had said. "But I enjoyed the work I did in Costa Rica, helping to build the infrastructure to support a broadcasting venture there. I haven't ruled out going back. It's important that we support communications growth in developing countries."

He had looked so handsome, she was sure hearts were breaking all over Atlanta at the news that he might not stick around for long.

Not my heart, of course, she thought while easing around the perimeter of the crowd. Her heart was perfectly intact and beating wildly at the thought of Gary being close by. Was he watching her, worried about her? Did he have a message for her?

Or was her mind playing tricks on her?

She kept her eyes peeled, but when Manolo launched into the history of his involvement with shoes, her pulse had begun to settle down. And then she saw Roger LeMon.

His head was turned and he wore sunglasses, but she recognized his profile. He was about ten yards away. The reporters and the guest of honor stood between her and him.

The breath froze in her lungs. It couldn't be a coincidence that she thought she'd seen Gary, and now LeMon was standing right in front of her. Before Jolie could decide what to do, LeMon turned his head and appeared to look directly at her. In fact, he took a half step forward before he seemed to remember where he was and stopped.

At that moment, the speech ended. Applause sounded and chaos reigned as Manolo Blahnik headed toward the line of shoppers waiting to meet him. In the confusion, Jolie lost sight of LeMon, and hoped he'd lost sight of her. Panic rose up in her stomach. Had Gary followed LeMon, or had LeMon followed Gary? She made a beeline for cosmetics and was almost in the clear when a shot rang out, then another, then three more in rapid succession. Startled screams sounded and Jolie dove under a hosiery display, covering her head and waiting for something to bleed.

She peeked through her fingers and saw people gathered around, gaping at her. It must be bad, she thought, because she couldn't feel any pain.

Suddenly Michael's face appeared above hers. "Jolie," he hissed. "You're causing a scene."

She patted various parts of her body. "But the gunshots . . ."

"They weren't *gunshots*, for God's sake—a few balloons broke free and hit the lights. Come out from under there."

She closed her eyes briefly and considered telling Michael to roll her out of the way. Instead she allowed him to help her to her feet, and gave a tentative smile to those standing around. Their guest of honor had paused, but Michael signaled that he should resume, then put his hand on Jolie's elbow and shepherded her toward the stockroom.

"What was that all about?" he asked when they were out of earshot.

Jolie glanced behind her, looking for Gary or Roger LeMon, but saw neither. She looked back and lifted her hands. "I . . . I've been jumpy . . . lately."

"Does this have anything to do with your boyfriend?"

"Indirectly," she murmured. "I'm sorry."

He sighed. "Why don't you call it a day? I'll see you Monday."

She nodded and went to gather her things from her locker. Michael must think she was a lunatic. Which wouldn't be surprising, considering she was starting to have her own doubts about her sanity.

"Hey."

She looked up and saw Carlotta standing at the door of the break room. "Hey."

"I heard."

Jolie inhaled and touched her forehead. "I thought I saw Gary, and I'm sure I saw Roger LeMon, and when the balloons burst—"

"You saw your boyfriend? Are you sure?"

"Not positively. But I did see Roger LeMon, and why would he be here?"

Carlotta shrugged. "He's married, isn't he? Maybe he's here with his wife." She bit into her lip. "Look . . . Jolie. I don't like Roger LeMon any more than you do, but . . ."

"But you think I'm being paranoid?"

The woman touched Jolie's arm. "You're in a bad place," she said softly. "Your boyfriend is missing, a woman is dead—no one would want to believe that someone they care about is capable of that kind of thing. You're starting a new job . . . Maybe the stress is just too much for you. Even if the two men knew each other, that doesn't mean that Roger LeMon had anything to do with what happened to your boyfriend . . . does it?"

Jolie looked into Carlotta's clear eyes and wondered how far out a limb her own imagination had taken her. She had thought the man with the car trouble was stalking her, and just a few minutes ago she had thought she was being shot at. The only true threat was Gary. He was the one who'd stolen her car, who had lain in wait to threaten her. She needed to talk to Salyers, to tell her everything.

Jolie exhaled. "You're right . . . You're right."

Carlotta looked relieved. "Now go home and get some rest." She grinned. "You're going to need it for the party tonight."

Jolie shook her head. "I don't think I should go."

"Of course you should go. It won't be fun for me and Hannah to crash without you. Besides, I'm going shopping for us later in sleepwear."

Jolie's eyes widened. "Carlotta, I don't want to do that again. I feel like it's stealing."

Carlotta dismissed her concerns with a wave. "How often do you get a chance to wear fabulous loungewear?" She grinned. "Come on, let's have some fun tonight—at your ex-boss's expense."

It *would* be nice to get one up on Sammy for once. Jolie mulled over that thought. And she was dying to see the woman's home. "Do you have another wig?"

Carlotta nodded emphatically. "Tell me where you live. Hannah and I will come to your place to get ready."

Jolie gave in to a smile and supplied Carlotta with the address and directions, then said goodbye and left by the back hallway that emptied into the men's department. She skirted behind the crowd, feeling a little better. She would let the police take care of everything where Gary was concerned, so she could concentrate on getting her brokerage company off the ground. Finding Beck Underwood a place to live would give her a tidy nest egg to draw from.

The fact that he might live there only temporarily was his business.

She left the store and walked to her rental car feeling closer to normal than she had in ages. She used her cell phone to call Detective Salyers.

The woman answered on the first ring. "Salyers here."

"Detective Salyers, this is Jolie Goodman."

"Goodman . . . You're the girlfriend in the Hagan case."

"Yes."

"Nice of you to return my call, Ms. Goodman. Finally."

Jolie ignored her sarcasm. "Do you have some information about Gary?"

"Maybe. We traced the hang-up call to your apartment on Monday to a pay phone three blocks away from your apartment complex. Have you had any more hang-ups?"

Jolie's pulse kicked higher and she spoke carefully. "No."

"Has Mr. Hagan called you?"

"No," she said, grateful she could answer truthfully. Crawling into the backseat of her car wasn't calling. "Has the woman in the car been identified?"

"No. We're still waiting on the medical examiner's report."

At the abrupt answers, Jolie swallowed. "Is there something else?"

Papers rattled in the background. "Ms. Goodman, do you know a Mr. Roger LeMon?"

Her heart jumped in her chest. "Yes. How do you know about him?"

"He came by this morning, said you've been harassing him."

Her eyes bugged. *What?*

"According to Mr. LeMon, you've been following him, asking him questions about Gary Hagan, whom he denies knowing."

Jolie clenched the phone tighter. "He's lying."

"You haven't been following him?"

"I . . . I mean he's lying about knowing Gary. He's one of the men in Gary's photos."

"Is he?" Salyers asked mildly. "You said you didn't know any of Mr. Hagan's friends."

"I d–don't."

"Then how did you find Mr. LeMon?"

"I went to a party in midtown Wednesday night and recognized him. I asked him if he knew Gary and he said he didn't."

"What made you think he was lying?"

"His body language. And when he excused himself, I . . ."

"Yes?"

Jolie sighed. "I followed him."

"Oh, you want my job, do you?"

Jolie frowned at her sarcasm. "I followed him because he said he was going to get a drink, but he walked right past the bar. When I found him, he was talking on a pay phone and I heard him tell the person my name, and that I'd recognized him."

She assumed the silence meant that the detective had perked up. "Do you know who he was talking to?"

"No."

"Did he see you?"

"I don't know. I left immediately, but he might have seen me."

"Hmm. Is that the only incident?"

Jolie squirmed. "I saw LeMon last night, and he was talking to another guy from the photos. Kyle Coffee."

"Where was this?"

"At another party."

"Another party, huh? You're really torn up over your boyfriend's disappearance, aren't you, Ms. Goodman?"

Jolie's stomach clenched.

"In fact, one might think that you aren't worried because you know he's alive."

Her inclination to tell the detective about Gary's late-night appearance in her car or her possible sighting of him in the store vanished. No way the woman would believe she hadn't helped him.

"I saw Roger LeMon again today," Jolie said, diverting the conversation. "He came to Neiman's."

"Did he approach you? Threaten you?"

"No," she admitted.

"What exactly did he do?"

Jolie bit into her lip. "He didn't do anything, I guess. He was just . . . there."

"Did you tell him where you worked?"

"No."

"I don't understand—was he shopping?"

"No. There was an event taking place in the store, a big crowd."

"So he was just standing in the crowd at a public event?"

Coming from someone else, it sounded harmless. "Yes, but . . ." But what?

The detective sighed. "Ms. Goodman, do you think maybe you're overreacting? Isn't it possible that Mr. LeMon, a wealthy man who probably shops in upscale stores, just happened into Neiman's to buy something?"

"Yes," Jolie admitted.

"Ms. Goodman, let me a give you some friendly advice. I don't know Roger LeMon, but I'm told that he's a wealthy man with a long reach." She lowered her voice. "He even donated money to buy bulletproof vests for the police department—do you get my drift?"

The woman's "drift" was unmistakable. "Yes," Jolie murmured, trying hard not to feel like a fool. "Was there anything else you wanted to tell me, Detective?"

"No, except to stay away from Roger LeMon before he slaps a restraining order on you."

Jolie disconnected the call with shaking fingers and acknowledged an instant headache. She touched her temples, trying to slow her thinking, to make some sense of things.

If Roger LeMon was up to no good, surely he wouldn't go to the police. She'd been hoping to talk to Salyers about the possibility that Gary had been framed, but the woman wasn't going to listen to a shoe clerk who stalked a pillar of the community.

She sighed, wishing for divine inspiration. Maybe she should just forget about Gary, forget about her car, and forget about the dead woman, whoever she was. Cut her losses and walk away. Before things got . . . worse.

The idea of going out with the girls tonight and crashing Sammy's party was starting to sound more appealing. What was it that Carlotta had said? That Jolie needed to add the word "fun" to her vocabulary.

"*Fuunnnnn*," Jolie said aloud, testing the word on her tongue. Then she tested a smile, suddenly anticipating the well-heeled pajama party.

At least she could wear house shoes.

Fourteen

"Are you sure it was Gary you saw in the crowd?" Leann asked.

Jolie sighed into the phone receiver and dropped into her favorite chair. "I thought so at the time, but now . . . I just don't know."

"Did he look as if he was trying to make contact with you?"

"I only got a glimpse of him, but he seemed to be looking at me."

"And who is this other guy you said was there?"

"Roger LeMon? Well, long story short, I recognized him from a picture in a photo album of Gary's."

"What? How did you get Gary's photo albums?" From Leann's tone it was clear she didn't approve of the kind of intimacy that having his personal items implied.

"The apartment manager gave me a box of things he salvaged from Gary's apartment after the fire. The album didn't have much in it, some childhood pictures, group photos from parties." She decided not to mention the *X*'d-out picture of herself.

"And this guy LeMon was in some of the photos?"

"Yeah." She told Leann about recognizing LeMon and following him to the pay phone, and the snippet of conversation she'd overheard.

"Maybe Gary is mixed up in something dangerous," Leann said, her voice solemn. "Drugs, maybe."

"That what's the detective insinuated. In fact . . ." She winced. "Gary has a record for selling cocaine."

"*What*? You're kidding, right?"

"No."

"And he never told you?"

"No, but then again, I never asked," she said dryly.

"What a slimeball," Leann seethed. "I can't believe he would deceive you like that, and now . . . *this*."

Jolie could tell she was pacing, and she was touched by her friend's concern. "Please don't worry about me—you have enough on your hands with your sister."

Leann sighed. "Jolie, I just wish you had taken my advice and stayed away from Gary Hagan. I told you he was trouble."

"You were right." Jolie laid her head back and stared at the water stain on her ceiling. "Why could you see that and I couldn't?"

Leann sighed. "Just a matter of experience, I guess. Gary seemed . . . too good to be true."

The water stain looked like a misshapen heart. "I'm gullible."

"You just haven't dated enough jerks to make you cynical."

She frowned wryly—linking up with a possible murderer had made her a quick study.

"Jolie, do you think Gary is still following you?"

"Yes," Jolie admitted. "I thought I saw my car drive by last night as I went into the hotel for the reception. I think he'll contact me again. For some reason, I think he feels that he can trust me. I can't decide if that's a good thing, or a bad thing."

"What will you do if he does contact you again?"

"Try to get him to go to the police."

"And if he won't?"

"I'll call them myself," Jolie said. "Stall him until the police get there . . . something." She pushed to her feet and walked to the desk to re-sort the mail, keeping an eye out for the alleged envelope Gary said he'd sent, but the only thing unusual was Mrs. Janklo's *AARP* magazine that the mail carrier had put in Jolie's box by mistake. "I just want this to be over."

"Me too," Leann said.

Jolie tried to smile. "I'm trying to forget about Gary, at least for one night. I wish you could drive up and crash the party with us." She glanced at her watch. "If you left now, you could make it."

"Yeah, right. Besides, you don't need me there, not with your new friends."

Jolie wasn't sure if the envious tone made her feel needed or crowded. She'd never before had multiple female friendships to maintain. She missed Leann, but she was grateful for Carlotta's companionship, especially since Leann would be in Florida for a few more months. Torn, she said, "Hopefully, by the time you get back to Atlanta, this mess will have blown over and *all* of us can be friends."

"Okay," Leann said, but she still sounded forlorn. "Hey, aren't you afraid that Sammy will throw you out of her party?"

"Carlotta is a master of disguise. Sammy won't recognize me." Jolie frowned suddenly, thinking she was getting way too blasé about deceiving others. This would be the last party she would crash, she promised herself.

"Is it a costume party?"

"No, actually, it's a pajama party. I think it's Sammy's version of a costume party."

"Sounds decadent."

Why the word "decadent" conjured up the face of Beck Underwood, Jolie wasn't sure, but she pushed him out of her mind. When she met with him tomorrow to try to sell him an expensive house, she would be all business. If the man had decided that she was his cause for the week, she would take it, but she wasn't going to risk more than her time. If there was such a thing as too good to be true, it was Beck Underwood. If nothing else, Gary had taught her a lesson about keeping her heart under wraps until her head caught up with it.

"With Sammy, I don't know what to expect," Jolie said. "I forgot to mention that she came by today, too. Tried to give me a bribe."

"For what?"

"I think she's in trouble for a deal that went bad and she's afraid I'll be questioned."

"Did you take the money?"

"Of course not!"

"You should have taken the cash and told the truth anyway. What's she going to do—fire you?"

"I don't want to have anything to do with the woman's money . . . unless I have to go back and beg for a job. And after the spectacle I made of myself today, I might get fired from Neiman's."

"So how is your brokerage business?"

She flipped on her computer so it could boot up while they talked. "Anonymous. But I'm sending out a mailing today to some of my former customers. And I'm meeting with a guy tomorrow who's looking for a house."

"That sounds promising."

"Uh-hm," she murmured casually.

"Anyone I would know?"

Because of her interior design connections, Leann knew almost everyone. "Er, possibly. Beck Underwood?"

"Of Underwood Broadcasting?"

"Yup."

"Oh, my God. How on earth did you meet him?"

"Remember I told you about running into a guy when I was carrying that armload of shoes my first day on the job?"

"Yeah . . . it was *him*?"

"It was him."

"Wow, what a coup. I can't imagine what kind of a house he's going to buy."

"Well, I don't have his business yet." She'd seen plenty of customers—especially wealthy ones—drop agents at the last minute to give their business to a buddy or to a buddy's wife, son, daughter, hairdresser.

"Oh, Jolie, I hate to go, but I have to get ready for a doctor's appointment."

"Sure," Jolie said. "Thanks for listening. Tell your sister that I hope everything is okay."

"I will. Good luck with Beck Underwood, and have fun tonight."

"Bye." Jolie hung up the phone reluctantly, conceding that she dreaded spending the afternoon alone. She leaned against the desk and surveyed her surroundings with an eye toward what Carlotta and Hannah would think when they arrived. The living room-slash-office, galley kitchen, breakfast area, all visible from where she stood. A sad collection of odd-lot furniture she had accumulated situated on gray builder-grade carpet. The layer of dust on every flat surface seemed to sum up her general mindset over the past few weeks—since Gary's . . . departure. Well, enough of that.

She unearthed the feather duster and gave everything a good going over. In the bedroom, though, she paused at the sight of finger marks in the dust on the top of the bookcase that was built into the headboard. She swiped her own fingers in a dusty patch, and the marks were much smaller. Her neck prickled with unease. Had someone been in her apartment, in her bedroom, or had she somehow made the marks herself when she'd reshelved the books strewn around the apartment? She experimented again, this time putting her weight on her hand, and, to her relief, the impressions were more similar. She wiped away the marks, telling herself that she truly was becoming paranoid.

After dusting and running her ancient vacuum cleaner, she looked around the small apartment where she'd lived for four years and tried not to feel depressed. Having worked in real estate for most of her adult life, she knew that the sooner she invested in a home, the better. Yet some small part of her resisted the idea of buying a home to live in alone. She had always envisioned that she and her husband would shop for a first home together. Between school loans and living expenses, she had managed to squirrel away a few thousand dollars, but when she'd opted to invest in her own brokerage firm, she had postponed owning a home for a while longer.

Now she wondered if that had been some kind of unconscious decision to wait for Gary—or someone else—before buying a home.

She shivered. The outside temperature had plummeted to an unseasonable low, and the apartment had acquired a distinct chill. Rebelling against turning on the heat in the middle of October, she donned jeans and a sweatshirt to work at her desk. To the tune of a smooth jazz station, she assembled a postcard mailing to a list of former clients, giving her new e-mail address and cell phone number if they had referrals. Sammy would probably shoot her if she caught her poaching clients, but Jolie reasoned that she had developed a relationship with the clients and had a right to ask for their future business. She welcomed the mindlessness of labeling and stamping the postcards. It was, she realized, the most normal thing she'd done in days and took her mind off the disturbing tangents her life had taken lately.

She was actually humming under her breath as she bundled the postcards into a bag and left to drive to the post office. A surprisingly cool wind gusted around her, tossing her hair into her eyes. Two young girls skipped along the sidewalk, holding hands, pigtails bouncing. Their pink cheeks and exuberant feet made Jolie smile. Had she ever been so carefree? At what point in life had she begun to accumulate baggage, to make poor decisions that had led her to this moment?

She dropped off the postcards, purchased more stamps, and on the way back to her apartment, pulled into a drive-through to pick up dinner. While she waited for her order, she leaned forward and peered through the windshield, squinting into the sun. The day was so luminous, it was difficult to imagine that anything was wrong with the world, much less the horrible mess that Gary had gotten himself into. When her order came through the window, she snagged a French fry from the bag and glanced in the side mirror in preparation for pulling away.

A gray Mercury Sable sedan sat behind her. With one occupant. A man whose build resembled Gary's. Was he following her?

She choked down the fry and looked harder, but the man wore a ball cap pulled low over his face. Coincidence or intentional? She kept her foot on the brake and reached for her cell phone. After retrieving Detective Salyers' number, she waited for the call to connect while her pulse climbed. Another car had pulled in behind the Sable, so as long as she stayed put, he would be trapped by a curb and some rugged landscaping. The young man in the drive-through window frowned at her.

At last the woman answered. "Salyers."

"Detective Salyers, this is Jolie Goodman. I think Gary Hagan is in the car behind me."

"What makes you think so?"

"It looks like my car, and a man is driving it."

"Are you sure it's Mr. Hagan?"

"No, I'm not positive."

"Is there some way you can get behind the car to check the license plate?"

"No. I'm sitting at a Wendy's drive-through."

"Where?"

"Holcomb Bridge Road."

"What's the cross street?"

She glanced around frantically, trying to remember. "East of Old Alabama Road."

"I'll dispatch a cruiser there. Can you sit tight?"

A horn blared a couple of cars back. "I'll try."

"Stay on the line."

More horns blared. She shut off the car engine, put on the hazard lights and locked her doors, all the while keeping the phone to her ear and her eye on her driver's side mirror.

The young man at the window waved to get her attention. She rolled down the window and said, "I'm so sorry—my engine light flashed, then it went dead."

From the look on the young man's face, it was clear the training manual hadn't prepared him for this. "I need to get the manager." Then he disappeared.

The horns kept blowing, although the man in the car behind her seemed calm enough.

"Ms. Goodman, are you still there?"

"Yes," she said into the phone. "But I have a bunch of angry, hungry people behind me."

"An officer is on the way, ETA less than five minutes."

Which sounded like an eternity to Jolie. Sweat gathered on her hairline and she felt nauseated.

"Can you still see him?" Salyers asked.

"Yes."

"What is he doing?"

"Just sitting there."

No sooner had she spoken than the door of the Sable swung open as far as the narrow driveway would allow. A jean-clad leg emerged.

"He's getting out," she said.

"Don't risk it," Salyers said. "Drive away."

She dropped the phone and fumbled to turn the ignition key. As the engine roared to life, she gunned the gas and vaulted out of the drive-through, tires squealing. When she looked in the rear view mirror, the man took off his hat to scratch his bald head. Definitely not Gary.

Relief flooded her limbs and she pulled into the next shopping center to retrieve her phone. "Detective?"

"I'm still here—what happened?"

"It wasn't him. Sorry."

"No problem," the detective said. "Hang on—let me cancel the call."

Jolie alternately berated and calmed herself until Salyers came back on the line.

"Ms. Goodman, are you okay?"

"Yes. I apologize for the false alarm."

"Don't worry about it. Gary Hagan is a fugitive. Even if you *think* you see him, I want you to call me, is that clear?"

"Yes."

"Because we both know he's still alive, don't we, Ms. Goodman?"

Jolie caught herself, then murmured, "Like you, I'm assuming that Gary stole my car."

"Ms. Goodman, when we spoke before, you neglected to mention the condo that Mr. Hagan owned."

Jolie frowned. "Condo? Here in Atlanta?"

"In midtown, on West Peachtree—ring a bell?"

"No. I don't know anything about it."

"Hm, that's interesting, since you're listed as the buying agent."

Jolie's mind raced. "That's . . . impossible. It had to be someone else named Goodman. I never handled a property for Gary."

Salyers sighed. "It won't do you any good to cover up business dealings that you had with Mr. Hagan."

"I'm not," Jolie said hotly. "Why would I lie about something like that?"

"Because when we raided the condo this morning, it showed signs of someone having been there recently. Plus, the freezer was full of coke—and not the cola kind."

Jolie's stomach roiled. "I . . . don't know . . . anything . . . about . . . anything."

"Of course you don't," Salyers said, and Jolie couldn't tell if the woman was serious, or if she was mocking her. "Will you agree to come down to the precinct to be fingerprinted?"

Her skin crawled just thinking about it. "What for?"

"Well, if you don't know anything about the condo, your prints won't be there, will they?"

Jolie swallowed. "No. I mean, yes—I'll be f—fingerprinted. I don't have anything to hide."

"In that case, you wouldn't mind submitting to a polygraph as well?"

Her breath caught in her chest. "A lie detector test?"

"Right."

Could she unwittingly incriminate herself? "I . . . this is a little overwhelming."

"It's nothing to worry about, unless of course you're keeping something from me."

Jolie closed her eyes, her heart hammering.

"There's my other line. I tell you what, Ms. Goodman— why don't you come by the precinct Monday morning at ten o'clock? We'll have another cup of coffee and discuss the new developments in the case, and I can take your prints, just for everyone's peace of mind."

She hesitated, already dreading the meeting. "What about the polygraph?"

"That will have to be scheduled—we'll talk more about it Monday."

"Okay."

"Meanwhile, Ms. Goodman, try to stay out of trouble."

Jolie disconnected the call and puffed her cheeks out in a sigh, thinking at least she would be safe crashing Sammy's pajama party tonight. The most trouble she and the girls were likely to encounter was unbridled pretentiousness in Realtor Barbie's funhouse.

Fifteen

"This is cozy," Carlotta said as she and Hannah walked into Jolie's apartment. The women's hands were full of shopping bags. "How long have you lived here?"

Jolie smiled. "Too long."

Hannah studied her shabby collection of furnishings as if Jolie were an oddity to the stripe-haired woman. She picked up a coaster that Jolie's mother had crocheted from orange yarn and scrutinized it. As a distraction, Jolie offered them something to drink, and Hannah helped herself in the refrigerator, emerging with a bottle of water each for Carlotta and Jolie, and a bottle of beer for herself.

With a start, Jolie stared at the bottle that Hannah lifted to her mouth. It was the premium label that Gary preferred. Hannah stopped. "Is it all right if I drink this?'

"Of course," Jolie said, recovering. She had bought a few to keep on hand and he hadn't had the chance to drink one before he . . . disappeared. She remembered thinking later that she had cursed the blossoming relationship with that casual act of intimacy—stocking his favorite beer.

"Wait until you see what I brought," Carlotta said with a grin, lifting a shopping bag. "We're going to knock 'em dead." From a bag she withdrew a burgundy-colored velvet robe with bishop sleeves. "I thought this would be perfect for you, Jolie."

Jolie petted the thick pile and began to salivate. "I hope you shopped the clearance rack."

Carlotta looked perplexed. "Why would I shop the clearance rack if we're going to be returning everything?"

"Will they let you return nightclothes?" Hannah asked, peeking into the bags.

"Robes they'll take back," Carlotta said. "And pajamas if they haven't been worn." She made a face. "Doris in Intimates actually sniffs things. It's disgusting."

"Uh, actually, I think it's a health code," Hannah said, pulling out a black high-necked satiny robe. "This is wicked."

"That one's yours," Carlotta said, then pulled out a teal-colored raw silk robe with a ruffled shawl collar. "This one's mine." She dug in a different bag and removed handfuls of colorful silk. "Pajamas for all of us: a cream chemise for Jolie, pink tap pants for me, a red gown for Hannah."

Jolie balked at the sight of the knee-length chemise. "Er, I was thinking more along the lines of cotton pajamas."

Carlotta looked horrified. "What? No!" She handed Jolie the chemise as if she were dressing a child who didn't know better.

Jolie rubbed the pale, thin fabric between her fingers with awe. "What if I ruin it?"

"You're not going to ruin it." Carlotta whipped out packages of what looked like shoulder pads. "Dress shields, so we don't sweat on the silk. And be careful what you eat and drink."

Jolie turned over the dangling price tag on the chemise and gasped. "Eight hundred dollars? You can't be serious."

"Your robe is twelve hundred."

Jolie looked at that tag, then dropped it as if it were dangerous. "You don't expect me to wear two thousand dollars' worth of pajamas to this party?"

"Of course not," Carlotta said, then reached into another bag, withdrew a shoebox, and flung off the lid. "Don't forget the two hundred dollar mules!"

Jolie gawked at the delicate burgundy shoes trimmed with feathers. "Two hundred dollars for house shoes?"

"*Designer* house shoes. The kind that Garbo and Hepburn used to wear." She sighed and angled her head. "It's one night—you'll look so fabulous."

Jolie chewed on her lower lip. "I promised myself I wasn't going to do this again."

Carlotta rolled her eyes. "Okay, just this last time. Think of how much *fun* it will be to pull one over on your ex-boss." She raised her eyebrows. "Who knows? Beck Underwood might even put in an appearance."

A ridiculous flush burned her face. "This sounds petty, but I really just want to see the inside of Sammy's house. When I worked at the agency, she talked about it nonstop. I actually drove by it once, but this could be my only chance to cross the threshold."

"All the more reason for you to look like a million bucks," Carlotta urged, then leaned in. "I brought you a

long red wig. We'll do your eyebrows, and with the contact lenses, she'll never know who you are."

"Are you wearing a wig too?" Jolie asked.

She nodded. "I'm going as Marilyn tonight, and Hannah
is going to wear the brown page-boy that you wore a few
nights ago." Carlotta looked at her watch, then shrieked.
"We only have two hours. Where's your bathroom?"

Jolie felt more than a little absurd leaving her apartment
wearing a nightgown, robe, and feathered mules, but
thankfully, the dipping temperatures necessitated a coat,
so her long, navy all-weather coat covered most of her
garb. Her new auburn tresses were stiff against her neck,
the green contacts, swimmy in her eyes. Thank goodness
it was close enough to Halloween so that anyone who
spied them might realize they were headed to a costume
party. Still, she already regretted not wearing a bra—the
slippery silk slid over her breasts like a constant caress,
with predictable results.

"Where did this cold weather come from?" Carlotta demanded, belting her own long coat—except hers was
black cashmere, and stunning against her blonde wig.

"It's called winter," Hannah snapped. With her blunt
page-boy wig, severe makeup and long black leather
duster, she looked every inch the dominatrix.

Carlotta frowned. "If you're going to be in a bad mood
all evening, don't come."

"Sorry," Hannah mumbled. "I expected Russell to call
before now."

Carlotta sniffed and looked like she wanted to say
something, but didn't. Jolie remembered that Hannah's
married boyfriend was supposed to tell his wife that he

wanted a divorce sometime this weekend. It appeared he was leaning toward the "end" of the weekend.

She locked the apartment door behind them and, out of habit now, looked left and right as they made their way down the sidewalk to the parking lot by lamplight. "Do you want to ride with me?" she asked. "Or are we driving separately?"

"I'm driving," Carlotta said, stopping next to a mirror-shiny dark Monte Carlo SuperSport parked in the handicap spot. "Like my new car?"

Remembering the woman's imminent rendezvous with the man who'd demanded two thousand dollars, Jolie's eyebrows went up. "What happened to the Miata?"

"I thought it was time to get a new ride."

Jolie opened the back door of the spanking-new sedan and inhaled the new-car smell. "Nice."

They were settled inside and fastening seat belts when Hannah, who sat in the front passenger seat, looked over at Carlotta. "Aren't you going to tell Jolie the truth?"

Carlotta started the engine. "She won't approve."

Jolie frowned and leaned forward as far as her seatbelt would allow. "What do you mean, I won't approve?"

Carlotta twisted in her seat and backed out of the parking place, then pulled toward the entrance of the apartment complex. "Well . . . some dealers are allowing customers to keep a vehicle for twenty-four hours before they actually buy the car, so . . . I'm trying it out." She grinned.

Jolie gave her a wry look. "You have no intention of buying this car, do you?"

"None whatsoever."

She couldn't be too self-righteous, Jolie reminded her-

self, not while she wore over two thousand dollars' worth
of jammies that she planned to return. She sat back in her
seat, marveling over the way Carlotta connived to get
what she wanted. On the surface, it didn't seem right . . .
yet she wasn't doing anything illegal. Besides, was it really so different from bending the rules on tax returns?

A small part of her admired Carlotta's cheekiness. The
woman's obituary was bound to be more interesting than
her own.

From the backseat, Jolie gave directions to a north
Buckhead neighborhood where the streets were narrow
and the homes were enormous. Old money had built the
McMansions, and new money had upgraded them.
Sammy Sanders' house was an expansive two-story white
home with yellow light blazing from the multitude of
windows. The structure sported a dozen different roof angles, various verandas and offshoots of smaller buildings
(the servants' quarters?) connected by breezeways, testi-
mony to at least a half dozen additions.

"It's a freaking compound," Hannah murmured.

Jolie nodded her agreement. She remembered it being
impressive in the daylight, but at night it was downright
imposing. With its circular drive lit by dozens of lights, it
resembled a country club more than a residence. "Looks
like things are in full swing."

"One of the party-crashing rules," Carlotta said. "Never
be the first person to arrive . . ."

"Or the last person to leave," Hannah said.

"She has a valet," Carlotta said, her voice ringing with
approval. She pulled up behind two other cars from which
coated people were alighting. Jolie felt a tiny surge of relief
that she wasn't the only person who felt compelled to cover
her sleepwear in public, but she was starting to get nervous

about crashing a private party . . . especially Sammy's party. She shifted, hoping the dress shields were protecting the expensive silk chemise from her nervousness.

A coated and gloved man was leaning down to address the drivers, then taking their invitations. The people two cars ahead appeared to have everything in order and were assisted from their car. The occupants of the Jaguar in front of them, however, after much head-shaking and shrugged apologies from the ticket-taker, were sent away. Jolie swallowed. "How did the invitations turn out?"

"My brother had to tinker with it some," Carlotta admitted. "The first pass looked better than Sammy's original, so he had to downgrade the print resolution."

Jolie bit back a smile as they pulled up and Carlotta zoomed down her window. "Hello," she said in a perfect imitation of the Buckhead bourgeois.

"Good evening, ma'am," the man said. "Invitations, please—one for each guest."

"Of course," she cooed, handing over the cards.

The man glanced at them, then nodded and smiled. "Leave your key in the ignition and the valet will park your car." He opened Carlotta's door, then tore off a ticket and handed it to her when she stepped out.

The man stepped back and opened Jolie's door. She gave him her hand and stepped out into the night air, which fell around her like a cold sheet, raising chill bumps . . . and concern. Suddenly spooked, she turned to look at the car behind them, half expecting to see Gary following her. But the driver was female . . . and wearing a fur coat, she noted wryly.

Because the winters in Atlanta were so short-lived, women who could afford fur broke them out at the first frost, without fear of the paint-throwing PETA people who targeted soirees in New York and Los Angeles. Jolie suspected the animal rights activists subscribed to the belief that everyone south of the Mason-Dixon Line was armed and that their red paint parties might get them shot down here.

Which probably wasn't too far off the mark, she thought, remembering the handgun tucked into Sammy's designer purse. She smoothed her hand over her trusty all-weather coat—so old, it bordered on retro. Unless there was a group of polyester activists that she wasn't aware of, she was safe from paint slinging—a bonus of belonging to the lower middle class. Then she frowned—since leaving Sammy's employ, she might have dropped into the upper lower class.

When they started up the steps to the glowing manor house, Jolie's nerve faltered. On the other side of the tall windows, people mingled, holding glasses and moving in that "let me slip through here" way that people use to sidle through parties.

"Come on," Carlotta hissed, waving her forward.

"I have a bad feeling about this," Jolie murmured, stepping up. Assailed again by the feeling that she was being watched, she turned to look back to the driveway, but no other guests had arrived. Then headlights from the street caught her eye. A car sat at the end of the sloping driveway, its nose jutting out past the brick pillars that flanked the entrance. In the darkness, she couldn't tell the model or the color. Gary? A lost driver, perhaps? A guest fumbling for their invitation? Or simply someone who had pulled to the side of the street to make a phone call? A dozen harmless possibilities, and one that unsettled her, yet seemed highly unlikely . . . especially in light of her paranoid scene at the drive-through today.

"What's wrong?" Carlotta asked. She turned her head

in the same direction, then frowned and reached for Jolie's arm. "Come on, let's go inside."

The woman's fingers bit into the back of her upper arm through the multiple layers of fabric. Carlotta herded her toward the door, on the heels of Hannah, and Jolie picked up on her unease. Had she recognized the car? Was it the man to whom Carlotta owed money, or perhaps someone else?

Carlotta released her hold on Jolie's arm, the gargantuan door opened, and Jolie watched as she morphed into a gracious guest, her smile wide and ready. A finger of disquiet nudged Jolie: If the woman could transform herself so quickly, who was the real Carlotta Wren?

Her thoughts were cut short by the haunting music and the sporadic blasts of voices and laughter. And blessed heat. Jolie looked up to see Sammy standing in the doorway, wearing a revealing leopard-print teddy topped by a long, transparent robe. Long, tanned legs ended at five-inch-high leopard-print satin mules. Her cleavage was precarious, and she looked perplexed as she glanced over the trio. "Hello," she said with a little squint. "I'm Sammy Sanders."

Carlotta laughed gaily. "I'm Carly, and these are my friends, Hallie and . . . Gwen." Sammy's gaze flitted over the other two women. Jolie nodded, but Sammy had already looked away. With a start, Jolie realized that she needn't have worried about Sammy recognizing her. The female bulldozer had never given Jolie credit, had never seen her for who she truly was. To recognize someone, you had to first know them.

Her former boss wavered, stealing a helpless glance toward the valet stand as another group of guests alighted from their car. Although it was clear Sammy had no idea who they were, Jolie suspected that neither did she want to create a scene. She knew they couldn't have gotten in without an invitation, so she was trapped.

Carlotta whipped a wrapped gift from her bag—the essential hostess gift. "Candles," she said sweetly.

After a brief pause, Sammy rearranged her face into a polite expression, stepped back and swept her arm toward the cavernous foyer. "Welcome, ladies. I hope this is a night you won't soon forget."

Jolie walked by Sammy and into the black-and-white checkerboard tile foyer of the palatial home. Her gaze traveled upward to the enormous chandelier, which looked as if it might have once belonged in a theater. She tried not to gape at the contemporary paintings on the soaring walls. Secretly, she'd hoped that Sammy would have tacky taste, and although her style was a little ostentatious, it was spectacular, in quality and in scale.

Meanwhile, her entire apartment would fit nicely within this entryway.

"May I take your coats?" a tuxedoed man asked a few feet inside.

Jolie unbuttoned the inexpensive navy coat and relinquished it self-consciously in return for a ticket. She turned the corner and glanced into a colossal great room where guests stood in happy clumps, clinging to champagne glasses and to each other. From this spot she could see the entrance to what appeared to be a French Country dining room, and across the great room, a wall of glass doors was open, leading to an indoor pool. Chlorine and perfume stung her nose.

She recognized a few faces from the night before, but she couldn't place them. The two attractive blondes standing next to the fireplace were sisters, she remembered, although she couldn't recall if their name was York, or if they were *from* New York.

The woman who had complimented her on the jumpsuit was talking to a man half her age, the man who had laughed at her joke talking to a woman half *his* age. Of course, they'd never recognize her in this getup.

Everyone, it appeared, had adhered to the suggested dress code. Most of the men wore silky pajamas—striped or paisley—and short robes or smoking jackets. The women, on the other hand, put a tad more skin on display. Teddies, tap pants and camisoles, shortie nightshirts, long gowns with high slits, gossamer robes. Breasts and Botox abounded. There were a few elaborate caftans (adult one-sies), but for the most part, Jolie felt overdressed. Still, when the lower part of her robe gapped and air rushed over her bare legs, she shivered and pulled the robe closer around her.

"Please, don't obstruct the view," a man said next to her.

Her nipples knew that voice.

Jolie turned to find Beck Underwood smiling down at her legs. He wore a plain black cotton robe a la Target that hit him mid-shin, and flip-flops that looked to be on their last flop. In one hand, he held a champagne flute that looked diminutive between his big fingers; in the other he held a bottle of champagne by the neck. The *V* of his belted robe revealed dark chest hair with golden ends. She'd bet her last dollar that the man had never worn a robe in his life. Obviously, he wasn't a pajama man. Jolie's gaze dropped lower and she couldn't help but wonder what, if anything, was underneath the robe.

When she looked up, Beck was staring at her as if she were his personal party favor.

Sixteen

Beck Underwood walked closer, his mouth pursed in an ironic smile. "I had a feeling you might be here."

Jolie glanced around. Carlotta and Hannah were standing a few feet away, their heads close in conversation. Sammy was greeting more guests. Jolie looked back to him and shook her bewigged head. "How do you always recognize me?"

He shrugged, then leaned in. "Did you crash?"

She crossed her arms, then nodded sheepishly.

He threw his head back and laughed. "That's great. Someday you're going to have to tell me how you do it."

Jolie bristled at the thought of being the man's entertainment.

"Who are you tonight?" he whispered.

Feeling more foolish by the minute, she mumbled, "Gwen."

"Ah. Well, Gwen," he said, picking up a lock of her long fake, red hair, "I've always had a thing for blondes, but in your case, I might make an exception."

Her heart fluttered irrationally until she realized that he was probably well on his way to emptying the bottle of champagne that he held. "You really shouldn't flirt with the person who might become your real-estate agent."

His teeth flashed white against his tan. "Why not?"

Jolie managed a watery smile that she hoped passed for coy. "B–because she might take advantage of you."

He lifted one eyebrow. "Careful, Gwen, you give a man hope."

Her heart skipped a beat, and she told herself he was teasing her, maybe looking for a rendezvous after the party . . . or *during* the party. And while she couldn't deny that she was incredibly attracted to the man, she wasn't about to put herself in the position of being one of Beck Underwood's groupies. She'd had casual sex before, but this situation was different. Besides the fact that she needed the man's business, she was dangerously close to caring what he thought of her. A caution flag was raised in her mind, warning her that there might be more at stake here than a missed commission.

"Is your sister here?" she asked, to change the subject.

He nodded. "Della's by the pool."

"Ah, yes, the pool."

"I suppose you've been here before."

"No, but Sammy talked about the pool, um . . . *occasionally* at the office."

"Ah. Then allow me to take you on a tour. It's quite the place." He winked. "Sammy gave me the full treatment earlier."

Jolie hesitated, then glanced over his shoulder and saw Sammy watching them with a proprietary eye on Beck, a warning eye on her. Revenge sparked in Jolie's chest and she looked back to Beck. "A tour would be nice. Maybe you can point out some things you do and don't like."

His gaze raked over her. "I like short, silky nightgowns and silly house shoes."

It was as if she weren't wearing a ten-pound velvet robe. "I meant what you like in a house," she added quickly, then nervously licked her lips. "Do you think I could have some of that champagne?"

His mouth curved into a grin and he flagged a passing waiter. "You, interesting lady, can have anything I've got. But," he added in a conspiratorial tone, "we need to work on getting rid of that troublesome boyfriend of yours." He juggled his own bottle and glass to snag a clean champagne flute from the waiter's tray, then held it out to her as if he were laying a kingdom at her feet.

Jolie swallowed. Why had she told him she had a boyfriend who was in trouble? She stared into his shining brown eyes and her knees felt loose, and then she remembered why she'd told him she had a boyfriend who was in trouble: To create enough distance to circumvent any possibility of developing a crush on him.

Giving herself a mental shake, she took the glass and held it with amazingly steady hands while he filled it with pinkish-gold liquid from his personal bottle.

"Why don't we start upstairs?" he suggested, and gestured toward the wide staircase—red carpet on white marble made the staircase itself a work of art. Other guests were walking down the stairs, returning from their own tours, she presumed, so she agreed. But she felt Sammy's stare when they moved away from the crowd.

As she climbed the stairs, Jolie sipped the champagne, cool and fizzy against her tongue, and studied the gold foil wall treatment on the massive curved wall. Despite the fact that she and Beck were in their bedclothes and drinking bubbly, Jolie was determined to be professional. "Is this the size home you'll be looking for?"

He lifted his big shoulders, straining the cotton fabric of his inexpensive robe. "I really hadn't thought about it—that's why I need you."

She refused to read anything into that statement. "I, um, saw you on the news last night. You didn't sound as if you were going to stay in Atlanta long enough to buy a home."

A pink stain crawled over his tanned cheeks. "Slow news night. Besides, if I buy a house and decide not to stay in Atlanta, I'll lease it out."

Hearing him say that he might not stay in Atlanta shouldn't have bothered her, but it did. Yet it was even more reason, she told herself, not to buy into his flirtation. Beck Underwood was looking for something to pass the time until he moved along, and she didn't want to be another short-term project.

At the second-floor landing, they stopped for a bird's-eye view of the magnificent chandelier and the grand entryway. Sammy was welcoming a male guest who was dressed in a red velvet smoking jacket reminiscent of the Rat Pack era, all the way down to the arrogant way he held himself. Jolie froze—she knew that pose. While she stood staring down, Roger LeMon looked up, directly at her and Beck. She gasped and stepped back.

"Is something wrong?" Beck asked, turning.

She couldn't very well tell him that Roger LeMon had reported her to the police, especially since Beck himself was aware of her tendency to stalk the man. "Um . . . the height," she lied with a laugh. "I had a sudden bout of vertigo." Her mind spun. Would LeMon recognize her tonight and accuse her of following him? Tell Sammy who she was? Call the police again? She looked around her. On the other hand, this house was enormous—maybe she could simply avoid him all evening.

"Feeling better?" Beck asked.

She nodded and tried to act normal. "Lead the way."

From the landing, two ten-foot-wide hallways split off in opposite directions. Honey-colored hardwood was covered with plush oriental-style carpet runners. Down the hallway to the right, a man and woman walked away from them, peering into rooms, apparently also enjoying a self-guided tour. The man who had collected her coat walked by, his face obscured under a mountain of coats—mostly furs. He disappeared into a room that she assumed had been set aside for a coat check. In the distance, doors opened and closed, voices oohing and aahing. The house appeared to go on forever, an astonishing amount of square footage for one resident.

She followed Beck down the hall to the left and glanced into a room that was perhaps an office or a den, although it was ornate to the point of distraction.

"The décor is too busy for my tastes," he murmured, "but I like the lines of the ceiling."

Jolie nodded. She'd learned to withhold her own opinion when working with a potential client, to listen as their likes and dislikes were revealed. Sometimes clients were unaware of their own tastes, although Beck Underwood did not strike her as a person who waffled. About architecture, anyway.

The next room was a feminine guest room with a daybed and overstuffed upholstered chairs. The textured wallpaper was perfectly coordinated to the comforter. "Why do people do that?" he whispered, his mouth close to her ear. "You have my permission to shoot me if I ever wallpaper a room to match a bedspread."

As if she would be around to witness his hypothetical case of hyper-decorating.

He walked to the next doorway and peered inside. "I believe Sammy said this was her spa room."

Tiled floor, ambient lighting, double massage tables, a whirlpool tub, ceiling fans and an abundance of plants. "Is this something you would be interested in having?" Jolie asked.

"Me? No way. The plants are nice though."

All told, on the hallway were four bedrooms and three den-ish rooms of ambiguous purpose but crammed with oversized furniture and electronic toys. One room was lined with glass display cases for Sammy's collection of crystal houses, most of them reproductions of famous buildings or antebellum homes. Jolie did some mental arithmetic and estimated the woman had tens of thousands of dollars invested in the fragile knickknacks. The outrageousness of it bordered on vulgarity, but before righteous indignation could set in, Jolie looked down at the twelve-hundred-dollar robe she was wearing and flushed with shame.

No more borrowing clothes, she vowed, and no more party crashing, no matter what.

The next room was a decidedly masculine guest bedroom stocked with beautiful hardwood furniture and expensive bed linens and curtains in muted animal prints. The walls were cocoa brown. She followed Beck into the room, although there was something distinctly intimate about being in this bedroom with him while they were both wearing pj's. She surveyed the windows, carpet, the faux finish on the walls—anything to keep from looking at the giant four-poster bed that sat in the room like a big pink elephant.

"Nice," he said vaguely, then turned and gestured toward the bed. "It's a little tall, don't you think?"

She glanced at the bed sideways. "It's tall," she agreed.

He stared at the bed. "I prefer sort of falling into bed versus having to climb up."

She took a drink from her glass. "Do you already have furniture that you'll need to fit into your home?"

"Such as?"

"Family heirlooms? A bed, perhaps?"

"A few things—a chest of my grandfather's, a bookcase I built when I was a teenager, but nothing big."

"You didn't bring things back from Costa Rica?"

"What little I accumulated there, I left there. It's a much simpler place to live."

"It sounds nice."

He nodded. "It is. I miss it. I felt like I was doing some good there."

She angled her head. "And what exactly was that?"

He drained his glass and refilled it from the bottle. "I was a teacher."

She couldn't keep the surprise from her face. "Really? What did you teach?"

"English, economics, math."

She pursed her mouth. "Is that your background?"

"No. My diploma from Duke says I'm an environmental engineer. But since Costa Rica has a greater need for teachers than for environmental engineers, I thought I'd give it a try."

"And?"

He shrugged. "And I'm pretty good at it."

She smiled, trying to visualize him in front of a chalk-board, pounding home an idea. "I'm sure you are. Will you teach here?"

He shook his head. "No, it's time to make amends with my father and step into the family business. My dad's going to retire soon, and I've left Della to carry the burden for too long." His laugh was dry. "Cry me a river, right?"

Bolstered by the champagne and his openness, she shrugged. "I guess most people would think that being heir to a family fortune isn't such a bad thing."

He nodded. "But what do you think?"

Her tongue stalled. "I . . . don't have an opinion. Besides, I have a vested interest in seeing you remain in Atlanta."

His eyes lit up. "You do?"

"My commission, remember?"

"Oh. Right."

"Shall we continue?" Jolie asked, eager to return to a larger group. She wasn't afraid of Beck, but she *was* afraid that the little twinges in her chest when she looked at him were bubbles warning her of emotional quicksand.

A little-boy smile climbed his face and he nodded toward the bed. "We could hang out in here."

Her thighs twinged, and her heart jumped with the optimism that every woman feels when she tries to justify the urge to let a man have his way with her: If the physical attraction is so strong, there must be feeling behind it. For him to be looking at her with such longing, he had to be feeling the same, overwhelming sense that he'd never been so attracted to another person, and never would be again. That sex with this person would be different. A religious experience. Lasting.

That with Roger LeMon afoot, she had a good reason to kill a few hours in Beck's arms.

Jolie came back to earth with a thud. The man was half drunk, after all. And it was up to her to protect her heart from a man who was undoubtedly just passing through— literally and figuratively. "We could," she said carefully, "but we won't."

His shoulders fell. "Okay. Can't blame a man for trying. I've been in the jungle for a few years."

She angled her head. "Something tells me you weren't lonely."

He gave a little laugh. "I've been lonely my entire life."

Jolie looked up, surprised to see the seriousness on his handsome face. She panicked—his teasing banter was so much easier to dismiss. In an effort to restore the light mood, she smiled. "Is that a pick-up line?"

He straightened, his solemnity gone. "Of course. Is it working?"

She smiled. "No, I don't feel the least bit sorry for you."

He made a rueful noise, then asked, "So, *Gwen*, where did you grow up?"

If he had planned to catch her off guard, he'd succeeded. She instantly missed the sexual tension. "Dalton."

"Really? On a farm?"

"No, although we did raise a small vegetable garden. Lots of green beans."

He smiled. "I like green beans."

"That's probably because you've never had to pick and string them."

"You could be right. Do you get back there often?"

She shook her head. "My parents are both gone, and I don't have any siblings."

His mouth parted slightly. "I'm sorry."

"It's not your fault," she said with a wry smile.

But he looked stricken. "You don't have *any* family?"

"There are a couple of great-aunts, and a few stray cousins," she said, trying to sound cheerful.

Concern clouded his eyes. "It's strange, but I can't remember having a conversation with my father that didn't end in an argument, yet I can't imagine him not being around."

Was she supposed to offer commentary on his family dynamics? "Arguing is a form of communication, I suppose."

He scowled, then lifted his glass. "I suppose you're right."

She walked to a window and looked out over the circular driveway. From this view she could see the rows of cars parked farther down the road, and distant lights from neighboring houses. "Are you like your father?" she asked, feeling brave.

He joined her at the window. "Everyone says so, but I don't see it." Then he looked contrite. "Don't get me wrong: My dad is a brilliant businessman, but he was a terrible father and—" He stopped, as if he realized he was revealing too much. "Well, no family is perfect, is it?"

She shook her head. "What's your mother like?"

"Oblivious," he said, his voice wistful. "Mother has been in her own little world for some time now. We all sort of move around her."

"I'm sorry," Jolie said.

One side of his mouth lifted. "It's not your fault."

"You and Della seem close," she ventured, feeling guilty that she was embarking on a fishing expedition.

"We are."

"What does she do for your father's company?"

"Besides sitting on the board, she's very good with the publicity department, which basically means she does public appearances, shmoozes advertisers, that kind of thing."

"And that doesn't interest you?"

"Not in the least."

"What *does* interest you?" She regretted the words before the vibration of them left her tongue.

His eyes trained on her, pulled at her. "*You* do, Jolie Goodman. You interest me, with your full-time dreams and your part-time job and your costumes and disguises and the little wrinkle of problems between your eyes that are normally hazel." He shook his head. "I can't figure you out, but I have a feeling there's a lot about you that you don't reveal to just anyone."

She glanced up and felt her heart opening to him, beckoning. *Look at me. Look at me and see me.* Her chest rose and fell, wondering if this man had any idea how uncomplicated she was, how remote she felt most of the time, how much and how little she needed from him at this precise moment.

"Yes," he murmured, as if she'd spoken aloud.

Even he seemed confused at his response as he leaned close, then closer. She had time to dodge the kiss, to step back or turn her head . . . but she didn't. Tonight she didn't have to be herself—and she decided to be the woman who was going to be kissed by Beck Underwood.

He lowered his lips to hers and she had the simultaneous impressions of champagne and warmth and firmness and desire. His hands were full, and she held her own glass out to keep from spilling champagne on Sammy's rug. With just their lips touching, the kiss seemed to grow in intensity as they strained toward each other. He stopped suddenly and pulled back, and before disappointment could settle in, she realized from the look in his eyes that he was surprised . . . but at her response or his own, she couldn't tell. Regardless, a split second later he was kissing her again, this time with hands-on features and sound effects.

And then slowly she began to grasp the fact that the sounds were coming from someone other than the two of them. They parted and Jolie looked up to see their hostess, Sammy, standing in the doorway of the bedroom with her arms crossed, looking, frankly, somewhat inhospitable.

Seventeen

"Why, Beck, I see you're having a good time."

"Great party, Sammy." Either Jolie was imagining things, or Beck inched even closer to her side. Was he afraid Sammy was going to recognize her?

She was afraid enough for the both of them, Jolie decided. At that exact moment, her left contact lens decided to revolt, folding onto itself and obscuring her vision. Jolie blinked liked mad and the thing finally righted itself, to bring Sammy back into view.

With her low- and high-cut (respectively) leopard-print teddy, severe makeup, and killer high-heeled mules, the woman looked ready to bare her fangs and pounce. "I'm sorry, what did you say your name was again?"

"Gwen," Jolie murmured, trying to disguise her voice.

"I didn't get your last name, Gwen."

Jolie's mind raced and came up with, "Yarborough."

"Gwen Yarborough," Sammy said, then shook her head. "When did we meet?"

"Gwen was at the media reception last night," Beck broke in. "The two of you must have met there."

"That's right," Jolie said. "You were wearing the most lovely pink dress."

Sammy's expression eased a smidgen. "Gwen, dear, you spilled champagne on my rug."

Jolie looked down in horror to see a wet spot next to the tip of her burgundy satin mule. In truth, though, she was relieved she hadn't spoiled the expensive shoes.

"I did that," Beck said quickly. "My apologies, Sammy."

The woman gave a dismissive wave. "I'll send someone to soak it up. That's why I don't serve red wine at my parties. Things tend to get a little . . . out of hand."

She stared at Jolie and she took a half step forward. "Are your eyes two different colors?"

Jolie's palm felt sweaty against the glass she held. "Uh—"

"Yes," Beck said. "Isn't that something? I'd heard of people having different-colored eyes, but I'd never met anyone who did, until Gwen."

Sammy was still staring at her and Jolie couldn't look away, like prey prior to being caught and eaten. Sammy's mouth parted slightly and something flickered in her eyes, then vanished. Suddenly, she smiled, then straightened. "Enjoy the tour, then come down and join the rest of the party around the pool. The games will begin soon."

"Games?" Beck asked.

"What's a party without games?" Sammy wet her lips, then turned on her five-inch heels and strode out, her sheer robe floating out behind her like a cape.

Jolie shivered, and the bad feeling she'd had when they'd first arrived descended over her again.

"Whew," Beck muttered. "That was close."

Jolie nodded absently, then glanced down. "I don't suppose you could help me find my contact lens?"

"Don't move. It's probably on that fuzzy robe that's covering practically every inch of you," he teased, setting down his glass and bottle. "This might require a little hands-on search." He lifted his eyebrows, waiting for her permission.

She pressed her lips together, then gave a curt nod. *Why hadn't she worn a bra?*

He took her glass of champagne and set it next to his. Then he gave her a sexy grin and skimmed his hands over her neck and shoulders in a slow sensual caress that made her wish the heavy garment wasn't between her skin and his hands. She swallowed hard against the pull of him, the memory of his kiss still on her lips. Longing pooled in her stomach, thighs. He must have felt it too, because his grin faded when he brought his hands down over her breasts, and his breathing increased.

Her nipples budded and she closed her eyes briefly. He continued to stroke his hands down the robe, spanning her waist and smoothing his hands over her hips, then down her thighs. When he crouched to lift the flowing hem of the garment for a closer inspection, cool air hit her exposed legs.

He took advantage of the opportunity to peek, grunting in satisfaction. She gave into a little thrill of pleasure, thanking God that she'd shaved. "Did you find it?" she asked.

"Find what?" he said, still peeking.

Exasperated, she reached down to close the bottom of her robe. "My contact lens, did you find it?"

"No," he said sadly, then stood and reached for her champagne glass. "Oh, but what do you know—there it is, floating in your bubbly." He grinned. "You would've thought I'd have seen that before I patted you down."

"Ooh!" She swatted at him and he clasped her hand, pulling her against his chest, stealing her breath. Beneath her palm, the hair in the opening of his robe felt coarse, and his heart thudded his intention. She looked into his eyes and realized miserably that Beck Underwood would be so easy for her injured heart to fall for. He was just the man to take her mind off her problems, to sweep her into his world, where his name opened doors and no material thing was out of reach. It would be so easy . . . and so dangerous, heaping heartache upon heartache when he tired of her or resumed his adventures.

Before he could kiss her again, she stepped back and inhaled deeply. "We should see the rest of the upstairs, then join the other guests."

He pursed his mouth, then nodded and handed her the glass with a wink. She retrieved the contact lens and stored it in the case in her bag. Beck disappeared into the connecting bathroom and emerged with her glass, empty and rinsed, which he replenished from the bottle. He didn't press her about what had happened between them, and she felt torn about the foregone chance to explore the chemistry. The irony was that Beck Underwood was intrigued by her aloof and bizarre behavior, but her aloof and bizarre behavior had been precipitated by Gary's disappearance, and it was Gary's disappearance that had left her in such emotional disarray.

But Beck was nothing if not resilient. Two minutes later, when they resumed the tour, he was whistling tunelessly under his breath, his gait easy, his smile ready. Jolie couldn't help feeling a little put out that one minute he was kissing her and the next he seemed unaffected. His behavior made her feel better about her decision to nip their budding attraction . . . but only a tad.

They crossed the landing to reach the second hallway. Laughter, music, and the occasional popped cork sounded from downstairs. Sammy had to be spending a fortune on champagne, Jolie decided. On this new corridor, they passed the converted coat check room and two additional opulent rooms before they reached the open French doors leading into Sammy's bedroom, a suite as large as a cottage.

White carpet, white walls, white linens, white built-in cabinetry, white leather upholstered furniture, a white-light chandelier. To the left, a doorway into a bathroom hinted at more of the same. A red ribbon had been secured across the opening as a polite reminder to guests that they could look, but not touch—or use—the facilities. To the right, a white door leading to yet another room was closed.

"I feel really creepy about being in her bedroom," Jolie whispered, although it was clear the woman intended for people to look—and to be in awe.

"I know what you mean," Beck said, then wagged his eyebrows. "Let's go look in her medicine cabinet."

"What? No."

"I'm kidding. But there is one thing I wanted to show you, the sitting room off to the right. I like the fireplace."

Apparently, he'd gotten the behind-the-scenes tour. She wondered perversely if he were the least bit interested in Sammy—beyond said fireplace. Especially now that Jolie had given him a bit of a brush-off.

Which, in hindsight, was starting to feel like a foolish decision.

Jolie followed him, but practically tiptoed across the snowy carpet.

Beck opened the door leading into the room that appeared to be another office—this one more functional by the looks of the complicated phone system. Most real-estate agents had home offices, and Sammy was no different—hers was just nicer than most. A massive, gleaming white desk and two white wood file cabinets to match, a white leather executive chair on rollers, 20-inch flat-screen monitor, with an impressive CPU tower on the floor. And the fireplace was indeed incredible—floor-to-ceiling gray stone facing with white masonry grout. Beck set down his glass and the bottle to inspect the hearth. No surprise, he also admired the on-wall plasma television and speaker system.

A five-by-seven picture frame on the desk caught Jolie's eye, and she circled behind it, curious as to whom Sammy would think enough of to display on her workstation. Her parents? Mrs. Sanders had died when Sammy was young, which was why Sammy was so close to her father. When Jolie saw the photo, though, she laughed to herself—only Sammy would have a picture of *herself* on her desk. The only surprise was that it wasn't a Miss America shot—instead Sammy was outdoors, dressed in a turtleneck, jeans, and sturdy boots, her hair pulled back into a ponytail, and she was sitting on a rock.

A familiar-looking rock.

Jolie picked up the frame and jammed her face closer. She studied the photo and tried to conjure up in her mind the photo of Gary sitting on a rock, mugging for the camera. Was it the same place, the same day? Was it possible that *Sammy* had been the woman who'd taken the photo of him? Her mouth went dry—did Sammy and Gary have a romantic history, or was this photo a mere coincidence?

She recalled introducing them at the agency and hadn't noticed anything more than a polite exchange. Ditto on the tube-float down the river. In fact, she'd gotten the feeling that Sammy thought he was unsavory because she'd commented once that someone who drove a nice car with no apparent signs of employment was either a trust-fund kid or a criminal.

Jolie scoured the photo, looking for any details that might help prove or disprove her wild theory, but in truth, the photo could have been taken anywhere, on any rock. She couldn't check the back for photo finishing details unless she took the whole thing apart . . . and that would take some privacy. She glanced at Beck, who was still mesmerized by a beautifully sculpted chrome remote control. Feeling like a bona fide crook, she slid the photo into her standard "biggish" party-crashing purse.

"We probably should go," she said abruptly.

He turned and nodded. "You're right—Sammy might think we're snooping."

A shamefaced flush climbed her cheeks as she left the office and strode across the bedroom. Amidst all the white, the edge of Sammy's green Kate Spade bag was especially noticeable sticking out from under the bed's dust ruffle. She detoured from her straight path to push the purse beneath the bed, thinking that would help assuage her guilt. She nudged the green bag with her shoe, but it wouldn't budge. She lifted the bed skirt, saw the bag was caught against a leg of the bed frame and reached down to push it out of sight. Just in case there were unscrupulous people about.

Party crashers, for instance.

"Something wrong?" Beck asked from the door.

"Nothing," she murmured, standing. Then she spied the bathroom. "Um, actually, I need to powder my nose. Do you think it would be okay to—"

"I'll be your lookout," he cut in, his tone as grave as a spy's.

The "keep out" ribbon had been affixed with tape. She unfastened one end, then entered the bathroom and closed the door behind her. The expansive whiteness was blinding—tiled floor, floating sink, slick cabinets, shiny garden tub, long, white sheers at the windows. Leann had once told her that white was a prestigious color among her clients because of the implication that one had to have money to maintain anything white. So true.

Jolie pulled the picture frame from her bag and studied the photo again. Hopefully she would find some innocuous description on the back like "Me and Dad at Yosemite," then she'd feel foolish and return it to Sammy's desk.

She turned over the frame to find the back held together with small screws. Cursing under her breath, she rummaged in her purse to find anything that would suffice as a tool. The screw heads were too small to be turned with a coin, and a paperclip wouldn't work. She needed a metal nail file or tweezers or something similar. She pulled out cabinet drawers, aware of the time ticking away. Lots of beauty products, combs, curlers, hair appliances, but nothing she could use as a screwdriver.

Jolie glanced toward the wide mirrored cabinet over the floating sink, remembering Beck's suggestion that they snoop in Sammy's medicine cabinet. She sighed and gingerly pulled open the mirrored door.

A second later, a shelf in the cabinet collapsed, sending its contents toppling and setting off a horrific, crashing chain reaction as bottles and jars and other personal toiletries landed in the sink. She cringed and counted to ten.

A quiet knock sounded. "Everything okay in there?" Beck asked, his voice muffled . . . and concerned.

"Fine," she returned shakily. "Just a little . . . accident. I'll be right out."

She slipped the shelf back into place with shaking hands, then scooped up the items and situated them back onto the shelves wherever they would fit. Men's toiletries were mixed in with the feminine items (a diaphragm, ew) and Jolie told herself that more men than Gary used Zirh brand premium shave gel. And old-fashioned razor blades. She fingered the packet and realized suddenly that a blade was thin enough and strong enough to loosen the screws on the picture frame.

Carefully, she removed a blade from the package and was successful in loosening one screw before the blade slipped and slashed the fatty pad of her left palm. She dropped the blade, instinctively pressed her hand to her chest, and puffed out her cheeks, knowing before she looked that the cut was deep . . . and bloody.

When she pulled it away, not only did the bleeding resume exuberantly, but the pain lit up her entire arm. She sucked air through her teeth, and looked for something to wrap around her hand. A stack of white fingertip towels sat on a cabinet. She grabbed one and held it against her hand until the bleeding slowed. Upon closer observation, the cut was only an inch long, but it throbbed unmercifully. Remembering the package of adhesive bandages she'd seen in a drawer, she appropriated three to cover the wound. Luckily, the damage was to her left hand, so she was able to restore order to the medicine cabinet, although

Sammy would have to be in a stupor not to realize that things had been rearranged.

She returned the picture frame to her purse, deciding it would go home with her. If it turned out to be unrelated to Gary's photo, she would return the picture to Sammy anonymously.

Now, what to do with the mess she'd made? A bloody towel, Band-Aid debris. The paper went into the step waste-can. She used the towel to wipe down the white counter and the white sink, then wrapped it inside another small towel and stuffed the whole kit-and-caboodle into her purse. Only then did she get a look at herself in the mirror and saw the big, bloody stain on the silk cream-colored gown where her robe gapped open. She shrieked, which elicited another knock on the door.

"Do I need to call someone for you?"

"No!" she called, then gulped a calming breath. She was no textile expert, but she had a feeling that the only way to get blood out of silk was to cut it out. She closed her eyes, chastising herself. Her amateur sleuthing had led to ruining an eight-hundred-dollar nightshirt. She whimpered, thinking how many shoes she'd have to sell. Served her right for stealing clothes, crashing this party.

She pulled herself up, thinking at least she had her commission from Beck Underwood's home to look forward to. If she hadn't completely blown it with him, of course. He didn't seem like the type of man who would take his business elsewhere because she wouldn't sleep with him, but then again, he didn't seem like the type of man who would do business with a nobody. So if this night was to be salvaged, she needed to leave feeling good about getting his business.

She pulled her robe together and tightened the belt, relieved to see the bloodstain was covered as long as she didn't flash anyone. She stuffed her aching hand into her pocket, retrieved her champagne glass, took a deep breath, and emerged with as big a smile as she could muster.

Beck straightened, his expression opening in relief. "If you ever want to make a man go crazy, go into the bathroom and start making a lot of loud, dangerous-sounding noises."

"Sorry," she murmured. "I was looking for an aspirin, and her medicine cabinet exploded."

That made him smile, and thankfully, he didn't notice her hand, or the fact that she kept glancing at her own chest every few seconds.

"I guess we'd better go," she said, "before Sammy sends out a search party."

He shuddered dramatically and she laughed as they walked into the hall.

"Thanks for the tour. Do you have an idea of where you'd like to live?"

"Maybe midtown," he said. "Or downtown." Then he grinned. "Or maybe a farm in Dalton."

Her heart flooded with intense like. "That really narrows it down."

He looked around and lifted his arms as they reached the landing that overlooked the enormous entryway on the first floor. Guests' voices carried up, bursts of laughter and clinking glasses. "Do you like this house?" he asked.

She took in the grandeur around her. "It's a beautiful house."

"Yes, but would you live here?"

Her cheeks warmed. "That's something I'll probably never have to worry about."

"Humor me. If you had the money, is this the kind of house you would choose to live in?"

"I . . . probably not. I have to admit that large houses seem . . . daunting to me. All that space demanding to be used." She blushed, thinking she'd probably offended him since the Underwood family home was near the governor's mansion in Buckhead, but was twice the size. She rushed to explain. "But what I think is missing most in this house is personality. Yes, it's beautiful, but it feels more like a showcase than a home. Anyone might live here. As a broker, I'm probably not supposed to say this, but owning a home is more than buying an address and filling it up with nice stuff. It should be personal, unique, symbolic even." She flushed because she thought she'd overstepped her bounds. After all, the man was probably looking for a tax shelter.

But instead of laughing at her, he looked at her in that dangerous fall-for-me way. "Do you have your own home?"

"Not yet," she said. "But someday."

"You're hired."

She grinned, but her pleasure over a potentially huge commission was cut short by a commotion on the first floor—Carlotta, flailing her arms, asking guests, "Have you seen a woman with long red hair?"

"Carlot—" Jolie stopped and cleared her throat. "Carly, I'm up here."

Carlotta looked up, then disappeared, apparently coming up after her. When she reached the landing, she was out of breath.

"What's wrong?" Jolie asked.

"There's been a little . . . complication."

Jolie frowned. "What?"

"Russell is here."

"Who?"

"Hannah's boyfriend."

"Oh."

"With his wife."

"Oh."

"Right," Carlotta said, her voice grim. "I tried to get Hannah to leave, but she wouldn't. She said she was going to make a scene. She was headed to the pool where they were, and I'm afraid someone's going to get hurt."

"What can I do?" Jolie asked.

"Find our coats, and meet me down there." Carlotta looked at Beck. "Would it be too much to ask you to run interference?"

"Who are we talking about?" he asked, scratching his head.

"Our friend Hannah, who came with us," Jolie explained. "She's been dating a married man, and apparently he's here—with his wife."

Beck winced. "Who's the stupid guy?"

"Russell Island," Carlotta supplied.

"I know him," Beck said. "And his wife. This won't be pretty." They started down the stairway and Jolie jogged toward the coat check room, thinking Hannah was likely to blow their cover and Sammy would toss them all out on their party-crashing behinds. Maybe even have them arrested for trespassing.

The attendant was gone, so Jolie undid the familiar and ineffective ribbon across the doorway and started her own search. The nicer coats—the furs, the leathers, the brocades—were hanging on portable racks. The jackets, hats, shawls, and assorted cheap coats had been draped over the bed—ten dollars said that's where her all-weather standby had been relegated. It was difficult to maneuver with her injured hand, but after searching three racks, she spotted Carlotta's black cashmere coat and pulled it off the rack. Hannah's leather duster was more elusive, but she finally found it. Then she turned to the bed to dig for her Montgomery Ward special.

She displaced a dozen hats and wraps and pulled three navy coats out of the tangle that weren't hers. She was starting to become frustrated when she touched something unexpectedly solid. Jolie frowned and pushed aside a pile of coats, then was struck mute with shock . . . terror . . . disbelief.

It was Gary. And from the hole in his chest, he appeared to be . . . checked out.

Eighteen

There are times in every person's life when they find out what they're made of. Looking down on Gary Hagan's body—lifeless eyes, gray pallor, unnatural position—Jolie discovered that she was made of soft, gooey, blubbery stuff. The only thing that kept her from collapsing entirely was the knowledge that if she did, she'd fall on a dead person.

She tried to scream, but no sound came out of her constricted throat. She stumbled backward on her high-heeled house shoes, twisting her ankle and ricocheting off the doorframe and out into the hall. Her mind reeled, rejecting what her eyes had just seen, and she was distantly aware that she was keening like a small animal.

She half staggered, half fell down the vacated stairs, grateful to the red carpet for sparing her knees from the marble beneath, and at one point thinking it would be faster if she just rolled down. Her hand felt wet and sticky and she registered the fact that she might be smearing blood down the handrail. By the time she'd reached the first floor, she was minus a shoe, and she still hadn't en-countered a live person.

Judging from the empty great room, everyone had mi-grated to the pool. She lumbered forward, heedless of anything except getting to Beck or Carlotta . . . or even Sammy. The good news was that Beck and Carlotta were standing together by the edge of the pool with their backs to her. The bad news was they were restraining Hannah, who was kicking at a cowering man as if they were in a Ninja movie. The guests were crowded around, fascinated.

At last the scream that had been caught in Jolie's throat erupted like a volcano, echoing off the surface of the aqua-colored water dotted with floating candles, reverber-ating around the glass-enclosed room. Every head pivoted her way. Beck took a half step in her direction.

"Help!" she bellowed, running toward them as fast as she could considering she was wearing one shoe.

The one shoe betrayed her. She hit a slick spot and skid-ded, flailing. A bewildered-looking Carlotta, who was closest, reached for her, and Hannah reached for Carlotta, and the next thing Jolie knew, she had entered the pool by way of a belly-flop chain.

The good news was the bracing water cleared the fog from her head. The bad news was she'd fallen into the deep end and the heavy robe instantly soaked up ten times its weight in water. She struggled with the tie belt, but only managed to pull it tighter around her ribs. Meanwhile, Carlotta floated by, her eyes wide, her mouth open—not exactly the safest expression for being underwater. She was in trouble. Jolie grabbed Carlotta's leg and shoved her toward the side of the pool while trying to kick her own way to the surface.

She yanked at the tie around her waist again and miraculously it loosened. She pushed her way out of the robe but it wrapped around her legs, immobilizing her, dragging her down. Red ribbons of blood colored the water around her—the wound on her hand had reopened. Panic clawed at her chest as she sank, and Jolie understood how Gary must have felt when he knew he was going to die. Petrified, helpless . . . remorseful. What had she done with her life, really? Would anyone care that she wasn't around? Drowning at a party that she'd crashed wasn't the way she'd hoped to make headlines. Her body jerked in preparation for taking a death breath.

Suddenly two big arms came around her from behind and jerked her upward. She inhaled water to satisfy her lungs, but her body rebelled, bucking. The robe fell away, brushing her feet. Air bubbles rushed past her face, then her head broke the surface of the water. She coughed and sputtered, thrashing her arms like a windmill.

"Relax," Beck said into her ear. "Don't fight me."

He eased her over to the side of the pool. Wheezing, she blinked the ceiling of glass into view, acknowledged the hard muscle of his torso and legs pressing against hers. Her brain must have been deprived of oxygen for a tad longer than was healthy, because the thought struck her that if she hadn't just seen the dead body of her boyfriend and hadn't almost drowned, this might have been a nice moment.

He boosted her up over the pool edge as if she weighed nothing and set her down next to Carlotta and Hannah, who were huddled miserably on the side of the pool like wet cats dressed in upmarket lingerie.

"Are you okay?" Beck asked, looking up at her from the water, his hand on her knee. His breathing was labored, his wet hair falling over his dark eyes.

She nodded, hugging herself in her transparent chemise. "Th–thank you."

"You're bleeding," he said, pulling her hand toward him for a look.

"It's not bad," she said between coughs. "Considering I could be dead right now."

A full-body shiver seized her.

"I'll get some blankets," he said, then hoisted himself up out of the pool. Once again she was struck by the inappropriateness of noticing the man's physique, but he was mesmerizing in blue cotton boxers molded by the water. She had wondered what he was wearing underneath the robe, but she hadn't planned on going to these lengths to find out.

They had managed to turn the pool into an ocean— their splashing had extinguished most of the floating candles. Their robes and purses littered the bottom. Their wigs bobbed on the surface like dead animals. Speaking of dead, she needed to tell someone—everyone—about Gary. She suddenly felt light-headed, and she couldn't stop shaking.

"My book," Carlotta whispered, gazing into the water.

"Your celebrity book was in your purse?" Jolie asked.

Carlotta nodded miserably.

"I'm so sorry," Jolie murmured. "Can you forgive me?"

"*Jolie Goodman.*"

Jolie looked up to see Sammy staring down at her. Unhappily.

The woman walked closer, hands on hips. "I *thought* that was you earlier, but I told myself that you wouldn't *dare* put on a disguise and *crash* my party! That was you last night at the media reception, too, wasn't it?"

Jolie could only wince.

"And you had the nerve to bring these two troublemakers with you!"

"I brought you a hostess gift," Carlotta muttered.

"Candles?" Sammy shrieked. "I ought to call the police."

"They're from Neiman's," Carlotta retorted.

"I mean to have you arrested for trespassing!" Sammy screeched, her volume off the chart in decibels. She jabbed her finger at Hannah. "And you, for assaulting one of my guests!"

Hannah glowered at a man across the pool touching his swollen eye. The woman next to him, presumably his wife, appeared ready to black his other eye. Russell Island seemed dazed . . . and vaguely familiar.

But enough stalling.

"Sammy," Jolie said, pushing herself to her wobbly feet. Water ran off her, splashing onto Sammy's shoes. "You do need to call the police."

"You're bleeding," Sammy said, looking disgusted, as if something might get stained.

"Yes," Jolie said, feeling bout of nausea coming on. "But it actually gets worse."

Re-dressed in his black robe, Beck walked up and settled a chenille throw that Jolie had seen on a couch around her shoulders. The warmth was heavenly, but having Beck behind her made her even more nervous—his desire to help her was about to change.

Sammy flinched at the sight of the expensive throw soaking up pool water. "Jolie, *what* are you talking about?"

"G–Gary Hagan is upstairs in the coat check room."

"Gary Hagan?" Sammy's expression turned lethal.

"What on earth is that criminal boyfriend of yours doing in my coat check room?"

"He's dead," Jolie murmured, seeing starbursts. She was going to faint. And God help her, she aimed herself at Beck for one last favor.

Jolie sat at a table in a holding room wearing an oversized gray "Property of Fulton County, Georgia" sweat suit and flip-flops since the police had confiscated her "borrowed" clothing. How she was going to pay for those nightclothes, she didn't know.

Of course, at the moment, paying for outrageously expensive clothes wasn't the biggest worry on her plate, but concentrating on the more mundane details helped her not to dwell on the fact that Gary was dead.

And that the police seemed to think that she and Carlotta and Hannah had something to do with it. The girls were elsewhere, in similar rooms, she assumed. Just like on television, the police had split them up so they couldn't devise a story. As if they would even try to come up with a better one.

Fatigue weighted her limbs, and her lungs felt raw. Her hair was a crusty nest. She had chewed her fingernails to the quick. She touched a goose egg on her forehead—Beck had caught her when she'd fainted, but she'd cracked her head when she'd gotten into the police car for the ride to the clink. The threesome was instructed by Salyers and her partner not to talk to each other, so Carlotta had cried the entire trip, and Hannah had conjugated her boyfriend's name with every expletive ever conceived. Jolie had concentrated on counting the squares in the metal grate between the front seat and the back, trying to forget the look on Beck's face as she was being stuffed into the cruiser. Condescension? Disappointment? He had turned away to put a comforting arm around Della's shoulder, and Jolie imagined they were saying how glad they were that Beck hadn't become involved with the poor-white-trash shoe salesperson-slash-real-estate-agent-slash-murderer.

The clincher was that she wasn't particularly good at any of those things.

The door to the holding room opened and Detective Salyers walked in, looking none-too-pleased to be awake at three in the morning. By the time she and other officers had been summoned to the scene and guests had been questioned, Carlotta's car impounded, and the three of them transported to jail, a few hours had slipped by.

"Hi, again," Jolie ventured.

"Alone at last," Salyers said, tossing a pad of paper on the table. "Ms. Goodman, I thought I told you to stay out of trouble."

"Trust me, this wasn't intentional."

Salyers blinked. "Was that a confession?"

Alarm blipped in Jolie's chest. "*No*. I meant that I was just going to a party. I had no idea Gary—alive or dead—would be there."

Salyers emitted a long sigh. "Why don't we start from the beginning. Want some coffee?"

Jolie nodded.

Salyers exited and Jolie glanced at the notepad—the first several pages were waffled with handwritten notes. Even upside down, she could make out "Goodmans" all over the page. She covered her mouth with her hand in an attempt to knock back the panic. This could be bad.

Salyers walked back in carrying two large cups of coffee. Jolie sipped with gratitude. It wasn't Starbucks, but it was hot.

The detective dropped in the seat opposite her. "Okay, Ms. Goodman, tell me everything that happened since you called me today—er, yesterday."

"Am I under arrest?"

"No."

Jolie swallowed another mouthful of coffee. "Do I need a lawyer?"

"That's up to you. If you want to call a lawyer, I can get you a phone."

"I don't know any criminal lawyers."

"Then I can get you the phone book."

Jolie shook her head. "I just want to get this over with and go home."

Salyers gave a curt nod, then removed a pen from her jacket pocket and clicked the end. "Ms. Goodman, what did you do after you left the drive-through yesterday?"

"I went back to my apartment."

"Did you talk to anyone on the phone—cellular or otherwise?"

"No."

"E-mail?"

"No."

"Did you go anywhere?"

"No."

"Then?"

"Then Carlotta and Hannah came over, and we got ready for the party."

"You were aware that the party was being given by your former boss?"

"Yes."

"And you were intending to crash the party?"

Jolie squirmed. "Yes."

"You didn't know Mr. Hagan would be there?"

"Absolutely not."

"Did Ms. Wren or Ms. Kizer know Mr. Hagan?"

"No."

"Do you have any idea why Mr. Hagan was at the party?"

She lifted her hands. "No . . . unless he followed me there. As we walked into the house, Carlotta and I both saw a car sitting at the end of the driveway."

"Could you tell what kind of car it was?"

Jolie shook her head.

"Were you and your friends wearing disguises?"

Jolie hesitated. "We were wearing wigs."

"And very expensive garments with the tags still attached—can you explain that?"

She swallowed. "We . . . were planning to return them."

"I see. Are you in the habit of buying expensive clothes, wearing them, then returning them?"

Jolie pursed her mouth. "I wouldn't say it was a habit, per se."

"But you've done it before."

Jolie nodded.

Salyers gave a little "the nerve" snort, then looked back to her notes. "Ms. Sanders said you were also wearing colored contact lenses."

"That's right."

"And Ms. Wren said she altered your features with makeup."

"It's true that I didn't want Sammy to recognize me."

"Because she wouldn't have wanted you at her party?"

Jolie flushed. "That's right."

"The two of you have a history. She said she fired you from her agency."

"That's a lie—I quit."

"When was that?"

"About three weeks ago."

"Why did you quit?"

"Because . . . Sammy asked me to do something un-ethical."

"What was that?"

Jolie sighed. "We were representing the seller in a commercial real-estate deal. She asked me to reveal to the buyer the amount the seller would settle for, which was much less than the asking price and confidential between the agency and the seller."

"And you refused?"

"Yes. And I quit."

Salyers leaned back, tipping her chair on two legs. "Ms. Sanders said that you came to her party to rob her."

Jolie gasped. "What? That's absurd!"

"Is it? Ms. Sanders said that some items are missing, including one thousand dollars in cash from her purse. She also said that her medicine cabinet had been ransacked, and a sterling picture frame was taken."

And the picture frame had been found in her biggish purse at the bottom of the pool. Jolie closed her eyes and when she opened them, Salyers was still there, unfortunately.

"Is there something you'd like to say, Ms. Goodman?"

Jolie steepled her hands over her nose. "I put the picture frame in my purse because of the photo, not the frame."

Salyers arched an eyebrow. "I understood it was a photo of Ms. Sanders."

Jolie frowned at the implication. "It *was* a picture of Sammy, but the rock she was sitting on and the background reminded me of a photo in Gary's album." She lifted her hands. "I thought maybe Sammy was with him the day it was taken."

"Meaning you think Mr. Hagan and Ms. Sanders were romantically involved?"

Jolie shrugged. "I don't know, but it seemed like too big of a coincidence to ignore. I thought if I could take the photo out of the frame, I'd be able to compare the film processing date and the paper. I went into Sammy's bathroom to remove the photo, but I couldn't find anything to use as a screwdriver."

"So you were the one who ransacked the medicine cabinet?"

Jolie nodded. "And the only thing I could find was a razor blade. It didn't work and I cut myself." She held up her re-bandaged hand.

"You said that's where the blood came from."

"The blood on my gown? Yes. Where is the photo now?"

"Taken into evidence, I would assume."

"Then you can look into my theory?"

Salyers gave her a skeptical look. "Sure. Okay, let's back up. What about the money that's missing?"

"I don't know anything about that."

"Ms. Sanders said you were aware that she normally carried a lot of cash."

"Anyone who knew Sammy well knew she carried cash."

"Did your friend Ms. Wren know?"

Jolie remembered the conversation she'd had with Carlotta about the hush money Sammy was trying to give her. Her heart sank when she realized that lifting cash from Sammy's purse would solve her friend's financial dilemma. "I might have mentioned it."

"The money was found in the pool filter. You, Ms. Wren, Ms. Kizer, and Mr. Underwood were the only ones who took a swim."

"We fell in," Jolie said.

"Are you sure you didn't jump in?"

She frowned. "Why would I have jumped in?"

Salyers shrugged. "Maybe you couldn't live with yourself."

Jolie's breath stuck in her throat. "You think I was trying to kill myself? That's crazy!"

"Or maybe you were trying to destroy evidence."

"I wasn't," Jolie said evenly.

Salyers leaned forward, settling her chair on the floor. "Ms. Goodman, how well do you know Carlotta Wren and Hannah Kizer?"

"Carlotta and I work together at Neiman's. Hannah is a friend of Carlotta's. I've known them for less than a week."

"So you really don't know them that well, do you?'

Jolie splayed her hands. "No, but they seem nice."

"Nice? They trespass for kicks. And the one with the pierced tongue, besides fooling around with a married man, looks like she's into some pretty kinky stuff."

"You'd have to ask her."

"Have either of them ever mentioned owning a gun?"

"No." Then a memory surfaced, and she snapped her fingers. "But Sammy owns a gun. She was at Neiman's yesterday and she paid for her purchase in cash." Jolie decided not to mention the five-hundred-dollar tip that Sammy had offered on the chance it might lead to questions she'd rather not answer. "When she opened her purse, I saw a gun."

But Salyers seemed unfazed. "Ms. Sanders informed us that she has a permit to carry a concealed weapon, that she kept a nine-millimeter handgun in her purse, and that it's missing. Do you know if the weapon you saw was a nine-millimeter?"

"I couldn't say—I'm not familiar with guns. Was that the kind of gun used to kill Gary?"

"Officers are still on the scene searching for the murder weapon."

"Everyone at the party had access to Sammy's gun," Jolie said. "I saw the green purse sticking out from underneath her bed. I pushed it back."

"Does that mean we'll find your fingerprints on the purse?"

Jolie closed her eyes briefly, then nodded.

"Did anyone see you push the purse underneath the bed?"

Loath to implicate Beck, she hesitated, but she'd seen the police officers on the scene talking to him. "Beck Underwood was in the room."

Salyers' eyebrow arched. "You and Mr. Underwood were in Ms. Sanders' bedroom?"

Her cheeks warmed. "We were taking a tour. Mr. Underwood had asked me to help him find a house—he was pointing out his likes and dislikes."

"Are you and Mr. Underwood friends?"

"Acquaintances," she said.

"No offense, Ms. Goodman, but how did you become acquainted with one of the richest men in Atlanta?"

So it was obvious to everyone that they didn't exactly move in the same circles. "I sold him a pair of shoes at Neiman's, and our paths crossed again at a couple of parties."

"Parties that you and your friends crashed?"

Jolie bit the end of her tongue, then nodded. "But I went to the parties looking for people who might know—have known—Gary." Her voice caught and she inhaled deeply. "That's when I ran into Roger LeMon."

"I see."

"*He* was at the party tonight," Jolie said, sitting forward on the hard chair. "LeMon's the one you should be questioning—he was probably the one who killed Gary."

Salyers nodded, but Jolie could tell the woman was only humoring her. "Why do you think that Mr. LeMon killed Mr. Hagan?"

"Because Gary was set up. He didn't kill that woman who was in his car."

The detective leaned forward on her elbows. "And how would you know that?"

She swallowed. If she told the detective about talking to Gary Wednesday night in her car, she could be in even more trouble for not coming forward sooner.

There was a rap on the door, then Salyers' dark-haired partner stuck his head into the room. "Got a minute?" he asked Salyers.

"Sure, Alexander."

He darted a worried look at Jolie that made her pulse pick up and handed a note to Salyers. After she read it, they had a murmured conversation, then he closed the door and left.

Salyers walked back to the table, note in hand, working her mouth from side to side. "Ms. Goodman, you were wearing a long, blue all-weather coat, Montgomery Ward brand, size six, is that correct?"

She nodded. "Did you find it?"

"Sure did. And guess what was in the pocket?"

Exhaustion was closing in. Jolie dragged her hands down her face. "Breath mints? Ticket stubs?"

"Try the murder weapon."

Jolie's mouth fell open. Tiny lights appeared behind her eyelids. A whining noise sounded in her ears.

Salyers crossed her arms. "Ms. Goodman, what do you have to say for yourself?"

That I'm gullible. "I . . . I m–might be needing that phone b–book after all."

Nineteen

Detective Salyers slid two three-inch-thick volumes of the Atlanta Yellow Pages across the table, then handed Jolie a cordless phone. Jolie stared at it and wondered if they were afraid jailbirds would hang themselves with a phone cord. Which, under the circumstances, seemed a preferable way to meet one's Maker than a needle in a vein.

"I'll be back in a few minutes," Salyers said, then left the room.

Jolie choked down her panic and gripped the phone so hard it made a popping sound. She had no idea how to go about choosing a criminal attorney—all the attorneys she knew represented irate buyers and sellers at mortgage closings. Generating enough paperwork to kill someone probably didn't qualify as the kind of experience she needed.

The L–Z volume had telltale curled pages near the beginning—countless other inmates had rifled through the "Legal Services" listings, which were handily categorized under "Attorneys, by Practice Area." She ran her finger down the page: Bankruptcy (she'd probably need an attorney for that later), Corporate, Criminal. She scanned the listings and the ads. Names (singular and multi-partnered), pictures (from stern to smiling), and slogans ("If you're in a jam, call Pam!") ran together after a while. Jolie was secretly hoping to find an ad offering representation for the wrongly accused, but conceded that in this situation that had to be just about everybody.

On the other hand, how many truly innocent people accumulated enough circumstantial evidence to incriminate themselves in a murder? Jolie had to admit that if she were the detective, *she* would arrest her.

Knowing that time was running out, she narrowed the choices to office addresses that sounded affluent (Buckhead, downtown, anywhere on Peachtree Street), and had launched into the scientific elimination process of eenie, meenie, miney, moe when the door opened suddenly and Salyers stepped in. "That was quick," she said to Jolie.

Jolie frowned in confusion as a woman who looked amazingly like Barbara Bush, except she was wearing a nylon running suit instead of a blue dress and pearls, strode into the room. She set a big, black briefcase on the table, and turned to Salyers. "I'd like a few minutes alone with my client before questioning resumes." Salyers nodded, then left.

Still holding the phone, Jolie looked up at the woman. "I'm sorry—who are you?"

"Pam Vanderpool."

Jolie squinted. " 'When you're in a jam, call Pam' Vanderpool?"

The woman grinned. "That's right. I'm your attorney, Ms. Goodman."

At a loss, Jolie shook her head. "How?"

"We have a mutual friend—Beck Underwood."

Jolie's eyes widened. "Beck called you?"

The woman nodded and pulled out a steno pad. "We go way back, Beck and I." With a rustle of nylon, she sat down in the seat Salyers had vacated. "Now, bring me up to speed. Tell me everything you told the police, and everything you didn't."

Jolie tingled with wonder, gratitude, and concern that Beck would take it upon himself to help her. Pam Vanderpool had a stern, motherly quality that comforted.

"I don't know where to start," Jolie stammered.

The woman shrugged. "Start at the beginning. How are you acquainted with the deceased?"

The deceased. Jolie's chest ached and her eyes blurred with unexpected tears. "I didn't kill Gary," she murmured. "I'm innocent."

The woman reached across the table and patted Jolie's arm. "I wish I could say that's going to make my job easier, sweetheart, but it's too early to tell." She sighed. "You're exhausted, so let's get through this real quick-like, so you can go home."

Jolie gave her a brief background and repeated the conversations she'd had with the police, startling with when she'd first filed the missing persons report to her most recent tête-à-tête with Salyers. Vanderpool wrote furiously, asking questions here and there. Jolie ended with Salyers' announcement that they'd found the murder weapon in her coat pocket.

"Do you know how the gun might have gotten there?" the woman asked, looking eerily calm for someone defending a murder suspect.

Jolie shook her head.

"Have you ever fired a gun?"

"No."

"And you have no inkling as to the identity of the woman found in Mr. Hagan's car?"

"That's right."

Pam Vanderpool played with her pen, turning it end over end. "Ms. Goodman, if there's anything you haven't been truthful about with the police, I need to know now, so there aren't any surprises."

Jolie swallowed hard and clasped her hands together. "Well, there's this one little thing."

Vanderpool squinted. "What?"

"Wednesday night when I left the party at the High Museum, Gary was waiting in my rental car."

The woman wet her lips. "And?"

"And he told me not to go to the police, that if I did, both of our lives would be in danger."

"Did he say why?"

"He said that he hadn't killed the woman found in his car, that he'd been set up, but he wouldn't tell me anything other than 'they' were out to get him, and if I went to the police, 'they' might come after me."

"Why would 'they' come after you?"

"He said because of an envelope that he'd sent to me. When I told him I hadn't received an envelope, he grew frantic and said 'they' must have intercepted it."

"Did he say what was in the envelope?"

"No. He wouldn't answer any of my questions about the dead woman or who he was afraid of. He said the less I knew, the better. He wouldn't even let me see his face."

"And you didn't report this to the police?"

She shook her head. "I convinced myself that he hadn't

said anything that would help them in their investigation and that I might actually make things worse."

The woman pursed her lips. "You still haven't received this alleged envelope?"

"No."

"Did you see Mr. Hagan again after that?"

"No, not until . . . tonight."

"You didn't see him at the party alive?"

"N–no."

"Okay, well, since you withheld information, no polygraph for you, young lady, but I'm going to try to convince the police that arresting you right now wouldn't be in anyone's best interests."

Jolie swallowed. "Okay."

"Is there anything else you'd like to tell me before I call Detective Salyers back in?"

"I . . . don't have much money . . . to pay you."

The woman winked. "But Beck does."

Jolie sat in stunned silence while her prepaid attorney summoned Detective Salyers. "My client wishes to go home."

Salyers smiled, tapping a rolled sheath of papers against her palm. "We all *wish* to go home, Ms. Vanderpool, but there's the little matter of a murder."

Vanderpool crossed her arms. "A man is shot at a party with dozens of people around—no one hears a thing. You're not even sure that the victim was actually shot at the party, are you, Detective?"

At Salyers' hesitation, hope bloomed in Jolie's chest.

"We're still waiting for the M.E.'s report," Salyers said. "Meanwhile, we want Ms. Goodman to take a polygraph test."

"No," Vanderpool said bluntly. "But my client is willing to submit to a gunpowder residue test."

Jolie's eyes widened. She was?

Salyers' mouth quirked to the side. "Your client took a swim in a pool. Any gun powder residue on her person or her clothes was washed away."

Vanderpool lifted her arms. "Then you got nothing."

"We have the murder weapon in Ms. Goodman's coat pocket."

"Which anyone could have placed there. Besides, if my client were guilty, why wouldn't she simply have left the party rather than raising an alarm?"

"Maybe she panicked."

"Detective," Vanderpool cooed. "Does Ms. Goodman strike you as a cold-blooded murderer?"

They both swung their heads toward Jolie. Her entire left arm throbbed from the cut in her palm. Her head felt as if it were in a vise. Every cell in her body sagged. If she looked half as pitiful as she felt, Salyers would give her a cookie and send her home.

Salyers frowned. "Looks can be deceiving. Case in point," she said, withdrawing a sheet of paper from the stack she held. "Ms. Goodman, you've just been served with a harassment restraining order, filed by Mr. Roger LeMon."

Jolie pushed to her feet. "What?"

"This is the man you told me about?" Vanderpool asked her.

Jolie nodded, fury burning in her empty stomach.

"What's this all about?" her attorney asked, taking the form.

"Mr. LeMon said he came to the party, but was forced

to leave because he was afraid Ms. Goodman would accost him."

"Accost him?" Jolie said. "That's ridiculous!"

Salyers shrugged. "Ridiculous or not, if you knowingly come within fifty yards of the man, you will be arrested."

"Don't you see?" Jolie asked, flailing her good arm. "He's giving himself an alibi! Roger LeMon killed Gary and is trying to pin it on me!"

"Another conspiracy theory?" Salyers asked, her eyebrow arched.

Jolie inhaled sharply and hiccupped.

Salyers considered her, then jerked her head toward the door. "You're free to go, Ms. Goodman. But I'll be keeping tabs on you—and your friends. Don't even think about leaving the city."

"Where are Carlotta and Hannah?"

"Ms. Wren and Ms. Kizer were released . . . with similar warnings." The detective hesitated, then said, "I think you should know that both of your friends have had run-ins with the law before."

Jolie blinked.

"Until this investigation is over, Ms. Goodman, you might want to steer clear of questionable company. And trust me, this investigation is only beginning."

On that ominous note, Jolie skedaddled before the woman could change her mind. She walked out of the room one step ahead of her attorney. They stopped at a counter to retrieve Jolie's personal effects which, since everything she'd been wearing and her purse had been confiscated as evidence, consisted of her keys and water-logged wallet. As they rode down one floor on the elevator, she asked, "Now what?"

"Now you sit tight," Vanderpool said. "Remember, the police and the district attorney have to build a case—let them do all the work." She handed Jolie a carbon copy of the restraining order. "And steer clear of Roger LeMon— I know the man, and he's formidable. Plus he's a friend of the police department, even lobbied the city council for raises for the force."

"Salyers told me as much," Jolie said.

"Don't fret. LeMon might be able to pull in a few favors, but that doesn't mean he can get away with murder."

"You think he might have killed Gary?" Jolie asked.

"I have no idea," the woman said, her expression stern. "But something has Mr. LeMon spooked enough for him to take out a restraining order on a girl half his size and half his means."

"*Less* than half his means," Jolie assured her.

As they walked off the elevator, Pam Vanderpool stopped. "Ms. Goodman, do you live alone?"

"Yes."

The older woman pressed her lips together. "Do you have a way to protect yourself?"

"What do you mean?"

"I mean there are already two people dead, and no one seems to know why. Maybe you should stay with a friend in town until this blows over."

Jolie nodded solemnly, embarrassed to admit she didn't have a friend in town with whom she was close enough to ask to hole her up. "I will."

"And here's my card. I sleep with my cell phone, so call if you need me, no matter what time it is."

Jolie gripped the business card in her hand as if it were a lifeline. "I don't know how to thank you for your help."

"Don't thank me," Vanderpool said as she resumed walking. "Thank Beck."

Beck. At the sound of his name, her nerve endings stirred. "How do you know Beck?"

"I've known Beck for years," she said, smiling fondly. "We've worked on many charitable causes together."

Jolie balked. She was a *cause*? She'd had similar thoughts herself concerning Beck's motivation, but to hear someone else say it was like a punch to the spleen.

"I will thank him," Jolie murmured, her cheeks flaming. "When I see him."

"Speak of the devil," the woman said as they entered the narrow lobby, which was deserted except for a security guard and Beck Underwood. Beck tossed aside a newspaper and stood. Jolie's heart beat wildly, and she had the crazy urge to run so she wouldn't have to face him. Since she'd last seen him, he had found jeans and a sweatshirt. His dark blond hair had dried at funny angles. Jolie suspected that she looked less cute after her own dip in the pool and subsequent air-dry.

"Hi," he said.

"Hi," she squeaked.

"She's free to go," Vanderpool said, all business.

He reached out to clasp her hand. "Thanks, Pam."

"You betcha," she said, then marched toward the exit as if she were accustomed to being summoned in the wee hours of the morning.

Jolie listened to the sound of the woman's retreating footsteps as if they were a ticking clock . . . counting down the time until she was alone with Beck. When the door closed with a resounding echo, Jolie finally found the nerve to meet his gaze. Abject mortification bled through her that she had allowed herself to become involved in such a mess . . . and had involved her friends and Beck Underwood by association. She was speechless with humiliation and weak from exhaustion.

He scanned her outfit with serious brown eyes. "How did they treat you in there?"

"Okay," she said, then pressed her lips together. "Ms. Vanderpool arrived just in time—I don't know how to thank you."

He winked. "We'll think of something. For now, let's get you home and in bed."

Since she looked like a ghoul and reeked of chlorine and now had this little murder rap hanging over her head, she was relatively sure that there was no innuendo intended. Still, that didn't keep her sleep-deprived mind from conjuring up a wonderful fantasy of crawling into bed with Beck Underwood and curling up next to his big body, reveling in the protection his presence and his name afforded.

The Buckhead Bubble, as Gary had always called it. The working-class girl in her railed against the double standard, but the nearly indicted girl in her longed to be included. She followed him to a side door, which he held open.

"How do you know Pam Vanderpool?" she asked.

But his answer was thwarted by the flash of a camera. "Mr. Underwood, over here!"

Flash! Flash!

Jolie blinked at the huddle of reporters and cameras gathered, her mouth opening and closing like a guppy's.

"Are you Jolie Goodman?" someone yelled.

"Are you under arrest for murder?"

"Mr. Underwood, is this woman your lover?"

"Come on," Beck growled, wrapping his arm around her shoulder, putting himself between her and the cameras. Frozen with shock, she stumbled to keep up with him, blindly walking forward to the parking lot until they stopped next to a dark-colored SUV. He swung open the door and helped her up into the seat. She didn't miss the concern on his face as he closed her door and glanced over his shoulder. The security guard had stopped the reporters at the mouth of the parking lot, but they were still shooting footage, and Beck would have to drive past them to get out of the lot. Dismay hit her like a slap when she realized how juicy a story it was for the media to cover one of their own. Rival networks of Underwood Broadcasting would be rubbing their hands with glee.

She covered her mouth with her hand, choking back a sob. The man had gone above and beyond the call of duty to help her for no legitimate reason and at great professional risk to himself.

He opened the driver's side door, climbed in, then slammed it shut.

"I'm so sorry," she said. "I'm sorry I got you involved."

"*I* got me involved," he said, his voice brusque. And regretful? "Put on your seat belt," he said, doing the same. "And look away from the cameras when we drive by."

Sensing that talking would only make matters worse, she nodded and stared at her shaking hands. By the time they drove to the exit, reporters were on both sides, so Jolie looked down and shielded her face with her hands. Beck slowed enough to take the curve, then they were speeding away. At the street, he slowed and gave her a wry little smile. "Where do you live?"

"Roswell," she said, pointing left, then gave him the street address and name of her apartment complex. She idly wondered how Carlotta and Hannah had gotten home, feeling yet another gush of remorse for involving them . . . and for trusting them. Their actions—and police records—made her look more guilty.

Beck pulled into the sparse pre-predawn traffic, slowing to allow an indigent pedestrian to cross illegally. "Hope he makes it until morning," Beck said ruefully.

With a start, Jolie wondered if that was how he saw her—as a poor person who needed a break? A handout? She gulped air. Pity? Waves of shame washed over her as they drove down the street. She didn't want the man's charity, but she was in no position to turn it down.

"I assume this will make the news," she said quietly. "You . . . with me, I mean."

He shook his head. "Don't worry about it. I'll make a couple of phone calls, pull in some favors. With any luck, it won't hit the air."

She leaned her head back on the headrest. "Is that how things are done?"

"What do you mean?"

"Favors are owed, favors are exchanged."

He shrugged. "I suppose that's life, isn't it?"

"I wouldn't want you to waste a favor on . . . me."

She felt his gaze on her, but she couldn't look him in the eye. "Oh," he said finally. "Well . . . there's my family name to think of, too."

Jolie wasn't sure if that made her feel better or worse. "I owe you an explanation—I . . . I didn't kill Gary Hagan."

"I suspected as much," he said. "And we can discuss everything later, after you've had a chance to recover."

Although she was grateful for the reprieve, Jolie had never been so thoroughly miserable in her life. Gary was dead, and the people who should believe in her innocence didn't, and the one person who shouldn't did. She felt like a glove that a hand had been ripped from—her right side turned in, her insides exposed. Her body ached with the intensity of a profound wound laid open, but she didn't have the energy to cry.

She concentrated on the rhythm of the engine and tires, the sound of her own breath entering and leaving her body. She closed her eyes, yielding to the hazy sense of nonbeing that sleep promised. Tension drained from her spine, sending the dead weight of her body into the seat.

Her next conscious thought was that the vehicle had stopped. A distant, dark feeling of dread came zooming back, jolting her upright. Moonlit hedges hemmed the nose of the SUV. Slowly Jolie became aware of streetlamps, sidewalks, connected two-story buildings. Her apartment complex.

"We're here," Beck said. "I think."

She nodded.

"You didn't say what your apartment number was."

She looked around to get her bearings, trying to shake the cobwebs from her brain, then pointed. "I'm in that building over there. We can walk."

She undid her seat belt and ran her tongue over her dry lips, moving gingerly to allow her sleep-laden limbs a chance to catch up. Before she realized what was happening, Beck was at the passenger door, helping her down in the dewy darkness. His hand against her waist, her back, sent a perilous feeling spiraling through her chest—she wasn't afraid of him, but she was afraid of how good his touch felt. She couldn't remember the last time a man had touched her just to comfort her instead of as a prelude to a sexual encounter. She leaned on Beck liberally while walking to her apartment door. She unlocked the door and pushed it open, overwhelmed with a sense of relief at being home.

Flipping on lights, she stumbled inside, not caring what Beck thought of her crocheted coasters and shabby furniture. He looked around, hands on hips, his expression unreadable, then he finally nodded toward her ancient sofa draped with a camouflaging throw. "Looks like a comfortable couch," he said, and from the tone of his voice she realized with a start that he was looking for a spot to crash.

"You want to stay?" she asked, unable to keep the surprise out of her voice.

He turned over his wrist to consult his watch. "Well, it *is* four in the morning." Beck cleared his throat. "And considering everything that's happened, I thought it best if someone stayed with you."

Was he afraid she would do something to hurt herself, or like Vanderpool, that someone else might? At the moment, Jolie didn't care. "That would be nice."

He returned to the door to check its security, then walked over to the picture window above the couch, pulled up the blinds, and tested the closing mechanisms. "Do you have any other windows?" he asked.

"Only in the bedroom," she said, pointing. "Come on, I'll get you a pillow and a blanket."

"Just a pillow will be fine," he said, following her into the bedroom.

He scrutinized the room where she slept, but his expression was devoid of personal interest in her intimate space—he seemed more concerned about the layout of the room. He strode to the window and nodded at the two-foot cactus she'd set on the floor beneath the sill.

"Nice touch," he said approvingly. He raised the blinds

and ran his hands along the closure, then frowned. "Have you had this window open lately?"

Jolie shook her head and walked over, her heart jumping in her chest.

"This latch is open." He leaned down to peer at the window sill, then indicated the clean scrape in the dust. "Looks like someone has either come in or left by this window in the past few days."

Her lungs squeezed as she remembered the finger swipe in the dust on her bookshelf headboard. She really needed to dust more often.

"Have you noticed anything missing?"

"No." Although she hadn't looked. She gasped and hurried to her hand-me-down dresser, lifting the lid of her jewelry box with trepidation. Her shoulders fell in relief when she removed the little felt bag holding her pearl choker. "Everything's here," she said.

She turned to find him studying her, and she flushed when she realized how meager her "everything" must seem to him. "They were my mother's," she murmured.

He nodded, then gestured vaguely toward the other rooms. "Any stereo equipment missing? Computer? Cash?"

She shook her head. "There's only the computer on my desk, and it's almost as outdated as my television. And . . . I don't keep cash here."

Nor in her bank account, but that was off topic.

He scratched his head, then spotted the fire extinguisher on her nightstand. "Have you had a fire recently?"

She flushed to the roots of her gritty hair. "That's the closest thing I had to a weapon."

He looked incredulous. "You've been sleeping here alone and afraid, with a fire extinguisher to protect you?"

She sagged onto the foot of her bed. "I didn't feel as if

I was in imminent danger." She nodded toward the window. "If someone was in my apartment, they obviously didn't mean me harm."

"This time," he added, his mouth drawn downward. "I've probably obliterated any prints," he said, but used the hem of his sweatshirt to refasten the window. The movement gave her a glimpse of the planes of his brown stomach, and she remembered the way he'd looked climbing out of Sammy's pool, his boxers clamped to his body, water streaming off his powerful shoulders. A wholly inappropriate pang of lust hit her, and she stood abruptly to distract herself, turning her back to remove one of the two pillows from her bed.

"You should report the entry to the police," he said, coming up behind her.

"I will," she said, then turned and smiled up at him. "Thank you for . . . thank you." She handed him the pillow and their fingers brushed. His eyes were dark with concern and other emotions she didn't want to investigate— regret? The most eligible bachelor in Atlanta probably could have found a more entertaining way to spend his evening, and with a less complicated partner. Or two.

"Try to get some sleep," he said. "But yell if you suspect that anything is wrong."

Everything was wrong, but Jolie nodded. He walked out, leaving the bedroom door ajar and a warm feeling of assurance in the cool air. She flipped off the light and crawled on top of the bed covers fully clothed. Hugging her remaining pillow, she willed her body to indulge in as much rest as possible, because she suspected the light of day would only reveal more and bigger dilemmas.

The dilemma sleeping on her couch notwithstanding.

Twenty

Jolie awoke to a sound alien to a single person—the shower running. Adrenaline shot through her, bringing her upright. Then she saw the "Property of Fulton County, Georgia" sweats she was still wearing, and the horrific events of the previous evening came crashing back down on her. Her first instinct was to pull the covers over her head, but her mother had once told her that the only thing that went away faster if a person ignored it was time.

The clock read 11:47 A.M. The day was already almost half gone.

She pushed herself up and took stock of her physical condition, running her finger over the knot on her forehead—better, but tender. The bandage on her hand seemed a little tighter, but the absence of dried blood indicated that the wound had not reopened during the night. Her throat and adenoids felt raw from the pool water she'd ingested and expelled violently.

She dared a glance in the mirror and cringed. Her fine, frizzy hair had exploded to new heights, and there wasn't

enough concealer in Neiman's makeup department to neu-
tralize the circles under her eyes. The sweat suit hung off
her like a feed sack on a scarecrow.

She had never been a woman who rolled out of bed
looking particularly good, and this morning was especially
unkind.

She straightened the covers on her bed and ventured
into the hall. The shower was still going full blast and she
hurried past so as not to dwell on the fact that Beck Underwood was standing naked in her shower, using her
soap and her towels. Her face burned when she thought
about the relative inelegance of her bath accoutrements,
but at least he would have found everything clean—it was
only dusting that she abhorred.

She scanned the couch where he'd slept and wondered
if the big, lumpy sofa had afforded him any rest at all. Her
extra feather pillow was still indented from his head. She
returned it to her bedroom, thinking Gary had been the
last person to share her bed or her pillow, although he had
spent the entire night on only one or two occasions.

Tears filled her eyes when the breathtaking sadness of
him not being alive hit her anew. Maybe Gary Hagan
wouldn't have saved the world, and maybe he'd been in
his share of trouble, but he didn't deserve to be shot in the
chest and abandoned under a pile of outerwear.

The cordless phone rang, jangling her nerves. She couldn't
think of anyone she wanted to talk to at the moment—unless
it was Detective Salyers saying the murder had been solved
and she was off the hook. But without caller ID, she had to
take her chances and hit the button to receive the call.
"Hello?"

"Jolie?" a man asked.

"Yes."

"This is Michael Lane. I just opened my paper—I called to see if you were okay."

"I'm fine," she said breezily, wondering if she should ask what the paper said. "A little shaken up, but fine."

"Yes, well, under the circumstances, I was thinking it might be better for you to take some time off from Neiman's."

She gripped the phone. "Michael, please—I *need* this job."

He sighed. "After the incident at the Manolo event yesterday—"

"Give me another chance," she pleaded. "Michael, to be blunt, I need the money." Else, how would she pay off the nightclothes?

He sighed again. "Okay, but only because I'm a wonderful person."

"Yes, you are," she said. "I'll see you tomorrow." She disconnected the call before he could change his mind, but the phone rang again almost instantly. She punched the TALK button. "Hello?"

"Jolie? This is Trini Janklo, upstairs."

Jolie rolled her eyes upward. "Hello, Mrs. Janklo. How are you?"

"Shocked, frankly. I opened the *Atlanta Journal-Constitution* this morning to find your name connected with the murder of a young man. Is that the same man I heard you arguing with?"

Her heart fluttered and she closed her eyes briefly. "We weren't arguing, Mrs. Janklo. This is all a big misunderstanding. You can't believe everything you hear . . . or read."

"It says you were so distraught that you tried to drown yourself."

Her eyes widened—no wonder Michael had been concerned. "That's simply not true—"

"I want you to know that I've already contacted management about having you evicted."

Her jaw dropped. "What? Why?"

"How am I supposed to sleep at night knowing there's a murderer living right underneath me?"

She pinched the bridge of her nose. "Mrs. Janklo, I'm *not* a murderer."

But the woman had already hung up, leaving an angry dial tone in her wake.

Jolie stabbed the DISCONNECT button and exhaled, dragging her hand down her face. She went to the door and unlocked it in search of her own Sunday paper. She opened the door and retrieved the paper, but when she straightened, a reporter was sprinting down the sidewalk toward her, his cameraman running behind him. "Ms. Goodman! Will you answer a few questions? Is there a love triangle between you, Gary Hagan, and Beckham Underwood?"

She was stupefied. "No!"

"Didn't Mr. Underwood spend the night here?"

She spun and scrambled back inside the door, slamming it hard. The door to the bathroom opened and Beck came out dressed in his jeans, pulling the sweatshirt over his head. He was frowning. "What was that?"

"A TV reporter," she said, distracted and comforted by his appearance . . . and self-conscious about her own.

He picked up his cell phone from a side table and began punching in a number. "What station are they from?"

"I didn't notice."

"Man or woman?"

"Man."

"What did he say?"

She wet her lips. "I don't think you want to know, but they're aware that you spent the night here."

He put down the phone before he finished dialing, then jammed his feet into his sneakers and strode toward the door. "I'll take care of this."

She wanted to watch, but decided she'd better take a peek at the paper. There she was, bottom half of page two: PARTY CRASHERS TERRORIZE BUCKHEAD HOME—BODY DISCOVERED.

Her heart dropped. Peppered with appropriate amounts of "allegeds" and "unnamed sources," the article mentioned her name ("questioned for the murder of the boyfriend for whom she filed a missing persons report a month ago"), Carlotta's name ("questioned in connection to widespread looting in the host's home during the party"), and Hannah's name ("reportedly assaulted a guest and held other guests hostage"). The article stipulated that no charges had been filed and hinted that it was due in part to "Goodman's unexplained association with Atlanta socialite, Beckham Underwood."

She closed the paper with a crunch just as Beck walked back in the front door. "That guy won't be bothering you anymore," he said.

"What did you do?" she asked, biting into her lip.

"Smashed his camera."

She held out the paper. "You might want to read this before you . . . do anything else on my behalf." She jerked a thumb toward the bathroom. "I'm going to take a shower. If you're gone when I come out, I'll understand."

He gave her a pointed look. "I thought we were going to talk."

"Oh." She tried to smile. "Right. I'll hurry."

She closed the door behind her and stripped off the offensive sweat suit, tossing it into a heap in the floor. Beck's towel was draped neatly over the shower-curtain rod. She withdrew a fresh towel from a tiny closet, then stepped under the shower spray and adjusted the head back down to her level. Her skin tingled at the intimacy of sharing a bathroom with Beck, and her mind reeled at the series of events that had brought them together in this—how had the newspaper worded it?—"unexplained association."

Protecting her bandaged hand from the water as much as possible, she scrubbed her hair and skin, then toweled off and shrugged into a long terry robe to make the dash to her bedroom to dress. When she opened the door, the smell of strong coffee reached her, as well as the sounds of cooking. She poked her head around the corner to see Beck, his back to her, tending to something on the stove that smelled wonderful. At least the article hadn't scared him off. He caught sight of her and waved her forward. "I made grilled cheese and tomato sandwiches—hope that's okay."

Jolie's stomach growled and she nodded. "Let me change."

"You're okay," he said. "Let's eat while the food is hot."

If he was so nonchalant about her being in a state of near undress, she didn't want to overreact. She joined him in the kitchen nook and withdrew plates and napkins from the cabinets, maneuvering around him with an ease that belied their impending discussion. A few minutes later they were settled at the rectangular plain maple table that doubled as her desk, sharing the space with her desktop computer. The chairs were mismatched, a collection of odds and ends from her parents' home that she'd painted white. Beck claimed a chair, seemingly unaware that he looked out of place in the quaint domestic scene.

Jolie sipped the coffee, murmuring in appreciation

when the warm liquid spread through her. She waited until she had eaten one sandwich and Beck had eaten two before she said, "I guess you read the article."

He nodded. "Want to fill in the holes?"

She set down her cup and retold the story, starting from when Gary had first disappeared.

"So the day I first met you, the detective had come to tell you about Hagan's car being recovered."

"Right." Then she told him about agreeing to attend the party with Carlotta on the chance she'd meet someone who had known Gary. "I didn't know we had crashed until we were already there," she felt compelled to explain, then realized the ridiculousness of minding that she'd been labeled a party-crasher in the larger scheme of things.

"I recognized Roger LeMon from a picture I found in one of Gary's photo albums. And later, Kyle Coffee."

"Do you have the photo?" Beck asked.

She nodded and rifled through papers next to her computer until she found it. "That's Gary next to LeMon, and Coffee is in the middle."

When Beck looked at the photo, he blinked.

"Do you recognize someone?" she asked.

He glanced up. "Besides Russell Island?"

She frowned. "Hannah's boyfriend? Let me see."

He pointed. "Different hair and he was heavier, but that's him. And that's his wife next to him."

She gasped. "So there were two more people at the party who knew Gary. Is the woman next to LeMon his wife?"

He lifted his shoulders in a shrug. "I never met his wife."

"How about the woman standing next to Kyle Coffee?"

"I don't know her either."

"Do you know the fifth man?"

He studied the picture, then rubbed his hand over his mouth. "I've seen him before. I want to say his name is Gordon something."

Jolie's head whipped around. "Gordon?" Gary's scribbled note on the pad rose in her mind: *Extra door key for Gordon.* It was too pat to be a coincidence. "Beck, please—can you remember his last name?"

He scratched his head. "I want to say it was a German name—something like 'bear,' but an unusual spelling." Then he shook his head. "I can't say for sure, but I can find out." He held up the picture. "May I borrow this?"

She hesitated, then felt foolish—Beck had done nothing but help her. "Sure. Do you know how these men are connected?"

He splayed his hand. "Movers and shakers, second-generation family businessmen. Like me," he added wryly. "They might belong to the same country club, or live in the same neighborhood."

"Have you ever heard of them doing anything illegal?"

Beck cleared his throat and sat back. "Like what?"

Surprised by his retreating body language, she spoke carefully. "Detective Salyers told me that Gary had a record for dealing cocaine in Orlando."

"And you think he might have gotten back into the business?"

"I don't know." She wet her lips. "Do you remember last Wednesday when you found me sitting in my car outside the High Museum?"

"Yeah, you were spooked."

"I was spooked because when I got in the car, Gary was waiting for me. He had just gotten out of the car before you walked up."

His head jutted forward. "Did he hurt you?"

"No. He told me he'd been set up, that he hadn't murdered the woman who was found in his car."

"I take it he didn't say *who* had set him up?"

"No. But I wondered if drugs might be involved."

Beck pulled on his chin. "I guess it's possible."

There was that hesitation again, that reluctance. Beck had a lot of money at his disposal—perhaps he had dabbled in drugs himself. Unease invaded her chest and she decided to change the subject. She pulled a sheet of paper and a pen from the office clutter on her table and did a rudimentary sketch of the tattoo on Roger LeMon's wrist. "Does this symbol mean anything to you?"

He squinted at the paper, then shook his head. "What is it?"

"A tattoo that LeMon and Coffee both have."

"Fraternity?"

"Friday night at the media reception, Carlotta and I cornered Coffee and asked him about the tattoo. He said it had ruined his life."

"What did he mean?"

"I don't know—Roger LeMon interrupted us, made some joke about Coffee's wife not liking the tattoo, then put Coffee in a cab. I think by that time LeMon had recognized me." She took a long drink from her mug. "Last night LeMon filed a restraining order against me."

"*What?*"

"He told the police that I've been harassing him, that he came to Sammy's party but had to leave because he was afraid I would 'accost' him."

"I was there, and it was clear you were trying to avoid him. Do you think he had something to do with the murder?"

She nodded. "I think he did it and set me up, then filed the restraining order to prove he left the party."

"To give himself an alibi."

"Right." Jolie stood and began clearing their impromptu meal.

He joined her, his expression thoughtful . . . and bemused. "So your theory is that LeMon killed the woman in your boyfriend's car and set him up for it, then killed your boyfriend and set you up for it?"

Jolie's hands stilled. When he put it that way, the story did sound too fantastic to believe. She flushed and leaned against the kitchen counter, her energy suddenly zapped. She was focusing on the puzzle pieces to detach herself from the fact that Gary was dead. She covered her mouth with her hand. "You're right. It's probably much simpler than I'm making it out to be—a debt owed, a drug deal gone bad. Roger LeMon might have nothing to do with it."

"Didn't you say that your boyfriend's apartment burned a few days after he disappeared?"

She nodded.

"Was the cause ever determined?"

"I don't know."

"Have you considered that the fire might have been directed toward Hagan as a warning? Or maybe to destroy evidence of, say, a drug deal?"

She shook her head, then sighed. "The thought hadn't occurred to me. I guess I didn't want to think that Gary could be involved in something that . . . sordid."

"So . . . were you in love with this guy?"

Startled, she looked up, and the air sizzled without the benefit of a fried sandwich.

Beck lifted his hand. "Never mind—that's none of my business."

Before she could agree or disagree, his cell phone rang. He stepped to the doorway to take the call, and Jolie decided to take advantage of the time to dress. She walked to the bedroom and closed the door, her mind racing with conflicting emotions—how *did* she feel about Gary . . . before, and now that he was gone?

Betrayed, mostly, on so many levels. She had genuinely believed that he cared for her, although she had sensed that Gary himself had been surprised by his feelings for her. It was almost as if he'd gone out with her on a lark—the handsome, eligible man about town who dates a quiet, spindly girl—with no pedigree or particular promise as a socialite—and becomes enchanted by her lack of pretense. At times she wondered if her conservative sensibility had attracted him because it helped to keep him grounded, or if he simply liked the idea that she would never compete with him. Regardless, she was beginning to think she loved the idea of Gary loving *her* more than she actually loved *him*. Had she mistaken flattery on her part for love?

And on those occasions when he'd looked at her with contrite eyes—when she'd thought that he was silently apologizing for underestimating her—had he instead been trying to think of a way to reveal the underhanded side of his life? She had sensed that he was struggling with something, but she hadn't asked.

Hadn't cared enough to ask. If she had, maybe he would've confessed the truth and she could have persuaded him to go to the police.

She pursed her mouth. On the other hand, she could have wound up as fish food in the Chattahoochee River.

She dressed quickly and opted for a few makeup basics to perk up her complexion while pondering Beck's interest in her feelings for Gary. Maybe he was feeling guilty over kissing her at Sammy's party. Or maybe if she admitted that Gary had been the love of her life, he could bow out with no pressure, no strings.

Jolie opened the bedroom door and walked into the living room quietly because Beck was still on the phone, his back to her.

". . . Jolie doesn't know," he said.

Her stomach plunged—at his words and at the guarded tone of his voice. She stepped back out of sight and strained to hear him, her heart hammering.

". . . You should be thinking of a story. Yes, I got it from her and I have it with me . . . I shouldn't be here much longer."

She tried to make sense of the words—a story, the photo he'd gotten from her . . .

The answer hit her so clearly that she almost laughed out loud at her stupidity—she'd just given an exclusive interview to a man who had his own news organization! Of course he was going to use it to his advantage. A part of her didn't even mind. Beck had saved her life, after all, and provided her with an attorney. But she felt so damn foolish, thinking he was helping her for altruistic reasons or maybe simply because he liked her.

She shook her head, blinking back tears. Then, it was as if something inside of her switched to "on." She straightened and inhaled deeply, filling her chest with resolve. She was almost relieved Beck was using the information she'd given him; it put their relationship on a professional plane. Neither of them would have emotional ties to the situation. She would no longer feel guilty about involving him, and she would no longer entertain fantasies about the man. Her head would be clear to navigate through the mess that Gary had left behind.

"Right," he said. "I'll take care of everything."

Jolie fumbled with her bedroom door to make noise, then acted as if she were just walking out.

Beck looked up and had the grace to blush. "Yeah," he said into the phone, his voice louder. "I'll be there as soon as I can. Okay." He closed the phone and looked apologetic. "I assumed you weren't exactly in the mood to take me house hunting today as we'd planned."

She nodded carefully, surprised that he'd remembered, then gestured to the computer. "How about if I print some listings to take with you? It'll only take a few minutes."

He glanced toward the door as if he were eager to leave, but nodded. "Sure."

She booted up the machine, trying to school her emotions as he walked over to stand behind her chair. She sensed the invisible barrier between them in the physical distance he maintained and in the rigid posture she maintained.

In her most professional tone, Jolie explained the search criteria—address, price range, amenities—then fed the program several scenarios of his responses and printed the results.

"See?" she said cheerfully, handing him the printouts. "That didn't take long."

He took the papers, but he averted his gaze. "Thanks."

"Beck," she said softly, "I will certainly understand if you decide to continue your house search without me."

He pursed his lips and nodded. "We both have other things going on right now."

"Right."

"Right." He pushed his hand through his hair. "Well, I'd better be going. Thanks for the sofa."

It was hard to smile, knowing the things that were going

through his mind, but she tried. "Thanks for the cheese sandwiches."

"You have Pam's number?"

She nodded.

He started to leave, then turned back. "Listen . . . I have a suite at the hotel. You're welcome to the extra bed."

She had to give him credit for trying to keep his source close by, and God help her, he was difficult to refuse. "Thanks, but I'll be fine."

He looked unconvinced. "I'll call you."

She followed him to the door, smiling until it was closed. Jolie leaned against the door and allowed herself a few seconds of quiet heartbreak, of wishing things could have been different, before forcing her thoughts to how to most constructively spend the afternoon. What was it Leann had said about her—that she always took things in stride? This was no time to break stride. Or to break down.

She gasped, realizing that Leann didn't even know about Gary, or that she'd almost been arrested. She called her friend's cell phone, relieved when Leann answered.

"Hello?"

"Hey, it's Jolie. Can you talk?"

"Just for a little while," Leann said quietly. "My sister . . . lost the baby early this morning."

"Oh *no*," Jolie said, her heart squeezing. "What happened?"

"Well, the doctors said all along that miscarriage was a possibility. I guess her body just couldn't handle the stress."

"You sound exhausted," Jolie said.

"I am," she said tearfully.

"How's your sister taking it?"

"Not well. You know at first she didn't want the baby,

couldn't bear the thought of raising it by herself, then she came around, and now . . . well, she feels so guilty."

The word of the day, Jolie decided. "Leann, I'm so sorry. Is there anything I can do?"

Leann released a shaky sigh. "No, but thanks for offering. What's up with you?"

Jolie couldn't bring herself to heap more bad news on her friend's personal tragedy. "I hate to ask, but I was wondering if you'd mind if I stayed in your apartment for a while."

"Of course not. Mrs. Janklo making you crazy?"

"Right," she said with a little laugh, although she suspected her friend sensed that other reasons were afoot.

"Sure, stay as long you need to. I probably won't be back for at least another couple of weeks, maybe longer."

"Thanks. Get some rest. Tell your sister how sorry I am. I'll call you later in the week."

"Okay. Bye."

Jolie hung up the phone feeling horribly self-centered. People all over the world were suffering through tragedies. She couldn't imagine the toll it would take on a person's mind to lose a baby at four months. And all this time she'd been selfishly thinking how Leann's sister's crisis had taken her friend from her, forcing her to make new friends.

Carlotta and Hannah. A knot formed in Jolie's stomach just thinking about her two party-crashing cohorts. They were all in a heap of trouble. She wanted to call Carlotta, but Salyers' warning to steer clear of the women's company reverberated in her head.

The phone rang again, and she picked it up with trepidation.

"Hello?"

"Jolie Goodman?" a woman asked.

"Yes."

"This is the Atlanta city morgue. A Detective Salyers gave me your name and number to contact for a next of kin for G. Hagar."

A lump formed in her throat. "Hagan," she corrected hoarsely.

"Hagan," the woman repeated. "The autopsy is done; the body needs to be claimed."

Jolie bit her tongue to keep from retorting that the woman needed to get a bedside manner. "There is no next of kin that I know of. What do I do?"

The woman sighed, mightily put out. "Somebody needs to let us know where to send the body to be embalmed. Two more days, and the state will start making decisions for you."

"Okay. What do I do?" she repeated calmly.

"Come down, identify the body, and fill out a form," the woman said in a bored voice.

Jolie swallowed hard. "I'll be there within the hour." She took down some directions and disconnected the call with a shaking hand. She didn't think she could do this alone, but who could she call? She hesitated, then found her purse and rummaged for a card. Working her mouth from side to side, she picked up the phone and dialed, nearly hanging up twice before the phone was answered with a groggy "Hell . . . o?"

"Carlotta . . . It's me, Jolie."

The woman moaned. "Christ, this had better not have anything to do with dead bodies."

"Well, actually . . ."

Twenty-one

"I don't believe I'm doing this," Carlotta muttered as they walked through the doors of the morgue. She wore dark sunglasses and looked like a movie star.

"I can't tell you how much I appreciate your coming," Jolie said. She wore a Band-Aid on her forehead and looked like a movie star's "person."

"If I so much as see a dead fly, I'm out of here."

"What can I do to make it up to you?"

"Get my car out of the police impound lot on a frigging Sunday afternoon."

Jolie winced. "They won't release your new car?"

"Not until tomorrow, *after* the twenty-four-hour trial period has expired."

"You're going to have to *buy* the car?"

Carlotta sighed. "Technically, I've already bought it. If I had taken it back this morning as planned, they would've ripped up the contract. Now I'm stuck, big time."

Jolie winced again. "If it's any consolation, the police have my car, too."

"The one that Gary stole?"

She nodded. "The police found it about a half mile from Sammy's house, but they're still 'processing' it." She tried to smile. "At least the car you got stuck with is a nice car."

"Yeah, well I've learned my lesson about borrowing things—I just wish I hadn't learned it all in one weekend."

Jolie had money concerns, too, but she knew the ruined clothes and now the car only heaped fuel onto the fire of Carlotta's financial problems. She felt responsible . . . sort of, but her hands were tied. "Have you talked to Hannah?"

"Briefly—she's prostrate with grief over her beloved Russell." Carlotta rolled her eyes.

"Remember the photograph I showed you with Gary and LeMon and Kyle Coffee? Russell is in it."

"He is?"

"Beck said he'd changed his looks, but it was definitely him."

"*Beck* said?"

Jolie flushed. "He took me home last night—er, this morning and . . . stayed. On the couch."

"Sure he did."

Ignoring the sarcasm, Jolie said, "And he said the fifth guy in the picture was named Gordon something, maybe Gordon Bear, with a German spelling?"

Carlotta shook her head. "Doesn't ring a bell. But I need to remember to ask Hannah if Russell has the same tattoo as LeMon and Coffee."

"May I help you?" a security guard asked in a funereal tone as they approached his desk.

Jolie swallowed twice before she found her voice. "I'm here . . . to identify a . . . person."

"Are they expecting you?"

"Yes."

"Third floor."

They moved toward the elevator in tandem and boarded the empty car. "Your boyfriend didn't have *any* family?" Carlotta asked.

Jolie pushed the button for the third floor and the door slid closed. "None that I know of, and none the police could find."

"Wow, that's kind of sad," Carlotta said as they were carried up.

Nodding, Jolie seconded her friend's observation. There was being alone in the world, and then there was being *alone* in the world. The door slid open and they walked out onto yet more tiled floor. The temperature here, though, brought to mind the phrase "meat locker." Jolie shivered at the implication alone.

"I mean, my family aren't the Cleavers," Carlotta whispered, "but at least someone in my tribe would claim my body if I got offed."

Jolie's eyes burned and she sniffed.

Carlotta looked over. "Ah, Jolie, I'm sorry. This has to be tough for you, seeing him again like this."

She nodded, terrified. Plus the chemicals in the air were killing her eyes. They walked toward a rounded counter reminiscent of a nurses' station. Two women in green scrubs were filling out paperwork and eating stromboli sandwiches—the source of the "chemicals."

"May I help you?" one of the women asked, then took a bite out of her sandwich.

Jolie rubbed her nose. "Yes, my name is Jolie Goodman. I received a call about an hour ago regarding . . . Gary Hagan."

The chewing woman frowned, then looked at the other woman, who was eating potato chips and licking her fingers. "Hagan?"

"Last night's gunshot," the licker said.

The chewer nodded. "Oh, yeah." She pointed down the hall with a tomato-sauce stained pinkie. "Ward Two."

"Gawd," Carlotta muttered when they started off in search of Ward II, "I may never eat again."

Jolie tried to smile through the panic that was beginning to build in her stomach. Since last night, every time she pictured Gary dead, she had forced the image from her mind. Now she not only had to relive it, but she would have brand-new images with which to torment herself.

They walked past Ward I, then located the stainless-steel double doors of Ward II. Jolie lifted her hand to knock, felt foolish and pushed one door open. Just inside, a young man in a white orderly uniform looked up from a computer. "May I help you?"

"I'm Jolie Goodman, here regarding Gary Hagan."

He looked over the top of his glasses. "Spell that, please."

She did, and while he tapped on his keyboard she looked around the room. The temperature was at least ten degrees cooler in here than in the hallway. Two opposing walls were lined with enormous stainless-steel file drawers . . . for cadavers. Her knees started to feel a little slack.

"Sign here," the man said, pointing to a line on a sheet of paper attached to a clipboard. "And I need to see a picture ID."

She signed her name, then removed her still-damp wallet and flashed her driver's license.

"Follow me."

She did, and Carlotta lagged a few steps behind. Carrying the clipboard, he consulted numbers on the sheet and the cabinets, finally reaching down to grab the handle of a drawer on the second row, about knee height. At the last second, he looked up.

"You should prepare yourself to see your loved one in what might seem like an unnatural state," he said in a rehearsed monotone. "Your loved one will be nude, but modestly covered with a cloth. In the event the person suffered wounds to the head, arms, or torso before they passed away, please know that those wounds will be visible."

Next to her, Carlotta grunted. "I'm not looking."

"Let me know when you're ready," he said.

Jolie nodded and steeled herself as the young man slid the drawer out from the wall. She stared at the still face of the dead man, her heart thumping against her breastbone.

Carlotta looked over Jolie's shoulder. "I thought Gary was white."

Jolie sagged. "He is—that's not Gary."

The young orderly's eyes widened behind his glasses, then he consulted his clipboard again. "Oh, you're right. Sorry 'bout that."

"Christ," Carlotta muttered.

He slid the first man back into the wall, then pulled open the next drawer over. A nauseating medicinal odor filled the air. As awful as it was to see Gary's ashen face, at least his eyes were closed and he looked peaceful, Jolie decided. If one's gaze didn't stray to the two-inch round black hole in the middle of his chest. Her own chest constricted painfully.

"Yes," she said, nodding. "That's Gary Hagan." Carlotta grabbed her hand for a surprising squeeze and Jolie was grateful.

"Okeydoke," the orderly said, closing the drawer with a metallic click. He pointed to the clipboard. "Sign here and here and I'll get the personal effects."

She did, blinking away the tears gathered in the corners of her eyes, then followed the young man back to the front. He consulted another computer screen and gave an exasperated sigh. "The personal effects are in police custody—sorry. But I need to know where you want the body to be sent."

"Leed Funeral Home." Jolie extended a card for the small funeral chapel on the northern side of Buckhead that she'd found in the Yellow Pages ("In your hour of need, lean on Leed.") When she got her broker business off the ground, she was definitely going to come up with a catchy slogan and take out an ad. "They're expecting the . . . Gary."

"Okay, you're all set." The orderly smiled. "Just go back out these doors the way you came. And have a nice day."

They exited into the hall and Jolie stopped to gulp fresh air.

Carlotta jammed her hands on her hips. "Ugh. I complain about my job way too much. Are you okay?"

Jolie nodded, trying to dispel the thought of Gary being warehoused like an auto part. They made their way past Ward I, where two uniformed police officers stood by and mournful cries were audible from inside the room. Jolie's heart went out to the family. The door opened suddenly and Detective Salyers emerged to speak to the officers. They nodded obediently, then left.

Salyers turned and her face registered surprise and recognition. "Ms. Goodman." Her gaze darted to Carlotta. "Ms. Wren."

"Hello, Detective," Jolie said.

"I suppose you're here to make arrangements for Mr. Hagan."

"That's right."

Salyers' face looked grave. "Well, this is opportune—I have news."

"What?"

"The woman found in Mr. Hagan's car has been identified."

Jolie glanced at the closed doors, her heart welling for the unknown family. "Who . . . who is she?"

"Janet Chisolm LeMon, wife of Roger LeMon."

Jolie gasped and covered her mouth.

"The man didn't know his own wife was missing?" Carlotta asked.

"According to Mr. LeMon, his wife was supposed to be on a spiritual retreat in upstate New York. She wasn't allowed to contact anyone and no one was allowed to contact her."

Jolie scoffed. "Who loses track of their spouse for a month?"

"Two of Mrs. LeMon's friends confirmed his story, and I have to say that he seems pretty torn up about her death."

"If he didn't know she was missing, how was she identified?"

"Her suitcase and purse were pulled out of three feet of mud at the bottom of the river. Ms. Goodman, you should know that Mr. LeMon has admitted that his wife was having an affair with Mr. Hagan."

Jolie gaped. "He told me he didn't even know Gary."

"He said he lied for his wife's sake because she had ended the affair."

"But doesn't that give him a motive for killing Gary?" Carlotta said.

Salyers crossed her arms. "Actually, Mr. LeMon seems to think that Mr. Hagan killed Mrs. LeMon because she ended the affair, then you, Ms. Goodman, killed Mr. Hagan in a jealous rage."

Jolie fumed, shaking her head. "That's insane."

"But it would explain your preoccupation with Mr. LeMon."

"I'm not preoccupied with Roger LeMon! Don't you think it's strange that his name keeps popping up in the investigation?"

"So does yours, Ms. Goodman."

Jolie frowned. "How did she die?"

"Gunshot. The weapon was also pulled from the mud, registered to Mr. Hagan."

Jolie was still digesting that troubling detail when the door to Ward I opened and Roger LeMon came staggering out, wiping his eyes. He immediately zeroed in on Jolie, pointing at her. "What's *she* doing here?"

"Ms. Goodman is here on a personal matter," Salyers said in a calming voice.

"Seeing about that killer boyfriend of yours?" he shouted. "You ought to see what he did to my wife!"

Jolie shrank back while Salyers put her hand on his arm.

"I should thank you for killing Gary Hagan! You saved me from killing the bastard myself!"

"That's enough, Mr. LeMon," Salyers said. "Come on, I'll walk you to your car."

She gave Jolie a look that said to stay put until they were out of sight, then she led him to the elevator.

"He seems upset all right," Carlotta murmured as the elevator door closed. "But is he upset about his wife being dead, or about her being identified?"

Jolie bit into her lip. "Good question. The thing is, for all

I know, Gary *could* have had an affair with Janet LeMon."

"Did he ever talk about his old girlfriends?"

"No, although he did refer to one simply as a fatal attraction, and I found a card in his things that looked as if it might have come from someone . . . clingy."

"Do you still have the card and the envelope?"

"The police do."

"Then they should be able to do DNA tests to see if Janet LeMon was his fatal attraction."

"Even if she was, that doesn't mean that Gary killed her."

"True."

Jolie mulled over the new information as they walked past Licker and Chewer.

"Talk about a bad day," Chewer said. "The man lost his best friend, then his *wife*."

"Death comes in threes," Licker said emphatically.

"Excuse me," Jolie said leaning over. "Did you say that Roger LeMon had also lost his best friend?"

Licker nodded and flipped through a stack of papers. "Here it is—killed in a car accident in Vegas just this morning. The body should be here any time now. Name was Coffee. Kyle Coffee."

Twenty-two

Jolie was a bona fide basket case on the drive home. She'd done her best to keep her panic at bay around Carlotta, but after they'd picked at a salad and she'd dropped her friend at her townhouse, Jolie had yielded to the shakes. Her mind ran in circles, shifting bits and pieces of the puzzle around to see if one detail would fall unexpectedly in place next to another. Only she kept coming up with the same scenario: Gary had killed Janet LeMon, and Roger LeMon had killed Gary in retaliation. It was a classic lovers' triangle, except LeMon was trying to position *her* as the third party.

The news of Coffee's death had shaken her. A car accident seemed too pat, too coincidental. Coffee was a loose cannon whose range was extended with each cocktail. Whatever he had been on the verge of telling them at that party had probably gotten him killed.

She flipped on her turn signal and veered right onto Roswell Road from Peachtree in the waning light, eager to arrive home . . . or rather, at Leann's apartment, located in another building in the complex. She had arranged to have her land-line calls forwarded to Leann's number, then packed a duffel bag of clothes and toiletries and tossed it in the trunk before leaving, so she wouldn't have to go back to her own place when she returned.

Last night's irregular sleep was catching up to her, along with the day's events. And her palm was throbbing again beneath the bandage. Being tired *and* nervous was a dangerous combination on any roadway, but in Atlanta traffic, the mixture was almost guaranteed deadly. She fought to stay awake.

Suddenly a pair of headlights came zooming up behind her. Adrenaline flooded her limbs at the reminder that something could go wrong so quickly. She tapped the brake and gripped the steering wheel tighter. The car moved into the left lane, presumably to pass her, but when the car came abreast of hers, it cut into her lane, scraping metal against metal.

Jolie screamed and glanced over at the other driver. The man sneered at her and recognition hit: the man from the parking garage who had been having "car trouble." He cut his wheel right again. He was trying to kill her. She hit the brakes, sending her car into a skid onto the grassy shoulder. She fought to regain control, then guided the car to a safe stop while the other car roared away, lost in the sea of taillights heading north. Her pulse pounded in her ears, and the bandage on her hand was bloody from gripping the wheel so hard.

She put on her hazard lights and checked to make sure that everything was in working order (on the car and on her person) before pulling back into traffic. This was perfect timing too—just when she was on the verge of returning her rental car and retrieving her violated Mercury, she had another insurance claim on her hands. Then there were the clothes, of course.

Top that with a funeral bill for Gary, and she was pretty much going to be in debt the rest of her life unless she could sell Beck Underwood a palace and get her brokerage business under way. Oh, and stay out of prison.

At the next traffic light, she made a U-turn into the southbound lanes. No way was she going back to the apartment complex tonight. And Carlotta's place was already crowded with her brother. She would simply have to get a hotel room. Then another solution presented itself.

She removed her cell phone and punched in a number with her thumb. After a couple of rings, a voice came on the line. "This is Beck."

"Beck . . . this is Jolie."

"Hi. I saw the news about Janet LeMon come over the wire. Are you okay?"

At least he sounded genuinely interested. "Um, not really. Kyle Coffee is dead, too."

"The guy I spoke to at the media reception?"

"Yeah, the one who was buddies with LeMon. Supposedly, he was in a car accident in Vegas, but—"

"But the timing seems pretty coincidental."

"Right. Anyway, I was wondering if that offer of your extra bed is still good?"

"Absolutely. Do you want me to come and get you?"

"No. I'm in my car—I can be there in a few minutes."

"Valet your car. I'll be waiting in the lobby."

"Do you think Ms. Vanderpool could join us?"

He hesitated, then said, "I'll call her," in a strained tone.

Jolie disconnected the call, feeling torn about using Beck for protection, but rationalized that they were using each other. During the drive, she dialed Salyers' cell phone.

"Salyers here."

"Detective Salyers, this is Jolie Goodman."

"Ms. Goodman, I apologize for the scene at the morgue. Mr. LeMon, as you can understand, is very upset."

"I could see that," Jolie said. "Detective, did you know that Kyle Coffee is dead?"

"Mr. LeMon told me that he was killed in a car accident this morning in Vegas."

"Right. Don't you find that suspicious since he's involved in this case?"

Salyers sighed. "The only reason Mr. Coffee's name came up in association with this case, Ms. Goodman, is because you mentioned it. People die in car crashes every day—it's a horrible coincidence." Papers rattled in the background.

"Did you check into the photo of Sammy Sanders I told you about?"

"Yes, but as it turns out, only the frame was taken into evidence. The photo was returned to Ms. Sanders, who said she threw it away because it was ruined."

Jolie grunted. "Great."

"But I did question Ms. Sanders, and she denied being romantically involved with Mr. Hagan."

And Sammy never lied, Jolie noted wryly. "Okay, here's something else—Russell Island, the man my friend Hannah, um, assaulted at the party is in the photos with Gary, Roger LeMon, and Kyle Coffee. The other man's name is Gordon Bear, possibly with a German spelling."

"Where did you get that information?"

"Beck Underwood identified them from the photo I kept."

"Hmm. While we're on the subject, Ms. Goodman, I have a waiter from the Sanders party who says he overheard you and Mr. Underwood say something about getting rid of your boyfriend."

Jolie swallowed past a dry throat. "That was a joke—I'd told Beck that I had a boyfriend who was in trouble. He had no idea who Gary was, or that he was missing."

"So are you and Mr. Underwood romantically involved?"

"No."

"Really? Because Ms. Sanders said she walked in on the two of you kissing in a bedroom at her party."

"I . . . trust me, that is irrelevant to this investigation."

"I'd say the fact that you have a new boyfriend could be damned relevant to your former boyfriend being dead."

She gripped the wheel tighter, sending pain shooting through her bad hand. "I didn't kill Gary, and I think you know that, Detective."

"Give me a better alternative."

She sighed. "*Roger LeMon.*"

"He has an alibi—a guest saw him leave the party a few minutes after he arrived."

"He could have returned. Have you questioned LeMon about his tattoo?"

"No."

"Why not?"

Salyers covered the mouthpiece and made a brusque comment to someone in the background, then came back on the line. "I'm sorry, where were we?"

"Roger LeMon's tattoo. And have you looked into the cause of the fire at Gary's apartment complex?"

Salyers emitted a long-suffering sigh. "Look, Ms. Goodman, I don't mean to be rude, but I have a file folder full of murders to investigate and limited resources to do it with. I can't chase down every tangent, especially when it's given to me by the prime suspect in the case."

Jolie fumed. "Well, here's another tangent: I was just run off the road—purposefully."

"Where?"

"Roswell Road, heading north just past Peachtree. The driver was a man I'd seen before, in the parking garage of the hotel where the media reception took place Friday night."

"Were there any witnesses?"

"To me being run off the road? Scores of them, but in Atlanta this kind of thing barely warrants a horn blow. Maybe the scratches and dents down the side of my rental car will convince you?"

"Are you injured?"

"No."

"Can you give me a description of the other car and the driver?"

Jolie squinted. "Dark-colored two-door . . . boxy . . ." Her voice petered out when she realized how little information she was giving the woman to act on. "The driver was dark-headed, maybe forty, possibly Hispanic . . . or not," she finished weakly.

"Okay, Ms. Goodman, I made a note of it, and I'll have units notified to keep an eye out for an errant driver of that er, description."

Frustration welled in Jolie's chest. "I don't blame you for not believing me, Detective, but I think there's something bigger going on, and Janet LeMon, Gary, and Kyle Coffee all died because they knew about it. Make a note of *that*." She disconnected the call, wondering too late if it was a crime to hang up on a cop. If so, maybe they would allow her to serve concurrent terms for murder and impoliteness.

Jolie flexed her aching hand and glanced in her rearview mirror. She might not have managed to spook Detective Salyers, but she'd managed to spook herself. Especially since she was returning to the same hotel where she'd first seen the driver of the car that had run her off the road. She took as winding a route as possible when traveling into the heart of Buckhead, exhaling a sigh of relief when she saw the canopy for the hotel.

The valet seemed slightly less happy to see her—or rather, her tin-can rental car, degraded even more by the freshly ruined paint job on the driver's side. She emerged with an apologetic look, then withdrew her decidedly inelegant duffel bag from the trunk. Beck came striding out, dressed in jeans and a different sweatshirt than he'd left wearing that morning. The sight of him was so comforting she felt a rush of sadness, although she took solace in the knowledge that he probably had the same effect on women everywhere.

She looked around. At various bellhops.

"What happened?" he said, inspecting the car.

She opened her mouth and burst into tears—God, that was the second time she'd done that around him.

"Hey, hey," he said, taking her bag and drawing her against his chest. He walked her toward the lobby. "You're safe now. Let's go in. Pam will be here as soon as she can."

She blubbered her story to him, letting the day's stress ooze down her cheeks. He wiped her tears with his thumbs, his expression troubled. "Did you call the police?"

She nodded. "But I think Detective Salyers is ready to lock me up just so I'll leave her alone."

"And you're sure it was the same guy you saw here?"

"I'm sure. He gave me the heebie-jeebies, so I didn't get into the parking garage elevator with him. I was going to wait until I saw him drive away before going to my car, but he came back down and supposedly was having car trouble. The concierge called an auto service for him."

"But you think that might have been a ploy?"

She shrugged.

"Come with me."

He walked across the hotel lobby to the concierge desk. Jolie recognized the attractive woman behind the counter. Her instant perkiness when she caught sight of Beck was familiar . . . Jolie'd seen that same look in her own mirror.

"Hello, Mr. Underwood. How can I assist you?"

"Can you help me track down some information about a man for whom you called an auto service Friday evening?"

She frowned. "That was at the end of the reception, wasn't it?"

He nodded.

She opened a log and ran her finger down a list of entries. "I don't have the gentleman's name, but here's the service I called—want me to write it down for you?"

"Please."

She gave him the information, then glanced at Jolie's duffel. "Will you be needing extra linens for your guest?" she asked slyly.

Jolie's face flamed.

"I'll let you know," Beck said easily, then guided Jolie toward the elevator bay. "Sorry about that."

"No problem," she murmured, following him into a mahogany-lined elevator.

When the doors closed, he lifted her hand in his. "You're bleeding again."

"I broke it open during the car-chase scene," she said with a little smile. His warm touch sent little thrills up her arm that made her forget the itchy pain.

He winked. "We'll get you fixed up."

They rode to a floor that was exclusive enough to require guests to insert their room key just to gain access. Jolie followed him down a plushly carpeted hallway and into a suite that was twice as big as her apartment, and decorated in a style that was at least two decades more current. Cocoas and creams and beiges and black, very masculine, very posh. His bed was enormous . . . she tingled with embarrassment over the thought of him bunking down on her lumpy sofa.

"Wow," she said, feeling a tad out of place standing there with her shabby duffel bag.

"The place is a little much," he said sheepishly, "but it's one of the company's corporate apartments, and since it sits empty most of the time, I thought I'd hang out here until I . . . decide what to do."

She looked up at him. "You mean until you decide if you're going to stay in Atlanta?"

He nodded, then pointed toward a door off the entryway. "There's a first-aid kit in this bathroom, let's take a look at your hand."

She followed him into a high-ceilinged, lavish cream-and-gold room. He found the first-aid kit and spread the items he needed on the vanity, then sat on a low stool and pulled her hand toward the sink. She stood and pivoted her head like a tourist while he carefully removed the blood-stained bandage from her hand.

"It looks puffy," he said. "It might be a little infected."

She sucked air through her teeth when he held her hand under a gentle stream of cold water from the faucet.

"Maybe you should go to the emergency room and get stitches."

"It'll be okay," she said. "I'll just be more careful."

"I'll put antibiotic cream on it," he said, then dabbed it on so carefully, she could barely feel it. The man was a paradox, raised in luxury but plainly uncomfortable with the idea of having so much. He could probably live the rest of his life off his trust fund, but his hands were calloused from physical work. And by right, no man so masculine should be so gentle. He wrapped her hand with a fresh bandage and taped it into place.

"There," he said, sandwiching her mended hand between his.

"Thank you," she murmured. "I feel like I'm always saying thank you to you."

He gave her a little smile. "You're welcome. You don't like asking for help, do you?"

"I don't like to take advantage."

"Asking for help when you need it isn't taking advantage."

She pursed her mouth. "That's easy to say if you've never had to ask someone for help."

He looked down at their hands. "Everyone needs some kind of help at one time or another."

She gave him a wry smile that belied the desire that coursed through her body. "This has been the neediest week of my life—you caught me at a bad time."

"Or a good time," he said, reaching for her other hand and pulling her between his knees. He curved his arm around her lower back and drew her closer. She wanted so badly to be kissed by him, but things were different now . . . Gary was gone . . . She was in real trouble . . .

Nothing good could come of an affair with this man. Well, nothing that would last longer than a few minutes . . .

When their mouths were a mere inch apart, he whispered, "Jolie Goodman, what am I going to do about you?"

Her lips parted involuntarily, and she leaned into his kiss. Their mouths met in a gentle exploration that grew in intensity as he slid his hands down her back. All she could think of was . . . nothing, actually . . . and it was nirvana to be lost in the moment. The fear, the sadness, the confusion she'd felt over the past few weeks and for most of her adult life, all of it channeled into pure passion for a man who was so compelling to her, she felt a little desperate around the edges.

He moaned into her mouth and stood, lifting her. She wrapped her legs around his waist and her arms around his neck, pressing her chest against his. He carried her to the bed as effortlessly as if she were a hat that just happened to be folded around him. Somewhere along the way, her shoes slipped off her feet. When he lowered her to the massive white bed, she'd never felt so reckless, her senses never so keen. His face was pained with desire, his dark eyes hooded as he pulled his sweatshirt over his head and slid onto the bed next to her.

She skimmed her fingertips over his collarbone and shoulder, captivated by the smooth muscle of his powerful torso, the mat of light brown hair over his chest that narrowed to a dark furrow over his stomach.

He unbuttoned her blouse, celebrating every liberated square of skin with his tongue. Jolie had always been modest, but with Beck she wasn't revealing her body— she was revealing everything she wanted to be and might never have the chance. Gone was any awkward-ness, any hesitation. Beck controlled his body with ath-letic grace, every movement intentional and effective. Anticipation coiled tighter between her thighs as each piece of their clothing was cast aside. At the sight of him nude, Jolie felt the shudder of Eve inside her, breathless with the necessity of him. This was the essence of life: a magnificent man, and hormones run amok.

But time was ticking, so when he parted her knees and kissed the heart of her, the frugal girl in her arched in ap-preciation of his attention to detail and economy of mo-tion. Determined to be more participatory than a hat, Jolie returned the favor with equal consideration, then after a few mental calculations regarding expansion, contraction, and overage, she straddled him in what proved to be a gradual yet successful maneuver. They found a natural glide, urging each other to higher heights. She came first, and second, and he arrived a gentlemanly third, breathing her name with an urgency that resounded in her defeated, gullible heart. She lowered her head to his chest, but his heart gave no indication of a similar distress.

He stroked her hair and made satisfied noises. She closed her eyes tightly, knowing that remorse was looking for her and would find her soon enough.

A knock sounded on the door, and her eyes flew open.

Beck lifted his head. "That will be Pam."

Remorse, remorse, remorse. Jolie disengaged herself from him as elegantly as possible, scooped up her clothes, and sprinted toward the bathroom.

"Jolie."

She turned back and raked her hair out of her eyes.

His head popped through the neck of his sweatshirt. "That was great."

That was inappropriate sprang to her lips, but it wouldn't be fair to drag Beck into her guilt event: *Goodman, party of one.*

Instead she nodded, then dove into the bathroom. After running a damp washcloth over key areas, she jumped into her clothes and gave herself a good mental shake. What was she thinking, entertaining the idea of having feelings for Beck Underwood? As if she didn't have enough to worry about right now—her reputation, her career, money, freedom. And how much more clear could he make it that he was a temporary . . . *benefactor?*

She opened the bathroom door just as the attorney he'd bought for her walked in wearing slacks and a black corduroy blazer, her phone to her ear, speaking in staccato phrases to the person on the other end. If-you're-in-a-jam-call-Pam Vanderpool was rattled.

"Okay . . . okay . . . *okay.* Keep me posted." She snapped her phone closed and sighed. "Not good news, I'm afraid."

Jolie hugged herself. What now?

Beck's hand brushed her waist. "Why don't we sit down?"

She saw Pam's gaze dart to the intimate gesture and a little wrinkle form between her dark eyebrows that contrasted so drastically with her white hair. "Good idea."

Jolie crossed the room, ignoring the blaring white bed, and purposefully sat in a chair, resisting the temptation to sit next to Beck on the loveseat. She looked down and saw, to her horror, one of her knee-highs rolled up in a little taupe-colored ball on the floor a few inches in front of her foot. How had she missed it when she re-dressed . . . and where was the other one? She extended her leg and flattened the ball beneath her loafer before Pam could notice.

"Okay," Pam said, sitting in a chair opposite Jolie. "I've been talking to the assistant D.A. Janet LeMon's death has a lot of influential voters upset. They've been lighting up the phone lines, clamoring for an arrest."

Jolie's mouth went dry. "They're going to arrest me?"

Pam sat back in her chair. "Not yet . . . but maybe soon. For the murder of Gary Hagan and possibly as an accessory to the murder of Janet LeMon."

The room tilted. Jolie grabbed the arms of the chair until the room righted itself, then expelled a shaky breath. "They can arrest me on circumstantial evidence?"

Pam nodded. "But remember—an arrest is one thing, a conviction is something else entirely."

Beck leaned forward, his handsome face wreathed in concern. "But they might make an arrest even if they know they can't get a conviction, just to quiet the public."

"And the media," Pam added pointedly.

Beck pulled his hand down his face. Jolie was distracted for the split second it took to register the fact that the great sex aside, she could fall in love with him based on this conversation alone. The one thing that kept this predicament from being even worse was the fact that Beck Underwood was in her corner.

"The one bit of luck," Pam continued, "is that the D.A. is on vacation and won't be back in her office until Wednesday. No one is willing to make a move without her go-ahead."

Jolie closed her eyes briefly and decided to throw up a quick prayer while she was in the proper position, then said, "There's nothing we can do?"

"Keep cooperating with the police, keep trying to remember details you might have forgotten."

"Do you happen to know what Janet LeMon looks—looked—like?"

Pam nodded. "I met her a couple of times. Seemed like a nice enough person to me."

"Beck," Jolie said, "do you have that picture? I'd like to see if Pam can identify one of the women as LeMon's wife."

He hesitated, then looked toward the desk. "I . . . put it in the glove box of my SUV. Sorry."

She nodded and looked back to Pam. "Okay . . . I'll try to remember details to tell the police. But short of a witness coming forward or someone making a full confession, the police will come to get me Wednesday?"

"There's a chance the D.A. will disagree with the charges," Pam said. "But if she doesn't, then I'll try to arrange for you to surrender yourself into police custody."

Bile backed up in Jolie's throat.

"I'll offer a reward for information," Beck said, standing. He reached for his cell phone. "Maybe that will shake something loose."

Pam Vanderpool studied him warily, then stood. "I have to go. Ms. Goodman, would you mind walking me out?"

Jolie pushed herself up and moved somewhat unsteadily toward the door. As they stepped into the hallway, Pam Vanderpool looked past Jolie's shoulder into the room, then leaned closer. "Ms. Goodman, do you know that Beck has been calling in favors all over town to keep your name and picture off the television and out of the papers?"

Her heart swelled. "No . . . I didn't know." And if that was the case, then who had he been talking to about a story yesterday morning at her apartment?

"His father isn't happy about the fact that one of his first acts in reestablishing himself in the broadcasting community is pulling in favors for a woman suspected of murdering her boyfriend and the wife of a successful Buckhead businessman."

Jolie bit down on the inside of her cheek. "I didn't ask Beck to get involved."

"I know you didn't—that's how Beck is. He sees a wrong and he tries to make it right, even if he hurts himself in the process." Pam wet her lips, and her eyes softened. "Ms. Goodman, I'm not suggesting that you try to stop him—when Beck sets his mind to something, there is no stopping him. But woman to woman, you're in a hell of a pickle here. Don't make things worse by giving the media more gossip for Beck to have to squash."

Jolie pressed her lips together and gave a curt nod. "I understand."

The older woman glanced down, then plucked off a staticky balled-up taupe-colored knee-high that had attached itself to her jacket and handed it to Jolie. "I hope so, for both of your sakes."

Pam turned and strode away, already punching in a number on her cell phone. Face flaming, Jolie walked back into the room, where Beck was ending one cell phone call, punching in another one.

"What was that all about?" he asked.

Jolie folded the knee-high into her hand. "Pam was just giving me some advice."

He nodded absently. "I'm calling the auto service to see if they have a record of servicing that guy's car."

"Beck, how exactly do you know Pam?"

He looked up. "She's my father's mistress." Then he

turned his back and leaned against a sofa table. "Hello, may I speak to the manager, please?"

Jolie studied him, then the rolled up knee-high. Not only had Pam given her advice from one woman to another, she'd given her advice from one woman who loved an Underwood man . . . to another?

She mulled over the revelation, then leaned one hip on the oversized desk that Beck had claimed as a work space. She looked down, frowning when she saw the edge of the group picture she'd asked about sticking out from beneath a newspaper. She looked up to see that Beck still had his back turned. From the sound of his voice, he was not having much luck with the manager of the auto service. Jolie removed the photo and replayed their recent conversation. Why would he have lied about its whereabouts?

This man who had captured her heart in a matter of days had a few secrets. Jolie glanced up to make sure he was still preoccupied, then tucked the picture into her purse. For now, she would keep a few secrets too.

Twenty-three

"Thank you for shopping at Neiman Marcus," Jolie said, handing a shopping bag over the counter with a smile. The woman glanced at the white bandage on Jolie's hand, then returned the smile warily.

"It's nothing contagious," Jolie assured her, instantly assailed by another bout of itchiness, which forced her to scratch her hand through the bandage before the woman looked away. "Really," Jolie said with a smile, still scratching.

The woman hurried away, and Jolie stared down at her hand, irritated. Which wasn't exactly fair since her hand also looked irritated. She made a fist and winced—Beck had made the bandage a little tight this morning when he'd dressed it for her. But after Pam Vanderpool's parting words last night, Jolie had concluded there could be no more hanky-panky between her and Beck. Since getting bandaged would be the extent of him touching her, she could tolerate tight. Tight was good.

To take her mind off her aching hand and off Beck, she

glanced around the nearly deserted shoe department, even willing to tackle an orthopedic-insert customer if necessary, to take her mind off her problems. She was just glad to be back to some kind of normalcy. The afternoon had passed, and she'd only thought of Gary lying in the morgue, oh, a few hundred times. But she knew that number would be much higher if she weren't working.

And then there was the one time that she *hadn't* been thinking about Gary that kept rising in her mind—when she'd climbed on top of Beck Underwood.

She cringed and tried to push aside *that* persistent memory.

She'd come in early to buy a suit for Gary to wear in his casket on her employee discount. Sending him off in style was the least she could do, and although she was a little dismayed when the funeral director had told her bluntly that they wouldn't be needing shoes, she conceded that her credit card couldn't have withstood much more.

The stark efficiency of finalizing the details for his memorial service over the phone had disturbed her. Generic burial plot with footstone? Check. Bargain-basement-priced casket? Check. Floral spray for the casket? Check. Preprogrammed organ music? Check.

To exorcise some of her own grief, she'd stopped at the card shop and written a short note to Leann's sister, and bought a sympathy card to mail to Kyle Coffee's wife later. Loss should never be overlooked, she decided, and although she doubted if anyone would attend, she'd sent a notice of Gary's memorial service to the newspaper.

In truth, though, she was half afraid his creditors might show up.

In the absence of customers, she began to tidy the counter.

"Jolie," Michael said, striding up. "I need to see you in the meeting room, please."

She glanced at her watch. "I still have twenty minutes on my shift."

His face grew stern. "Right away."

"Okay," she murmured, thinking this couldn't be good. Especially since Michael stalked ahead of her the entire way, forcing her to trot. But when they reached the meeting room and Carlotta was there along with Lindy, the store's general manager, she knew they either were getting big raises or were in big trouble . . . She suspected the latter.

Lindy, the redhead with a reedy voice, invited them to sit, which they did. But she and Michael remained standing.

"We received a phone call today," Lindy said. "A tip that the two of you are buying clothes on your employee discount, wearing them, then returning them."

Carlotta looked outraged. "That's ridiculous."

"Carlotta, I must say the high volume of returns that you process for yourself is very suspicious."

Carlotta gave a dismissive wave. "I never try anything on here in the store because I know I can bring it back if it doesn't fit."

Lindy and Michael swung their gazes to Jolie. "Jolie?" Michael prompted.

They weren't going to have to torture her. "There was a jumpsuit—"

"That was my fault," Carlotta cut in. "I talked Jolie into buying the jumpsuit and a great pair of shoes, but she simply couldn't afford them, so she returned them the next day." Carlotta pointed to Michael. "You can attest to that, Michael. The shoes that Jolie returned didn't look worn, did they?"

Michael turned to the manager. "She's right—they were in perfect shape."

Lindy pursed her mouth and looked suspiciously back and forth between the women. "Carlotta, from now on, you'll be limited to one returned item a week, so make sure you try on clothes before you buy them."

"I will," Carlotta said, with just the right amount of contriteness, innocence, and obedience.

"I also read the Sunday paper," the woman said, "so I know that the two of you were questioned in connection with a murder investigation and a robbery during a party over the weekend."

Jolie swallowed hard. Next to her, she could feel Carlotta's nervousness rolling off in waves.

"Both of you are certainly presumed innocent until proven guilty, but I must inform you that if you are arrested, you will be placed on unpaid leave until the matter is resolved."

Carlotta nodded and Jolie joined in.

"That's all," Lindy said. "Ms. Goodman, please accept my condolences on your friend's . . . passing. If you need to arrange time off for a service, we will accommodate you, of course."

"Thank you," Jolie said. "The memorial service is tomorrow evening, so I don't need any time off, but I appreciate the offer."

The woman nodded curtly, dismissing them.

They filed out silently. When they were out of earshot, Carlotta turned on Jolie and glared. "You told!"

"Told what?"

"About the *system!*"

Jolie held up her hands and gave the bandage a scratch.

"I didn't tell. It must have been an employee . . . or what about Hannah?"

"Hannah would never do that to me," Carlotta said.

"Neither would I," Jolie said. "Besides, why on earth would I incriminate myself? So I can add a shoplifting charge to my rap sheet?" She frowned. "And don't act so innocent—I know you took that money from Sammy's purse."

Carlotta's eyes rounded. "I did not!"

Jolie sighed. "Carlotta, I've heard you make comments about what easy pickings a party would be for a thief, and I know you saw the money in Sammy's purse when she paid for her shoes Saturday morning. And," she said more quietly, putting her hand on Carlotta's arm, "I know about the money you owe."

Carlotta frowned. "What?"

"The day I was taking a nap in the dressing room upstairs, I heard voices through the vent—I heard that man threaten you."

Carlotta blanched, looked around, and pulled her aside. "You haven't told anyone about the man, have you?"

"No."

"The police?"

"No."

Her shoulders sagged in obvious relief.

"Who is he? And why do you owe him money?"

"I don't." Carlotta massaged her temples. "My brother owes him."

"Your brother?"

"He had a gambling problem. He's reformed, but he still has a lot of debt. We were able to consolidate some of it and set up payments, but this one guy that he owes ten grand to is breathing down my neck."

"Why *your* neck and not your brother's?"

"Because this guy knows that my brother doesn't care if they rough him up . . . but I do."

"Do you have the money?"

She shook her head. "I scraped together a few hundred dollars and bought another week, but by next Friday I have to have another two grand."

"What are you going to do?"

"As soon as I get my Miata out of the shop, I'm going to sell it. I'd hoped to put the money back into a new car, but right now I need the cash flow."

Her eyes glistened and Jolie's heart went out to her. "Your parents can't help?"

Carlotta gave a little laugh. "My parents are bankrupt upper-class drunks who move around the country staying with any friend who hasn't yet figured them out. I mean, it's no wonder my brother and I are misfits, right?"

"You're not a misfit."

She gave another laugh. "What do you call someone who borrows clothes to crash parties and assume alternate personalities?"

"Creative. It's a shame you can't find a way to make a living at it."

Carlotta looked away. "Look at all the trouble it landed you in."

"I don't believe it—is that a guilty conscience?"

Carlotta looked at Jolie and rolled her shoulders sheepishly. "I have a conscience—just don't tell anyone."

"Carlotta, unless you shot Gary, what happened Saturday night isn't your fault. And crashing the first two parties helped me to get a lot of information I otherwise wouldn't have." *Plus I got to know Beck*, her mind whispered.

"That lady detective told me that Hannah and I made things worse for you because . . . we both have records."

Jolie pressed her lips together.

Carlotta sighed. "Hannah got busted for selling pot when she was in her twenties, and a bookie was trying to get my brother to go off the wagon, so I hit him."

"Oh."

"With a tire iron."

"*Oh.* Well . . . still." Jolie cleared her throat. "But if you did steal Sammy's money, I might be able to talk her into not filing charges."

"You mean *blackmail* her into not filing charges?"

"Well, let's just say I have some dirt on her."

Carlotta smiled, shaking her head. "That would be great, except . . . I didn't take that money. I would tell you if I did, but I didn't!"

"The money was found in the pool filter, and there were only four of us in the pool—you, me, Hannah, and Beck."

"I think we can strike Mr. Moneybags," Carlotta said dryly.

"That leaves Hannah—would she have done it?"

"Only one reason that I could think of—come on, let's go call her. I need to ask her if Russell has that tattoo." They started toward the break room. "So, what's going to happen to you?"

Jolie inhaled deeply, then exhaled. "My attorney seems to think they'll arrest me Wednesday when the D.A. gets back into town."

"Aren't you scared shitless?"

"Well . . . pretty much. The police don't seem to have

the manpower to look into all the leads, at least not right away. But I have a good lawyer, and I hope that some of the leads will pan out before there can be a trial."

"You seem remarkably calm."

Jolie tried to smile. "Give me an alternative."

Carlotta spun the dial on her combination lock and shook her head. "We need to take matters into our own hands, start making phone calls and taking names."

"I'm game."

Carlotta opened her locker and withdrew a pack of cigarettes and a box of matches. "I think I'll go out on the loading dock for a smoke before I call Hannah. Want to join me?"

"No, thanks."

"Oh, Christ!"

Jolie looked up from her own locker to see Carlotta staring at the box of matches. "What is it?"

"I just remembered where I saw that picture on the wall—the pig in the suit that's in your photograph."

"Where?"

She held up the matchbox. "Manuel's Tavern down on North Highland Avenue. It's a hangout for politicians, reporters, cops, attorneys." She grinned. "I've met lots of famous people there—Jimmy Carter." She sighed. "He was in my book."

Jolie nodded absently, aware of a memory stirring just below the surface of her consciousness. "Manuel's," she repeated. "Where have I heard that name . . . word . . . lately?" In the crazy way a person's subconscious teases, she knew it wasn't in association with the bar. It was out of context . . . In a conversation? She shook her head. Maybe on one of the matchbooks in Gary's box of belongings?

No! It was the note he'd scribbled illegibly on the back of a brochure: *hardy manuals*. At the time she had thought it was nonsensical, but maybe there was a connection.

On impulse, she withdrew her cell phone from her bag. "Is there a number on the matchbox?"

Carlotta recited it as Jolie dialed.

The phone was picked up on the second ring. "Manuel's Tavern."

"Yes, is um, Hardy, working tonight?"

"Yeah, he takes over for me at the bar in about an hour."

Jolie's pulse picked up. "Thanks." She disconnected the call. "Want to take a field trip?"

Carlotta shrugged. "Sure. I got my new wheels from the impound lot this morning—that was a degrading experience. Are we going to Manuel's?"

Jolie nodded, more excited than she'd been since . . . last night, with Beck. She pushed the thought from her mind. "Why don't you call Hannah and have her meet us there?"

Manuel's was a neighborhood tavern, full of customers who moved around the bar and the crowded tables with familiarity. The furnishings were old and eclectic: scarred tables, mismatched chairs, a beer can collection, faded photographs. The patrons themselves ran the gamut from suited businessmen shooting pool to dusty laborers ordering from menus. Even so, Hannah stood out, dressed in what could only be described as gothic guerilla. She was sitting at the bar glaring at her cigarette as if she might simply eat it and dispense with the formality of smoking.

"You're going to have to work on looking more approachable," Carlotta commented wryly as she and Jolie slid onto stools on either side of her.

Hannah blew smoke into the air. "I managed to save you seats, didn't I?"

Carlotta winked at Jolie. "Bad day in cooking school, Hannah?"

She ground her cigarette in an ashtray, twisting it until it broke, exposing the fibrous filter. "Russell filed assault charges, the wimp."

Jolie winced.

"I thought that's why you liked him," Carlotta said lightly. "Because he's a wimp."

Hannah gave her a wry smile. "Ha ha."

"You're going to get the last laugh," Carlotta said. "Can't you visualize the courtroom? He'll be in his Brooks Brothers special, and you'll soar in like Elvira and he'll be a big fat laughingstock. The courtroom regulars will crucify him from the gallery."

Hannah managed a little smile. "You're right. That *will* be a rush."

"Hannah," Jolie asked, "does Russell have a tattoo on his wrist?"

She nodded. "Yeah, a tiny thing, four hands or four arms or something. I remember teasing him that it looked like some kind of sissy Boy Scout badge." She looked at Jolie. "Did you bring the picture Carlotta told me about?"

Jolie nodded and withdrew the photo from her purse.

Hannah studied the picture, shaking her head. "Can you believe that your boyfriend and my boyfriend knew each other? Small world, isn't it?" She frowned, then flicked her finger against Russell's wife's face.

Carlotta gave Jolie a sideways glance, lifting her eyebrow.

A plump woman bartender came down to the end of the bar and gave it a swipe with a hand cloth. "What can I get for you ladies?"

"Gin and tonic," Carlotta said.

"Same for me," Jolie said. "I was told that Hardy was working the bar tonight."

The woman looked across the room. "Har-dee!"

A slender middle-aged man serving a tray of drinks looked up.

The bartender pointed to the women. "Fans of yours."

The man tucked the empty tray under his arm and ambled over, sporting a communal grin. "What can I do you for, ladies?"

Jolie leaned forward. "Actually, I was hoping to ask you a few questions."

His eyes narrowed. "You a cop?"

"No. I'm looking for some information about a friend of mine, Gary Hagan."

He nodded, his expression more congenial. "Yeah, Hagan. Likes fancy beer. I haven't seen him around here for a while. How is he?"

"Um, not well," Jolie said ruefully while trying to control her excitement at finding someone who actually knew Gary. She took the photo from Hannah and extended it to him. "I understand that this photo was taken here. I thought you might help me identify some of the people in it."

He squinted at the picture. "Yeah, it was taken here all right. Let's see—that's Hagan, right?"

She nodded.

"This guy's name is Coffee, I think, and that's Russell Island." He looked up. "He's kind of a pansy-ass, always orders a frozen drink."

Carlotta snickered and Hannah gave her a deadly look.

Hardy shook his head. "I've seen these other guys in here, usually with Hagan, but I don't know who they are."

He grinned. "I can remember the drinks people order better than their names."

"Did you happen to overhear any of their conversations?" Jolie asked carefully. "How they might have known each other?"

He drew back a couple of inches, and she sensed his retreat. "You're asking a lot of questions."

"It's for a good cause," Carlotta said, then nonchalantly unbuttoned the top button on her blouse and held the drink the bartender had delivered to her long, slender neck. Because of course, it was so hot in mid-October.

Hardy stared at her cleavage. "Well . . . I don't remember any specific conversation."

Another button came undone. "Do you remember seeing tattoos on their wrists?"

He dragged his gaze up, then pointed his finger. "Yeah. In fact, I think they were all in here celebrating after they got them. I remember thinking they were grown men acting like a bunch of fraternity boys." He laughed. "In fact, I think I might have said something like that, and one of them remarked that they had their own fraternity house."

"What did you think they meant by that?" Carlotta asked, playing with the next button.

Fascinated, Jolie held her breath, wondering what would give first—Hardy, or Carlotta's bra.

Hardy's Adam's apple bobbed. "I'm not sure, but I took it to mean that they had a playhouse, you know, somewhere to take their girlfriends, some place their wives didn't know about. That's pretty common, actually."

Jolie and Carlottta's gaze swung to Hannah.

"Did Russell have a playhouse?" Jolie asked, her heart beating faster.

She nodded. "A condo on West Peachtree. We went there a few times."

Jolie's heart beat faster as a few more pieces of the puzzle fell into place. Gary was a services broker, and he owned a condo on West Peachtree. The four men used it as a playhouse. Hannah could provide the link between the condo and Russell Island, and the tattoos would provide the link between the four men. Hope flowered in her chest. She gave Carlotta a triumphant nod, barely able to contain her excitement.

Carlotta rewarded Hardy with a glimpse of her navel. "Thanks, Hardy."

He grinned, then looked back to the photo, as if hoping to find more details he could expound upon—Carlotta was, after all, wearing a skirt that buttoned up the front.

He pulled the picture closer, squinting.

"What?" Jolie asked, thinking at this point any information would be pure gravy.

Hardy shook his head. "I can't say for sure—this is an old picture, taken before we repainted—but . . ."

"But what?" she prompted.

"I swear this dark-haired lady staring off to the side looks like Della Underwood."

Jolie's heart dropped. "What?"

Carlotta grabbed the photo and jammed it close to her face. Jolie looked over her shoulder and broke into a full-body sweat.

Carlotta nodded. "I think he's right. Della went through a brunette phase in the mid-nineties. Tragic, really."

Jolie fairly buckled under the sense of betrayal—Beck had recognized his sister in the photo. That explained the phone call he'd made from her apartment. "*. . . you* *should be thinking of a story. Yes, I got it from her and I have it with me . . . I shouldn't be here much longer."*

He'd called Della to warn her. That was why he was trying to keep the story out of the papers and off television: for Della's sake, not for hers. He hadn't wanted to show the photo to Pam Vanderpool because he knew she would recognize Della.

All this time, Della might have known something about LeMon that would exonerate Jolie . . . or is that what Beck was afraid of? That his sister was somehow involved? He said he'd come back to Atlanta because his sister was going through some things that he wanted to be here for. Had she gotten in over her head with her old lover Roger LeMon?

Her heart shivered in disappointment. She'd imagined the connection between her and Beck, had wanted it to be so. Was she so starved for love that she couldn't recognize the real thing from a come-on? She swallowed hard. No, not a come-on, but worse: *pity.*

She drew in a shaky breath, determined not to cry.

"Do you know Ms. Underwood?" Hardy asked them, handing back the photo.

"Indirectly," Jolie murmured, feeling Carlotta's perceptive gaze all over her. "Excuse me—I need to make a phone call."

"To Beck?" Carlotta asked in a low voice.

"No," Jolie said. She was finished with being gullible. "To Detective Salyers."

Twenty-four

Jolie stood staring down at Gary, glad she'd gone with the blue tie instead of the red one. It seemed more tranquil, and hopefully, more indicative of the resting place he'd made for himself in eternity.

Her eyes filled with sudden tears, and a sob caught in her throat from the guilt over not having cared enough about him. Somewhere there was probably a pretty girl who had been Gary Hagan's first love, who wondered how he had turned out, hoping she would run into him again someday, not knowing that he was dead unless she happened to subscribe to the *Atlanta Journal-Constitution*. Somewhere there was someone who was more qualified to bury him.

At the sound of footsteps behind her, she brushed away tears and turned.

Detective Salyers, wearing her uniform of chinos and jacket came walking toward her.

Jolie tensed. "If you've come to arrest me, can you wait until after the service?"

Salyers gave her a little smile. "I didn't come here to arrest you, Ms. Goodman. I came to pay my respects to Mr. Hagan . . . and to you."

"Oh. Thank you."

Salyers cleared her throat. "Ms. Goodman, I know this isn't exactly the time or the place, but I wanted you to know that I've made this case my top priority—on the clock and off. I truly appreciate all the leads you've sent our way. The information you got from the bartender at Manuel's last night will go a long way toward linking these two murders by way of more than an affair gone bad. We're looking into Kyle Coffee's death, and we're re-examining the West Peachtree condo." Salyers sighed and averted her gaze.

"But?"

Salyers looked back. "But you're still the prime suspect, and my boss is going to recommend to the D.A. tomorrow that an arrest warrant be served."

Panic pumped through her limbs. Jolie massaged her throbbing hand through the bandage. "Okay . . . okay . . . okay."

"I thought this would be better coming from your attorney, but I contacted Pam Vanderpool; she said that you had fired her."

Jolie nodded. Beck had left her a half dozen messages. "I'll find another attorney in the morning."

At the sound of more guests, Jolie turned. Carlotta and Hannah walked in, their footsteps careful and uncertain. Carlotta, always the trendsetter, wore yellow head to toe. Hannah looked surprisingly feminine in a flirty ruffled skirt. Jolie smiled, grateful for their presence. They spotted her and made their way toward the front of the chapel.

"He looks better than the last time I saw him," Carlotta murmured. "Nice suit—everyone should be buried in Prada."

Jolie nodded. She'd paid almost as much for the suit as she had the casket.

Hannah gave Jolie's hand a squeeze. "How are you holding up?"

Her gaze flitted to Detective Salyers, who had taken a seat in a middle pew. "Fine."

Hannah shifted from foot to foot. "Jolie, I stole that money from your boss's purse the night of the party." She puffed out her cheeks. "I was going to plant it on Russell."

Jolie frowned. "Why?"

She shrugged. "To discredit him, to show him that I could. I was trying to get close enough to put it in his jacket pocket when Carlotta grabbed me and we went into the pool."

Jolie bit into her lip. "Hannah . . . have you considered counseling?"

She nodded miserably.

"Omigod," Carlotta whispered. "Jolie, your ex-boss just walked in."

Jolie lifted her head and sure enough, Sammy had arrived, toning down her usual pinkness with a splash of gray.

"Excuse us," Carlotta said. She and Hannah turned and claimed a pew equidistant between Salyers and the back of the room.

God help her, but Jolie looked at Sammy and immediately pondered the woman's motivation. Did she feel obligated to attend because the body had been found in her house? Had she been fooling around with Gary behind

Jolie's back and developed genuine feelings for him? Or was she here simply to give out business cards? (A trick of the trade.)

Sammy stopped in front of Jolie and after an awkward hesitation, leaned forward to give her a stiff one-armed hug. "I'm really sorry about Gary," she said, and she sounded like she meant it.

Jolie felt unexpectedly misty. Was it possible that she and Sammy had simply fallen into a habit of disliking each other? She hadn't exactly behaved well herself, sneaking into the woman's house, ransacking her bathroom, filching a photo frame, then bringing the party to a screeching halt. She was touched that Sammy seemed to be extending an olive branch. "Thank you for coming, Sammy."

Sammy's expression was pinched with compassion. "I wouldn't have missed it." She linked her arm in Jolie's and stared down at Gary. "So young, so handsome, such a tragedy."

Jolie nodded, biting into her lip.

Sammy patted her arm. "Jolie, I have a little confession to make."

At the sound of Sammy's "cajoling" voice, a red flag raised in Jolie's mind. "Confession?"

Sammy looked contrite. "Gary called me at the office a little while after you all started seeing each other and asked me to broker a deal. He wanted to buy a condo that he'd been renting for a couple of years." She gave a little laugh. "He said it was going to be a surprise and he didn't want you to know about it, but he wanted you to get the commission for the sale."

Her stomach gurgled. "So you forged my name on the contract?"

She nodded and winced. "And that was wrong, but

Gary was adamant that he wanted you to have the money." She lifted her manicured hands in the air. "I thought he was getting ready to propose and that the two of you would live there. Since I couldn't cut you a commission check without you knowing the source, I tried to give you the money in little spurts, but you simply wouldn't take it."

Jolie wet her lips. "That's why you were trying to give me money Saturday morning?"

"Yes. I felt terrible that you'd left the agency before I could get you to take it." She laid her ice-cold hand over Jolie's—or maybe it only felt cold because her wounded hand felt feverish. "Jolie, I just wanted you to know the entire story from my point of view."

"In case anyone asks me?"

The woman's smile was poignant. "Yes."

Salyers had been asking questions about the property—was Sammy telling the truth, or covering her tracks? Jolie gave her a noncommittal smile. "I appreciate your concern. And about the money that was taken at the party—"

"It's forgotten," Sammy said emphatically. "It's just money, and it was recovered. This memorial service is a good reminder that life is short, and we can't be consumed by material things."

Said the woman with a room in her home dedicated to crystal dollhouses.

But with her own emotional receptors misfiring, Jolie couldn't decide if the woman was a big fraud, or if kindness was just so foreign to Sammy that she hadn't gotten the knack of it yet.

The funeral director, a pear-shaped, slump-shouldered man with glasses on the tip of his nose, walked into the doorway and signaled that it was time for the service to begin. Sammy patted Jolie's hand, then settled herself in a back pew.

Jolie conjured up a smile for the handful who had gathered for the service and lowered herself to the front pew. The funeral director meandered to the front of the room and flipped a switch. Organ music wafted in from the speakers—a sickly sweet melody meant to wring the emotion out of the most stoic observer.

A cell phone rang, piercing the mood. Jolie pivoted her head to see Detective Salyers reaching into her pocket and ducking out of the pew. She hurried out of the room, and Jolie couldn't be irritated. The woman had come because of her and had other emergencies to attend.

The song finished playing and another song began, this one more mournful than the last. When she looked at Gary's chalky profile, she was overwhelmed with helplessness, assailed with thoughts that things might have ended differently if she'd simply started the car and driven off while he was in the backseat.

Another cell phone rang, and Jolie turned her head to see Sammy jump up and run out, reaching into her purse. Another lead, another sale. Jolie couldn't figure out Sammy, but deep down, she thought the woman was too dim to be truly dangerous. She looked back to the casket and sighed. What-ifs plagued her and she felt torn because she didn't entirely trust Gary. Had he been sleeping with Sammy? Had he been sleeping with Janet LeMon? Selling cocaine to the men who used the condo as their getaway? All of those things were hard to reconcile to the gentle, laughing man she'd known, but what if Gary had only let her see the side of him that he wanted to reveal? Was that why he hadn't wanted her to meet his friends, so she wouldn't see the smarmy side?

At the end of the second song, the funeral director made his way to the front of the chapel to a small podium and began to read the seventy-five-word obituary he'd asked her to write. "Gary Hogan—"

"Hagan," Jolie corrected.

He squinted over the podium at her. "Huh?"

She wet her lips. "It's 'Hagan,' with an 'a.' "

He pointed to the paper. "This says 'Hogan.' "

Another cell phone rang. Jolie turned her head to see Hannah sidling out with her phone to her ear. Jolie turned back with a sigh. "Trust me—it's 'Hagan.' "

"Okay." He cleared his throat, then started again. "Gary Hagan was on this earth thirty-six short years. Born in Germany to a U.S. airman, Gary lived the life of a soldier's son."

Another cell phone rang and Jolie turned to frown at Carlotta, who mouthed, "I'm sorry, I have to get this," and ran out of the room.

The funeral director looked around the room, then looked back to Jolie. "Do you want me to finish?"

"Yes." She'd spent hours on that obituary, hoping to come up with seventy-five words that would have pleased Gary, if he were within earshot. She wanted them to be heard. "And then I'd like another song, please."

He looked over his glasses at her. "You only paid for two songs."

"Bill me."

"Okay." He looked back to the sheet of paper. "Where did I leave off? Let's see, Gary Hagan, blah, blah, blah, soldier's son. Ah, here we are: More than anything, Gary liked to make people laugh. He was known as a person who could make things happen. He loved sports, especially the Braves. He was preceded in death by his beloved parents,

Alvin and Polly Hagan. He is succeeded by an army of friends." The man glanced over his glasses at the empty chapel, then looked back down. "Then it says here 'Magic of thinking big.'" He squinted at Jolie. "Is that supposed to mean something?"

"It was his favorite book," she said wistfully. "And I only had four words left."

The man looked at her as if she were a kook. "Here's your extra song." He flipped the switch, then lumbered back down the aisle.

Jolie sat perfectly still while the song played—it was the first song again, but she didn't care. She sat unmoving until the vibrations of the last note had died, then pushed to her feet and walked to Gary's casket. She broke off one of the white roses from the casket spray and tucked it inside his jacket pocket.

"Gary," she murmured, "I'll bet when you got to the Pearly Gates, you had Braves tickets for St. Peter." She smiled, then bit into her lip. "I want you to know that I'm going to try to figure all this out. I don't know what's going to happen, but I know I was never this brave before, so thank you." She inhaled deeply, bringing the scent of live flowers into her lungs, then exhaled and turned to leave.

A movement in the empty chapel caught her attention. Beck. He was sitting on a rear pew, wearing a suit and tie and a solemn expression.

She stopped, shot through with anger, remorse, shame. Her only solace was in the fact that he didn't know how much he'd trampled her heart—and why would he even guess that he had in such a few short days? It wouldn't make sense, so she was safe from that ultimate humiliation at least.

He stood, shoving his hands in his pockets, and Jolie realized that eventually, she was going to have to move forward. She walked toward him and he stepped out into the aisle.

"I got here a little late," he said, his tone apologetic.

"Thank you for coming anyway," she said. "Detective Salyers was here, and Carlotta and Hannah. Oh, and Sammy."

"She left a stack of business cards by the guest book."

"Sounds like Sammy."

"She's persistent—she called me twice this week trying to get my business."

An awkward pause followed. Beck scratched his temple. "I, uh, was hoping we could talk."

She angled her head. "About the fact that your sister is in the photo I showed to you? And that you deliberately concealed information that might have helped me in some way?"

He nodded, pressing his lips together. "You're right, I did conceal that information from you, and I hope you can forgive me for wanting to protect my sister. But I didn't keep the information from the police."

She blinked. "You didn't?"

He shook his head. "When I left your place Sunday morning, I picked up Della and we went to talk to Detective Salyers. I convinced Della it would be better if the police knew everything."

"What's everything?"

He sighed. "My sister has been in love with Roger LeMon most of her adult life. I don't understand it, but she's blind to the fact that he's not a good guy. They were off and on, off and on. Even after he married, LeMon called Della. She wouldn't have anything to do with him, but I knew she was still crazy about him."

"I feel for your sister," Jolie said, "but wouldn't that make her a suspect in Janet LeMon's murder?"

"It might," he admitted. "Except Della was in a psychiatric clinic in Vermont all summer, up until I got back in town a couple of weeks ago."

"Oh."

"Yeah," he said. "As you can imagine, that's not the kind of thing Della wants everyone to know, especially since she seems to finally be getting back on her feet. So . . ." He gave her a little smile. "I just wanted to apologize and let you know that Pam is willing to take your case again."

She shook her head. "Thanks, but . . . no thanks."

"So . . . you won't accept my help."

Her heart thrashed in her chest like a wounded bird. "No. There are just too many . . . complications—your name, your sister. You're my alibi at the party. How's that going to look to a jury if you're also paying for my attorney and—"

He lifted an eyebrow. "Sleeping with you? Not good. You're right, of course."

Jolie exhaled. The day was catching up with her. "Look, Beck, I've had a long day, and something tells me that tomorrow is going to be even longer. So if you don't mind—"

"Where are you staying?"

"At my neighbor's. She's out of town and said I could use her apartment for a few days."

"Let me get you a hotel room."

With him in it? "No, thank you. Good night."

He reached out to clasp her arm. "Jolie, I can make things easier for you."

Anger blazed through her. "Do you think I'm blind, Beck? I know what I am to you—I'm a project. I'm a 'before.' I'm the damsel in distress that you can swoop in to save and feel good about yourself for a while. Until you get bored and start looking for a new project, or decide to go back to Costa Rica." She pulled away from him. "Go find another charity case."

She sidestepped him, marched out of the funeral chapel, and unlocked her pitiful rental car door. She climbed in and started the engine, then looked heavenward. "God, I'm broke, barely employed, a suspect in two murders, I drive a ramshackle car, and the man I love might as well be living in your galaxy. Please let me know that this is a low point. Send me a sign." She leaned forward, looking for shooting stars, a burning bush, a two-headed goat . . . something.

And she got nothing.

She drove to the apartment complex counting road signs to keep her mind occupied . . . off Gary . . . off Beck . . . off jail. It was just before 8 P.M. when she pulled into the parking lot.

Residents had already decorated for Halloween, putting lighted jack-o'-lanterns in their windows and corn fodder shocks in the common areas. Her hand felt warm and tight beneath the bandage. Maybe Beck was right—maybe it was infected.

Beck.

She worked her mouth from side to side, conceding it would probably take some time to get out of the habit of thinking about him.

She drove past Leann's apartment to check her own mailbox. After a couple of days, it probably would be full.

She parked and walked to the bank of mailboxes, looking right and left, ever aware of her surroundings. Fatigue pulled at her lower back—the shoe department had been much busier than usual today.

The night air was cool—in the forties, she guessed. And so cloudless, the stars took her breath away. A rustling noise behind the boxes also took her breath away, until she realized it was the dry husks of the corn fodder shocks rubbing together. Still, she didn't dawdle checking the mail. As suspected, her box was full—one reason was because Mrs. Janklo's bank checks had been delivered to her by mistake. She looked up at the woman's window and noted that the lights were on. If she knew Mrs. Janklo, she'd be looking for these checks and worried that they hadn't arrived.

Jolie heaved a sigh and opted for the elevator over the stairs. A couple of minutes later, she was ringing Mrs. Janklo's doorbell. She stood in front of the peephole and waved. "It's Jolie, Mrs. Janklo—I have your checks."

The door opened and Mrs. Janklo squinted at her through the chain. "What do you want?"

"Here are your checks," she said cheerfully. "The mail carrier put them in my box by mistake."

The woman's plump hand appeared in the six-inch opening and Jolie gave her the box. "Thank you," her neighbor said begrudgingly.

"You're welcome. Good night."

"Wait, I have something for you." The door closed.

Jolie tried to smile. Mrs. Janklo was famous for her frozen zucchini bread wrapped in layers and layers of aluminum foil. It was god-awful, and Jolie had lost a toenail last year when she'd dropped one on her foot.

The door opened and Mrs. Janklo's disposition seemed much improved. "Here you go—some nice zucchini bread. It'll need to thaw for about three hours."

Jolie juggled her mail and took the icy brick, which actually felt good against her injured hand. "Thank you, Mrs. Janklo."

"And here's something for you that was put in *my* mailbox by mistake . . . a few days ago." She extended a lumpy, padded manila envelope.

Jolie frowned. "When did you say it arrived?"

"One day last week," the woman snapped. "I'm a little forgetful these days." She slammed the door.

But Jolie barely noticed because she recognized the handwriting on the return address: Gary's. Her heart beat wildly. This was the envelope that he'd said "they" had intercepted. He couldn't have known that in this instance, "they" were a nearsighted mail carrier and her nosy, forgetful neighbor.

She raced down the stairs and decided it would be faster to step inside her own apartment to examine the envelope. With a bum left hand and a right hand that shook from excitement, it took her a few seconds longer to unlock the door and the deadbolt. Just as she turned the doorknob, a man's gloved hand clamped over her mouth from behind.

Jolie's cry died against his hand. Terror bolted through her as he shoved his body against her back, his mouth to her ear. "Welcome home."

At the sound of Roger LeMon's voice, she almost lost control of her bladder. His fingers covered her nose too, so she was bucking to breathe. The door opened in front of her and he pushed her inside, sending her sprawling in the darkness against the gray carpet, which was much harder than she'd ever imagined. Everything in her arms scattered and rolled. The front door slammed closed and she heard him fumbling with the deadbolt. Precious time, and she knew her way around in the dark. She pushed herself up and ran for the bedroom. LeMon abandoned the door and lunged after her. He caught her by the arm, pulled her to him, and covered her mouth again.

"Time to die," he growled in her ear, dragging her backward. "After your boyfriend's memorial service, you couldn't live with yourself anymore. You left a note on your computer about the little love triangle between you and Gary and my wife, about how Gary killed my wife, then how you killed him."

She fought him furiously, struggling left, then right.

"It's not going to hurt, you'll be out from the sleeping pills when I slash your wrists."

He released her mouth for a second and when she gasped for air, he shoved capsules into her mouth. She clamped down, refusing to swallow, her screams sounding like mere grunts. Tears streamed down her cheeks. Would anyone question her death? Leann . . . Carlotta . . . Salyers . . . Beck? He had offered her a safe, secure place to sleep and she'd thrown it in his face. She gagged as the bitter powder from the broken capsules began to dissolve in her mouth.

She heard a loud boom, the distant sound of wood splintering. "Jolie! *Jolie!*" a voice shouted.

Beck?

Suddenly LeMon released her. She fell to her knees, gagging, spitting out the capsules, pulling them out with her fingers. Gasping, she dragged herself up a wall and slapped at the light switch. The two men were crashing against walls, floors. Beck had the bulk, but LeMon, to her

horror, had a blade. Beck's shirt was cut and he was bleeding. Jolie was terrified at the thought of losing him . . . of
him losing his life because of her. She looked around for a
weapon. She remembered the fire extinguisher in the bedroom, and then she spied the great frozen zucchini brick at
her feet. She hefted it, rushed forward, and brought it
down on the back of LeMon's head. The sound of frozen
bread connecting with flesh was . . . satisfying, actually.

LeMon dropped like a stone, his knife clattering to the
floor.

Beck was at her side in two strides. He cupped his
hands around her face. "Are you all right?" he demanded,
his voice rasping.

She nodded, then burst into tears. Third time and
counting.

Twenty-five

Carlotta's eyes widened. "They were going to do *what*?"

"Murder their wives," Jolie repeated. "Among other things."

"I don't believe it," Carlotta said, setting her bottle of Pellegrino on the table.

Yesterday Jolie had spent most of the day with the police, this morning, she and the girls were at the Crepe House playing catch-up.

"I don't believe that *Russell* would do it," Hannah said.

"Supposedly, his wife was next," Jolie said. "That's why Gary was at Sammy's party—to warn Mrs. Island."

"So that's why he was with Roger LeMon's wife at the river?"

Jolie nodded. "Gary said on the audiotape that after he stumbled onto the fact that the four men were going to get rid of their wives, he told LeMon *he* would do it, then he picked up Janet LeMon under the pretense of taking her to the airport to go on her retreat. He took her to the river to tell her what her husband was planning to do and taped the conversation so she could have a copy for protection. But LeMon had followed them to make sure Gary did it, and when he saw he'd been double-crossed, LeMon shot his wife himself. Took a shot at Gary, too, but it only grazed him. He dove into the water and floated downstream until he thought it was safe to get out, then hiked to my place and took off in my car."

A mistake, he'd said on the tape, because by doing so, he'd gotten her involved. He'd wept, apologizing. That had been the hardest part to listen to. He'd been surprised when Jolie had filed a missing persons report, surprised that she'd cared enough. He hadn't wanted to expose her to his shady friends, hadn't wanted to put her in danger. But when she'd filed that report, she had implicated herself irrevocably. That had tortured him, he'd said.

"He stayed hidden because he wanted LeMon to think he was dead?" Carlotta asked.

"Right."

"So how did Gary get involved with them in the first place?"

"On the tape, he said he met LeMon and started doing little things for him—getting game tickets, that kind of thing. LeMon gave him a lot of referrals, introduced him to Kyle Coffee, Russell Island, and their other pal, Gordon Beaure. After a while, he was working for them almost exclusively. He rented the condo on West Peachtree for their leisure, then handled the sale when they decided to buy the property. He arranged for hookers, bought drugs for them—he even bought a gun for LeMon and taught him how to shoot it."

She swallowed, remembering the desperation in Gary's

voice on the tape. *"I've done some bad things in my life and I've done business with some bad people, but Roger LeMon is a cold-blooded killer, as cold as they come."*

"Who is Gordon Beaure?"

"He owns a liquor distribution company. He wasn't around as much, but Salyers said he had just taken out a multimillion-dollar life insurance policy on his wife."

Carlotta shuddered. "Creepy."

"Yeah," Hannah said. "I wanted Russell to leave his wife; I had no idea he was planning to kill her."

"Or to have her killed, more likely," Jolie said. "Gary said they were all planning accidents. In fact, the police are looking into the possibility that Kyle Coffee might have been killed in the 'accident' that had been previously arranged for his wife. Apparently, he was having second thoughts."

"LeMon will probably get the needle for killing his wife and Gary," Carlotta said.

Jolie pursed her mouth. "And possibly Coffee. Plus he hired the guy who tried to run me off the road. And Gary's tape probably seals LeMon's fate for shooting his wife, but there's still no physical evidence linking him directly to Gary's murder."

"But the creep is going to be charged with attempted murder too, right, for what he did to you at your apartment?"

She nodded solemnly. She could still feel his fingers pressed against her mouth, could still hear his voice in her mind. *"Time to die."* The man's ruthlessness was stunning, even more so considering the fact that he moved comfortably in such polite circles.

"Beck saved your life," Carlotta said pointedly.

Jolie nodded and stared at her hands. Beck.

"So what's going on with you two?"

Twice they'd met to talk, and twice they'd wound up making love instead. Jolie adopted an innocent expression. "Nothing."

"Liar."

She flushed. "I *am* supposed to meet him in a few minutes to show him a house before my afternoon shift, but that's the extent of our relationship—strictly professional."

The fact that he'd had his secretary call that morning to arrange the appointment seemed like a clear indication that he was trying to create distance between them. She knew she should just be grateful for the commission she would earn, but now that she had her life back, her imagination appeared to be running full-throttle with possibilities: a successful business, lively friendships, a love for all time . . .

The girls were staring at her, and for a moment she was afraid she'd said that out loud. "I need to run," she chirped, springing up from her chair. She left cash for her meal and waved, thinking she shouldn't have eaten anything on her nervous stomach. One thing that lifted her spirits was the sight of her Mercury sitting at the curb—Detective Salyers had pulled a few strings. It was nice to have a piece of her old life back, although admittedly, she didn't want *all* of her old life back. She felt as if she'd been given a second chance, and she was going to live life more largely than before.

Minus the party crashing, of course.

At red lights, she reviewed the listing that Beck wanted to see. The house was in the most exclusive neighborhood in Buckhead—Sammy's favorite, in fact. She'd be cross-eyed with jealousy if Jolie managed to sell one of the elite properties. The home was enormous and chock full of amenities, with a price tag to match. Secretly, she was disappointed that Beck had gone the "bigger is better" route, although her inner agent told her to keep her idealistic mouth shut. It wasn't as if he were buying a home for them to share. Besides, a tiny voice inside of her promised, *If he buys a big house, he might stay in Atlanta.* Not that she'd be running into him at the country club.

She pulled up to the house a few minutes early, which would give her time to scout out the uber-structure. From the looks of it, she was going to need a map. She removed the door key from the lockbox device and let herself in the front door.

Huge. Colossal. Gargantuan. She toured the first floor quickly to get a feel for the layout and the yards (plural), then she climbed the stairs and checked the rooms for the best views. She heard the front door open and close, and her heartrate kicked up in anticipation of seeing Beck again. She walked to the landing and looked over, then felt her smile dissolve.

Sammy was frowning up at her.

"What are you doing here?" they asked in unison.

"I'm showing the house to a client," Jolie said.

"Who?" Sammy asked suspiciously.

"Beck Underwood."

Sammy frowned harder and Jolie had the distinct feeling that Sammy wanted to stamp her foot.

Jolie crossed her arms. "What are *you* doing here?" she asked again.

"I just finished showing a house two doors down, and I saw what I *thought* was your car in the driveway."

In other words, it drew attention because it wasn't a

nice-enough car to be in this neighborhood. Jolie checked her watch. "I don't mean to be rude, but my client should be here any minute."

But Sammy walked across the foyer and up the stairs. "While I'm here, I'll just look around."

Jolie glared as the woman sashayed by her on the landing. Her cell phone rang and she pulled it out of her purse, thinking it might be Beck saying he was running late. But when she saw the 904 area code, she smiled—Leann. She had so much to tell her.

"Hello?"

"Is this Jolie Goodman?"

Jolie frowned. "Yes, who's this?"

"This is Rebecca Renaldi, Leann's sister. I'm calling about the card I just received."

Jolie smiled. "You didn't have to call—I hope you're recovering well. I'm so sorry for your loss."

"Jolie, one of us is confused. I didn't lose a baby—Leann did."

Jolie blinked. "What?"

"Leann lost her baby early Sunday morning. Personally, I think it was the long drive."

Gripping the phone tighter, Jolie said, "I thought Leann went to Jacksonville to take care of you."

"No, she came here so I could take care of *her*. Gary was going to join her later."

Starbursts flashed behind Jolie's eyelids. "Did you say 'Gary'?"

"Yeah, Gary—the father of her baby."

Jolie grasped the rail in front of her. Gary and Leann? Bits and pieces of conversations came flooding back to her: Leann telling her to stay away from Gary, exhibiting irritation if Jolie shared personal tidbits.

"I would've thought Leann had told you about the baby and about Gary, but she was probably waiting to see if it would work out this time."

"Th–this time?"

"They dated for about a year, then he broke it off, but she never really got over him. Actually, I was worried about her."

Gary's fatal attraction girlfriend. Leann had moved to the apartment complex within a couple of weeks of when she and Gary had started dating. In the laundry room, Leann had initiated a conversation and fostered a friendship.

"When you see her, you might not mention that I told you all of this."

"When I see her?" Jolie asked, her voice shaky.

"She left this morning to drive back to Atlanta, for good this time."

Jolie's pulse raced. "Earlier, you said something about losing the baby after a long d–drive."

"She drove back to Atlanta last Saturday, against my wishes. But she said she and Gary had some things to talk about."

"I wish you could drive up and crash the party with us. If you left now, you could make it."

Apparently, Leann had made it.

"Jolie, was I right to tell you about the baby?" Rebecca asked.

"Yes," she murmured. "I, um, need to go, though."

"Okay. Nice talking to you."

Jolie disconnected the call, completely numb. She needed to call Salyers. She flipped up the phone.

"Drop the phone, Jolie."

She looked over the rail and her heart stalled at the sight of Leann holding a handgun pointed up at her.

"I said drop it."

Jolie obeyed and the phone bounced down several steps. Leann hadn't told her to, but for some reason, it just felt right to hold her arms up while having a gun trained on her heart.

"That was my sister, wasn't it? I heard the tail end of your conversation. Did you call her?"

Jolie searched for her voice and found it cowering behind her liver. "No. Sh–she called me. I s–sent her a sympathy card. She was confused."

"Ah." Leann laughed. "I'd forgotten how damn polite you are." Her smile was squinty and mean. "It must have been one of the things that Gary loved about you."

"I d–don't think that Gary was in love with me."

"Sure he was," Leann said. "I could tell. Remember the day we all floated down the river? I could tell by the way he was around you."

Oh, God—she had invited them both. Although, in hindsight, Leann had finagled an invitation, no doubt gleeful at being able to torment him all day, reminding him that she could cozy up to any future girlfriend, keep tabs on him.

"The fire at his apartment?" Jolie asked.

"Me," Leann said, proudly.

"The *X* on my face in the photograph?"

"Me."

"The lipstick note to Gary?"

"Me, me, me."

And she'd thought that *Hannah* was scary. "Leann, I don't know how you found me, but my client will be here any minute. Why don't you put down the gun before someone gets hurt."

"You mean Beck Underwood? The man you took up with before Gary was even in the ground? He's not coming."

"The call from his secretary?"

"Me."

Okay, now she was truly terrified. Alone in the house with a crazed gunwoman, and no one around except Realtor Barbie, who was probably lost somewhere in the right wing. And her arms were getting really, really tired. She seriously needed to work on her upper body strength.

"Leann, what do you want?"

"You dead." Quick and to the point.

"What will that accomplish, except to mess up your life?"

Leann smiled. "It will mess up *your* life. Gary and I could have been together if you hadn't come along."

Out of corner of her eye, Jolie saw Sammy walking in front of the house, hands on hips, scowling at the dusty domestic car that Leann had arrived in. She must have found a back staircase and was walking the grounds.

"Leann, can we talk about this? If I had known that you were in love with Gary, I would never—"

"Shut up. I tried to like you, I truly did. Sometimes, I *did* like you. Do you know how many times I could have hurt you? Gary threatened me not to, but he's gone now. Come down here."

"I don't think—"

Leann fired a round into the wall behind Jolie.

"Okay," Jolie said. "I'm coming." She started down the stairs, half relieved, half terrified when she realized that the shot had caught Sammy's attention. The woman scowled at the house and was no doubt thinking about how they could keep out the riffraff agents and lookey-loos.

And she must have thought of something, because she was charging toward the house, a thundercloud on her brow.

Jolie was halfway down the stairs when Sammy pushed open the door like a bad wind, catching Leann between the shoulder blades. The gun went off as Leann went down—Jolie heard the *zwing* of the bullet going past her head.

"Sammy, she has a gun!" Jolie yelled.

But Sammy barely missed a beat as she stepped on Leann's back, reached into her Prada bag, and came out with her own gun, long and blue and a caliber that Clint Eastwood might carry. "Mine's new and it's bigger." She dug the heel of her Manolo Blahnik ankle-tie suede pump into Leann's spine. "I don't know who you are, but move and I'll blow your effing head off."

"She killed Gary," Jolie gasped, reaching for her dropped phone to dial 911.

Sammy glared down at her detainee. "You ruined my Ralph Lauren comforter. You're going to have to pay for that."

Twenty-Six

"It's like, I can't decide between the Ferragamo wedges and the Stuart Weitzman boots, you know?"

Kneeling on carpet-burned knees, Jolie peered at the tortured coed over a mountain of boxes. "Why don't you take both and decide when you get home? You can always return a pair later—if they don't show signs of wear."

The young woman's shoulders fell in relief. "You're *right*. I'll take them both."

"And the Dior sandals?" Jolie encouraged.

"Sure, why not?"

Jolie nodded with approval, scooped up the boxes, and trotted to the checkout counter before the girl could change her mind. Michael eyed the three boxes in her hands with an arched brow. "You're catching on," he murmured. "You just might last after all."

"He says again on my last day."

"Jolie, I understand why you're going back to your old

job, but it's not going to be nearly as exciting around here without you."

"It's not my *old* job," Jolie declared. "I'll be a partner." She smiled at him over her shoulder. "Someday maybe I'll be able to afford to buy a pair of shoes from you."

But Michael's remark rankled Jolie. Returning to the Sanders Agency felt as if she were taking a step backward. Not in pay, of course, but in life experience. Still, she would be secure . . . and alive. That was important, considering that just a few days ago her prognosis for living had not been encouraging.

She rang up the sale and thanked the customer, then glanced around the showroom, a little wistful about leaving after only two weeks.

The most eventful two weeks of her life. Leann had been charged with various and sundry crimes ranging from arson to murder to trespassing, but was already enjoying a nicely padded room at a psychiatric facility just outside of Atlanta. According to her sister Rebecca, Leann had suffered a lifelong history of mental instability, and the pregnancy had only exacerbated matters. Leann had told the police that after Gary disappeared, she was sure he was going to join her in Florida. When she discovered that instead of coming to her in his hour of need, Gary had sought out Jolie, Leann was incensed, and became increasingly distraught after her conversations with Jolie that Gary was not only still alive, but was watching Jolie—protecting her—while Leann waited in Florida, pregnant with his baby.

Suspecting that Gary would follow Jolie to Sammy's party, Leann had made the long drive to Atlanta and had disguised herself as one of the hired help for the evening.

Apparently, after listening to Jolie's party-crashing stories, she had decided to give it a try. Leann had heard Jolie say on numerous occasions that Sammy carried a gun in her purse—finding it had been a cinch, Leann said. She'd skulked around until Gary had appeared. When he sneaked upstairs carrying an armful of coats to the coat check room to follow Jolie, Leann had tailed him and confronted him about the baby. She said that when Gary had refused to accept the fact that the baby was his, she'd shot him through a fur stole to silence the gun and then stuck the gun in Jolie's coat pocket—Leann said she'd have known that shabby coat anywhere.

Ouch.

Jolie touched her temple. Leann was insane, but she wasn't devoid of feelings. The trauma of what she'd done had led to her miscarriage when she returned to Florida. The sadness of it all was so profound, Jolie could scarcely believe it had happened. She decided she might never know why Gary hadn't told her about Leann—had he been afraid it would incite Leann even more? Had he enjoyed taunting the poor woman? Had the baby truly been his? Endless questions had plagued her over the past three days since the incident that had exposed the group of conspirators, which the papers, every bit as slogan-savvy as the Yellow Pages, had dubbed the "Buckhead Brotherhood."

Roger LeMon was being held without bail in the murder of Janet LeMon. Russell Island had wasted no time turning state's evidence and spilling his guts about the foursome's evil plans to inherit their wives' trust funds. The story was a media sensation—part of the reason Jolie was leaving her job at Neiman's was that the security detail had to be increased to keep reporters and assorted weirdos from dogging her.

Strangely, Leann's appearance at the house had been a turning point for Jolie and Sammy. Sammy had admitted that she'd always been jealous of Jolie's relationship with her father. But since the agency's business had been sliding without Jolie's organizational skills to keep things moving, she'd made Jolie an attractive offer to come back. Jolie had held out for a partnership, and Sammy had finally agreed. There had been no hanky-panky between Sammy and Gary, although Sammy had admitted in a rare, sheepish moment that it wasn't for lack of trying on her part.

Beck had called a couple of times. Once they'd talked for a few minutes until the conversation had trailed off awkwardly. The next time, she had listened to his voice message but hadn't returned his call. She knew when to make a graceful exit. Of course, that hadn't kept her from lying awake at night thinking of him. Beck had been her first experience with full-on love, no doubt because her emotions had been running full-tilt since the day she'd met him. But eventually the bewilderment over the mess that Gary had introduced into her life would dissipate, and so would her intense longing for Beck Underwood.

"Hey, short-timer."

Jolie looked up to see Carlotta striding toward her wearing her trademark gapped grin. "Hey yourself."

"I can't believe you're leaving us to go back to Realtor Barbie."

Jolie gave her a wry smile. "Well, she did save my life."

"Is that all?"

"And I'm better at selling houses than I am at selling shoes."

Carlotta nodded. "As long as it's what you truly want."

A little laugh escaped Jolie's throat. "Who gets what they truly want?"

Carlotta studied her for a few seconds. "Are you okay?"

Jolie nodded. "Just a little sad, I suppose, about leaving." About returning to her previous life.

"If it makes you feel any better, I came to tell you that you've inspired me."

Jolie frowned. "How?"

Carlotta's hands fluttered with excitement. "I don't have all the kinks worked out yet, but I want to start a business to place products at high-class functions. I'm calling it Product Impressions. A designer would come to me with, say, a fabulous coat, then I'd hire a model to wear the coat to important places."

Jolie grinned. "And to crash parties?"

A sly smile crawled over Carlotta's face. "Let's just say I would take advantage of any advertising venue that presented itself."

"I'm sure it will be a raging success," Jolie said, then lowered her voice. "How's the other . . . situation?"

Carlotta's smile faded. "Don't worry—my brother and I will work it out." Then she winked. "Call me Monday and we'll have lunch next week, okay?"

Jolie nodded and waved goodbye, glad to have one good relationship to show for her ordeal. She crossed the showroom floor to clean up a few cardboard fillers and stray boxes. Time to clock out and go home.

"Excuse me, ma'am."

"I'm sorry," she said, turning. "My shift . . . just . . . ended." Her mouth went dry. Beck, looking much the same as a few days ago, but so good to her eyes that she was embarrassed for herself.

"Hi," he said.

She swallowed painfully. "Hi."

"How are you?"

"I'm good." Desperate for something to do with her hands, she gestured vaguely toward the showroom. "This is my last day."

He lifted his eyebrows. "Oh?"

"I'm going back to work at the Sanders Agency, except this time it will be Sanders and Goodman."

He grinned. "That's great. I'm . . . happy for you . . . if that's what you want."

Why did everyone keep saying that? She nodded cheerfully, pleased that she at least could share that news before she never saw him again, but wishing she could be as enthusiastic about going back to the agency as she rightfully should be. Jolie manufactured a smile, trying to steel herself against the physical sway he still commanded over her. "Are you shoe shopping?" she asked.

"Actually, yes." He shifted his big body from foot to foot and glanced around at the displays. "I'm going to be needing a couple of pairs of rugged shoes to take back with me."

Her heart jerked sideways. "You're returning to Costa Rica?"

He nodded. "Della is doing great, and she always was much more interested in the family business than I was. I'm just not cut out for Atlanta, at least not at this phase in my life."

She nodded. The not-ready-to-settle-down phase. "Well . . . congratulations." Talking was the best distraction for her stupid heart. She swept her arm out like a game-show hostess. "Perhaps you'd like to see our Gortex boots?"

"Sure . . . how about two pair?"

"Okay."

He captured her hand. "One pair of men's and one pair of women's."

Jolie startled at the bolt of desire that his mere touch summoned. "I don't understand."

His Adam's apple bobbed. "Jolie, I was wondering if you might like to . . . come with me."

Her eyes widened. "To visit Costa Rica?"

"No . . . to live there . . . with me."

She blinked. "Live there . . . with you?"

He nodded, then entwined their fingers. "Oh, I know it's not a partnership in a brokerage company, but I was thinking of a different kind of partnership: Underwood and Goodman."

She was struck mute.

"Jolie," he said softly, "do you remember when you said that people like me don't need anything?"

"I think you're paraphrasing."

"Humor me."

"Yes, I do."

"Well, you were right—partially. I've lived a charmed life, and I've never known what it felt like to need something." He pressed his lips together. "To need . . . someone." A flush rose on his cheeks. "The truth is, you were also right when you accused me of viewing you as a project."

Jolie's heart dipped to her stomach.

He squeezed her hand. "I'm ashamed to say that you were a project to fill a void in my heart. I was selfishly trying to force my affection on you when your life was crazy. Now, I'm being selfish again, but I want to take you away from the bad memories where we can learn everything about each other in a beautiful, exotic land." He lifted her hand and kissed her fingers. "Come with me. Think of what an adventure we'll have."

Her heart vaulted to her throat. "What if I say no?"

"Then I'll have to stay in Atlanta and pester you until you say yes."

"But . . . what would I do in Costa Rica?"

He shrugged. "Sell real estate, sell shoes, sell coffee beans." He pulled her closer. "You can start over . . . *We* can start over. The truth is, Jolie, I'm crazy in love with you."

"You are?"

"Since the day you crashed into me." He lowered his mouth to hers for a slow, sensuous kiss, and Jolie felt herself crumbling, wanting, hoping. Her mind reeled at the possibilities . . . and the risk.

When he pulled back, he squinted. "What's going on in that pretty head of yours?"

"I . . . don't have a passport."

His mouth quirked. "That we can fix. Is that all?"

"I . . . don't have boots."

"Good thing we're in the middle of the shoe department."

Jolie felt engorged with emotion, yet paralyzed with uncertainty. The words were shouting in her heart, but cowering on her tongue. Could she dare say them? Snatches of scenes from the past few days flashed in her mind. Life was so fragile, so random . . . she had nothing to lose, except everything. She could stay in Atlanta and live comfortably and quietly.

Then something Carlotta had said came floating back to her. *"You're too young to be comfortable."*

"Jolie," he said, his eyes questioning. "Is that all?"

"No." She wet her lips. "I . . . I love you too, Beck." She said the words on a long breath that left her lungs empty.

"You do?"

She nodded. "Since the day *you* crashed into *me*."

He whooped and lowered another kiss to her mouth. She poured all her hopes and dreams into the kiss. Beck seemed to understand the leap of faith she was taking and his mouth promised she wouldn't be sorry.

"Get a room!" someone shouted.

Beck lifted his head and grinned at her, his dark eyes shining. "What do you say? My room is five minutes away."

Jolie laughed. "I say . . . let's go crash."

Epilogue

"Take these for sure," Beck said, holding up a pair of miniscule pink lace panties and wagging his eyebrows.

Jolie bounced a rolled-up pair of socks off his arm. "*I'll* sort through my underwear drawer, thank you very much." Then she looked around and sighed. Her bedroom floor was covered with cardboard boxes and crates bound for Goodwill. "Besides, I won't have room in my suitcase for something so impractical."

Beck tucked the panties into the pocket of his T-shirt and gave it a pat. "I got you covered." He grinned and swooped in for a kiss. "In fact, I will personally see to the safe arrival of any sexy underwear you want to take to Costa Rica."

She lifted her arms around his neck and leaned into him for a slow, rocking kiss. She could scarcely wait until they were in Costa Rica together. Long, warm nights lying heart to heart. She couldn't have hoped to be this happy.

"The Goodwill truck will be here soon," he said. "I'm going to start carrying boxes to the curb."

Jolie nodded. "I just have a few more things to sort through." She watched with bittersweet excitement as he hoisted a box of her former life to his shoulder and maneuvered his way through her bedroom door. She turned and caught sight of herself in the mirror of the bureau that was bound for storage. Wild, blonde curls, wide eyes, pink cheeks—she'd never looked or felt so alive.

The past week had been a flurry of packing and planning. Sammy had told Jolie she would have a job at the Sanders Agency if things didn't work out in Costa Rica, and while Jolie was grateful for the offer, she had no doubt that she and Beck would be together always. Since the day he'd come to the department store to ask her to go with him, they had scarcely been apart. After the first couple of days of marathon lovemaking and nonstop talking, she had prepared herself for Beck to take an emotional step back, but instead, to her heart's joy, had discovered that Beck reveled in sharing details of his thoughts and experiences now that he had found someone like-minded. They were two people who had held themselves in check emotionally until each found the person who had the same bone-lonely look in their eyes. Jolie had felt herself unfolding more every day, like a party dress that had been left in a drawer, waiting for the special occasion that had finally arrived.

With a smile on her face, she sorted through her underwear drawer, and, remembering the gleam in Beck's eyes, threw out the sensible in favor of the sensual. Her cheeks warmed at the thought of their physical chemistry, how Beck was able to stir her senses with a look or a murmured word. At first she had to keep reminding herself that she deserved this chance at happiness, but the affirmation seemed to be working, because she had relaxed into the idea of accepting Beck's love.

Having exhausted the drawers in her bureau, Jolie turned to the bookshelf that made up the headboard of her bed. She pulled out *The Magic of Thinking Big* and a rueful smile played over her face at the book that Gary had insisted would change her life. In hindsight, it had: The book had given her confidence to quit the Sanders agency and try her hand at something new, and she wouldn't have met Carlotta or Beck otherwise. On her nightstand lay a padded envelope containing a new pink leather-bound journal that she was going to mail to Carlotta—perhaps she would send her Gary's favorite book as well to encourage her to pursue her idea for a product placement business.

Jolie thumbed through the book, and halfway through the pages stopped to reveal a white envelope simply marked "Jolie." Frowning, she removed the fat envelope and slid her finger beneath the flap. She gasped at the stack of cash inside—all large bills. Folded sheets of notebook paper cradled the money. Jolie withdrew the sheets, hands trembling. It was a handwritten letter from Gary.

Dear Jolie,

I'm leaving this letter in case something terrible happens to me. I'm sorry I got you involved in the mess of my personal life and the mess of my business dealings. Since you didn't get the envelope I sent earlier, these notes explain the crimes that were planned. I'm innocent of murder, but I'm not an innocent man—I figure if I die young, it's payment for other things I've gotten away with in my lifetime.

You see, Jolie, I really loved you . . . or maybe it was the thought of you. You reminded me that there are people in the world who are truly good, and I wanted to feed on your goodness. Unfortunately, I'm in too much trouble to extricate myself. I should have told you that your friend Leann Renaldi is a former girlfriend of mine with obsessive tendencies, although I don't think she'd ever hurt anyone, except maybe me. And if she does, I probably deserve it for the way I dumped her. I can be a real jerk, even though I tried hard not to let you see that part of my personality. You made me want to be a better person, Jolie.

Enclosed is repayment for your car I took the night Janet LeMon was killed, and a little extra for all the trouble I caused you. I hope you can put it to good use. I wish I had met you sooner, Jolie. I hope your life is long and full of happiness.

Gary

Jolie wiped at her eyes, grateful to have some explanation of why Gary had become involved with her in the first place, and what motivated his secretive behavior toward her. He must have entered her apartment and planted the envelope some time after he had talked to her from the backseat of her rental car . . . which explained the finger marks in the dust that she'd found, and the indications that someone had climbed through her bedroom window. She scanned the notes he'd left and decided they would go to Detective Salyers immediately to help fill any holes in the case against Roger LeMon. Then she counted the cash with growing wonder—fifteen thousand dollars.

Since her car had been returned to her, the cash Gary had left seemed extraneous.

Then an idea occurred to her. Jolie picked up the padded envelope containing the leather journal she was sending to Carlotta, and tucked two thousand dollars inside—enough to get the threatening collector off her friend's back. The rest she bundled into another envelope and addressed it to Rebecca Renaldi. A posthumous gift from Gary, Jolie explained, to put toward Leann's treatment. She sealed the envelope with mixed feelings pulling at her—incredulity over the randomness of how people's lives crossed and changed each other, remorse that the same human dramas seemed to play out over and over—greed, ambition, love and hate—with unpredictable results.

"Everything okay in here?" Beck asked from the doorway.

Jolie looked up and felt a rush of love for this amazing man. She set the envelopes aside and crossed the room to slip into his embrace. Tilting her head she smiled up at him. "Yes, everything is okay."

A little scoff escaped him and his eyes darkened with sudden desire before he lowered a kiss to her neck. "We have a few minutes before the truck gets here—what do you say we bypass okay and shoot for spectacular?"

Jolie arched into him and grinned. "Wow me."